KT-461-362

ABIGALE HALL

BLACK & WHITE PUBLISHING

ABIGALE HALL

'A deliciously creepy tale with a strong sense of menace.'
CRIME PIECES

'A beautifully written novel full of rumours, intrigue, love and loss.'
THE WELSH LIBRARIAN

'Forry ratches up the tension expertly, until we don't know if it's madness, ghosts, someone toying with Eliza, or her own imagination that makes the mansion such a place of fear. Whatever it is, it works - keep the lights on when reading!'
CRIME WORM

'*Abigale Hall* starts in London in 1947 and is an old-fashioned tale of terror and horrors of the mind. The book tells us the tale of two sisters who are sent away into service in deepest Wales. All is not right, however, when they reach their final destination and their new home holds many secrets. The story's limited cast of characters are well written and once the tale hits its stride it is a compelling read. Forry sets up the mystery well and the tension builds to a climax with a gruesome outcome'.
NORDIC NOIR

'The mansion is something of a gothic horror in its own right, and there's even a sinister housekeeper something along the lines of the terrifying Mrs Danvers.'
CRIME FICTION LOVER

'Forry is obviously well versed in nightmares... This debut novel is one to watch.'
THE SKINNY

'This is a SERIOUSLY good read. *Abigale Hall* has a sense of intrigue and mystery running throughout which meant I kept turning the pages long after I should have gone to bed.'
READING WITH A VIEW

B000 000 017 7

ABERDEEN LIBRARIES

ABOUT THE AUTHOR

LAUREN A. FORRY was brought up in the woods of Bucks County, Pennsylvania, USA, where her FBI agent father and book-loving mother raised her on a diet of *The X-Files* and RL Stine. She spent a summer working as Zooey Deschanel's personal assistant whilst they filmed M. Night Shyamalan's horror film *The Happening* and has worked on the film sets of *Limitless* and *The Last Airbender*.

After earning her BA in Cinema Studies from New York University, she moved to London where she earned her MFA in Creative Writing from Kingston University. There she was awarded the Faber and Faber Creative Writing MA Prize for her dissertation, which would become her debut novel, *Abigale Hall*. Her short stories have since appeared in multiple anthologies. She currently resides in the woods with her dogs Harry and Gizmo.

ABIGALE HALL

Lauren A. Forry

BLACK & WHITE PUBLISHING

First published 2016
by Black & White Publishing Ltd
29 Ocean Drive, Edinburgh EH6 6JL

1 3 5 7 9 10 8 6 4 2   16 17 18 19

ISBN: 978 1 78530 009 7

Copyright © Lauren A. Forry 2016

The right of Lauren A. Forry to be identified as the author of this work
has been asserted by her in accordance with the Copyright, Designs and
Patents Act 1988.

All rights reserved. No part of this publication may be reproduced,
stored in a retrieval system, or transmitted in any form, or by any means,
electronic, mechanical, photocopying, recording or otherwise, without
permission in writing from the publisher.

A CIP catalogue record for this book is available from the British Library.

ALBA | CHRUTHACHAIL

Typeset by Iolaire Typesetting, Newtonmore
Printed and bound by Nørhaven, Denmark

To Mom, for giving me the time and space and support to become what I wanted to be.

ACKNOWLEDGEMENTS

I owe thanks to many people for many things. These are a few of them. Thank you Jonathan Barnes, Anna Faherty, Judith Watts and the rest of the Creative Writing and Publishing faculty at Kingston University for helping me learn the craft and the business. Thank you Serina Gothard and Hannah Tuson for reading early drafts and later drafts and helping to make it better.

Thank you Sandra Sawicka for your notes and your guidance and for making this a real thing. Thank you Karyn Millar, Campbell Brown and the entire Black & White team for everything you've done to make this the best book it could be.

Thank you David Raynor, Claire Raskind and Jose Rodriguez for giving me amazing opportunities and being all-around wonderful people when I had no idea what I was doing.

Thank you Hyun Davidson for the inflatable mattress, brunch, *The X-Files* marathons and the years of support, even after I dropped pre-med.

Thank you Jannicke de Lange for being who you said you were. Thank you for being the best roommate, the best collaborator, the best evil twin and the best friend. Thank you to the rest of my Norwegian family: Cathrine de Lange, the first to read the finished version, for being the little sister I never had, and Margaret M. de Lange and Harald J. de

Lange for letting your daughter meet people on the internet and welcoming them to your home. Thank you especially for the crabs.

Finally, thank you to the people that have been there from the very beginning: Cherie and Lindsey, for putting me in the laundry basket and including me in your shows; Dad, who thought everything was wonderful; and Mom, for everything.

PROLOGUE

In a hidden corner of the Welsh countryside, beneath the dark green hills and stretching deep underground, lies a secret. Though few know of its existence, all feel its presence, for above this secret rests a house. One would be forgiven for believing it abandoned. Long grasses choke the overgrown gardens. Boards grey as the old mare grazing behind the rusted gates cover the highest windows. The house sits alone, its crumbling façade a pox on the hills it once commanded.

No one lives there, though a few reside within its walls: a caretaker who tends the grounds, too young for this damnation; a housekeeper who will never be satisfied, not until . . . ; and an old man who sits and thinks round the holes in his mind. If one were at the house now, one would see the caretaker smoking in the carriage house and the old man watching the world with eyes closed. The housekeeper cleans in the cellar. Flames dampen as she throws frocks into the furnace, then grow again to devour the thin fabrics. Next she adds the shoes, undergarments and, finally, the diary. She watches as the fire envelops the journal's pages, the leather cover melting and blistering in the intense heat. Satisfied, she shuts the furnace door, wiping her hands on her apron before ascending the cellar steps and returning to where the old man waits.

'It's all done. I told you I'd take care of it, didn't I?' She brushes the lint off his shoulder. 'She was no different than the others, was she? There was no reason to worry. Now, shall you retire until dinner?'

She escorts him through the house, making note of her chores as she goes: light the fire in the bedroom, order more coal for the east wing, scrub the blood from the floorboards. There is much to do in a large house such as this.

The door to the veranda jams as she opens it. A firm yank and the frame yields. This house always yields to her. She leaves the old man there to admire one of his favourite views – the little cemetery in the west. The sun will soon be setting, casting crimson light over the ageing gravestones where another waits, watching.

The housekeeper returns to her wing, leaving footprints in the disturbed dust of the bloodied servants' passage, pausing only to wipe a damp, crimson handprint from the peeling wallpaper. Ensconced in her small office by the kitchen, she settles at her writing desk and produces his familiar grey stationery from its drawer. Upon taking up her pen, she dips the worn quill in a jar of red ink and composes the letter as it has been done so many times before, and as it will be done again. The names are all that change. Tomorrow she will travel to the village and post it. She hates the delay, but all will be taken care of in good time. A few weeks and Mr Brownawell will have his new ward. She smiles as the sharp edge of the envelope slides beneath her fingers.

In the cemetery, as the dimming light casts the house in darkness, the other watches, weeping for those who will join them in the shadows of the dark green hills.

1

'One. Two. Three.'

The slow, methodical taps punctuated the air, asynchronous to the beat of the morning traffic that filtered through the single-glazed kitchen window.

'Four. Five. Six.'

Each pat of the brass door handle, underscored by a whispered number, tightened Eliza's nerves like the winding of a clock. Each pause in between lasted longer than a second, providing a brief respite before the next number dutifully struck.

'Seven. Eight. Nine.'

She glanced at their grandmother clock, eyes wandering past the singes around the plinth and body before settling on the clock face: half past ten. They would be late, again, but Aunt Bess would need to accept that. There was no such thing as being on time in Eliza's world, only varying degrees of late.

'Ten. Eleven. Twelve.'

Rebecca, her face wrinkled and pinched in serious concentration as her breathy voice echoed through the small flat like a ghostly whisper, could not be rushed.

In the mirror above the wireless, Eliza spotted a smudge of coal dust on her cheek and scrubbed at it with her thumb until her skin turned red. Behind her freckles, she recognised her mother's round face but none of her beauty. At Rebecca's age, she dreamt of being glamorous at seventeen, like the women in Mother's fashion magazines. There was nothing glamorous about freckles or straight brown hair too heavy to perm. She looked past her reflection and watched her sister. Rebecca would be beautiful at seventeen, Eliza knew. Though only twelve, she already possessed delicate blonde curls that perfectly framed the sharp cheekbones of Father's side of the family. Boys would gawk at her, trip over themselves asking her to the pictures, compare her to the beauties on the screen.

'Twenty-one. Twenty-two. Twenty-three.'

Eliza wrapped her dishevelled hair in a clean headscarf and turned away from the mirror. She preferred books to films, anyhow.

'Have everything?' she asked as Rebecca skipped across the room.

'I think so.' Rebecca checked her bag. 'Are we going to be late?'

'Course not, dearie.' Eliza placed her arms around her sister's shoulders and guided her out the door. 'Just remember, leave Auntie Bess to me.' As Rebecca's eyes flitted to the lock, Eliza checked for herself that the door was secure behind them. 'Come on then. We may have to run.'

Eliza manoeuvred round the fermenting rubbish that crowded the halls and staircases. With the cool air outside, the smell wasn't so bad today. 'We can head down through Fieldgate Street to save time. Cut over at Romford. They've started clearing the rubble there. Careful. Watch your step. Good girl.'

The heavy front door banged shut. Eliza grabbed Rebecca's hand as she reached for the latch and dragged her down the steps to the pavement where the queue for List's blocked their path. Rebecca's protests were lost amidst the din of a busy Whitechapel morning. Though Rebecca tried to withdraw her hand, Eliza gripped it ever tighter as they forced their way through the empty baskets and shabby overcoats in the queue.

'What's the point, he said, if the bomb's just going to kill us all? Only fourteen and he thinks it's the end of the world.'

'And that's his excuse for stealing, is it? You tell him, it's not the bomb he should be worried about. Nationalisation, now that . . .'

Eliza's coat sleeve caught on a wicker basket. She apologised as she backed into the street, narrowly dodging the number fifteen bus as she and Rebecca hurried to the other side, where the queue for the haberdasher's waited. After inhaling a lungful of exhaust smoke, she paused to cough while Rebecca fiddled with her shoes.

'Horrid time for it. And with the shortage and all. I'll tell you, it'll be for nought. I've lived through two wars now and there's a third just round the corner. Wait and see.'

'Oh, don't get your back up. It's only a bit of lace! I've been waiting months for new . . .'

A delivery truck lumbered past, drowning out all conversation. Eliza tried to rush them past the collapsed Anderson shelter on Romford Street, but Rebecca slowed to a near stop.

'Eliza, wait! I can't keep up.'

'You can if you try harder.'

'No, I can't. My shoes are too tight.'

She tried to pull Rebecca along. Every second lost was another second she would have to explain. 'Well you should've mentioned it before. I could've given you my old pair.'

'But your feet are too big.'

'Thanks very much.'

'I'd flap about in them. They wouldn't be any use at all!' Rebecca stopped and stomped her foot. Eliza took her arm and kept her moving, dodging a man on a bicycle.

'All right, enough! We'll ask Auntie Bess if she can spare any clothing coupons. Perhaps if we're not so late she'll be kind enough to give them to you.'

'But you said we weren't late!'

'We will be if you don't keep up.'

'It's not me. It's the shoes!'

Already Eliza was behind in the day's chores, which meant after work it would be straight back home, instead of a late meal with Peter. There wasn't time for Rebecca's complaints. Only five minutes from the office, she stopped at the queue for Dyson's.

'Bread rationing, of all the things. This wouldn't have happened if Churchill were still in charge. My Charlie, he says . . .'

Eliza shouldered her way through the crowd and stopped on a thin strip of unoccupied pavement.

'Here.' She bent down and untied her shoes. 'Hurry up. You, too.' Eliza stuffed their handkerchiefs into the toes of her larger shoes and handed them to her sister. 'Put these on.' Eliza slipped the too-small shoes into her bag while Rebecca laced up Eliza's pair. 'Better?'

'A bit. Yes.'

'Good. We'll switch back when we get there.' They ran to the next street, Eliza ignoring the wetness seeping into her stockings, the feel of the dirt soaking into her feet. It was only a month since the big freeze. Grey snow long pushed into the city's crevices melted in the cool March air, leaving the ground damp and slippery. She could wash her stockings. It would be fine.

After exchanging shoes outside the office, Eliza pushed Rebecca into the building, preventing her from touching the door. The scent of grime and sulphur in the narrow stairwell threatened to choke her. A sweet, smoky odour lingered in the air. Unable to breathe, she felt her pulse quicken. The pressure around her neck made her head heavy as the smell pulled at unwanted memories. When they reached the crowded planning office, she inhaled deeply, savouring the rank odour of fag smoke and old coffee.

Aunt Bess stood halfway across the room, devouring another cigarette and wearing that awful red dress – the one she said brought life to their drab world. Eliza thought it garish. That V-neck brought life only to the bulge in Mr Mosley's trousers.

'And that lovely floral dress I had, remember? With the pale pink . . .' Aunt Bess stuck the cigarette between her lips.

'Oh yes,' her co-worker nodded. 'Yes, with the corseted bodice?'

'Yes, that's the one. Would you believe a tear, right there . . .' With the cigarette, Aunt Bess pointed to her shoulder.

'Now how on earth . . . ?'

'No idea. Think I'd been gaining weight, as if that were possible with the . . .'

'They should up the butter ration. It simply isn't—'

'Fair. No, not fair at all. Oh.'

Eliza smiled as she was finally noticed.

'I expected you an hour ago.' Aunt Bess searched through her handbag.

'The clock is slow,' Eliza said.

'Then wind it.'

'I did.'

'Well, you're only hurting yourself, aren't you?' Aunt Bess retrieved her tattered ration book and dropped it into Eliza's hands as if ridding herself of a dead rat. 'Woolworths will be completely out of cooking fat by now and Harriet told me they already sold the last of the rabbit half an hour ago.'

The co-worker, Harriet, crossed her arms and nodded.

'I don't like rabbit,' Rebecca mumbled. Eliza elbowed her.

'What did you say, young lady?'

'Nothing, ma'am.'

Aunt Bess blew smoke out of the corner of her mouth. 'Well, I happen to adore rabbit and was very much looking forward to it this evening.'

'Sorry, ma'am,' Eliza and Rebecca replied in unison. Aunt Bess flicked ash into the tray beside her elbow.

'Right. Well, Eliza, you'd better leave else it'll be offal again tonight. Rebecca, Mr Mosley needs your help running files to the City. Go on.' She nodded to the office behind her.

Rebecca hurried off while Eliza took her time placing the book into her bag. Aunt Bess sat behind her typewriter, already ignoring her.

'Auntie Bess?'

'You have that job of yours tonight, don't you? Cinema cigarette girl or whatever it is?'

'Theatre usher. Yes, ma'am.'

'You'll make sure all the food is prepared before you go out?'

'Yes. Of course. I'll have everything ready, ma'am.'

'Good.' She stubbed the cigarette butt into the ashtray and fitted a piece of paper into the typewriter. She looked at Eliza, the circles under her eyes the same shade as the soot in the tray. The dress didn't do anything for her at all, Eliza thought.

'Why are you still here?'

'I had a question.'

'There aren't any jobs here. Already told you. Harriet can't even get her bloody daughter one and she worked as a clerical assistant in the war rooms! The daughter, you know. So, there's positively no hope for you.'

'No. It's not that.'

'Well, what is it then?' She sighed, pulling another cigarette from the near-empty pack.

'Rebecca needs new shoes.'

'Don't we all?' She struck a match and lit the fag.

'Hers are too small. She's grown quite a bit in the past year . . .'

'Then use your clothing card and get her some.'

'The Post Office still hasn't replaced the ones we lost during the move and they said . . .'

'And that's my problem, is it?' She tossed the extinguished match onto her desk and slumped back in her chair. 'I'm sorry, Eliza. Really I am. But she'll have to wait. Maybe next month. She can wear your other pair for now.'

'But they're too big.'

'Damn it, child, what do you expect me to do?'

'Miss Haverford?' Mr Mosley, lanky and balding, stood in the doorway of his office. He looked as if God had made him by stretching a short man's skin over a too-large skeleton. His black suit, the same one he wore every day, was short around the wrists and ankles, like it belonged to the skin but not the man.

'Yes, Mr Mosley.' Aunt Bess smiled, her teeth a muddy brown from her strict tea-and-fags diet.

'I need those papers on Spitalfields.'

'Right away, sir.' She rose from her desk. 'If rabbit's out of the question, find some Spam. I'll only be a minute, Mr Mosley!' Aunt Bess disappeared down the hall, leaving Eliza alone with her open handbag.

Without thinking, Eliza thrust her hands into Aunt Bess's bag, fingers digging beneath the empty cigarette boxes, headache pills and make-up before brushing paper at the

9

bottom. She pulled out an unopened grey envelope and her aunt's clothing card. The envelope she stuffed back into the cluttered bag. The coupon book went into her jacket pocket.

*

The human wall outside their flat had changed faces, but its structure remained the same. With her heavy burlap bags, Eliza forced a path through the fortress of worn overcoats and shouldered her front door open. The trek to the third floor was slow as she navigated round the rubbish. On the first landing, she passed hobbling Mrs Hodgkins, who was struggling down the stairs.

'Tell you what, child,' Mrs Hodgkins coughed. 'If these bags here aren't gone by tomorrow, I'll chuck them out myself!'

'You do that, Mrs Hodgkins, and I'll be right beside you with an armful of my own.'

Mrs Hodgkins' creaking laughter followed Eliza all the way to her door.

She wasted little time preparing the dinner, sparing herself a crust of bread and some margarine for her luncheon. If she was quick enough, there might still be time for Peter to buy her dinner after work. She thought of Peter in his ill-fitting usher's jacket and allowed herself a smile.

With dinner stored in the larder, she pulled the final package from the shopping bags and scribbled a note inside its lid.

Don't tell Auntie Bess.

Eliza shoved the parcel under their bed, knowing Rebecca would find it during her nightly count. A thump from the floor above caused the books on her shelf to shift. *Peter and Wendy* fell over with a slap. Eliza carefully rearranged it, propping it up with one of Mother's porcelain figurines. Eliza had dozens

10

of books saved from their old house, some still wrapped in brown paper and tied neatly with string. She ran her fingers over the delicate spines, rereading the titles as she checked that all remained in their proper place. As soon as she received her pay this month, she would be back at Foyles adding another to her growing collection. She straightened a dancing figurine so that the woman's outstretched hand fell perfectly in line with the book spines.

The laundry she'd hung in the sitting room that morning was still damp. Nothing dried inside, but it wasn't worth hanging it out the window. It would either be stolen or coated in coal dust. She saw in a magazine that every home in America now had electric dryers. They had everything in America – nylons, chocolate, chewing gum. Mrs Hodgkins received a parcel from her son over there every month. If only they had family there, a friend. Electric dryers. She sighed as she felt the wet sleeve of Rebecca's brown dress. Might as well be science fiction, she decided.

Eliza dropped her hand and took a breath. For the first time that day, there was a moment of quiet. She stood still, surrounded by the dank stench of drying clothes mingling with the fatty scent of cooked bacon. The sound of the cars below crept in through the cracked kitchen window. *Thunk thunk.* There was a crater in the street below. A present from Jerry. The buses could never avoid it.

There it was again.

Thunk thunk.

Every bus. Every cab.

Thunk thunk.

They chose to ignore it. Pretend it wasn't there. Pretend it didn't matter, even if it did.

Thunk thunk.

11

The noise was constant. Eliza heard it in her sleep.

Thunk thunk.

Even when all else was quiet, there was always . . .

Thunk thunk.

The heartbeat of the building.

Thunk thunk.

A horn screeched and other sounds trickled back – the conversations in the queue outside, Mrs Granderson's wireless above, the constant drip in the sink.

Eliza looked at the clock. She had just an hour before she was needed at the theatre. It would take her that long to cross London. She changed into her uniform, freshened her face and made her way onto the cluttered stairs. Halfway down, her foot landed in an open bag of tea dregs, mouldy bread and fish waste.

Fighting the urge to be sick, she tried to dislodge her foot but accidentally kicked the mess. The rotting muck exploded, spraying bits of fish-flavoured tea over the wooden stairs and cracked walls. After the bag settled, she straightened her jacket, checked the bun in her hair and proceeded down, nodding to Mrs Hodgkins, who, now struggling up the stairs, stopped to taste a bit of the fish that had landed in her hair.

*

On her hands and knees, Eliza stretched under the seat, her fingers brushing the greasy newspaper. She felt her stockings stick to the unwashed theatre floor as she strained to grasp the edge of the paper. When was the last time Jessie washed these floors like she was meant to? Eliza glanced at her palm. Unidentifiable dark specks pressed into her skin. A shiny brown stain marred the heel of her hand. She could almost picture the filth sinking deeper and deeper into her palm, worming its way through the muscle and bone, finding a way into a vein . . .

'Try this.'

A wooden cane hovered over her head. Holding it was Stephen, his bulldog face caught somewhere between a smile and a grimace, a piece of meat stuck between his crooked teeth.

'Cheers.' Eliza took the cane and guided it under the chair, unable to rid the feel of dirt from her skin.

'Last to leave again, eh, ducks?'

'You're still here, aren't you?'

His horrid aftershave was worse than the smell from under the seats. Stephen bragged how his cousin sent it from Canada, but that scent was nothing to be proud of.

'Well, I can't possibly leave you here on your own, can I? Want me to . . . ?'

'No.' She accidentally knocked the paper further away.

'It would go a lot quicker if—'

'I didn't ask for your opinion.'

He leaned closer, his sour breath warm on her neck. 'I'm only trying to help.'

'That's very kind of you, Stephen, but I can manage.' She hooked the cane behind the paper and dragged the rubbish towards her.

'Well, I wouldn't be a gentleman if I didn't offer.' He placed a heavy hand on her shoulder. She felt it creeping towards her neck, his thumb stroking her through her blouse.

'Eliza?'

She jumped at the sound of Peter's voice.

'Over here!' she called, grabbing the rubbish.

Stephen leant back against a seat as Peter tripped down the aisle towards them, his wavy ginger hair matted down with Brylcreem, light freckles nearly invisible in the dim light. Freckles didn't look so bad on him, she thought. Flecks of white lint peppered the unkempt uniform that hung from his lean frame. She resisted the urge to reach out and pick each bit off one by one and settled for scrubbing her dirty palm against her thigh.

'I couldn't find you anywhere,' Peter said, struggling to juggle the heavy bin bags in his arms.

'Purvis had me clear Jessie's rows.' She tossed the greasy newsprint into her bin bag.

'That's the second time this week she's missed her shift.' Peter dropped one of the bags on his feet. 'Good Lord.'

'Easy, Lamb.' Stephen laughed.

'I don't see you helping.'

'Enough, boys.' Eliza picked up one of Peter's bags along with her own. 'And don't be so hard on Jessie. Think she's finally got herself a new job. Wants to tell me all about it on Saturday. She's been saying for weeks how much she hates this place.'

'I'm beginning to see her point,' Peter sighed, noticing a stain on his vest.

'You're going to see her?' Stephen yawned, baring his teeth like a dog. Eliza hooked her free arm through Peter's, resting her head against his shoulder.

'She rang yesterday. Wants my advice on how to break the news to Purvis. Come on, Peter. Let's toss these out and go to dinner.'

Stephen leapt to his feet. 'Is the invitation open?'

'Couples only.' Eliza smiled, escorting Peter up the aisle and away from that revolting aftershave. Alone in the lobby, she pulled him closer.

'Is everything all right?' he asked.

'Yes. Fine. I'm tired, that's all.' Eliza peeked over her shoulder to see Stephen watching them from the darkened stalls. He picked the food from his teeth and spat it onto the floor.

*

A church bell chimed the hour as Eliza entered her building. Two years on and it still warmed her to hear the bells again. Eleven o'clock – Rebecca would be in bed and Aunt Bess complaining about the laundry. Maybe Eliza would tell her about electric dryers. She slipped her key into the lock, pushed open the door and got slapped in the face.

Aunt Bess radiated fury and fag smoke.

'In.'

Cheek stinging, Eliza bowed her head as she closed the door behind her. Rebecca sat on the edge of the ratty sofa, the box of new shoes at her feet. If Rebecca had cried, her last tears were already smacked out of her.

Aunt Bess reached out her hand.

'Well?'

Eliza pulled the clothing card from her handbag and handed it over without a word. She wanted that to be the end of it. She knew it wasn't. Aunt Bess threw the card onto the side table and grabbed the shoebox lid from the floor.

'*Don't tell Auntie Bess?*' she read. 'Don't tell Auntie Bess!'

'Rebecca had nothing to do with it. It was my idea. Please . . .'

'Of course it was your idea! I bloody well know she wouldn't do anything like this on her own.' She waved the lid about her head, threatening to bring it down like an axe.

'Please let her go to bed.'

Aunt Bess dropped her arm, fingernails gouging the pulpy

flesh of the lid as stiff tendons protruded from the thin skin of her tightened hand.

'You do not tell me what to do. Not in my home. You're bloody lucky to have a home at all. Would you rather be squatting at Bedford House? No heat? No running water? Or should I chuck you out and send her to the orphans' home?'

Rebecca remained still. Eliza trembled. She wanted to run to her sister, sit by her, hold her. Aunt Bess blocked her path.

'What? Nothing to say for yourself this time?'

'I'm sorry,' Eliza whispered. She kept her eyes on the ground.

'Oh. Yes. Sorry is going to get my coupons back, is it?'

'I'm sorry,' she repeated. She stared at the blackened floorboards beneath her feet. Soot was embedded deep into the wood grain. No amount of washing would ever get it clean.

Silence overtook the room. A bus hit the pothole outside. *Thunk thunk.* Aunt Bess's rage receded. She took a seat at the kitchen table, tossing the box lid onto the warped surface. She lit a cigarette and avoided Eliza's eye.

'Take Rebecca and go to bed. I'll decide your punishment in the morning.'

Eliza felt the release in those words. Her paralysis was gone, but Rebecca's remained.

'Come, Rebecca. Time for bed.' Eliza held out her hand. Rebecca did not take it; her eyes remained fixed on an unseen point. Eliza crouched before her. 'Rebecca?' She stroked her sister's soft hair. 'It's time for bed, dearie. Aren't you tired? Rebecca?'

Rebecca turned her head and met Eliza's gaze. Eliza could see nothing in Rebecca's eyes. They were so like their father's, those eyes – large and brown and empty.

'Come on. Bedtime,' Eliza repeated. Rebecca's hand snaked

into hers. She guided her to their bedroom as Aunt Bess's cigarette burned in her hand, the filter never raised to her lips. The key turned stiffly in the door. Eliza double-checked it was locked then sat Rebecca down on the shared double bed while she changed out of her uniform.

'The weather was nice today. They said on the wireless it was only supposed to get warmer. I bet we could have a picnic soon. We could head across town and sit in St James's Park and feed scraps to the ducks. Wouldn't that be lovely?' Eliza finished changing and helped Rebecca lie down underneath the threadbare blankets, pulling them up to her chin the way Mother used to.

'Eliza, are you cross with me?' Rebecca asked, her voice distant. Eliza neatly folded her uniform.

'Why would I be cross? You've done nothing wrong.' She slid the uniform into their dresser, rearranging the collar and sleeves before shutting the drawer.

'Suppose I did, would you still love me? I don't think Auntie Bess does.'

'Oh, Rebecca.' She switched off the light, already feeling the pull of sleep, and crawled into bed beside her sister. 'We're not like Auntie Bess, you and I,' she said, wrapping her arm around her. 'We'll always love each other no matter what.' She kissed Rebecca's cheek then rolled over and stared out the window, unable to see the clear night through the grime-covered glass. Rebecca whispered to the darkness.

'Onetwothreefourfive.'

Eliza couldn't block it out.

'Sixseveneightnineten.'

She remained awake, focusing on the flickering street lamp outside.

'Eleventwelvethirteenfourteen.'

Its orange glow filtered into the room, becoming more pronounced as Eliza's eyes adjusted to the dark.

'Fifteensixteenseventeeneighteen.'

A chair scraped against the kitchen floor.

'Nineteentwenty.'

The stool tipped over. She smelled sulphur and marrow liqueur. Eliza cried.

'Twenty-one.'

No. No stool.

'Twenty-two.'

A chair. Aunt Bess.

'Twenty-three.'

It was only Aunt Bess rising from her chair. Eliza stopped crying and closed her eyes. Rebecca began counting again.

2

Mother stood on the shore, watching them from across the sea. Far, far away she was, but Eliza could see her clearly, see her smiling. At the dock was a little wooden boat, rocking gently back and forth. Father picked up Rebecca and sat her inside. He offered Eliza his hand, but she could not move. Peter held her, anchoring her to the grassy bank. Father turned his back on her and climbed into the boat. The dock faded and he rowed in long, even strokes, taking Rebecca away. Mother waited, solemn. Eliza wanted to tell them to wait but she had lost her voice and did not know if it would return. The boat became a pinprick in the ocean, so small Eliza could hold it in her hand. She balanced it on her palm. A mighty screech startled her. She dropped the boat and it broke at her feet.

The bus honked again, and Eliza startled awake. She checked the mattress was dry then slipped out of bed, careful not to wake Rebecca, as the scent of the ocean still lingered in her mind. Pulling on Mother's dressing gown, she crept out of the bedroom to find Aunt Bess cooking breakfast. A cigarette butt burned in the cracked ashtray beside her.

'Good morning,' Eliza said.

Aunt Bess dropped the wooden spoon. She picked it off the floor and stuck it straight back into the porridge.

'Morning.'

'Did I oversleep?' Eliza approached the table, keeping her arms tucked around her waist.

19

'No. I had to wake early today.'

'Oh.'

The contents of Aunt Bess's handbag were dumped across the table. Eliza's eyes were drawn to the grey envelope, now opened, that she had glimpsed yesterday. The stationery was thick – expensive – with Aunt Bess's name and address scrawled in red ink in a neat, slanting hand.

As if sensing Eliza's gaze, Aunt Bess forgot the porridge and grabbed the letter. Then she cleared the rest of her things. 'Set the table, would you?'

'Of course.' Eliza retrieved the plates from the cupboard. 'Would you like me to wake Rebecca?'

'No. Let the girl sleep. Pour us some tea, would you?'

Eliza obliged, retrieving the pot and two cups. They were both eating before either spoke again.

'Rebecca needn't come to work today,' said Aunt Bess.

'She hasn't been let go?'

'She's getting the day off. I've already discussed it with Mr Mosley.'

'But she'll be allowed back? She loves the work. It keeps her—'

'That's not for you to worry about, Eliza.' Aunt Bess dabbed her mouth with the edge of her apron then rose from the table. 'I need to change. Keep her busy today.'

'I have to leave for work at five o'clock.'

Aunt Bess hesitated as she pushed in her chair.

'No. You don't.'

'But . . .'

'I've spoken to Mr Purvis as well. Perform your household duties as per usual and I'll be home for dinner at six.' She went to the sitting room to change into her work clothes while Eliza remained at the table.

20

'Is this our punishment? Taking away our livelihoods?'

'Working as a cigarette girl is hardly a livelihood.'

'Auntie Bess, I know what I did was wrong, but—'

'There's to be no further conversation on the matter. Now do as you're told and be here at six. Understood?'

Eliza stared into her bowl. The porridge was runny, tasteless.

'Understood, Eliza?'

'Yes, ma'am.'

'Good.' She finished applying her lipstick then dropped the make-up into her handbag and stared inside the small handbag. 'Good.' She snapped it shut. 'Six o'clock. And I expect you to be on time.'

Eliza stared at the closed door, feeling Mother's old dislike for Bess Haverford threatening to escalate into her own absolute hatred. The floor creaked behind her. She turned to see Rebecca standing in the bedroom doorway, tapping the handle.

*

'What's she planning, then?' Peter asked as they strolled down Charing Cross Road. Eliza held a new book from Foyles under one arm, the other threaded loosely through Peter's, as Rebecca skipped beside them.

'I don't know. I never know.'

'All over a pair of shoes . . .'

'Peter, please. Can we talk about something else?'

'Yes. Sorry. Course we can.'

They continued their walk, neither saying a word. Rebecca darted ahead to look in a shop window, then ran back to Eliza and Peter. A pigeon flew low over their heads and landed on a nearby ledge. Rebecca ducked and laughed, sticking her tongue out at the bird.

'Well. This is exciting,' Peter said.

'I'm sorry. I'm just . . .'

'Worried? Tired? Angry?'

'Do I look worried, tired or angry?' Eliza fussed with her limp hair.

'No. I think you look . . .'

'Normal?'

'I was going to say beautiful.'

'Thank you.' She blushed.

'Well, I mean it. By the way . . . I was thinking . . .'

Say it, she thought. *I'll say yes if you ask*. She spun the Claddagh ring on her finger.

'I'll be finished with my apprenticeship soon. Uncle Marvin says I'll be a fine accountant, earning a good wage. I won't have to work at the Palladium any more . . .'

'Yes?' She squeezed his arm, encouraging him. *Say it . . .*

'Thought I might go on holiday. Leave London for a bit . . .'

For a honeymoon, she thought. *Please say . . .*

'If you'll be all right without me.'

She stopped walking.

'Oh. Well,' Eliza started. 'If it's what you . . .'

'Hard to get abroad, but I thought maybe the Isle of Wight or the Lake District. Could be difficult, but can't hurt trying, can it?' He smiled and checked his watch. 'That can't be the time. Suppose I should be off or Uncle Marvin will have my head.'

'Peter, wait.'

'Work and all. You know.'

'Just . . . thank you. For wasting your luncheon hour on us.'

'Waste? Nonsense. What else would I do?' He pressed his lips to Eliza's cheek. The lingering warmth of his kiss remained as he walked the opposite way down the street. Eliza watched him, pressing her hand to the still-tingling spot below her cheekbone.

'He will. One day,' she whispered. 'Rebecca, let's go home. Rebecca?' She could not spot her sister in the crowd. 'Rebecca?' She clutched her book with both hands.

A squeal of tyres ended in a sick thump.

'Rebecca!'

A small crowd gathered by the street was already dispersing as Eliza ran towards it. Rebecca stood safe on the pavement, looking down. A dead cat lay by a sewer grate. Fresh blood seeped from under its carcass, the neck broken. A dark red blotch stained its chin where its mouth was frozen in a permanent scream.

'Leave it. Come away. Rebecca, come away.' Eliza grabbed her sister by the wrist and pulled her down the street.

'What's wrong, Eliza?'

'Nothing.'

'It was only a body, wasn't it? What made it a cat was gone. That's what you said when . . .'

'Yes. I did. But I told you not to stare then, too, didn't I?' She walked quickly, straightening the collar of her blouse as she dragged Rebecca behind her, slowing only when she heard her sister crying.

*

Six fifteen p.m. Aunt Bess was late. The only logical explanation was that something awful had happened to her. Rebecca was too busy counting the cutlery to notice. The beef stew grew cold. All her life, Eliza had never known Aunt Bess to be late, not even by fifteen minutes. She focused on her knitting. Her mother had made the most beautiful gloves and scarves. Eliza hadn't inherited her natural ability. The current project was a blue scarf for Peter that she had started in January. She hoped to have it finished by Christmas.

6.20 p.m.

What if something had happened to Aunt Bess? She was the only family Eliza and Rebecca had left. And there had been so many muggings lately. The papers blamed mothers who continued to work after the war – said there was no one to look after children, who now ran rampant through the streets.

6.25 p.m.

'Liza, can't we eat yet?'

'You know we need to wait. Why don't you practise your cross stitch?' Eliza handed her the sewing basket. Rebecca sat beside her on the couch and pulled out a scrap of fabric, a needle and some thread. In the flat above, the muffled sounds of *It's That Man Again* drifted down from Mrs Granderson's wireless.

6.30 p.m.

What if Aunt Bess had been attacked? What would happen to them if she died? Would they be separated? Rebecca wouldn't bear being away from her again. Eliza could see Aunt Bess walking home down the street, pausing to search through her handbag for a cigarette, unaware of her surroundings. Unaware of the man sneaking up behind her. He would grab her, his meaty hand covering her mouth, preventing her from screaming as he dragged her into an alley. Aunt Bess would kick and scratch, desperate to fight him off but not possessing the strength. Her neck could snap so easily . . .

The front door clicked open. Eliza sprang to her feet, the scarf slipping to the floor as Aunt Bess appeared, unharmed.

'Good. You're here.' She twisted her red gloves in her hands as she avoided Eliza's gaze.

'Yes. Are you all right? We were . . .'

A man stood behind Aunt Bess. He was tall – taller even than Mr Mosley – his great height causing his broad shoulders to slouch forward. His left arm hung loosely at his side, drawing attention to its missing counterpart, the right sleeve of his dirtied flannel shirt pinned up at the shoulder. He looked no more than thirty, but his face was a patchwork of scars, reminding Eliza of the crumbling Egyptian statues she'd seen at the British Museum as a child.

The door smacked shut behind him.

Aunt Bess spoke first. 'This is Mr Drewry. He's taking you to Wales.'

Eliza must have heard wrong, must have still been imagining things.

'I'm sorry?' she asked.

'You have an hour to pack your things. Then Mr Drewry will escort you to the train station. I've secured you work at a house in—'

'We have work. Here. In London.'

'You had work in London,' she said, removing her thinning burgundy coat. Her hands were shaking. 'Now you have work in Wales.'

'What . . . Who gives you the right?'

'Your father.'

Eliza felt Rebecca grow still beside her. She kept her attention on Aunt Bess.

'He never said you could send us away from everything we've ever known. He never—'

'He made me your legal guardian, which means I can raise you however I see fit. But, as you are an adult now, Eliza, I suppose I can't force you to go. Yet I needn't let you stay. From this point on, you're no longer permitted to live here.'

They didn't have to leave London, she thought, thank God.

And they didn't have to live with Bess, either. Peter's parents. They could stay with them in Shepperton. Peter was right about his apprenticeship. He'd be earning a good wage soon. Surely then he'd propose. That was all he was waiting for. She and Rebecca would pack tonight. Leave this wretched place forever. Live with people who truly cared for them. This was a blessing, really. A blessing . . .

'As for Rebecca,' Aunt Bess interrupted her thoughts. 'She is under my care until she is of legal age. I am her guardian. Not you. And, regardless of what you choose to do, she will be going to Wales.'

'No!' Rebecca threw herself at Aunt Bess, stabbing her in the leg with the sewing needle then scratching at her stomach and face. 'No! No, you won't take Eliza away! I won't let you! No!'

'Rebecca!' Eliza pulled at her sister's shoulders, tried to get her arms around her waist, but the girl's wiry frame was tense with rage. She could not get a hold of her.

'Bitch bitch bitch!' Rebecca screamed, now kicking Aunt Bess's legs. Aunt Bess raised her hands in front of her face but otherwise did nothing to defend herself.

'Rebecca, stop!' Eliza begged. Feeling a hand on her shoulder, she turned and saw Mr Drewry standing next to her. He pushed her aside and reached for Rebecca, but Eliza shoved him back.

'No!' She threw her entire body over Rebecca and dragged her away from their aunt.

'I hate you!' Rebecca screamed. 'I hate you, I hate you, I hate all of you!' She broke free from Eliza's hold and ran into their bedroom.

The slam of the door was the full stop to her outburst. The room went quiet. Laughter from Mrs Granderson's wireless trickled through the ceiling.

Eliza watched as Aunt Bess bent over and extracted Rebecca's sewing needle from her thigh. A sheen of red glistened on the thin metal. Aunt Bess went pale then carried the needle to the kitchen sink. Eliza retreated to the bedroom. She closed the door softly behind her and rested her head on the cold wood, listening to Rebecca sobbing on the bed.

She could leave all this behind tonight.

She turned to her sister. 'You know you mustn't use such language. It's very rude.' She took her handkerchief and wiped Rebecca's face clean of tears.

'You won't leave me, will you, Eliza?'

Rebecca was so small for her age. Such a fragile thing, easily broken. Eliza could still see the cracks from before. Rebecca absolutely wouldn't survive being away from her again. Eliza took a breath.

'Never, dearie. We'll stay together. Always. I promise.'

An hour later and the room was empty save a ratty blanket, their gas masks and Aunt Bess's derelict furniture. Their entire lives fitted into two brown suitcases, except her books. There wasn't enough room. They remained on the shelf, abandoned, begging to be brought with them. The paperback Peter had bought her that afternoon lay abandoned on the shelf, unread and out of place. Eliza had to look away, unable to bear the sight. She wrapped up her hair in a headscarf and slipped on her ragged mauve coat. Into the pocket, she slipped one novel – a gift from Father. Forgotten in that pocket was a government pamphlet, one she received during her evacuation – *Information on Bed-wetting for Householders Taking Unaccompanied Children*. She considered saving it, then tossed it into the bin instead.

Aunt Bess sat in the kitchen, smoking, when they emerged. Eliza helped Rebecca carry her luggage to the door, where

Mr Drewry waited. Rebecca had become vacant, the way she often did after a fit, and made no protest when Mr Drewry took her arm. Before Eliza could wrench her sister from him, Aunt Bess called from the table. Eliza would not look at her.

'Aren't you going to say goodbye?' Aunt Bess asked.

Eliza picked up both suitcases and motioned for Mr Drewry to exit the flat.

'No.' She closed the door calmly as she left. Mrs Hodgkins was carrying a bin bag downstairs.

'Going on a trip, love?'

Eliza ignored her.

Outside, a cab waited for them. Mr Drewry opened the taxi door and climbed inside with Rebecca. Eliza followed with the suitcases. Their escort sat close to the driver while the girls settled in across from him. A layer of grime coated the floor, and the thin seats had little cushioning left. A spring jabbed into Eliza's upper thigh. She tucked in her legs and arms, attempting to touch as little of the filthy car as possible. As the cab drove off, Eliza saw a tall, skeletal man enter their building – Mr Mosley.

'May it be an unhappy union,' she muttered, and looked away.

With Rebecca leaning against her, Eliza stared out of the window as the cab made its way through the streets. She watched the buses and pedestrians, admired the old Victorian homes now pockmarked from bomb blasts and glanced down narrow side streets where spivs stood selling their wares. She watched the damp pavements speeding alongside her, empty of queues now the shops had shut.

Eliza watched it all as the cab took them further away from home. She was still here yet missing it already. She did her best not to think about Peter. As soon as she could, she would write to him. Rebecca kept silent. She wasn't counting, at least not aloud. It was the best Eliza could hope for. Mr Drewry also remained mute, staring out of his window for the duration of the ride. If he was familiar with London, Eliza couldn't tell. He expressed neither the interest of someone visiting the city for the first time nor the apathy of someone who'd seen it all before.

The cab stopped outside Paddington Station. Mr Drewry paid the driver then led Rebecca out, leaving Eliza with the suitcases. When Peter went on holiday, would he leave from here, she wondered as she followed Mr Drewry and Rebecca inside. Would Peter think of her as he travelled alone, or would there be another girl at his side?

She followed Mr Drewry to Platform 4, where a train awaited them underneath the high, vaulted arches. The ticket collector directed them to a first-class carriage, for which Eliza was grateful. Returning to London after the war, she and the other children were packed in the coach compartments so tight there was no room for anyone to sit. A little boy had vomited on her only pair of shoes.

Mr Drewry chose an empty compartment and slid the door shut behind them. Only then did he help Eliza with the luggage. Together, they lifted the pieces onto the racks above their heads, his solitary arm proving remarkably strong. Once finished, he sat across from the sisters and went back to staring out of the window. Eliza could no longer bear the silence.

'My name is Eliza. This is Rebecca.'

She waited. He said nothing.

'What part of Wales are we going to?'

No answer.

'Could you at least tell us how long the journey will take?'

'Seven hours, fourteen minutes,' he replied. Eliza expected

his voice to be soft, lilting and Welsh. Instead, it was hard and English. Possibly Northern, though it was difficult to tell since he spoke so little. She thanked him then leant Rebecca against her shoulder and began her silent goodbyes to home.

*

It did not take long for the city to disappear. Eliza watched as the lights faded away into fog. Once they were rolling through darkened fields, she felt Rebecca's heart beat faster.

'Better than last time we left, isn't it?' she said. 'Don't have to worry about bombs falling on us before we get there. And no awful luggage labels on our coats, either.'

Despite Eliza's words, Rebecca remained tense and unresponsive.

Now three hours had passed since the train left. Eliza thought Mr Drewry would fall asleep, maybe pull his hat down to block out the carriage lights, like Father used to do on long journeys, but Mr Drewry did nothing. Every once in a while he'd smoke a cigarette but that was all. He didn't appear to mind Eliza and Rebecca talking, however.

'Why don't you read to me?' Eliza asked when, for lack of something to do, Rebecca began kicking the underside of her seat. She pulled the tattered copy of *Mrs Miniver* from her handbag and gave it to her sister.

'Where should I start?'

'Oh, why not the beginning?' Eliza replied, closing her eyes. 'We have plenty of time.' She heard Rebecca open the book and fold back the pages.

'"For my girls. No day is complete without a story. With love, Father."'

Eliza smiled. Rebecca turned the page.

'Eliza, does Aunt Bess hate us?'

30

'Hate is a very strong word. I think maybe she grew tired of us.'

'Do you hate her?'

Eliza sighed and opened her eyes. 'Right now, I'm very cross with her. But I don't know if I've ever hated anyone.'

'You hate Hitler.'

'Well, that's true.'

'For what he did to Mother.'

'For what he did to lots of people. Now go on and read. I can't remember how it starts.'

Rebecca began the opening chapter but stopped after the first paragraph.

'I hate Aunt Bess,' she said.

'You're too young to know if you hate anyone.'

'No I'm not. And I do, I hate her. I hate her and I'm not sorry for hitting her.'

'Well, if you're not sorry now then you will be,' Eliza said.

'Why?'

'Because you'll realise it was wrong. Are you going to keep reading or shall I do it myself?'

Rebecca continued then stopped when she reached the end of the page.

'Liza?'

'Yes, dearie?'

'Will you grow tired of me?'

Eliza wrapped an arm around her sister's shoulders. 'I can't. It's against the law for sisters to grow tired of each other.'

'It is not.'

'Is too. Mr Attlee passed it through parliament just the other day.'

'You're fibbing,' Rebecca giggled.

'Am not. The king asked for it. The princesses had an

argument and he wanted to make sure that – no matter what – they would always remain friends.'

'Liar.'

'Saw it in the papers.'

'Well, I don't believe you.'

'Well, I think you should keep reading.'

They shared a smile and Rebecca returned her attention to the book, reciting page after page as the train continued forward through the fog.

*

Eliza rummaged through her purse. All she had was £2 12s 8d. Pay day would never come after all.

'I'm hungry, Eliza.'

'I know.'

'We didn't get dinner.'

'I know.'

'I haven't had anything to eat for ages!'

'Hush!'

Mr Drewry appeared to have fallen asleep, and Eliza was afraid of waking him. Slowly, she rose, pressing her finger to her lips to keep Rebecca quiet. Her hand was on the carriage door when a train thundered past in the opposite direction. Mr Drewry shot up in his seat, using the stump of his missing arm to search for something at his side. When he couldn't reach, he looked at the missing limb as if seeing it for the first time. The panic only lasted a moment, already dissipating when he saw Eliza at the door.

'Would it be all right if we went to the dining car?' Eliza asked, hoping he wouldn't notice they had already been leaving. Mr Drewry glanced at the floor then at the window, touching his hand to the glass.

'Mr Drewry?'

'Suit yourselves,' he said, keeping his gaze on the window.

Eliza thanked him then exited the compartment with Rebecca. They had just passed the five-hour mark of their journey and Eliza's legs were cramping, her back stiff. A headache was brewing and her stomach sent hunger pains up into her chest as her dry eyes itched. She wanted a bed – a double, no a king – where she and Rebecca could both stretch out and fall asleep and not wake for a very long time.

Instead, she stood in the dining car, Rebecca clinging to her arm for support as she pleaded with a waiter.

'Please, sir. We didn't realise what time the kitchen closed. We'll take anything you have. It can be cold. I do have money. We'll pay for anything. Please. My poor little sister is famished.'

As they spoke, the train pulled into a station. *Swansea*, read the sign. On the platform was a telegram office.

'How long will our stop be?' Eliza asked.

'At least half an hour. We're changing engines here.'

'Rebecca, wait here.'

'Where are you—?'

'If Mr Drewry comes, tell him I went to the toilets.'

Eliza ran out of the carriage and onto the platform.

'Please, please be open,' she whispered to herself as she weaved her way through the crowd of disembarking passengers. The telegram office was indeed open. A bored young man waited behind the counter.

'How much to send a message to London?' she asked, digging through her small purse.

'Six pence per ten words.'

Eliza grabbed the form. Mr Drewry grabbed her arm. Rebecca stood outside the office, the suitcases beside her.

'I . . . I was . . .'

'We're changing trains.' He took the blank form from her

33

hand and set it on the counter then pulled her from the office. Eliza looked for the young clerk, but he had disappeared.

On the platform, Mr Drewry shoved Eliza's suitcase towards her with his foot. It bounced against her shins. He picked up Rebecca's case and walked to the platform opposite. Eliza took Rebecca's hand and the other suitcase and went after him.

As they waited in the bitter cold for the connecting train, she glanced often at the telegram office. One message, that was all Peter needed and he would come running after her. How else would he be able to find her? And who would help Mrs Hodgkins carry her shopping, or look after Mr Pendleton's canary when he went to Blackpool? She was to meet Jessie on Saturday for tea. How long would she wait at the Corner House before deciding Eliza had abandoned her?

There was so much left unfinished and nothing she could do as their new train pulled into the station. Only a handful of passengers climbed aboard its four coaches. They settled into an empty compartment in the last car. Mr Drewry lapsed back into silence, but Eliza could see he was keeping a closer eye on them. Once they were seated, Rebecca elbowed her. In her hand was some cold ham and bread wrapped in newspaper.

'When he saw Mr Drewry,' she whispered, 'he said we could have it.'

Eliza grabbed a piece of the bread and took a bite, closing her eyes as she chewed slowly.

'God bless the waiters,' she sighed.

*

Click-clack-clack.

Eliza listened to the rhythm of the train as it carried them deeper into Wales. It was well past midnight. Usually, she would be home from work now.

Click-clack-clack.

Rebecca was already asleep, but Eliza fought to remain awake. She wanted to stay alert. She could sleep when they arrived.

Click-clack-clack.

She had to keep an eye on Mr Drewry. She had to pay attention.

Click-clack-clack.

She had to stay awake.

*

Rebecca did not scream. Even as Eliza shouted, Rebecca said nothing. Nor did she move. Eliza grabbed her, tried to push her up the stairs. Eliza did not want to look. All she could hear was her own voice, crying. All she could smell was dust. Dust and marrow liqueur, spreading across the cellar, the brown syrup seeping into the dirt floor. Dust and marrow and . . .

Her screams became the screeching of the train lurching to a stop. Eliza jolted awake and placed a hand to her throat. It was not bruised. Nor should it have been, she reminded herself.

'Only a dream,' she whispered. Rebecca stared at her. Eliza looked away and saw that they had stopped at a dimly lit station.

Mr Drewry pulled their luggage down from the rack then carried Eliza's suitcase out of the cabin. Eliza took Rebecca's case in one hand and Rebecca's hand in the other then followed him onto the platform. As the train pulled away, Eliza realised they were the only ones to disembark. The tiny station had one sheltered waiting room where a solitary lantern hung above a rotting door. The name *Plentynunig* was painted in whitewash on an old wooden sign. Mr Drewry led them down a few creaking stairs that led to a patch of grass beside an unpaved road.

Across the way was a pub, a light still on despite the lateness of the hour. Mr Drewry headed directly for it. He set down the suitcase and rapped several times on the pub door. Eliza heard the bolts being thrown back. The door cracked open. A balding head appeared, saw Mr Drewry and nodded. The door then closed; the bolts slid back in place.

Mr Drewry picked up the suitcase and walked the girls back to the road.

'Eliza,' Rebecca whispered. 'I'm still hungry.'

'Me too. I'm sure they'll have something for us when we arrive.' She squeezed her sister's hand. It was colder here than in London, and Eliza found herself pulling her coat tight around her. A chilling wind cut through the stillness of the night and a light mist coated the girls in fine droplets of rain. Eliza remembered when she was evacuated, how the Littletons had immediately filled her with Ovaltine and sponge cake and told her she was going to be just fine as she warmed herself by the fire. And she had been, until her evacuation ended.

Around the corner of the pub came an open-top carriage driven by the balding publican. He stopped the weary grey horse in front of the trio and hopped down. Mr Drewry handed the man some money then tossed the girls' luggage into the back.

When he offered them a hand into the carriage, Eliza climbed up by herself then helped Rebecca in. Mr Drewry ignored her refusal and hoisted himself into the driver's seat. With a flick of his wrist, the horse moved steadily forward. Eliza glanced behind her, watching the man's silhouette fade as they disappeared over the first hill.

'Excuse me, Mr Drewry, may I ask how long till we arrive?'

'Twenty minutes.'

A single lantern hanging towards the front of the carriage was all the light they had. Eliza searched around them for something to keep warm and eventually found an old wool blanket under their seats. She tucked it around herself and Rebecca. There was nothing to see in the dark. Eliza began humming to keep her nerves steady. She didn't realise what song it was until she reached the refrain – 'We'll Meet Again'. She stopped mid-phrase. Memories came unbidden into her mind. Memories of that song playing on the wireless when Mr Littleton had handed her the telegram that informed her of Mother's death.

Eliza let the journey continue in silence. The biting wind prevented her from falling asleep. She focused on finding signs of life in the unfamiliar landscape. A house, a shop, a stray dog, anything. All she could see was the road they travelled on and the grass either side. The effort drained her and exhaustion tired her body. The increasing pulse of a headache created a growing pressure behind her eyes.

Despite her vigilance, Eliza didn't notice the stone and iron gates until they were passing through them. She turned round to try to get a better look, but they had already disappeared into the darkness. Facing forward, she saw a speck of light in the near distance, growing stronger with each pull of the carriage.

From the light emerged the outline of a manor house. Like Carroll's Cheshire Cat, it came into being piece by piece – there a window, there a chimney, there a hedge. The carriage drew closer. There appeared a door and, by that door, a thin, unmoving figure.

Mr Drewry pulled the carriage to a stop in front of the house. The still figure remained in the doorway. It was a woman – Eliza could see now – her hair pulled back in a loose bun, dark dress swaying in the night-time breeze. Eliza had barely enough strength to climb down from the carriage and nearly fainted as she and Rebecca waited to follow Mr Drewry into the house. As they did so, the woman stepped aside, allowing them entry, then approached the girls, a lantern held above their heads as she inspected them.

The shadows from the flame fell on her face, exaggerating the wrinkles around her mouth and eyes. Grey flecked her dark brown hair, and her serious manner reminded Eliza of their long-dead grandmother. When she spoke to Mr Drewry, her breath smelled of aspic and her voice sounded much younger than such a face should allow.

'Why,' she asked, 'are there two of them?'

3

Eliza lost her grip on Rebecca's hand as they walked through the serpentine halls. Gilded frames decorated the walls, reflecting the light from the lantern's low flame. The paintings themselves were near-black, swallowed by darkness, the lantern too weak to illuminate the full images within.

Her body, damp from the rain and heavy from exhaustion, lacked the strength to reclaim Rebecca's hand. Each step threatened collapse. The boiled ham she had eaten on the train sat undigested in her stomach, weighing her down. All she could do was follow the warm orange light and allow herself to be led deeper into the labyrinth.

The housekeeper seemed oblivious to Eliza's exhaustion. She strode ahead at a steady pace, weaving her way effortlessly through the house. Eliza's head pounded in time to her pulse. She focused on that pain, willing the rest of her stiff body numb. No longer could she feel her feet hitting the floor. Any moment her legs would give out beneath her.

Without warning, the housekeeper stopped. Holding the lantern up to an unmarked door, she removed a set of heavy iron keys from her waist. She spoke, but Eliza's tired mind made no sense of the words. What she saw through the opened door was a bed neatly made and waiting. She could feel the warmth of her sister's body beside her, but her head felt so light that if she turned to look, she knew she would faint.

There were more words, more things Eliza could not

understand. Instead, she forced herself forward and fell onto the bed, her body spiralling into sleep as she felt Rebecca climb in beside her.

*

Rusty curtain rings scraped against a metal rod. Eliza jerked awake.

'It's six thirty,' said a sharp voice. 'Breakfast is in half an hour. Out, turn right. Third door on the left. The kitchen doors lock precisely at seven. Chores begin at seven thirty. From the kitchen, I'll give you a full tour of the manor then set you your list for the day. Your luggage is in the hall.'

The door banged shut.

Eliza sat in a momentary stupor. She felt queasy, her left leg only pins and needles, and the headache that saw her to bed remained to greet her this morning.

'Rebecca, wake up.' She nudged the lump beside her.

A grunt sounded from beneath the blanket.

'Yes,' Eliza said. 'We have to eat.'

The lump would not move.

'Come on, dearie.' Eliza prodded what she thought was a shoulder. An arm swung at her face. Eliza caught it before it could strike. 'No,' she said firmly, looking Rebecca in the eye. 'No.' When Rebecca relaxed, Eliza released her. 'Let's get dressed.'

They pulled their suitcases into the bedroom and rummaged through them for something to wear. Dawn was just breaking and there was little light in the room. 'Room' was a generous word, Eliza thought as she slipped on clean dungarees. The place was little more than a cupboard, barely able to accommodate even its few pieces of furniture – the single bed, a water-damaged wardrobe and a wobbling side table. The wardrobe and table were stained a dark brown, except where they were scratched or chipped. The bed frame, made of metal, had rust accumulating at the welds, reminding Eliza of the beds at Rebecca's former hospital. The curtains were a faded olive green patched together in several places. Dust circulated in the damp air, swirling in patterns illuminated by the oncoming dawn. Eliza sneezed and her head throbbed.

Rebecca struggled with her shoe. 'Liza, I want to go back to sleep.'

'Well, we can either sleep or we can eat. And I don't think we'll be able to get through today on empty stomachs.' Eliza finished lacing up her own shoes and rose from the bed. Rebecca remained seated.

'I don't want to be here. I want to go home.'

'I know. But there's nothing we can do about that right now.'

Rebecca refused to move. Eliza sat back down beside her.

'We're still tired and we're hungry and we're grumpy. And that makes everything seem more awful than it is. But we'll eat well today, sleep well tonight, and tomorrow, everything will be a little bit better.'

'I don't want to be here tomorrow. I don't want to be here at all!'

'Neither do I and I promise I'll do whatever I can to get us home. But for now, let's make do as best we can.' Eliza stood and held out her hand. 'All right?'

Rebecca rose from the bed but walked past Eliza into the hall, counting as soon as Eliza closed the door. Eliza's eyes, itchy and red from so little sleep, struggled to focus. She stared at blue floral wallpaper coated in coal dust as each whispered number aggravated her headache. So much dust lingered in this place. How much did she inhale with every breath? How much had she swallowed while she slept? Rebecca counted as Eliza pictured her lungs blackening. Mites lived in the dust, Mother once told her, too small to see. But Eliza could feel them, dancing up and down her arms, making their way into her hair, her eyes, her ears.

Once Rebecca counted to twenty-three, she started towards the kitchen. Eliza followed. The faded wallpaper peeled at the edges of the chipped moulding, revealing the cracked brown wall beneath. Eliza could almost see the mites crawling underneath the paper, up to the ceiling stained with yellow and brown water spots. The mites could fall on her from above. She brushed them off her skin and clothes, but more dust greeted her as she walked. She tried not to breathe, afraid of further poisoning her lungs, but this made her light-headed. She felt herself teetering as if balancing on the edge of a pier. Before she could recover, she swayed and lost her balance. Her palms smacked into the thin carpet as she narrowly avoided cracking her chin. Her pulse quickened and her breath caught in her chest. The high walls loomed over her, pressing in from either side. She tried to stand but had no strength in her legs. Eliza closed her eyes, rid her mind of thoughts of mites, and took a deep breath before trying again. This time her legs did not fail her.

Rebecca continued down the hall, blind to her sister's need. Eliza frowned. While she went out of her way to ensure Rebecca was safe and happy, soothing her over something as simple as a splinter, she could be sat bleeding on the pavement and Rebecca would walk past her without a second look. As she brushed off her red palms, she remembered the time Rebecca caught her crying in their bedroom. Instead of asking what was wrong, Rebecca told her they were out of jam and vanished. Eliza knew Rebecca loved her, but Rebecca had no grasp of how to care. Caring was Eliza's responsibility and, before that, Mother's. It was Mother who would sing to Rebecca when she cried. Mother who would cradle her after a bad dream. Mother who would tell her that everything would be fine. Eliza's songs and comforts never had quite the same effect. Whenever Eliza said everything would be fine, something would go wrong.

The kitchen door mirrored the state of the hall. Clumps of unappetizing pea-green paint clogged the once intricate carvings decorating the door's border, while specks of gold peeked through the muddy brown of the tarnished brass knob. Rebecca started tapping the door before Eliza could stop her.

The war taught her to be patient, to remain calm in the most dire situations, but with her legs like jelly and back aching like a witch's hump, the memory of imagined mites still tickling her skin, all she wanted was for Rebecca to stop her incessant counting and let her have some breakfast.

Twenty-three.

The opened door released a harsh morning light. Eliza raised a hand to shield eyes accustomed to the dim hall.

'This must be the east wing,' she said, trying to enjoy the sun's warmth instead of focusing on how much it burned.

'Well spotted.'

The housekeeper, her hair in an elaborate plait, stood by a square wooden table that sat in front of a set of long windows. Sunlight illuminated the multiple counters and cabinets. Their white paint reflected the light and revealed the dirt and grease which had accumulated over the years. One cabinet door was missing from its hinges.

Rebecca started tapping the doorknob. 'One, two, three, four . . .'

'What is she doing?' the housekeeper asked.

'She's making sure the door is closed,' Eliza replied. It was time yet again to explain. Eliza prepared the oft-said words in her mind. By now she could almost say them without the fierce flush which accompanied shame.

'Eight, nine, ten . . .'

'It is closed. I can see that from here.'

'Thirteen, fourteen . . .'

'She'll be done in a moment. We weren't properly introduced last night. I'm Eliza Haverford, and this is my sister—'

'I know very well who you are. I hired you, didn't I?'

'Eighteen, nineteen . . .'

'You – girl! Stop that.'

Eliza stepped to the side, trying to block the woman's view of Rebecca.

'Please, it's better if you . . . if she's left to it.'

'So your aunt sent me an extra mouth to feed who's a simpleton as well.' She turned to a large bowl on the counter beside her.

'Twenty-three.' Rebecca joined her sister by the table.

'She's not—'

'Sit down.' The housekeeper pointed to a chair.

'Excuse me, I . . .'

'You sit or you don't eat.'

The chair wobbled as Eliza sat. She grasped the table to steady herself. Cold, congealing porridge was ladled into each of their bowls. A thin skin had already formed across the top.

'My name is Mrs Pollard. I run the estate. I'll handle the cooking until you prove yourself adequate. Luncheon is cold meats and bread. Dinner, the daily menu approved by Mr Brownawell. Luncheon is at precisely twelve thirty and dinner at seven. If you're not here by then, you don't eat.'

Rebecca stared into her bowl. Eliza kicked her under the table before she could make a face.

'I'm sorry, Mrs Pollard, but who is Mr Brownawell?' Eliza asked.

Mrs Pollard swivelled round and fixed her gaze on Eliza. Her eyes were a deep brown and sparked as she spoke. 'Mr Brownawell owns this house and most of the surrounding land in Carmarthenshire. Didn't that aunt of yours tell you anything?'

'No, ma'am. I'm afraid she didn't.'

Rebecca nibbled at her porridge. Eliza kicked her again, and she started taking bigger spoonfuls.

'Then you'll have to learn quickly. Hurry up and eat. There are plenty of jobs that need doing today.'

Eliza and Rebecca ate in silence while Mrs Pollard cleaned the breakfast dishes. When the clock on the wall read precisely seven thirty, Mrs Pollard returned to the table.

'Done? Good. Leave your bowls. Since you're unfamiliar with the kitchen, you're liable to cause a mess. Don't expect the same courtesy tomorrow. Now follow me.'

As they rose from the table, Eliza reached to straighten Rebecca's dress, which had crumpled in the back, but Rebecca darted away.

'Hold still. Let me fix it,' Eliza said.

'I'm fine. Leave it.'

Eliza grabbed Rebecca's arm and held her while she sorted out the fabric. 'This is getting to be too small. Give it to me tonight and I'll let down the hem. Look, it's too tight in your arms as well. No, you simply cannot wear this again until I've altered it.'

The plain brown dress coupled with her unruly hair made Rebecca resemble a peasant. Mother had dressed them in beautiful, bright colours – frocks with matching bonnets, shining black shoes without the slightest scuff. To see them both now – rumpled, fraying clothes, colour faded from too many scrubs on the washboard – she would not recognize her daughters.

Rebecca tugged her arm free. 'If you hadn't lost our clothing cards, I could buy a new dress.'

'With what money, may I ask?'

'Girls!' Mrs Pollard glared at them. 'If you do not wish to be locked in this kitchen for the rest of the day, I suggest you do as you're told.'

They entered a wide hallway where dusty wood panelling covered the bottom half of the walls while on the top hung the paintings Eliza had glimpsed last night. They were idyllic scenes reminiscent of the Sir Fildes paintings Father once showed her at the National Gallery, the flowers and fields painted in intricate detail while a woman in a ghostly-white muslin gown drew the eye. This same woman in the same gown was at the centre of every painting. In one she picked flowers; in another she stood with a small, scruffy dog.

Though once beautiful, the paintings were uncared for. The paint was cracked, the lines filled with dust. The woman's brown plaited hair possessed a dull grey sheen as if she had aged with the painting.

When Father had walked her through the National Gallery, it frightened Eliza – the way the eyes of those painted figures followed her wherever she went. This woman was different. Every painting depicted her with her back to the observer, and it was she who seemed scared, shielding her face from the living figures passing through her hall. Eliza wanted to reach out a hand and tell her everything would be all right.

There was no plaque on any of the paintings to indicate who

the woman was, and it saddened Eliza that no one deemed her important enough to identify.

Mrs Pollard's voice broke the silence which, until then, had been punctuated only by the padding of their feet on the floorboards. 'This is Thornecroft, built in 1793 by Mr Brownawell's great-grandfather, Sir Charles. This is indeed the east wing. We use mostly this and the west wing. Mr Brownawell's rooms are the only areas open on the first floor. The second floor is completely shut. The main entrance is located in the south hall. Though fitted for electricity, we've had none since the generators broke several years ago. You must learn to do without.'

'Were any soldiers billeted here during the war?' Eliza asked, trying to make friendly conversation.

'I should certainly think not,' Mrs Pollard replied.

'Oh. Only, it's such a grand house, I would've thought the government had forced some on you.'

'Child, His Majesty's government has no concern with Plentynunig, so long as the coal keeps coming.' She stopped in the middle of a great circular foyer where passageways darted off in four directions. 'This is Abigale Hall,' she said. 'Named for Sir Charles's wife. Above you is a glass dome installed by John Nash himself. He designed most of Thornecroft, with the late master's help.'

'It's beautiful,' Rebecca whispered, staring up at the magnificent structure. The morning light shone through the iron and glass, illuminating the large room below before spilling into the surrounding halls and tapering off partway down each corridor. To Eliza, it felt like standing in the centre of the sun.

While Mrs Pollard started back down the east wing, Rebecca remained in the centre of Abigale Hall unable, or unwilling, to look away from the dome. Eliza watched as her sister turned slowly on the spot, face slack, eyes unblinking. Eliza had witnessed her stare that way only twice before – at the Royal Pavilion in Brighton and the last time they saw Father. Drawn in by her sister's trance, Eliza made no move towards her. The sunlight was so warm, the silence of the house so soothing, she could not move for fear of shattering the much-needed sense of calm. For the first time since arriving at the manor, she felt welcome. It was as if the hall fought against the ravages that had overtaken the rest of the manor – forcing the damp and mould into retreat, illuminating the blackened corners. Like the warmth of her mother's arms, Abigale Hall wrapped itself around her, shielding her from all that was dark and terrible.

A loud groan ejaculated from the bowels of the house, spoiling the illusion. Hunger, headache and hurt clawed their way back into her consciousness. Her senses now acute, she listened again for the sound. Rebecca took no heed of it; nor did Mrs Pollard, who continued to glide down the hall. Eliza listened a moment longer.

Nothing. Perhaps it was the pipes. Her hand shaking – from exhaustion, nothing more – she pulled Rebecca away from Abigale Hall and hurried after Mrs Pollard.

'Every morning I'll have a list of duties for you to complete. And they must be completed that day. I assume you can handle basic household chores? We'll travel into the village tomorrow. There may be occasions when I'll need you to run errands. Sundays are days of rest in this house. Breakfast is served at seven thirty, after which I take Mr Brownawell to church. You may do as you like. If you require any other holidays, you must ask me in advance. The answer will be no.'

They arrived at their bedroom door.

'Any questions?'

Eliza had several but knew none were wanted.

'Good. Now, your first task will be to unpack your things. As for you . . .' She looked at Rebecca. 'Your room will be here.' Mrs Pollard showed Rebecca to a door up the hall.

Eliza held her panic in check. They never had separate bedrooms except during the evacuation and Rebecca's hospitalisation. Sleeping alone increased Rebecca's anxiety, as did sleeping in new places. Eliza could only do so much to keep her sister's nerves under control.

'Excuse me, Mrs Pollard?'

'You'll have to clean the space first then you may unpack.'

'Mrs Pollard?'

'We'll bring an extra bed round this afternoon.'

'Mrs—'

'I gave you your task for the morning. Get on with it.'

Eliza mustered all the patience she learnt from dealing with Aunt Bess and countered Mrs Pollard's cold disposition with her own wavering conviction.

'I was only wondering if it was necessary for us to have separate bedrooms. We're quite used to sharing and—'

'Those are Mr Brownawell's rules. They must be abided by.' She waited for Eliza to retaliate, but Eliza could not find the words to form a sensible argument. The way Mrs Pollard's body stiffened, she seemed to be using every ounce of her self-control to refrain from slapping Eliza. The memory of Aunt Bess's sharp palm across her cheek was enough to keep her mouth shut.

'Now,' Mrs Pollard said, 'do you have any more questions, Miss Haverford, or am I allowed to continue with my day?'

Eliza looked past Mrs Pollard to Rebecca, but Rebecca kept her eyes to the floor. Perhaps if they both objected to the sleeping arrangements, Mrs Pollard might acquiesce. As usual, Eliza received no help from her sister.

'I'll see you at luncheon, ma'am,' Eliza said.

'Till luncheon.' Mrs Pollard took Rebecca inside the second bedroom, leaving Eliza with only a fluttering stomach for company.

*

All morning, Eliza cleaned the bedroom. Climbing on top of the wobbly side table, she took down the curtains and hung them out the open window. She remembered helping Mrs Littleton stitch her blackout curtains when the bay window shattered during a night of bombing. Broken glass made numerous cuts in the fabric, the sunlight peeking through the small holes like a hundred fairy lights.

The respite brought from the thorough cleaning was mitigated by how utterly filthy she felt underneath her clothes after so much dusting. It felt as if the little mites were again crawling all over her skin. She hoped she would be allowed to bathe tonight. Not only was her body covered in grime, she could still smell the sweat of the train journey on her. If Peter could see her now . . . She stopped herself. She was too worn down to think of Peter or London without crying. She twisted the ring on her finger. Tomorrow would be better. That was what she had told Rebecca. She had to believe it herself.

As she re-hung the curtain, she noticed the time on her alarm clock. Almost twelve thirty. She wiped her hands on a dusting rag and made her way into the hall. Rebecca was there already, tapping her bedroom doorknob.

'Twenty-two, twenty-three.'

'How is it in there?' Eliza asked, wrapping an arm around her sister's shoulders. Rebecca was often able to lose herself in work. By focusing on chores or cleaning, she had less energy to spend on her worries. If they had plenty of work to do, as

50

Mrs Pollard implied, perhaps Rebecca wouldn't be as anxious here as Eliza originally believed.

But Rebecca did not answer, her attention on something in the pocket of her cardigan.

'What do you have there, dearie?' Eliza asked.

Rebecca turned away. 'Nothing.'

'Go on. Let me see.' Eliza pulled Rebecca's hand from her pocket.

A dead mouse fell to the carpet, its head twisted backwards in a grotesque fashion.

'Why on earth are you carrying that around?' Eliza shuddered, looking at the tiny, lifeless body on the floor.

'I found it.'

'In your room? Well, you should have left it or put it in the bin. Not your pocket. It's still warm . . . Never mind. It's time for luncheon.'

'We can't leave him there!'

'And what do you suggest we do? Give it a proper burial?' Eliza felt her headache, which had receded over the past few hours, make its return. This time it pulsated at the back of her head, drilling its way towards her eyes. 'No. I suppose you're right. Mrs Pollard will have a fit if she sees it lying there. Is there a wastepaper basket in your room or . . .'

'A small one.'

'Put it in there then. We'll chuck it out later. Go on.'

Rebecca knelt beside the mouse and placed it in her palm as if coaxing an injured chick. Her lips were moving. She whispered, but Eliza could not hear what. After disposing of the mouse, the girls made their way to the kitchen.

Mrs Pollard addressed them the second they entered.

'You were almost on time. Sit.'

On the table was a small spread of boiled ham, cheese and

bread. Rebecca lunged for the food while Eliza attempted to be more demure. Mrs Pollard busied herself by rolling out a pastry shell.

'When will we get to meet Mr Brownawell?' Rebecca asked.

'It will depend on when he wants to meet you. If he does at all.'

'Does he live here alone?'

'I live here. As does Mr Drewry. And now you.'

'Doesn't he have a wife?'

Eliza couldn't kick her in time.

Mrs Pollard paused in her movements then continued working the pastry. 'That opportunity passed a very long time ago,' she answered.

'But doesn't he have any children?'

'Rebecca! Apologise to . . .'

Mrs Pollard slapped her rolling pin onto the counter. She was at Rebecca's side in an instant, clutching Rebecca's chin in her fingers.

'Nosy children are severely disciplined in this house.' She released Rebecca and returned to the counter, taking up the rolling pin as if the outburst had never happened. 'Finish your luncheon. There are chores to complete.'

The silence was oppressive. It reminded Eliza of the times Mother and Father fought then refused to speak. Like there was something invisible in the air, coiled and waiting to strike. Eliza could feel the tightness in her stomach. The strength it took to remain calm strained her nerves. She felt like she was waiting for a bomb. She could even smell the reeking sweat of an air-raid shelter. Across the table, Rebecca reached into her cardigan and stroked something within her pocket.

4

The city was bright. Rare sunlight had burned off the morning fog and, from his office window, Peter could see far down the Thames, all the way to Tower Bridge. With no barrage balloons blocking the sky, the light was free to reflect off the brown water. Tiny crests caused by the current glistered in myriad compositions, shining a secret code only the river understood.

Uncle Marvin coughed, and Peter's attention was drawn back to his work, but the numbers in his accountancy book brought him no joy. He spent his last hour tracing over the same number eight until he wrote through the paper to the next page, waiting for the clock to reach five.

Once it did, he made his way to the Palladium, reciting his favourite Sid Field jokes to cheer him. As he turned off the Strand and cut through Covent Garden, a pigeon flew past and any accumulated joy vanished as he remembered yesterday's walk with Eliza. He kicked at a loose chunk of pavement but missed and tripped, catching himself on a nearby lamppost.

He had upset her yesterday, all that talk about a holiday he would never take. The idea had hit him suddenly after that awful morning in the office, and he'd been giddy to share it. Yet he shouldn't have shared it with Eliza, who could never take a holiday, not with her responsibilities to her aunt and sister. There he was waxing on about relaxing in the Lake District when inside she must have been fuming. It was a stupid mistake, she had to know that, and he had to make it up to her. He passed a Lyons Corner House and knew exactly what to do. Dinner followed by a night of jitterbugging at the dance hall. That was just the thing. They hadn't been dancing together in ages.

In better spirits, Peter shoved the last of a sausage roll in his mouth as he entered the stage door, tipping his cap to the evening watchman. He let his eyes adjust to the low lighting before venturing further. The narrow halls held only a quarter of the electric lights they should on account of Mr Purvis conserving the bulbs for Vera Lynn. The lady required a fully lit dressing room more than the ushers needed to see where they were going, or so he said.

The call sounded, 'Twenty minutes, twenty minutes to curtain!'

Peter entered the staff room and quickly traded his account-ant's suit for an usher's vest.

'Oi, curly ginger!' Stephen sauntered in, dropping a ciga-rette butt into Peter's teacup. 'Cutting it fine again, are we?'

'I've plenty of time. Have you seen Eliza?'

'Not tonight. That's two shifts in a row. Bit queer, isn't it?'

How could he apologise if she wasn't here? Peter tried not to let his concern show. 'Maybe she's sick.'

'Aye. Sick of you. Did you finally propose? That'd be enough to scare any girl off.'

The little box in his sock drawer, when would he bring it out? Peter shook the image away as the next call came – fifteen minutes till curtain. He and Stephen hurried out of the staff room, dodging frantic make-up girls and a rehearsing warm-up act before a decapitated papier-mâché horse rolled into their path.

'Evening, gentlemen. Supposed to be at the doors, aren't

you?' Purvis rested his flabby elbows on the horse's body, transforming himself into a hideous centaur. 'Well, now I know why there's such a long queue to get in the stalls. There's no one there to collect the bloody tickets!'

'But Eliza works the stalls,' Peter said. His vest seemed to tighten.

'Worked. Past tense. Haverford's quit, like that no-show Rolston. Which is why you two incompetents need to be on time! Now hurry up. Miss Lynn will be quite displeased if her show is delayed because of two irresponsible ushers.'

Peter froze as Purvis's words bounced off a brick wall in his mind, refusing to be understood. As he walked to his post, the news pummelled that wall until its meaning slipped through the cracks. The sausage roll in his stomach began to spoil. Eliza had never mentioned she was handing in her notice. Dinner and dancing might not be enough.

As soon as work ended, he travelled as quickly as possible to the Haverfords' flat. He had to apologise now, in person, let her know what a fool he was before it was too late. He knocked on the door for a good fifteen minutes before the overweight bachelor across the landing shouted at him to leave it. The Haverfords weren't home.

*

A normal evening would see Peter at the theatre, preparing for the night's performance. He would finish his cup of tea then walk up the aisles, ensuring all the floors were clean, before taking his post at the dress circle. It would be warm in the theatre, the heat of the stage lights working in tandem with the coal to counteract any chill encroaching from outside. But this was not a normal evening and, instead of taking tickets from the warmth of the Palladium lobby, he was huddled against a brick wall, wearing the thickest coat he owned and blowing on his hands, trying to create a facsimile of warmth.

Jessie and Eliza often worked the stalls together and on their days off would go to the Majestic or for a meal before Eliza needed to get home and help with Rebecca. Peter thought it odd that the two of them should up and leave like that, especially when jobs were so scarce. Perhaps they had confided their plans to each other, as girls tended to do. As another day passed and he couldn't get hold of Eliza, Peter wouldn't know the truth unless he found Jessie, and he couldn't find Jessie until someone came to the house. So, he waited, something his brothers told him he was good at. Michael used to joke that waiting was Peter's only skill. Michael didn't joke much any more.

No one had answered the first time he knocked on the door of the maisonette, but he was determined to wait out the cold. The last time he stood here was when he picked Jessie up for their first and only date. There was something about her blue eyes and the way she smiled, he had to ask her out for a dance. The evening was a disaster for them both, but it ended up being for the best. Jessie soon found another boy to latch on to and Eliza started work at the Palladium.

Peter stuffed his frozen hands into his pockets, wishing for the first time that he was wearing the knitted mittens his mother had given him for Christmas. He shifted his weight from foot to foot, clapped his hands together and sneezed into his sleeve. He searched for his handkerchief then realised that, too, he had left at home. He was kicking a stone about when an older couple approached the maisonette, their hands laden with shopping baskets. They stopped when they saw Peter. He removed his cap.

'Good afternoon. I'm terribly sorry to bother you, but I was wondering if I could have a word with Jessie?'

The couple said nothing.

'Jessie Rolston? She lives here, does she not?'

The woman dropped her shopping and burst into tears.

'Oh. Oh dear. Here, let me help you.' Peter scurried after the rolling potatoes, gathering them from the gritty pavement. He tripped over his own feet but managed to maintain his balance as he bagged her groceries. 'I'm terribly sorry. I didn't mean to . . .'

The man spoke. 'Are you with the police?'

'No, sir. Only a friend. Peter. Peter Lamb.' He extended his hand, but the man kept hold of his sobbing wife. 'We work together at the Palladium, but I haven't seen her in a few days. I thought she might have fallen ill or . . .'

'Why don't you come in, son?'

Inside a small kitchen, Mrs Rolston busied herself lighting the coke in the grate and making tea. Cracks riddled the walls and many windows were boarded up. Shrapnel had taken chunks from the bricks in the fireplace. The sitting room was blocked off with an old sheet, and Mr Rolston's armchair was positioned awkwardly between the larder and the cooking range. He sat there now, fiddling with the small, broken wireless in his lap.

'How do you like your tea, dear?' Mrs Rolston asked, her voice weak and tired.

'Milk, two sugars, please, ma'am.' Peter smiled. It brought no joy to the room. 'Please don't trouble yourself about the sugar.' Though he spoke to strangers every night at the theatre, he had no idea how to begin this conversation, not without making Mrs Rolston cry again. Mr Rolston cursed at the wireless.

'Any good with electrics?' he asked Peter.

'No, sir. I'm doing an apprenticeship in accounting.'

Mr Rolston stopped listening as Mrs Rolston served the tea, adding a small spoonful of powdered milk to each cup. Peter thanked her and sipped the tea. The Rolstons left theirs untouched. It was a bitter, watery mixture, the teabags reused too many times.

'Where is Jessie?' he asked quietly. Mrs Rolston began scrubbing the range. Mr Rolston buried his face deeper into the wireless.

'Do you know where she is?'

Mrs Rolston sniffled, and Mr Rolston sighed.

'Moved out a few months ago, didn't she?' Mr Rolston said. 'I'm sorry. I didn't . . .'

'Said she wanted to be an independent woman,' he continued, his voice mocking. 'Whatever the bloody hell that means. Not even married and she leaves us, goes to live in some brothel. Don't even write.'

Mrs Rolston slammed her fists onto the range. 'Because she can't! She can't. She can't.'

Peter looked between them. 'Why can't . . . ?'

'Don't you start, woman! I'll hear no more of that rubbish.'

'No! I need someone to listen. Someone needs to listen.'

'To what? How you've gone mad?'

Mrs Rolston flung herself at Peter. His tea spilled over the table top. 'She came to me in my dreams. Begged me for help.'

Mr Rolston threw the wireless aside and grabbed his wife's arms as she held onto Peter's hands.

'They won't let her write. They won't. "Help me, Mummy," she said. "Help me!"'

Mr Rolston slapped her across the face. The second time, she stopped crying. Mr Rolston smoothed back his hair as his wife prodded her bleeding lip.

'Go and lie down,' he ordered. She did as she was told,

disappearing behind the sheet. 'You must excuse my wife. She's ill.' He took up a newspaper. Peter feared he would be struck with it. Instead, Mr Rolston scribbled something in the margins.

'That's where she is.' He handed it to Peter. An address in Camden. 'You do see her, tell that whore she's no longer welcome here.'

*

It was after eleven by the time Peter made his way home, thoughts of Eliza and Jessie still distressing him. Home was a small flat in a quiet area of Earl's Court. The majority of residents should have already been asleep by the time Peter shuffled out of the Underground station, so he thought it odd when he sensed someone behind him.

He didn't see anyone the four times he peeked over his shoulder, but the feeling – that pressure on his back, as if something was staring into his soul – refused to dissipate.

Peter kept a steady pace, ears keen for the slightest sound. He never liked walking down empty city streets at night. It reminded him too much of being caught out in an air raid. Too young to fight, most of his war days had been spent at the family cottage in Shepperton. Though it was much smaller than London, they heard their fair share of sirens thanks to the nearby aircraft factory. Many cold nights had been spent cowered in the Anderson shelter at the bottom of their garden, wondering if they would have a house to return to come morning. His family had been lucky. His father was too old to enlist and all three of his brothers returned home safe to English soil. His mother's disposition had been Peter's greatest challenge, but Peter understood her nervy feeling. He had it now.

It was the feeling one had whenever a telegram was delivered to the door. The drop even the heartiest of stomachs would take as fingers tore open the envelope with silent prayers of 'not Casualty Services, please God, not that'. It was a feeling which remained under the skin all day, even after good news. That one had escaped this time, but the next would bring Death to the door.

Something hit the back of his shoe. Peter's chest constricted as he turned round. It was a stone. Just a small grey stone. Yet the way it hit was as if someone walking behind him had kicked it forward. He looked. There was no one he could see. Though only a few doors from his building, Peter walked faster.

He tried to imagine what it must have been like for his brothers walking across the fields of France, their packs weighing them down as they waited for a German attack. How they would peer over their shoulders, ensuring it was a comrade behind them, not a *kommandant*. The longer they went with no attack, the more heightened their senses would become. Every snapping twig or barking dog would become the enemy. Every scent would mean danger. Or death.

A pot shattered.

Peter ran to his door, fumbled with his keys. He leapt inside, locking himself in before someone could follow. Leaning against the door, short of breath, he paused and listened. No sound came from the other side of the door. The panic in his chest threatened to escape as a nervous laugh until the door shook.

The handle twisted and rattled. Peter backed away, the swallowed laugh stuck in his throat. He did not wait for the door to still before running up the stairs to his flat. His foot slipped on the second landing, and he caught himself against

60

a neighbour's doorway. Peter clung to the wooden door jamb. A fall in the other direction would have sent him tumbling onto the hardwood floor below, the wrought-iron banister having been long since removed to support the war effort. He continued to the third floor, keeping his body pressed against the far wall until he safely reached his door.

As soon as he unlocked his flat, he ran to the sitting room, slipping on the day's post as he went to the window which overlooked the street below. All that moved was a shadow in the mews opposite. It could have been anything – a cat, a neighbour, anything. Peter drew his curtains and waited several minutes before switching on the lights. His nerves, though stilled, remained fragile as he scooped the post from the floor. The first envelope gifted him a paper cut as his uncoordinated fingers slit it open. He sucked on the sharp sting as he read the brief missive, his nerves returning tenfold as his eyes pored over the unwanted words.

*

It was late, but this would not wait till morning. He needed answers now. He pounded his fist on the door. He wouldn't stop until it was opened.

'Miss Haverford. Miss Haverford!'

'Who is it?' Bess's voice carried into the hall. So she was home now.

'Peter. Peter Lamb.'

'It's late, Peter.'

'I know. But I need to speak with you. Urgently.' He straightened himself up, tried to sound like his father.

'I'm in no state for visitors. Please, go home.'

'Not till you tell me about Eliza. Where is she? Where has she gone?'

There was a pause. The door barely opened, stopped by the chain. Bess seemed disinclined to remove it. Peter was about to demand entry when he noticed her face. She was without make-up, and her pale complexion and unpainted lips drew more attention to the bloated black bruise under her left eye. Conscious of his staring, she turned her head away.

'Eliza is no longer your concern.'

The door closed, leaving Peter standing there alone, the letter from Eliza crumpled in his fist.

5

Only a sliver of moonlight shone through the dirtied windows, but it was all Eliza needed to see the framed photograph on her bedside table. Despite her exhaustion, she was unable to sleep. She was accustomed to having her sister beside her and, while grateful for not having to share this tiny bed, she couldn't shake the sensation that a part of her was missing.

A shadow passed by the window. Eliza shrank back. There were all sorts of stories about what lurked in the Welsh hills, legends easily conjured up by her tired mind. She focused on the photograph instead – she with her mother, father and baby Rebecca outside the Royal Pavilion in 1935. She was five years old and Rebecca about six months. Eliza remembered the smell of salt water, a seagull leaving a mess on her pink dress and Rebecca crying at night. They went to Brighton every summer up until the war. It was where her parents had met. They had taken hundreds of photographs over the years, had bought dozens of souvenirs, and this was all that survived. The war took the rest.

Unable to sleep in the bright moonlight, Eliza rose to shut the curtains. Her fingers froze around the fabric, unable to draw them closed. Outside stood a beast. It possessed the outline of a dog, but one larger than any natural animal of the earth, its bristled fur black and matted. Hellhound, she thought. The beast that appears to those about to die. It turned its misshapen head towards her, eyes glowing red, white fangs reflecting the night-time glow. It lifted its muzzle upwards, prepared to howl.

She yanked the curtains shut and cowered beneath the window, hugging her knees to her chest while she waited for the sound which would pull her soul from her body and send it to the demons below. Silence rang in her ears. Steadying herself, she peeked through the curtains. Only the empty lawn remained. Two days of exhaustion must have been playing tricks on her mind. A nervous laugh did little to ease her frantic heartbeat.

Eliza crawled back into bed and drew the covers up to her chest. Though the curtains blocked the moonlight, she could still see the silver outline of the picture frame. She closed her eyes, telling herself Rebecca was fine, and tried to smell salt water and listen for seagulls. She could not hear the child crying.

*

The alarm clock announced the hour with a screech. Eliza silenced it as quick as she could. Six a.m. She could either sleep another half an hour or finally take the bath she desperately needed. With a groan, she forced her body out of bed.

Carrying a clean dress and undergarments, her old towel and some soap, she crept up the hall to the bathroom then locked herself inside. With her measuring tape, Eliza made a careful five-inch line along the tub. She missed the days when Mother would fill the tub to the brim, and she and Rebecca would spend hours playing in water scented with Coty's bath salts.

'If it's good enough for the king and queen, it's good enough for me,' she sighed. The taps, nearly rusted shut, turned after a few hard twists, and the pipes spluttered to life. When was

64

the last time Thornecroft had a housemaid, she wondered. The first water to emerge was brown and carried a stench of sewage, but the pipes soon cleared. Eliza bathed slowly, letting the tepid water massage her aching neck and stiff limbs. Despite the lukewarm temperature, it was better than the cold baths she was accustomed to at Aunt Bess's flat.

As she climbed out of the tub, a rasping groan echoed from the hall – the same as she had heard in Abigale Hall. She listened but, like yesterday, it did not repeat itself.

Shaking off the chill, Eliza dressed then opened the bathroom door only to have it yanked shut, catching her fingers in the jamb. She gasped, pulling her hand back as she listened to Rebecca shouting in the hall.

'No! You've ruined it! You've messed it all up.'

'Rebecca. Open the door,' Eliza said, cradling her injured hand against her chest.

'You know you mustn't do that. You know you have to wait!' Rebecca started counting.

Eliza's hand throbbed, the pain causing her to hold her breath. Tentatively, she tried flexing her fingers. Pain made movement difficult.

Rebecca reached ten. Fifteen.

All she wanted was a calm morning. One without shouting or tears.

Twenty.

One without . . .

The door opened. Eliza grabbed Rebecca with her good hand.

'You know you can't run about slamming doors! Look what you've done.' Eliza showed Rebecca her already swollen fingers.

'I need a bath.'

'You need to apologise.'

Rebecca kept her eyes on the slight bulge of her cardigan pocket. Eliza extracted the dead mouse. It was cold and stiff now.

'This is filth. I told you. Do you want to go back on medication? Do you want to go back to hospital?'

Rebecca shook her head.

'Take your bath. There's already water in the tub. Don't waste it.'

Without looking behind her, Eliza marched to her bedroom then hefted open the heavy window and tossed the little corpse outside. She heard it land somewhere in the grass then pulled the window back down. The cold morning air had snuck in and, with her hair still wet, she began to shiver. She wanted to wash her hands, but the basin in her room was empty. She rubbed her hand against her towel until her skin turned red.

As she chose a dress from her wardrobe, she realised how unsatisfied she was with the arrangement of her clothing. She pulled everything out, refolded and refitted it, ignoring the throb in her hand and her clumsy swollen fingers.

Still unhappy, she took the clothing out again, noticing how much ironing she needed to do. Everything was wrinkled, a shambles, unsuitable for service – the phrase from Father's letter whispered inside her head.

She threw the clothes into the wardrobe and shut its doors. She would never get it right. It would always be a bit off.

It wasn't until after she finished dressing that she realised Peter's ring had fallen from her finger. She searched the wardrobe, the windowsill, the floor. It had to be here somewhere. She couldn't lose that, too. Down on her hands and knees, she peeked under the bed and saw the gold band. The sight of it calmed her. Unable to reach it, she moved the end of the bed, exposing the floor beneath.

As she bent down to collect the ring, she noticed a crack in the floorboards. The edge of something thin, like a piece of paper, protruded from the crack like a new tooth pushing through the gum. Eliza reached for it when someone pounded on her door.

'Eliza! Liza! It's breakfast. We're going to be late!'

She slipped the ring onto her finger and moved the bed back into position, forgetting her discovery.

*

According to Mrs Pollard, the blue towels Eliza carried belonged in the north hall linen cupboard. This was all well and good except that Mrs Pollard never told Eliza where the linen cupboard was. Which of the seemingly hundreds of doors was it? She balanced the stack in one arm as she tried yet another knob with no success. As she went further down the hall, she was reminded of when they had first moved in with Aunt Bess. So often she was given tasks without being told the necessary information.

Put that pan away. Away where?

Take this letter to Mrs Granderson. Where did Mrs Granderson live?

Give this money to the butcher. Which butcher?

Eliza learnt to ignore Aunt Bess's annoyance and ask the necessary questions. Asking a question and receiving a rebuke along with an answer was better than spending an hour running up and down the steps of their building searching for the old woman who lived directly above them.

This part of the manor was like ice, as if no fires had been lit here for decades. The cold froze Eliza's joints.

That noise, again. That groan. Eliza stopped.

Maybe it was the pipes, but pipes didn't normally make her heart beat faster. Pipes didn't remind her of the patients in Rebecca's hospital. She tried another door. Brooms and buckets but no linens. She continued down the corridor. Every door remained the same. The wallpaper repeated an endless pattern. Eliza had no idea where she was. She clasped the towels tightly, the throb returning to her sore fingers. There appeared to be no end to the hall before her. Behind her looked the same. From which way had she come? Which way should she go? She could not even tell which door was the broom cupboard she last opened. She felt like she was on an assembly line being pulled through a never-ending tunnel. She was dizzy and, when she closed her eyes, felt herself spinning down and down.

She braced herself against a door. Its carvings pressed into her back, helping to steady her. When her head cleared, she turned to examine them. The image of books lining a bookshelf decorated the dark wood. Balancing the towels in one hand, she ran her fingers over the etchings. She thought of her lone copy of *Mrs Miniver* and wished she could pull a carving from the door, have it transform from solid wood to soft pages in her hand. Surely a decoration such as this would be for a library. Old manor homes like Thornecroft all had libraries, didn't they? Eliza reached for the curved gold handle.

Mrs Pollard's voice sounded from down the hall. Eliza dropped the towels then hurried to pick them up. In the distance, she noticed Abigale Hall. Why had she not seen it before? Towels in hand, Eliza followed the sound of the housekeeper's voice, hoping to find the location of the linen cupboard.

'. . . making a mess of things . . .'

Halfway down the hall, a door to her right was partway open. Eliza crept closer.

'. . . she can't interfere. Leave it to me . . .'

A light in Abigale Hall distracted Eliza. She thought it was a reflection, but it hovered above the ground, beckoning her.

'. . . won't be any trouble . . .' Mrs Pollard said.

She stepped towards it.

'. . . nothing like the last one . . .'

The light glided away.

'. . . leave her to me . . .'

The light rose towards the ceiling then sank to the floor.

'. . . she'll regret . . .'

It spiralled out of sight, down the hall to the west wing. Eliza moved to follow it when a rasping groan stopped her. Mrs Pollard had fallen quiet. Eliza turned to see the housekeeper standing in the doorway. Behind her, a dry cough came from an antique library chair of red calfskin. Mrs Pollard blocked Eliza's view before she could see any more.

'Why are you hovering?'

'The linen cupboard, ma'am. Where . . . ?'

Another chest-scraping cough interrupted her.

'Give them to me.'

'I can . . .'

'I said give them to me.'

Eliza did so.

'Tell Mr Drewry to ready the carriage for one o'clock. I trust that's not beyond your abilities.'

'I . . .'

The door closed in her face.

Eliza walked towards Abigale Hall, hoping to catch another glimpse of the strange light, but there was nothing. More coughs issued from the closed room behind her, the noise reminding Eliza of Rebecca's stay in the hospital. One of the patients, Aggie, had coughed in that way. She had sat by the entrance in a rocking chair, spindly legs tucked beneath a red flannel blanket, her hacking breaths greeting visitors as they arrived. Eliza passed through the hall, suddenly chilled.

It was soon after Father died that Rebecca was sent away. She was worse, then, tapping everything, counting under her breath, never stopping. Her voice was so quiet, it had taken Eliza a week to realise it was always twenty-three – Rebecca's number – and even longer to understand why. Aunt Bess took her to the hospital in Portsmouth. She said it was her doctor who recommended the treatment, but Eliza knew how much Aunt Bess wanted rid of her.

Eliza could still hear the low murmur of voices drowned out by classical music played through tinny speakers. What she remembered most was white – white walls, white uniforms, white sheets. White made it easy to see the filth. Rebecca's ward was so damp. Patches of black mould lived on the ceiling and the corners of the walls. Sunlight was unable to reach through the dirt-glazed windows into the white rooms. Eliza felt moisture gathering in her lungs just by standing there, as if she inhaled mould with every breath, causing spores to incubate in her lungs, making them black as the walls.

The first visit itself was unremarkable. Rebecca had been sleepy, from a 'special treatment' the nurse said, and spoke little. Eliza remained cautiously optimistic after seeing her sister so relaxed and sedated, but this minor relief evaporated when she accidentally wandered into the custody ward. These were the long-term patients, those who could never be cured. Here she saw more white – white-padded rooms, white straightjackets, white skin of those never allowed outdoors.

Here, they screamed. Here, they cursed. Here, was Rebecca's future.

Eliza paused at the latticework doors which opened on to the garden. Inhaling the fresh air cleared her nose of the phantom smell of disinfectant. The hospital was nearly two years ago. Rebecca was fine now.

The sun hid behind a layer of clouds and the morning chill hung in the air as she stepped onto the garden path that led to the carriage house. It must have been a beautiful garden once, Eliza thought, as she followed the dirt footpath, but its splendour was, like most of the manor, a victim of years of neglect. There was a crumbling grey fountain, its ornate top broken off and lying in the overgrown grass while the still water in the basin grew a thick coat of green scum. The long, dead grasses tickled her ankles as she manoeuvred round deep, muddy puddles.

Thrushes and warblers sang from nearby trees, but Eliza longed for noise – sputtering car engines, honking cabbies and bicycle bells, shouting children and chattering housewives. A few birds and some rustling leaves were not enough. To Eliza's ears, all was silent.

The door out of the gardens was built into a brick wall covered in lush green ivy. The carriage house sat in the high shadow of the garden wall. Built of the same brick as the manor, it was isolated from the main house like a cast-off appendage. Two windows rested above a set of barn doors, their bevelled markings from a glassblower's pipe like sightless eyes staring down as she approached. They watched her step onto the wider tongue of dirt that led to the mouth of the house. She could hear no birds on this side of the wall, only the scraping of her shoes against the gritty path.

'Mr Drewry?'

The shadows swallowed her voice. She pulled her cardigan tight and listened for a reply. There was none. She took another step towards the open doors then stopped. She saw nothing inside the carriage house.

'Mr Drewry?'

The wind died, the clouds ceased moving. The world stilled around her as if she had wandered into one of the east wing paintings.

A heavy weight tackled her to the ground.

Warm liquid coated her neck as claws dug into her shoulders. The hellhound had her now. She could not breathe.

We'll meet again . . .

And Mother was gone and Father did not care. Perhaps the devil would let her see them once more . . .

'Kasey! Heel!'

The pressure disappeared.

'All right?'

Trembling, she put her hand to her neck to staunch the wound, stop the bleeding. Although her neck was wet and sticky, it felt whole. She drew back her hand. The liquid was clear – not blood. Saliva.

'All right?'

Mr Drewry stood above her, hand outstretched. A black wolfhound sat beside him. Eliza scrambled to her feet without his assistance. Moments ago, she could not breathe. Now, she could not stop gasping. Mr Drewry, with his tanned, cracking face, his vacant expression, this Frankenstein's creature, stepped towards her. Eliza staggered back.

'Are you all right?' he asked again. She could not bear to look at him.

'Mrs . . . Mrs Pollard. Carriage. One o'clock.'

Without waiting for confirmation, she ran back through the

garden and into the manor, unable to catch her breath until she reached her room. By one o'clock, she had nearly stopped shaking.

*

The low fog parted as the old grey horse pulled them towards Plentynunig. The hills on either side were a brownish-green, the foliage hardened from a harsh winter, fighting to revive for spring. In the distance stood the rusted red pithead and brick boiler chimneys of a coal mine that poured smoke which mixed with the grey sky.

Rebecca sat beside her, tapping her knee. There had been no time for reconciliation this morning and Eliza wouldn't try now, not with Mrs Pollard sitting there across from them. Ever since they climbed into the carriage, Mrs Pollard had not removed her eyes from Eliza. She said nothing but raked her gaze up and down Eliza's body, occasionally pausing on her face.

If Eliza had done anything to offend her, she did not know. Perhaps she was displeased with Eliza's choice of clothes – brown utility coveralls and a white shirt. She had been wearing a dress this morning but changed before they left. She couldn't go into the village covered in dog slobber and dirt. Yet Eliza could not quell the feeling that it was not her clothes that Mrs Pollard was examining. Hers was the same look Mr Purvis had given her before she was hired as an usher. The same look Peter's parents had showed when meeting her the first time. The look which decided one's worth. Since Mrs Pollard would not look away, Eliza kept her eyes on the passing landscape. Every quiet, sheep-dotted hill looked the same. What she wanted to see more than anything was a bright-red double-decker bus bursting with harried businessmen and busy shoppers.

Eventually, they approached a crop of buildings. Eliza

thought they were passing through a small farmers' village on the way to Plentynunig. It wasn't until Mr Drewry slowed the carriage that she realised this was it. The village was only half a mile wide and about two miles long. There were no street signs but vacant wooden poles. Markers removed during the war had not yet been replaced.

Mr Drewry parked the carriage in front of an ashen wood building whose fading painted sign read *Davies Market*. A pack of muddy dogs raced around the corner. Eliza tensed. Mrs Pollard took a sip of something from a small glass bottle then slipped the bottle into the pocket of her coat.

'Follow me,' she ordered.

Unlike the shops of London that even with bare shelves managed to project a semblance of life, Davies Market appeared dead. A whiff of rot hung in the air, its source unseen. The wood, old and untreated, was a faded grey, like the remnants of a fire left to cool till morning. Indeed, the place looked as though a fire had swept through, burning out the life it contained and leaving the building a frail skeleton. Eliza feared one touch would turn the splintered shelves to ash.

While Mrs Pollard was distracted by the grocer – a man as ghastly grey as his store – Eliza turned to speak to her sister, but Rebecca was not there. She ducked outside, hoping to see her in the carriage. It was empty, save Mr Drewry.

A warning siren sounded in Eliza's head. While Mr Drewry busied himself with a cigarette, Eliza took off down the road, looking down every side street and calling out Rebecca's name. It started raining, a soft but heavy misting that permeated her trousers and beaded on her wool coat.

'Rebecca!'

The dirt on the road changed to mud, which clung to her black shoes and kicked up on her ankles and calves.

'Rebecca!' She should've known better than to take her eyes off her sister. Why had she not paid more attention when they arrived?

'Rebecca!'

Eliza looked down the next street and stuttered to a stop. There, at a crossroads, a young girl anxiously tapped her thigh while a man kneeled before her, clutching her wrist.

'Rebecca!'

Eliza grabbed her sister away from the man. He smiled, revealing a mouth of broken, yellowed teeth and red, blistering gums. His face was covered with deep wrinkles which Eliza first mistook for scars. When he spoke, his breath was choked with beer and tobacco. She noticed the bottle of Wrexham lager in his gnarled hand.

'Want a sip, little girl?' he asked Eliza, holding up the bottle.

'Rebecca, we're leaving.'

'Ah, another English rose. Working for Master Brownawell? He does love his roses. Mm, yes.' He wrapped his flaking lips around the mouth of the bottle and took a sip. 'Yes, loves 'em. Loves 'em bright and red. Red, red roses.' He coughed. Yellow sputum flew from his mouth onto Eliza's shoe.

Still holding Rebecca, Eliza hurried back to the main road, the old drunk shouting at them as they left.

'No runnin' from Thornecroft, is there? *Pob luk*, little roses! *Pob luk*.'

Eliza watched the faces in the doorways and windows – faces that didn't bother turning away when caught staring. Tired mothers in grey aprons holding silent children wearing nought but rags. Young girls picking undernourished vegetables from small gardens. Old men peering down from dirtied windows, cigarette smoke clouding their faces.

Eliza wanted to yell at them to leave her alone, go about

their business, ignore her. She squeezed Rebecca's hand so tight her sister winced, and turned her own eyes to the grey dirt, listening to the whispers of those they passed. The name Thornecroft followed them through the streets.

As she climbed into the carriage, Eliza caught the eye of a girl across the way. The damp mist plastered her wavy auburn hair to her head. She did not sneer or frown at Eliza, like the others had. Her face was, instead, etched with lines of worry. Mr Drewry watched all, his back to the wall of the market. He started at small sounds but kept his position, moving only to follow Mrs Pollard as she approached the carriage.

'There you are.' Mrs Pollard dropped her filled basket onto Eliza's foot with a heavy thud. Eliza drew back her leg, making space for the packages. Mrs Pollard took no notice as she lifted herself to her seat. 'When I was a child, those who did not listen had their ears sliced off.'

Rebecca huddled close to Eliza.

'And that, if it failed, was followed by their tongues.' She snapped her fingers. 'Home, Mr Drewry.'

The carriage started with a jolt. When Eliza looked again, the auburn-haired girl was gone.

*

Tonight, no moon illuminated the grounds. Though she left the curtains open, a thick cover of clouds blocked the sky. The clock read one thirty, but Eliza was not tired. She lit a candle she found at the bottom of her wardrobe and watched the changing shadows reflecting off the photograph. Sometimes the shadows would enshroud Mother and Father. Sometimes Rebecca. Eliza remained in the light.

Another trip to Brighton – their last trip, the summer of 1938 – was the one Eliza wished she could forget. She was eight, Rebecca three. They were sitting on the beach. Eliza was too small for the red and white striped chairs but wanted to sit in them nonetheless. She wanted to feel grown up. Father read his paper, while Mother prepared the tea and sandwiches. Rebecca finished another tantrum and played calmly in the sand until she asked if she could play by the water. Mother made Eliza take her.

Eliza wanted to relax and sunbathe, like the models she saw in *Woman's Own*. She pouted and whinged but did as she was told and took Rebecca to the water, where she jumped and played in the shallow waves, laughing as the water covered her toes. Eliza stood there with her arms crossed, glaring at the water as it came near her feet. When she looked up, Rebecca was gone. Eliza searched all around her but could not see her. She called her name, but the crowd and ocean were too loud.

She couldn't remember how long she searched before she heard the scream. This wasn't the scream of people playing on the beach. It was a scream of terror. Eliza ran towards it. A woman fainted and others cried as lifeguards pulled the body of a small girl – a girl Rebecca's size – out of the water. Before Eliza could see the poor child's face, she felt a tiny hand slip into her own.

Rebecca stood beside her, giggling.

'She had a pretty shell.' Rebecca smiled and showed Eliza a small, pearlescent seashell.

'Come away,' Eliza whispered. 'Come away, Rebecca.'

When they returned to their parents, Mother asked what the screaming was about. Eliza said she didn't know. She never told her parents about the little girl's death, Rebecca's disappearance or her younger sister's behaviour upon seeing the body pulled from the water. She carried those secrets inside her, afraid if she spoke of them she might be implying something untrue, that her parents would believe she was ascribing some terrible misdeed to Rebecca to get her in trouble. Yet ever since that day, Eliza began keeping Rebecca at a distance, not wanting to stay close to this child that giggled at death.

Eliza extinguished the candle and turned away from the photograph. It was just as she was closing her eyes that she heard another scream, one not in her mind. She ran out of her bedroom and into the hall. It was dark, but she could see the small figure standing there. Eliza threw her arms around her.

'Shh, it's all right. It's all right, dearie. Was it a nightmare?'

'I want to go home. I want to go home, Liza. Why can't we go home? You said Peter would come for us, but he hasn't and he won't. I hate it here. I hate it. I hate it. I hate it!'

'Shh. Come now. Let's go back to bed. Here, come in with me.'

Nestled together in the small bed, Eliza listened as Rebecca fell asleep. In the hall, a door slammed shut, while outside, the wolfhound howled.

6

The pint glass released with a sticky snap as Peter tugged it from the table. A few drops of bitter sloshed over the brim and onto his hand. He shook them off, adding to the congealed beer stains already coating their table, before wiping his hand on his trouser leg. Cigarette smoke eddied above the punters, the various plumes mingling in the air much in the way the men commingled around the bar. The chatter this evening was low, broken only by the occasional guffaw from the large, drunken Scotsman at the darts board.

Peter was content to stay at the small corner table and send Stephen to get the fresh pints, a trade made possible by Stephen's never-ending lack of cigarettes and Peter's ready supply. Tonight, he didn't feel much like drinking yet couldn't stop his hand from lifting the glass and tipping the beer down his throat.

Stephen returned, nearly dropping his fag butt into Peter's pint.

'Watch it, Stephen.'

'Just a bit of ash. Don't get cross with me. I'm not the one what left you. Now, cheer up. There are loads of lovely ladies here in London.' Stephen held out his hand. Peter gave him another cigarette.

'She didn't write it.' He lit a cigarette for himself and watched as Stephen's Guinness settled.

'Oh, she didn't? And what sort of nutter makes up letters from girls and sends 'em to their boyfriends?'

'The words – it wasn't how Eliza would have written it. She's better with her words.' Peter's fingers pinched the end of his cigarette so tight it was nearly flat.

'Unless she were told what to write.' Stephen turned his attention to the darts match, but Peter saw him continuously glance in his direction.

'What are you thinking, then?' he asked. Stephen turned towards him with such eagerness, Peter could almost see his tail wagging.

'What if it were the sister?'

'Rebecca?'

'Aye. What if she went a bit, you know, nervy again and they had to send her off to the country and Eliza went along, but her aunt were too embarrassed to let her say so? So, she tells Eliza to make up this running-off story instead. Me gran's sis, she went mad after me uncle were killed in the trenches. Stood facing the sitting room wall for hours at a time. Great Uncle Albert found her with her head in the oven, but the dozy cow forgot to switch the gas on. They sent her to this place near Edinburgh where—'

'Rebecca's a good girl.'

'Right. Yeah.' Stephen sipped his Guinness and turned back to the darts match. 'All I'm thinking is maybe it's best if you leave it alone. Probably nothing to concern yourself with.'

'Yeah. Maybe.' Peter rose and grabbed his coat.

'Oi, where you off to?'

'Nowhere. I just . . . I have an errand to run.'

'But I just got you a pint.'

'Keep it.'

Stephen called after him. 'I don't like bitter!'

Peter jostled his way through the crowded pub and onto the cold street outside. He walked to the bus stop that would take him north to Camden, checking over his shoulder every few steps. It was impossible to see anything through the fog, and he nearly missed the bus.

The Camden flat sat hidden in the basement of a three-storey Georgian nightmare. Peter passed it three times before locating it. The houses on either side had been bombed and the rubble remained where it had fallen. A child's toy pram stuck out from a pile of broken bricks.

He wanted to come during daylight, but Uncle Marvin wouldn't let him leave the office early. Now here he was, pacing in the fog and dim light, lost in an area of London he did not know well. Lights were on in the basement, and Peter could hear music blaring from within. He walked down the steps to the door, careful of the empty milk bottles.

No one heard him when he first knocked. He tried again, and the door was opened by a blonde in a tight dress, a long cigarette between her fingers. Behind her, a party seemed in full swing – loud music from the wireless, raucous chatter from numerous guests. The sound of glass breaking disturbed no one.

The blonde took her time looking Peter up and down before speaking. 'Yeah?'

'I . . . that is . . . I'm here, I was wondering . . .'

'Out with it, love.'

'Is Jessie here?'

Expressionless, she pulled on her cigarette. 'Another of her suitors?'

'Suitors? Oh, oh no. No, I'm a friend.'

'Okay.'

'No. Really. I am. We work together.'

'Never said I didn't believe you.' She smiled. Peter felt his palms go sweaty.

'Is she here?'

The girl tapped ash onto the welcome mat. 'Jessie's not been round the past couple of weeks. Couldn't pay her share of the rent so we chucked her out.'

Someone called from inside. 'Who's at the door?'

'It's no one!'

'Did she leave a forwarding address?' he asked.

'Told me she were going back to Mummy and Daddy's. Try them.' She went to close the door. Peter put his hand out to stop her.

'I have.'

'Shame. Tell you what . . .' She walked away, leaving the door open, and returned a moment later with a brown carrier bag. 'You find her, give her this. I ain't a storage cupboard.'

The door closed for good.

There wasn't much in the bag, merely a few pieces of clothing, a notebook and a green and white poker chip with a joker's face on one side. Defeated, Peter tucked the bag under his arm and began the long journey home to Earl's Court.

*

Peter only made it as far as Euston. Warm blood mingled with cold rainwater, the rust-coloured concoction seeping into the gutter as he tried to stand. Blood poured from his forehead into his eyes, obscuring his vision. He made it to his knees – like a dog, he thought – and was struck again, this time on his back. He collapsed onto the pavement, splayed out in his own vomit. He didn't remember being sick, but he could taste the sweet acid in his mouth.

Someone spoke to him, but he could hear nothing over the air-raid siren. As he rolled onto his back, he realised there was no siren, only his own head ringing. He wiped a clumsy hand over his face and smeared some of the blood away. His attacker loomed over him, face darkened by the backlit shine of the street lamp, but Peter recognised the flat pug nose.

'S-Stephen?'

'Told you to leave it, didn't I?' his friend said, holding a lead pipe at his side.

'I . . .' Peter tasted blood in his mouth. He swallowed instinctively as consciousness ebbed away.

'Leave her, mate. For your own good.'

Peter's eyes blurred as the pipe dropped by his head, its clatter muffled by the rapid beating of his heart. He felt his head lower to the pavement, the damp seep into his cheek. He watched as Stephen fixed his checked cap and turned away, but then the strength to keep his eyes open became too much. The sound of the pipe rolling towards the gutter was the last he heard before he gave in to the darkness.

7

The absence of warmth in the bed beside her woke Eliza
before the alarm clock could. Rebecca was gone. She felt
the blankets. They were cold. The clock read quarter to six,
and no sunlight yet peeped through the open curtains. Eliza
rubbed her eyes, trying to remember if she had closed the
curtains last night. She tossed back the blankets and let out a
scream. She wasn't alone in bed after all.

A dead mouse lay beside her leg.

Rebecca came running into the room. 'Eliza, what is it?'

'I . . . Did you put that there?' she asked. It was the same
mouse Eliza had thrown out yesterday, or at least looked it.

'Of course not. This one is a girl. Mine was a boy.'

'Rebecca, don't be absurd. How else would a dead mouse
end up in my bed? Get rid of it.'

'I said I didn't do it. You're always blaming me for things I
didn't do.'

'So a ghost put it there, is that it?'

'Maybe. Or maybe it crawled into your bed and you suffocated it while you slept. Then it would be your fault for once,
not mine.' Rebecca started to pout, and Eliza recognised
the onset of a tantrum. This early in the day, she could not
handle it.

'Fine, I'm sorry. But could you please do something with it?
I've handled enough dead mice for a lifetime.'

Rebecca picked it up by its tail.

'Not your pocket,' Eliza warned.

'Where am I supposed to put her?'

Eliza opened the window and Rebecca gently dropped it outside. She stood there looking at the spot where it had landed.

'Where were you?' Eliza asked.

'I went to my room. Mrs Pollard said that was a rule and I didn't want her to catch us.'

'Rebecca, what makes you think Mrs Pollard would check on us in the night?'

Rebecca ran away from the window. 'I'm going to get dressed. I hope breakfast is hot. I always like your hot breakfasts. Are you doing the washing today? I'll bring you my soiled things.' She darted out of the room as a cold wind flooded in, freezing Eliza in her nightgown.

At breakfast, Mrs Pollard dropped an empty bucket and scrubbing brush at Eliza's feet. Eliza dreaded what new dust-filled room she would have to clean next, until Mrs Pollard announced, 'Today, you'll be cleaning the library.'

'The library?' A lightness filled her, one she had not experienced since Peter's final kiss on Charing Cross Road.

'Are you deaf?'

'No, ma'am.'

'Good. Then you'll understand me the first time when I tell you to go there immediately after breakfast.'

'Yes, ma'am.'

'Now, will you be able to find your own way or shall I have to draw you a map?'

'That won't be necessary, ma'am. Mrs Pollard . . .' Eliza caught her attention before she could drift away. 'After I clean the library, would it be possible to borrow one of the books?'

Mrs Pollard regarded her through half-lidded eyes and,

although her expression did not outwardly change, Eliza suspected a laugh was hiding in her thin chest.

'I doubt anything in Mr Brownawell's collection will be of interest to you. You, girl.' She stared at Rebecca. 'Come with me now. I'll show you the henhouse.'

Rebecca left her half-eaten porridge on the table and followed Mrs Pollard, head low, arms stiff at her sides. Now alone, Eliza hurried to finish her own breakfast and clean her dishes. Mrs Pollard had not technically said no to her request and, even if she did not find books which interested her, simply being in their presence would help her feel more at ease here.

Eliza hummed as she carried the bucket and brush to the library. The pain of leaving her books behind continued to lessen as she thought of the stacks she'd be caring for now. Shelves reaching from floor to ceiling would be filled with original leather-bound copies, their titles embossed in real gold; paper thin as a butterfly's wing with shining, gilded edges; red velvet bookmarks creased in forgotten chapters. Yet it was the smell she looked forward to most – the welcoming mustiness that would fill her nose and permeate her whole self, reminding her of home, of Mother reading to her by the fireplace, Father taking her to the British Library. Eliza saw herself spending hours curled up in a chair with an old book in her hands. She could fill her free time hidden away in her own corner of Thornecroft, away from Mrs Pollard. The work here might be bearable now, she thought. This place might begin to feel like home.

She ran her fingers over the engraved doors as she had yesterday, though this time with less fear. The heavy doors opened with a hard push, but no electric light meant she had to open all the curtains before she could admire the room. Resting her Tilley lamp on the floor, she tied back the heavy

Victorian curtains and opened the Holland linen blinds. Rain pattered the windows as grey daylight entered the room in rectangular slabs. With the final window exposed, Eliza turned to face the massive bookshelves.

The massive, empty bookshelves.

They went from floor to ceiling like she imagined, but they held no books. None at all. There was a large oak desk with a reading lamp, a calligraphy pen and a bottle of dried ink, but not a single book.

Eliza ran her finger through the inch of dust on a barren shelf, bitter disappointment forming inside her. All she wanted was this one thing – one thing to make life in this empty place bearable – yet this, too, had been snatched from her. And Mrs Pollard had known yet said nothing. She had been laughing at Eliza. Eliza grabbed the filled bucket from the hall and let it clatter angrily to the floor. On her hands and knees, she scrubbed the brush into the wooden boards, working up a thin sweat that kept her warm in the cold, cavernous room. She focused on her cleaning, unwilling to look at shelves that mocked her with their open, empty mouths. Peter once referred to her as Aunt Bess's Cinderella, and Eliza chided him for mocking her aunt. Now his remark was all too accurate. She slammed the brush into the floor.

Where was Peter? Shouldn't he be trying to track her down, hounding Aunt Bess for answers as to her whereabouts? She rinsed the scrubbing brush in the warm water and slapped it down again. No, Peter would not be playing detective. When he left his keys at a Corner House, he couldn't even ask the waitress if anyone had turned them in. She had to do it for him.

Eliza scraped the brush back and forth, her arms sore from the effort as a stronger pain formed behind her eyes. Another headache. Peter was wrong. Aunt Bess demanded much of her but allowed her to lead her own life. Not until now was she truly a slave, every second of her day devoted to the demands of a decaying house. When would she have time to do the things she needed? When would she have time to rest? The brush hit the floor with a wet slap.

Scrub, sweep, cook. Mend this. Fix that. Scrub, scrub, scrub.

Water sloshed over the side of the pail.

Do the ironing. Unpick the mattress. Find more soap flakes.

Her fingernails were cracked, caked with dirt.

Bottle more fruit. Find a nylon to hang the marrow. *Father's homemade marrow liqueur, its jar broken, glass in pieces, as the smoky syrup seeped into the dirt floor. The smell of that damn marrow as he tap-tap-tapped* . . .

Eliza dropped the brush and stopped. Stopped cleaning, stopped thinking. Curled her knees to her chest like she had as a child. She felt warm tears on her cheeks but did nothing to wipe them away. She stopped, and needed the world to stop with her.

A wetness in her undergarments moved her. She felt her face flush, but as she clambered to her feet, she realised she'd not had an accident. The washing bucket had tipped over and she was sitting in the dirty, soapy water. Her relief was short-lived for, when she picked up the bucket, she spotted the blood.

Dried onto the gold handle of the desk drawer, it was so old it was nearly black. Yet Eliza had seen old blood before. She could recognise it for what it was. As she examined the drawer more closely, she realised it was slightly ajar. With her handkerchief, she opened it. Inside was a copy of *The Mammoth Book of Thrillers, Ghosts and Mysteries*. The only book in an otherwise empty library. Eliza took it from the drawer. More brown streaks stained the crisp pages.

The book fell open to the first page of a story entitled 'The Woman Who Rode Away'. Yet the page was unreadable, as it was covered in smears of bloody fingerprints.

*

'I don't want to go on holiday with Rebecca. She ruins everything.'

That was what Eliza said when her parents told her about the evacuation. She sat on the Oriental carpet in front of the hearth, staring up at Father while Rebecca played on the floor with her wooden Noah's Ark and paper animals. Two by two she made them trot – a giraffe with a polar bear, a ram with a camel. Eliza explained many a time that the animals were meant to go with their own kind, like with like. Rebecca did not care.

'Be nice to your sister,' Father answered, his face hidden behind *The Times*. The bold headline read WAR IMMINENT. 'She's your responsibility.'

A crack of lightning lit up the room. Rain pelted the windows.

'Yes, like I'm yours, Freddie.' Aunt Bess smiled, a glass of orange gin in one hand and a cigarette in the other. Eliza could tell she was planning on going out that night, her scarlet dress neatly pressed and cinched at the waist, her hair freshly permed that morning. All Aunt Bess needed was her soldier. She'd be waiting all night. 'It'll be like an adventure,' she said. 'Don't children like adventures?'

Another roll of thunder.

'I do!' Rebecca raised her hand.

Eliza crossed her arms. 'No.'

Mother entered from the kitchen, her apron stained with cooking fat and flour.

'Eliza, won't you help me with the pies?' she asked.

Eager to leave, Eliza followed her mother and was soon set to work, kneeling on a stool and flattening the pastry with the heavy wooden rolling pin.

'Wonderful,' Mother said, kissing her on the top of the head.

'Mummy, why do I have to leave? Why aren't you and Father coming?'

Mother stopped slicing the carrots and sat in one of the kitchen chairs, beckoning Eliza into her lap. Soon, she would be too big for her mother's lap. Before then, her mother would be dead.

'Do you know who Hitler is?' she asked.

'He's the man from Germany. The one they talk about on the wireless.'

'Well, he has been doing some very bad things to his neighbours. We've asked him to stop, but . . . it doesn't appear that he will. So, we must stop him ourselves.'

'Father says there's going to be a war.'

'That's right. And when the war starts – which may be very soon – Hitler is going to drop bombs on London. They're going to hurt people and it's going to be very dangerous. So, you and Rebecca and all the other children, we must send you somewhere safe.'

'Until the bombs stop?'

'Until the bombs stop.'

Eliza toyed with the string of her mother's apron. 'Why doesn't everyone leave? Then Hitler can drop all the bombs he wants and no one will get hurt.'

She remembered the scent of her mother's perfume emanating from her soft neck as she sighed.

'There are many people in London, dearie. Too many to move elsewhere. You children have priority, always. And, well, if we all left, that would be like running away, wouldn't it? And we mustn't run, Eliza, ever. We must stand and fight. Say it with me: we mustn't run.'

'We mustn't run.'

The storm outside made the lights dim and the house shake. It would be the worst storm they would have in all of September. They sat at the dining table together, the crackle of the wireless barely audible over the storm as they ate in silence. Eliza did not know then that it would be the last time her family would ever eat dinner together. At nine years old, one did not yet understand things such as ending or change. Life was as it was before and always would be.

Now, years later, as she hurried down a dusty corridor, clutching a bloodstained book to her breast, Eliza remembered how naïve she had been as her mother's words repeated in her mind.

We mustn't run. We mustn't run.

And yet she had, hadn't she? She had left Mother and Father there, left them to suffer the horrors of the Blitz while she remained safe and sound in the country. Now she had run again, from Aunt Bess and Peter and everything she loved in London.

The paintings passed in a blur, their faded colours melding together as she maintained her focus on the fixed point ahead of her. She had to get to her bedroom. There she could hide the book and decipher it later.

'Miss Haverford.'

The words struck her like a knife to the back. She heard the footsteps approaching, the clang of keys hanging from the waist, but could not move. Her palms began to sweat, her grip on the book slipping.

'Yes, ma'am?'

'Finished in the library, I presume?'

'Nearly, ma'am.'

'Turn around. It's impolite to speak to one's back.'

Her heart flapped wildly in her chest, desperate to escape its cage of bone. There was no place to hide the book. As she turned, she could only adjust her fingers to cover the bloody smears.

'Nearly finished because you're stealing Mr Brownawell's property?' Mrs Pollard put out her hand. Her eyes were cold and focused. Before them, Eliza could be nothing but obedient.

'I wasn't stealing—'

'I packed and catalogued the entirety of Mr Brownawell's collection the other year because of a silverfish infestation,' Mrs Pollard interrupted, reading the spine. 'Books must be carefully monitored. If not properly maintained, all sorts of terrible ideas could come spilling out. This must have escaped my notice. Or . . .'

Cradling the spine in her palm, her eyes fell on the blood-stained pages. Eliza felt her whole body shaking as Mrs Pollard stared at the blood.

'Pip Vlasto,' she whispered, then quickly shut her mouth as if surprised she had uttered the name aloud.

'Who is Pip Vlasto, ma'am?'

Mrs Pollard regained her composure and straightened her spine. 'Your predecessor. She must have stolen this from the reading room. She was always snooping about.' Her fingers traced the line of the blood on the pages' edges.

'A weak child, Miss Vlasto was. Very sickly. Suffered horrible nosebleeds. I'll take care of this. Resume your duties, Miss Haverford.'

'I can dispose of the book, Mrs Pollard. It's no trouble.'

'I said resume your duties. I thought you told me you weren't deaf?' Mrs Pollard turned on her heel and marched down to the kitchen. Yet the lack of her presence did not lessen Eliza's fear as the memory of the blood imprinted itself on her memory.

*

The Spam salad – a dish barely edible at the best of times – turned Eliza's stomach before she even swallowed the first bite. She chewed slowly, tasting every bit of the limp lettuce and flavourless mash. They were supposed to have better food in the country. That was what she heard every day in London. And it had been true during the evacuation. Her first night at the Littletons', the dining table had been covered – a full roast with fresh carrots, peas and broccoli from the garden; sweet toffee pudding; thick custard made with real eggs from pet hens. Eliza ate her fill and then some, and still Mrs Littleton apologised for having so little to offer.

Mrs Pollard appeared to have opened a tin and plopped this gooey, pale pink chunk onto a bed of browned salad plucked from the compost pile. Still, Eliza ate every bite. One couldn't waste food, no matter how awful it tasted. Yet the food provided no distraction from her thoughts. After spending the day cleaning the useless library, the image of every empty shelf was ingrained in her memory, along with the sight of the brown blood.

'Excuse me, ma'am,' she said, her throat so dry it ached to speak. 'But I wanted to enquire about the books.'

'Yes, what about them?' Mrs Pollard stood at the sink, again not eating with them.

'Well, I was hoping I could get the chance to read them. You see . . .'

'They're packed away.'

'Yes, I understand. But earlier you mentioned a reading room, and I thought . . .'

'No, I didn't.'

'When I saw you in the hall, you said . . .'

Mrs Pollard dropped the washed knife onto the drying board. The plait draped over her shoulder quivered in warning, like a rattlesnake's tail. 'How many times must you be told no? Mr Brownawell's collection isn't meant for your eyes. And you will never ask me about it again. Do you understand?'

Eliza finished her dinner in silence.

Now, as she sat on her bed dabbing Mendahol to a hole in her stockings, she felt the undigested lumps of salad threatening to escape her stomach. She considered going to bed, but the thought brought no comfort. Every time she closed her eyes, she saw the book's black cover and Pip Vlasto's blood.

Father hadn't allowed them to read ghost stories. He said they were nonsense, but Mother would read them to her. They would stroll into St James's Park on a breezy, warm day and, while Rebecca chased the pigeons, Mother would read Eliza the tales of Poe and M.R. James and Bram Stoker. In her warm voice, they hardly seemed frightening at all. They were only stories, Mother would smile. Such stories never did any harm.

Where had Pip retrieved that book? And why had Mrs Pollard lied about the reading room? Despite the housekeeper's insults, Eliza could hear perfectly well. If only this Pip were here to question. What had happened to her? How long had she been employed? Had this, too, been her room? Then Eliza remembered the paper stuck in the floorboards beneath her bed. Like Poe's tell-tale heart, it began to call to her. Eliza set her stockings aside.

Wind blew against the window as another rainstorm passed through the valley. Eliza moved the bed and, with the tips of her fingernails, was able to pull the paper from the crack. It was a photograph. A group of women stood together in light dungarees and dark shirts, their hair pinned back or wrapped in headscarves, baskets hooked on their arms – the uniform of a Land Girl. In the back row was the auburn-haired girl from Plentynunig.

'Liza!'

Rebecca knocked at the door. Her darning. Eliza had completely forgotten.

'Eliza!'

She quickly returned the bed to its proper position.

'Eliza!' Rebecca opened the door as Eliza stuffed the photograph into her pocket. 'You said . . .'

'Yes, I know. Look, here I come now.'

Rebecca had piled her clothes outside Eliza's door.

'See? I put everything together for you.'

'Well, good. Now go and fetch your sewing kit so you can help.'

'I can't. I'm busy.'

'Doing what, may I ask?'

'Things. But I promise to help you later with the washing.'

'Promise?'

'Of course!'

Eliza picked up a dress. A mutilated face stared back at her. She gasped, but a second glance showed her it was only a doll.

'Rebecca, what is this?' she asked, picking it up. It seemed familiar, yet it wasn't any toy Rebecca had brought with her from London. The closest thing Rebecca had to a doll was her large plastic cat. This toy was much older and felt fragile in Eliza's hands. It was a bisque doll, made of hard porcelain, its face painted with rosy cheeks and red lips. The hair was dark brown and coarse, long and tangled after years of neglect. She wore a yellowed dress which Eliza imagined must once have been a brilliant white.

Eliza knew then why she recognised it – its hair and dress matched that of the woman in the paintings. But what truly unnerved Eliza was the empty space where its eyes should have been. They had been scraped out of its head. Deep scratches were laid into and around the empty eye sockets.

Rebecca wrapped her arms around Eliza's waist. 'I was hoping you could fix her.'

'Oh. Well . . .'

'You always say we can't waste and you're so good at fixing things, you really are.'

Rebecca did have very few toys, Eliza thought, and there wasn't much wrong with the doll except for the eyes. Yet it was the eyes she couldn't ignore. They weren't simply missing, having fallen out due to age or accident. Someone had violently torn them from the innocent face. She handed it back to Rebecca.

'I'll see what I can do, but I won't get to it tonight. You keep her for now.'

Rebecca hugged it tightly then disappeared into her room.

It was only a doll, Eliza told herself as she gathered the clothes. The sick feeling she had was due to the Spam and nothing more. Nothing more.

8

Leather-skinned spines stacked the solitary shelf that towered high into the storm clouds above. A book slipped into Eliza's hands like silk as the ground beneath her swayed with the tide and sand snuck into her shoes.

'Rebecca, look.' Her voice drifted on the breeze. The beach was empty.

She opened the cover. A mouse scurried from the pages. The book curdled at her feet. Pages dissolving, cover blackening.

One, two, three, four . . .

The pink sky dimmed. A second shelf appeared behind her and Eliza chose a rose-pink cover with a shimmering gold trim. Mice crawled up her arms. She brushed them away and the book fell into the sand, rotting as the tide carried in compost that rose to her ankles.

Five, six, seven, eight . . .

A third shelf brought her another book, soft and red. Mice burst through the cover. She clung to it as boils marred the leather, the pustules filling and bursting.

Nine, ten, eleven, twelve . . .

The mice counted, running figures of eight between her feet on the bare wooden floor as the clouds drew the ceiling lower with books now made of bone. Rats gnawed through the spines, yellow teeth crunching brittle tissue.

Thirteen, fourteen, fifteen . . .

Across the library was a door, but the floor was filled with rodents as a waterfall of fur and fleshy tails poured from the shelves. The mice crunched underneath her wooden shoes. They squealed and bit her ankles and she could not walk.

Sixteen, seventeen, eighteen . . .

They came together and formed a wolfhound-shaped beast. Mice flowed from its mouth. It ate them with glee, swallowing bits that fell from its undulating stomach. It retched and the doll came forth from its snout and it held onto the hair while the little head turned towards Eliza and smiled.

'Nineteen, twenty, twenty-one . . .'

Mice crawled over her arms, over her legs, into her hair.

'Twenty-two, twenty-three.'

She felt them but saw nothing. She flipped back the covers, searched under the pillow. No mice. No rats. She was fine. It was fine. Everything was fine.

'One, two, three, four . . .'

The butchered doll stared at her from across the room. Eliza hurried out of bed and turned it round to face the wall. The doll couldn't have moved on its own.

'Five, six, seven, eight . . .'

Her sister's voice came from the hall. Rebecca must have slipped it into her room during the night.

'Nine, ten, eleven, twelve . . .'

Eliza climbed back into bed. Sunlight peeked through the tattered curtains. Morning. Sunday morning. There were no chores today. She could lay here and rest, doze through the quiet hours, find the dream-world where London lay beyond the curtains. No. She sat up. Sunday morning. It was time to dress. Today was her only chance to speak to the auburn-haired girl, the one who must be Pip. Eliza needed to know where the blood in the book had come from. Maybe then the nightmares would slip away.

When Eliza finally emerged, Rebecca was still in the hall, counting the flowers in the wallpaper. 'Twenty-two. Twenty-three. Where are you going?'

Eliza buttoned up her coat. 'Into the village. I have errands to run.'

'But it's Sunday. Everything will be closed.'

'Not for what I need.'

'Can I come?' Rebecca followed her, her bare feet like the pitter-patter of mice. Eliza saw them running down the shelves.

'I need you to do a job for me. Can you have a look round the manor and see if you can find any books? Anything that might be the reading room?'

'Mrs Pollard said there isn't a reading room and that you can't have them.'

'Mrs Pollard says a great deal of things. Just like Aunt Bess. And we didn't always listen to her now, did we?' The paintings blurred in the corner of her eye as she passed them.

'But Mrs Pollard is different. The way she looks at me and grabs my arm and what she whispers to me when I'm sleeping . . .'

'No one whispers to you when you're sleeping. Dreams aren't real, remember? Besides, Mrs Pollard is at church all day. Now, I'll only be gone a few hours . . .'

'But . . .'

Eliza stopped. There was no time for this. She cupped Rebecca's cheeks in her hands. 'I need you to do this for me, dearie. We need to work together. As soon as I come back, you can tell me what you found while I work on your . . . your doll. How does that sound?'

'Promise?'

'Promise.' Eliza kissed the top of Rebecca's head then

continued on alone. If the woman in the paintings were to turn, would she, too, be blinded? Eliza suppressed a shudder. She had no intention of ever touching that doll again, except to throw it away.

A misting rain fell as she stepped onto the gravel drive. Fog hovered over the ground, curling round her ankles as she passed through Thornecroft's stone and iron gates. The cold prickled her skin. She kept her hands warm in her pockets, rubbing her fingers over the smooth photograph.

No one else walked the road, human or animal. She listened for an engine. She had yet to see a motor since leaving London. Perhaps in Wales such a thing did not exist. A horse, then, or carriage, but there was nought save her wooden soles hitting the hard ground, their staccato rhythm echoing through the dead air like nails into a coffin. Eliza sang to fill the silence.

'*You always hurt the one you love . . .*'

She had first heard that song while wrapped in her old blue coat with Rebecca's hand squeezing hers, her nose itching from the smell of coal smoke and chip grease.

'*The one you shouldn't hurt at all . . .*'

Wrapped up like a present with a luggage label pinned through her top buttonhole, Mother's hands holding fast to hers until the train whistled.

'*You always take the sweetest rose . . .*'

Loaded on the carriage, special delivery, the last glimpse she had of Mother a flash of yellow coat being swallowed by the crowd.

'*And crush it till the petals fall.*'

The same song crackled through the wireless when Eliza heard of Mother's death. When Father drank, he told how he watched her body burn, said he could still hear her screaming. Eliza could still hear that song.

100

She stopped singing.

The walk to Plentynunig took over an hour. The exertion caused her hands to swell, and she rubbed them together as she turned onto the main road, hoping to ease the pain. From the other end of the village, tuneless church bells chimed. Was the service beginning or ending? Would she pass Mrs Pollard and Mr Brownawell in the road? Eliza kept her head down, although Mrs Pollard would surely recognise her faded mauve coat, so vulgar amongst all these greys and browns.

She hurried to the house where the auburn-haired girl had stood, and knocked. Though she could hear someone moving inside, the old brown door remained closed. When she raised her hand again, the door swung open.

The old drunk smiled, baring his rotten teeth. His breath stank of yeast. 'Hullo, English rose. Hullo, hullo. You find Brownawell? Tell him Kyffin says hullo, he says. Hullo to all the roses.'

'Enough, Berwin.'

The drunk shuffled into a shadowed room, muttering to himself as the auburn-haired girl took his place, arms crossed over her chest.

'He's not well,' she said, her accent Irish. Though not many years older than Eliza, she bore the marks of one who suffered a hard life. Her pinned-back hair revealed a deep worry line across her forehead and there were already crow's feet at the corners of her eyes. A scar graced her chin and there was a small bump in her nose, as if it had once been broken. A decade ago, she would have been beautiful.

'Can I help you?' she asked, blocking the doorway.

'Pip Vlasto?' Eliza held out the photograph.

The wrinkles grew more severe as she frowned. Eliza

101

thought the door would shut in her face. Instead, the girl stepped aside.

'Did you walk all that way? I'll fix us some tea.'

Her tidy dress belied the condition of the house. Papers were scattered everywhere, some tied in bundles and stacked on the stairs, others spread loose through the sitting room, where a plethora of sewing supplies – stacks of fabric, a pedal-operated sewing machine, baskets of bobbins – mingled with the newspapers, journals, magazines. Most were old and damp, yellowed and green from age and mildew. A glance at the titles and headlines revealed many to be medical texts. Their sheer number filled the house with a fusty odour that made Eliza sneeze.

In the kitchen, the warmth of the fire did little to dry out the damp, yet there were no papers here, only near-bare shelves and curtains gone grey from coal dust. A clay vase bearing white flowers like those in the fields around Thornecroft sat in the centre of the table, surrounded by the bread crusts and soiled dishes of a finished breakfast for two. One open text sat on the table – a copy of *Gray's Anatomy*. The girl dropped the photograph by the vase then filled an old iron kettle and hung it from a rod above the fire.

'Milk?' she asked. 'We're out of sugar. Probably won't see any till it comes off the ration, 'less we start growing that ourselves, too.'

'Yes, please. I'm sorry for coming unannounced.'

'We don't get many visitors here. Makes for a nice change.' She fussed about the kitchen, moving flannels, brushing away crumbs. Her hands were never still – playing with the pins in her hair, wringing themselves together, untying and retying her apron. Eliza sensed she didn't appreciate the change at all.

102

'The tea will be lovely, thank you. You like to read?' She pointed at the book.

'Not much else to do around here.'

'Do you know du Maurier?'

'We don't have a cinema.'

'She's an author.'

'Oh.' Pip plopped a mug on the table.

Eliza spotted the drunk wandering round the back garden. 'Is he your father?'

'A friend. This house is too big to go without company. Though you'll know all about that. Living at Thornecroft.'

'So you know who I am.'

Pip paused. 'Everyone knows the new housemaids.' She pulled an already clean dish from the drying rack and began washing it. 'You found that photograph on the estate?'

'In my room.' Eliza waited for some reply. None came. 'You were a Land Girl?'

'For most of the war.'

'And when it ended, you went to work at Thornecroft?'

She left the plate in the sink. 'I think the kettle's ready.' It had not yet whistled.

'How long were you employed there?' Eliza asked. 'Did you ever find the reading room?'

'Why does it matter?'

'I don't mean to pry, but—'

'Then don't!' With a heavy thud, she dropped the still-cool kettle on an iron trivet. 'What's your name, girl?'

'Eliza Haverford.'

Pip gripped the counter's edge as if it were the only thing keeping her upright. 'Well, Miss Eliza, if you want any advice about Thornecroft, all I can say is keep your head down, stay out of Pollard's way and ask yourself what horrible thing it is

103

you've done to be there.' She took a flannel and wiped where the kettle's water had spilled. 'It was a mistake to let you in.'

Eliza looked away. Aunt Bess had said the same once. Their first of many rows.

She rose. 'Then I had better go. Thank you for the offer of tea.'

Eliza waited, but Pip remained silent.

'Whatever happened to you, I'm sorry for it. I hope your nosebleeds are much improved.'

At this, Pip reached a hand to her face, covering her mouth as if to keep herself from crying.

'Good afternoon.' Eliza saw herself out. The heat of the kitchen fire was stifling compared with the fresh, cold air outside.

The fog thickened as she returned to Thornecroft, matching her increasingly heavy mood and making the road invisible. It was not the yellow, putrid kind of London, but a pure, thick cloud cocooning her from the Welsh countryside. She felt the dirt road beneath her feet and inched her way forwards. Now and then she would veer off course onto the soft grass. The journey was slow, and she doubted she would reach Thornecroft by dinnertime. She should never have made the trip. How could she explain her absence to Mrs Pollard? Would Rebecca give her away? She hadn't told her this should remain secret. How could she forget something so important? Her mind was full of so many things. Too many things. She felt she needed to drill a hole in the side of her skull and allow some of the thoughts to drip out. Maybe then the headaches would stop.

A soft glow emerged from the fog – a small ball of light floating ahead of her, too small for a lantern, too large for a candle. Its colour and size matched the light she glimpsed in Abigale Hall. She stepped towards it.

A horse whinnied.

Eliza turned from the light but saw no sign of any animal.

'Hello?' She listened. No reply came.

When she turned back, the light had moved further away. Secure in the feeling of gravel beneath her feet, she inched closer. The light remained static. She closed her eyes, cleared her head and looked again. No movement. It had never moved at all. It must be Thornecroft, she thought. The gravel meant she reached the main drive. With greater confidence, she quickened her pace. Her foot met only air.

Her body pitched forward, unable to stop its momentum.

Something yanked her back. She collapsed onto her side, patting the firm ground, ensuring it was real.

'What're you doing all the way out here?' Mr Drewry appeared from the fog, the grey mare behind him.

Eliza panicked. He would tell Mrs Pollard she had gone, and she would be punished, Rebecca too.

'I'm sorry . . .'

'It's a thousand-foot drop to the bottom of that quarry!'

'Quarry?' Eliza scurried backwards as she climbed to her feet.

'You'd be dead soon's you hit the ground. Be lucky if there was any body left to bury.' He towered over her, his animated face making his scars alive and angry.

'The light . . . I thought . . .' There was nothing in the fog save the mare and Mr Drewry.

'Light? So you were chasing corpse candles, eh? Think they'll guide you to Thornecroft? Daft girl. You're miles away. Corpse candles only show you to your death.' He grabbed her arm. Manure from the stables was caked under his fingernails. 'But maybe that's what you're hoping for?'

'No, no I . . .'

'Are you certain? What's your life worth, then? Better men than you die every day. I've seen it. Men you'd lay down your life for. There beside you one minute then BANG.' He shook her hard. 'All that's left is a pair of boots with your mate's feet tied up neat inside. But it's not the sight that gets you. No, it don't look any worse than owt at the butcher's. What gets you is the smell. Crawls inside your skin and stays there. Ain't no smell like burnt flesh, fresh blood and gunpowder. The Devil's Dinner. That's what we called it, that smell. And even here – out here where there's nowt – it creeps up behind you. Takes you by the throat.' He gripped Eliza at the base of her neck. 'Takes you and never lets go. Ever known a smell like that?'

Eliza felt the increasing pressure, smelled sulphur and marrow. He released her.

'Thought not.' He spat tobacco chew onto the ground. 'Get on the horse.'

As Mr Drewry turned them around, she caught a glimpse of the cliff edge through the fog. She clung tightly to the saddle, picturing her bloodied body lying at the foot of a crevasse.

Her hands were still shaking when they reached the manor. She struggled to unwrap her hair as she made her way through the halls, the knot of the headscarf getting tangled in her loose strands. She ripped it from her hair with a shout, then froze.

The doll stood in the centre of the passage, balanced on its worn leather shoes as if interrupted in its midday walk. It fell onto its side.

Eliza waited for it to move again. All was still.

'Rebecca?'

No answer. She sidestepped the doll but went no further.

Her bedroom was torn to pieces. The wardrobe hung open, her clothes strewn across the floor and windowsill. The suitcase sat overturned on the bed and the wash basin lay in two jagged pieces. Eliza rushed to the bedside table to find their family photograph on the floor, the silver picture frame damaged beyond repair. She gripped it with her fingertips, careful of the glass. The jagged edges had scratched Mother's face.

'Rebecca!'

'Yes?' Rebecca stood in the doorway, cradling the doll.

'What happened?'

'I was looking for your sewing kit,' she said, her face impassive.

'You did this?'

'Don't worry. I found it.' She walked away.

'Rebecca. Rebecca!' Eliza ran after her. 'Rebecca Haverford, you look at me when I'm speaking to you.' She grabbed her arm. 'Apologise. Now!'

'What for?'

Eliza yanked the wretched toy from Rebecca's hold and threw it against the wall.

'Look what you did. Look!' She forced the damaged photo into Rebecca's hands. 'This was our only picture of Mother. It's ruined now. Ruined because of what you did. You're exactly like Father! You have absolutely no consideration for anyone's feelings. Never think how your actions will affect others. You didn't even do what I asked of you, did you? Well?'

Rebecca counted under her breath.

'Of course you didn't. Go to your room. I don't ever want you in here again. Do you understand?'

'Eight, nine, ten . . .'

'Rebecca.'

'Eleven. I understand. I ruin everything. Twelve . . .'

Rebecca dropped the photograph – 'Thirteen, fourteen . . .' – and went into her room, leaving Eliza alone in the hall.

Her anger receded as guilt swallowed her bit by bit. Rebecca would count all night now because of her. Eliza scooped up the doll. Her careless throw had left a scratch on its cheek. She could still fix it, if Rebecca wanted. Holding it by the arm, Eliza returned to her room. Mr Brownawell's coughs reverberated through the manor.

9

Blood ran into the gutter, slipping away like the voices in his head. They were important, the voices. Without their words, he would fade into nothing. Yet he could not understand them. They came from the sitting-room wireless while he slept in his bedroom above. A bright light blinded him and sleep disappeared. Shouting tore his paper-thin throat. A gentle pressure on his shoulder returned him to sleep. He snuck to the top of the stairs to better hear the voices and found himself walking along the Strand towards Trafalgar Square. Nelson's column never came nearer. Barrage balloons floated across the sky, turning day to night.

The air raid sounded, but Peter did not worry. He was almost there. He saw her in the distance, by Charing Cross. She was dressed as Dorothy, but her feet were red from blood not rubies. He thought it funny. She did not. She had never been to Kansas. Eliza pointed to the silver sky. The balloons began to pop, showering them in a thick confetti of rubberised cotton. He opened his umbrella, but it floated away. Cables spiralled to the ground, cracking into buildings and breaking off bricks that fell as bodies. The pavement turned silver, peach and red. A cable came towards Eliza, but she was Jessie now and that was okay but not the same. He shouted to her, but she pointed above his head. A steel rope crashed down upon him.

Peter jerked his hand to catch the cable but felt nothing,

only an itch on the back of his hand that mirrored the tickle in his throat. He coughed. A cool, smooth surface was pressed against his bottom lip. He coughed again and felt water trickle past his lips. After a moment's rest, he opened his eyes. The light was dim but still it burned, and he saw only indistinct blurs. A yellow and red shape tipped more water into his mouth. He drank until it was taken away. The form moulded into a woman. His mother, Peter thought, but his mother was not blonde.

He tried to say her name, but his voice sounded wrong – too soft, too high – like it had when he was a little boy. She hushed him, stroking a hand through his hair. Peter inhaled deeply, breathing a strange mixture of ether and cabbage. It choked him. When he coughed, the angel comforted him again. Did angels wear perfume? Her blonde halo obscured the water-damaged ceiling, but he could not force her face into focus. His eyes grew tired of trying, so he closed them and sank into the safe abyss.

*

Having been asleep for two days, Peter thought he should be able to remain awake for visitors. Instead, after five minutes with his family, he already felt the strain of consciousness. His mother sat beside him, speaking to him, but he had lost the conversation long ago. John and Samuel, his two eldest brothers, relaxed at the end of his bed, laughing at a magazine borrowed from a sleeping patient. Only Michael was silent, perched on the windowsill by Peter's head, chewing on a fingernail as he watched the street below. Peter remembered when they were young how people would confuse them as twins even though Michael was three years older. They still looked so alike.

Mother squeezed his hand. 'Peter? I said the police gave me your wallet and ration card. I'll return them when you're discharged. It's not that I don't trust you, but you never know with . . . other people nowadays.' She eyed a passing sister.

'Might as well hang on to them, Mother.' John grinned. 'He'll be moving back home now the big city's roughed him up, won't you, Petey?'

'Nonsense. Only a slight setback.' Samuel stole a grape from Peter's plate. 'Think of it as your first war wound.'

'Enough, boys,' Mother scolded.

Peter's eyelids slid shut. He blinked them open, hoping she hadn't noticed.

She had. 'We should be off. Peter needs his rest if he's to give the police his full statement.'

'But I already have.' He sunk into the mattress. He enjoyed his family's company, the sight of familiar faces. There was something inside him urging him not to remain alone.

Mother sighed. 'All you've told them is you can't remember a thing. That's hardly helpful, is it?'

'It's the truth.' Memories of that night hovered just beyond his reach. Only fragments came to greet him.

'Well, there must be more to it than that,' John said.

Orange light.

'Indeed,' Samuel added.

Damp pavement.

'If you try very hard, I'm sure you'll remember something,' said Mother.

Blood down his face.

'What did the fellow look like?' John asked.

Vomit beside his cheek.

'Was there more than one? Two? Three?' Samuel leant closer.

Sweat gathered in his palms as their questions bombarded him faster than German doodlebugs, firing image after useless image across his vision.

'Was it a whole gang?'

'Did you get in with the wrong crowd?'

'Do you owe anyone money?'

Round and round they spun, buzzing inside his head. A carousel losing control.

'You can't remember a fig what they looked like?'

'Where had you been?'

Vomit. Light. Jessie.

'Where were you going?'

'Where was that girl of yours?'

Blood. Fear. Eliza.

'He said he doesn't know!' Michael's voice flung itself into the gears of Peter's mind. The madness halted as the ward grew still. Patients, sisters, doctors – all stopped to watch Michael's pacing.

'If he says he doesn't remember then he doesn't remember. Leave him alone. You must leave him alone!' When Michael spoke, no one listened but everyone watched. That's how it was now, Father said. Watch until he quiets then ease him back into the world, that's what you had to do.

Mother addressed him too soon. 'Michael, please.'

'Please what, Mother? Please stop harassing my brother?'

'Easy, Michael.' John approached him, palms up, placating. 'We were only trying to help.'

'We didn't mean to upset him,' said Samuel.

'Here, what say we go to the pub? Let Mother and Peter have a few minutes' privacy?'

'Why, John, a splendid idea. Shall we, Michael?'

They clasped Michael by the shoulders, patting him on the

112

back as they escorted him from the ward. Michael itched at his arms, muttering about injustice as he allowed himself to be led away. The look on Mother's face was an echo of the one she had worn during his brothers' deployments. She watched them even after they were gone.

'Mother?'

'Yes? Oh, I'm sorry, Peter.'

'No. I am. That I can't remember anything. I'll try. I promise I'll try.'

'I know you will. Only . . . promise me you won't try too hard, my poor boy.' She looked towards the ward door. 'My poor, poor boy.'

*

Peter regained his strength over the next few days with little to do but ponder his mother's words – did he remember what happened? When he tried, all he found was a black space between walking from Jessie's flat to waking in hospital. The harder he tried to fill that gap, the larger it became. He imagined he could lose his entire self to it, if he allowed it to grow. His only options were either to brick up that part of his life and forget it ever happened, or find the memories to close the wound. Both seemed impossible lying in a hospital bed, surrounded by sad faces awaiting the end.

The day of his release, the air was clear and fresh as he leaned heavily on his cane and limped out of St Bart's. He filled his lungs and looked back at the building, admiring the statues on the Greek colonnades. Somehow, like St Paul's, these survived the war. Not all was lost. Across the street, the council were clearing rubble from a bomb crater. It would take time, but everything could be rebuilt.

His landlady fussed over him when he arrived home,

113

insisting she carry his bag and help him up to his flat. She promised to get new banisters installed right away, as soon as she could find someone with the proper iron. Wouldn't it be a nightmare, she said, for poor, young Mr Lamb to be limping up and down the steps with only that cane for support? The missing banisters had almost never bothered Peter. Now he felt their lack with every step as he climbed behind her, inhaling her strong French perfume. He remembered another perfume, one at hospital, so different, like lavender and fresh linen.

Promising to join her and her husband later for tea and biscuits, Peter stepped into the stillness of his flat. Though nothing had changed, there was an emptiness which hadn't existed prior, one he knew would linger in the rooms for days following his return.

His post lay strewn across the floor and, gently, he lowered himself to gather the mess. There were a few bills and a letter from his mother sent before the attack, but nothing from Eliza. She would have visited him in hospital if she were near. If she had known. With a sigh, he used the cane to push himself up and dropped the post onto the counter. The larder and cupboards were empty of anything he felt like eating, so he put the kettle on instead. Eliza's last letter said nothing as to where she was, only that she needed to go away, that she would never return and he would never see her again.

If Eliza was still in London, someone would have told her about his attack, wouldn't they? And Jessie, what about her? All those days in hospital and he barely spared her a thought. The morphine had clouded his thoughts. Now he was home, he could refocus his efforts. Maybe John or Samuel could help him. Michael, too, if he was feeling well.

With a cup of tea in hand, Peter settled into his armchair. Today he would rest, but tomorrow he could start his search again. He switched on the wireless and, as it warmed up, he caught a flash of red amongst the blues and greys outside.

Bess Haverford paced the pavement opposite his building. Peter wanted to run down to her, but his sore leg made it impossible. Unable to lift the heavy window, he knocked on the glass.

'Miss Haverford!' He saw her jump and look about. He called again, and this time she noticed him through the glass. Peter waved to her, indicating she could come up. Bess hesitated then stepped one foot off the pavement.

A cab sped past. She leapt back, paused, then hurried off down the street, never glancing again at his window.

Peter collapsed into the armchair. Billy Cotton and his band started playing, but it was only background noise to his thoughts on Bess Haverford. Theory after theory on why she had been there passed through his mind. He could come to no decent explanation.

He thought he would forget her visit come morning, but even in the busy nine o'clock rush, he could still picture her waiting on the pavement. The image kept playing in his mind, even when he moved away from the window. Had she seemed tense? Excited? Had she waved? His mind kept adding new details until he couldn't remember what he truly saw and what he imagined. Yet she had come, and a nagging thought said it wasn't to see if he was well. There was something else Bess wanted.

It was dinnertime when Peter took up his coat, cap and cane and made the exhausting trip to Whitechapel. His steps were stilted and stiff by the time he reached Eliza's building, and he stifled a groan when he saw that the stairs to her flat were again covered in rubbish bags. Despite his best efforts to avoid them, he tripped upon the landing. His bad leg gave out under him, and he fell against the wall opposite their flat. The sound of his cane rolling down the stairs echoed through the building.

His vision blurred. The smell of sick accompanied the flash of a lead pipe rolling into a gutter.

As his sight cleared, the image faded but the smell remained. It wasn't sick, he realised, but it wasn't the rubbish, either. Peter hoisted himself to his feet and limped to the Haverfords' door. It was unlocked.

'Miss Haverford?'

No answer. He tried pushing the door open, but it was blocked from the inside. Bit by bit, he forced it open.

The smell of gas hit him. As he covered his mouth and nose, he saw the towels stuffed at the bottom of the doorframe. Peter inched his way inside but stopped after crossing the threshold.

Bess Haverford was on the kitchen floor with her legs splayed out behind her, her head in the oven.

10

Eliza covered her nose to block the metallic smell of blood emanating from the butchered sheep carcass that swung rhythmically from the ceiling. For a moment, it was not a sheep she saw. She helped Mrs Pollard carry the slab of meat from the larder. They dropped it on the butcher's block with a thud. The raw pink body of the headless skinned animal was marred in places by patches of mildew.

'Mr Drewry slaughtered it last week. He's very good with a gun.' Taking a cloth soaked in vinegar, Mrs Pollard rubbed the green patches away. 'Have you ever made curried mutton?' She pressed two fingers against the flesh and plunged a boning knife into the top of the sheep's pelvis.

'No, ma'am.'

'What a travesty. Curry powder is the first item one learns to cook with when living in India.'

'I've never been to India, ma'am.'

'Well, I suppose we can't all be so fortunate.' The boning knife sliced around the pelvis, perpendicular to the spine. 'Fetch me two small onions, a sour apple and the curry powder.'

Mrs Pollard wanted to see how Eliza would get on with the cooking, wanted to see if she could take on the added responsibility, speaking to her as if Eliza had not been the sole cook for her family for two years. As if she had not put meals on the table three times a day despite the ration. As if she wouldn't know the difference between rabbit and pork, lamb and mutton. She would show her just how well she could 'get on'.

The larder was dark except for the light leaching in from the kitchen. Tinned fruits and vegetables lined the granite countertops while empty metal hooks were screwed into brick walls which held in the cold. Their larder in London was no more than a small pantry, but it was large enough for the little she managed to buy when going to market in Whitechapel. The jellied, pickled and preserved foods here could feed them in London for weeks, perhaps months. All of it for one old man and his housekeeper.

She set down the items with a heavy smack. 'Was Miss Vlasto a good cook?'

'Why the interest in poor Miss Vlasto? Get that pot.' Mrs Pollard tossed the boning knife onto the table.

Eliza dropped the pot onto the counter. 'I suppose I'm interested in why she left. Jobs must be few in Plentynunig, what with the coal mines closing. They said on the wireless—'

Mrs Pollard took a cleaver to the sheep's spine. 'The master's mines will never close. Get the lid.'

Eliza tossed the lid beside the pot. 'So you fired her?'

'Don't be silly. Help me cut the meat.' Mrs Pollard handed Eliza a knife, blade first. 'Miss Vlasto died before I had the chance.'

The knife nearly sliced her palm.

'In your bed, as it happens. Very sickly, I told you. The Welsh air did not agree with her.' Mrs Pollard stuck her hands under the butchered ribcage. 'Don't look so concerned, Miss Haverford. I changed the sheets before you arrived.'

*

118

Blood stuck under Eliza's fingernails. She stood at the bathroom sink, scrubbing at her hands with a nail brush. Washing them in the kitchen had not been enough.

How could Pip be dead? Had she not seen her the other day? Either she was speaking to ghosts or that girl with the paper-riddled house lied to her. Was she really as gullible as Father said?

Her skin was raw but the germs remained, embedded in her pores. She had to get them out. The tap ran so loudly that Eliza almost missed the singing.

'*Run rabbit, run rabbit, run run run . . .*'

'Rebecca?' She turned off the water. The soft padding of small feet crossed in front of the bathroom. Eliza opened the door and caught a glimpse of a brown dress darting around the corner. She followed.

'*Bang, bang, bang, bang goes the farmer's gun . . .*'

Rebecca dashed into the north hall.

'*Run rabbit, run rabbit, run run run . . .*'

A shadow ascended the staircase that led to Mr Brownawell's private rooms.

'Rebecca!' Eliza ran up after her.

The first floor of the north hall wore the same faded carpets and peeling wallpaper as downstairs. Though fitted for electricity, there were no bulbs in the sconces. A window at the end of the corridor allowed the only light. Eliza listened.

'Rebecca? Rebecca, you know you shouldn't be here. You're going to be in an awful lot of trouble if Mrs Pollard catches you.'

When she reached the end of the hall, there was still no sign of her sister, only empty passages either side leading to destinations unknown and large windows that lined the back of the manor. Thinking she perhaps misheard – could the singing have come from outside, her glimpses of a child merely shadows? – she leant over a bare oak table to peer onto the north lawn below. The grass was overgrown and a lone, gnarled tree pocked the otherwise flat land. The wolfhound barked and galloped across the field, followed by Mr Drewry, a rifle slung over his shoulder. He stopped mid-stride and turned his head towards the north hall window where Eliza stood.

She spun away from the glass, pressing her body flat against the wall. She wouldn't return to the staircase until she could be certain he was gone. Eliza waited, counting her breaths, until she felt it safe to look again. Mr Drewry walked towards his carriage house, giving no sign he had seen her. Eliza dabbed the sweat from her brow. She needed to return downstairs but hesitated.

If Mrs Pollard wanted to keep the bloodstained book from her, why not hide it up here? Eliza needed to find it, scour it for clues as to what had killed Pip Vlasto. If Mrs Pollard were to lie about something as innocuous as mentioning a reading room, what lies was she telling about Pip? About the blood in the book? What else was the auburn-haired girl hiding, apart from her real name? No longer would Eliza take anyone in Plentynunig at their word. She'd discover truths for herself.

Every room she tried was empty. She discovered a few pieces of scattered furniture but nothing more. No boxes. No books. So much empty space, it was overwhelming. At Aunt Bess's they had been three people crammed into a one-bedroom flat. There was never any peace, not even in the bathroom, with only one per floor. Mrs Hodgkins would occupy it for hours, soaking her back, or Mr Pendleton would bang on the door complaining he never got his fair chunk of time. When Eliza did have a spare moment, Rebecca would seek her out or Aunt Bess would holler. So many voices calling out for her attention.

Another empty room.

Three people in Aunt Bess's flat and the whole building felt claustrophobic. Here, there were so many rooms and passages, they could go days and never so much as glimpse one another. Yet Eliza could never shake the sensation that there was always someone with her.

She turned the corner, and a massive set of wooden doors – more elaborate than anything she'd seen at Thornecroft thus far – stood before her. As she inched closer to the towering panels, Eliza felt small, plain, insignificant. She ran her fingers over the intricate carvings in the wood. It felt warm against her skin. The handcrafted images depicted scenes of men ploughing fields, women cooking, sheep in fields, dogs and children playing – an illustration of what a plentiful Plentynunig could be, of perhaps what it once was. Every carving was smooth and polished. Unlike so much in the manor, these doors were in perfect condition. They could have been made yesterday. Eliza wanted to open them, split the scene in half, discover what lay behind. She placed her hand on the curved brass handle.

Coughing rattled the hall – a deep, dry hacking that made the handle vibrate in Eliza's hand.

'Handkerchief! Hurry up now. We must get moving.'

Mrs Pollard stood behind those doors.

Eliza ran, the carpet silencing her steps. The staircase she needed wasn't there. She made a wrong turn.

A door opened and slammed. She turned left. More doors and no exit. The slaughtered sheep came to mind, Mrs Pollard with cleaver in hand, the blood on the butcher's block.

Heavy footsteps pursued her.

121

She slipped inside the nearest room, holding her breath as her eyes adjusted to the dark. The footsteps, louder now, were accompanied by a light creak and the brush of something heavy sliding against the carpet.

'. . . close it until the autumn. I warned them. Nationalisation would mean death . . . may have to sell . . . but we'll keep the Cware entrance open, of course. Still . . .'

A dry cough brought the footsteps to a halt outside Eliza's door. She kept perfectly still.

'Use your handkerchief.'

The muffled coughs continued for another minute. Eliza held her breath, afraid of making the slightest sound.

'Better? Good.'

Eliza thought the loud thumping of her heart would give her away, but the steps and creaks recommenced. She remained huddled by the door, listening for any more sounds.

It was then she spotted the portrait. It hung uncovered above the fireplace. Dust blanketed the paint. Yet even in the grey darkness of the room, Eliza could tell it was the woman in the muslin dress. In the downward gaze, she saw a forlorn look cast by deep brown eyes. The face was round and soft, much like Eliza's. If she let her hair grow longer, Eliza could almost pass the portrait off as her own, albeit a more beautified version of herself.

A nameplate was screwed into the bottom of the frame. She stepped onto the foot of the fireplace. Leaning over the mantle, she wiped away the dust, but the plate was unreadable in the dark. She pulled the box of matches from her pocket, lit one and held it close to the frame. Someone had tried to scratch out the inscription, but the words remained legible.

Beloved Victoria

Eliza reread it till the match burnt her fingers.

When she returned to their wing, she found Rebecca sitting in the hall with her toy cat. Without a word, Eliza took her by the arm and pulled her into the bedroom.

'You told me I'm not allowed in here,' Rebecca said as Eliza closed the door.

'What were you doing on the first floor? You know we're not permitted up there. What do you think Mrs Pollard would've done had she found you? You must think about consequences, Rebecca.'

'But I didn't do anything.'

'It doesn't matter. Simply being where you're not allowed—'

'But I wasn't!' Rebecca sat on the bed beside the body. Eliza blinked. There was only Rebecca.

'Stop being silly. I won't let people lie to me any more.'

'I wasn't on the first floor, Liza. I wasn't! I've never been up there.'

'Then where were you this afternoon?' Eliza crossed her arms, trying her best impression of Mother.

'I was where Mrs Pollard told me to be. At the henhouse.'

'All afternoon?'

'I had to collect the eggs, change the straw, sweep the coop, feed the chickens. It took ages. And they kept squawking at me and flapping their wings. All these feathers got in my mouth . . .'

'You never went up on the first floor?'

'No.'

'Mrs Pollard didn't ask you or . . .' A pulsing pressure formed behind her eyes. She wanted to sit but not on the bed.

'Eliza, what's wrong?'

'Tell me the truth. Swear to me you weren't there.'

Rebecca stood beside her. 'I swear. Do you really think I'm a liar? Well, do you?'

'No. No, I . . .'

'I'm trying to be good. Really I am.'

'I know, dearie.' Eliza regarded her another moment then hugged her. Though Rebecca wore the same brown dress she had on at breakfast, she smelled nothing of the henhouse.

*

Mrs Pollard slopped a hunk of mutton onto Eliza's plate. The curry powder smelled too strong for her liking and the meat was overcooked. While Rebecca had no trouble eating, Eliza only nibbled. She had never regained her appetite after the butchering.

'Not to your liking?' asked Mrs Pollard. 'This is one of my favourites.' Despite her words, Mrs Pollard ate only a small portion, leaving most of her plate untouched.

Eliza tried a larger bite. It was like eating a hunk of dried liquorice root. Her jaw became sore trying to grind it down.

'Tomorrow, I need you to sweep the north hall. The dust is exacerbating the master's condition. You remember where the north hall is, don't you, Miss Haverford?'

Eliza fumbled her fork. It clattered against the stoneware. 'Of course,' she said, picking it up off the plate.

'Good. I do like a maid who remembers what she's told. Miss Vlasto was troublesome like that. Very forgetful. Reminds me of a maid I knew in India. A native called Bimali. Pretty girl, for a coolie. Unfortunately, her intelligence did not match her appearance. Miss Haverford, since dinner appears to be beneath you, go and stir the stock on the stove.'

Being away from the table was a relief. The mixture of broth and vegetable juices smelled better than what was on her plate and cleared her nose of the awful curry. Eliza's stomach grumbled.

124

'What did the maid do?' Rebecca asked and, this time, Mrs Pollard did not rebuke her curiosity.

'Bimali was ordered to serve only the lady of the house, as her appearance distracted the master from his work. One night, as she passed by while bringing tea to her mistress, the master saw her. Of course he could not resist such beauty, so he took her into his room and had his way with her.'

There was something large in the pot that struck the wooden spoon every time Eliza stirred.

'The master was furious, of course, for Bimali had used her wicked ways to lure him into sin. So he told her family of her indiscretion.'

Eliza coaxed the large chunk to the surface.

'They took her to the bazaar and stoned her to death.'

A set of teeth smiled at her from the brown water. Eliza dropped the spoon. The sheep's head sunk to the bottom of the pot.

'She didn't even scream as they pelted her with rock after rock. She knew she had done wrong and let the stones beat away her wicked soul. I remember how the bruises marred her face and the blood pooled by her head.' Mrs Pollard's voice became soft and distant, the way Aunt Bess's did when she spoke of her ex-fiancé. 'I remember, though her eyes were swollen shut, how she stared at me while I held my mother's . . .'

The room fell silent save the quietly bubbling stock.

Mrs Pollard laughed. 'I just remembered. Her name meant "pure". Wishful thinking on behalf of her parents, wouldn't you say? Oh, Miss Haverford. I nearly forgot. Mr Brownawell would like you to join him for dinner this Friday. You'll need a proper dress. The master always dresses for dinner and none of the frocks you brought will do.'

'Have you gone through my things?' The story had so angered Eliza that she didn't fully understand what Mrs Pollard said. Such stories shouldn't be told, not in front of her sister.

'I'll send you into town with Mr Drewry so you can purchase some suitable fabric. Mr Brownawell is very much looking forward to meeting you, Miss Haverford.'

The housekeeper's announcement began to sink in. She was to see him, the master, Mr Brownawell. 'And what of Rebecca?'

'He has no need of her. Not yet.'

She was to see him, alone. Eliza expected Rebecca to pout over her exclusion, but instead she simply smiled.

'Very well.' Unable to eat, Eliza took her plate to the compost pile outside. Aunt Bess had never gone through her things, not once. She valued privacy, Aunt Bess, even in that tiny flat. Eliza had never known what it was like to have absolutely none, until now.

As she turned to go back inside, she heard a scratching near the back door and found a young rabbit caught in a snare.

'Poor thing. Hang on.'

Before she could release it, Mrs Pollard was by her side.

'Ah. So it's you who's been nibbling at my garden. Rebecca, come here. What do you think of that?' She pointed to the struggling rabbit.

'Is it hurt?' Rebecca asked.

'I don't think so,' Eliza said. 'Here, you can help me free him.'

'Free him? When good meat is hard to come by?' Mrs Pollard asked. 'That seems a waste, don't you think? Or are you city folk happy living off sardines and Spam?'

'We have plenty of meat on the estate.'

The panicked animal was frozen in fear beneath Eliza's hand. She could feel the frantic beating of its tiny heart through the soft brown fur.

'So we allow it to eat most of our vegetables? We've had a hard enough winter without having this vermin destroy what little we have. Go on, Rebecca. You know what to do.'

Rebecca knelt by her side and replaced Eliza's hand with her own.

'It's all right, Liza. I've done this before. You don't have to be scared.' Rebecca petted the rabbit with one hand while she reached for the stone doorstop with the other. 'Hello, little rabbit. Don't worry. It'll all be over soon. Shh.'

The rabbit watched Eliza until Rebecca smashed the stone once, twice, three times against his head, crushing his small skull. Bits of blood splattered their dresses. Eliza watched the rabbit's long feet twitch, again hearing the song as its fur became brittle with blood.

Run rabbit, run rabbit, run run run . . .

11

Their house grew to Thornecroft's size, but the rooms shrank once she stepped inside. Mother was in the kitchen, stirring explosives in the mixing bowl. She let Rebecca taste the dough. Eliza wanted to help but was shooed away.

You're needed elsewhere, said Mother's voice, and she put the bomb in the oven.

Eliza left the kitchen and entered Mr Brownawell's small parlour which should not have been there, but it was part of her life now, and she needed to accept that. The red calfskin armchair was by the fire with Beloved Victoria curled upon it, a bandage round her eyes. Her hair kept her dry from the water dripping through the ceiling, though it wasn't meant to rain tonight.

Read to me, said Father's voice, so Eliza chose a book from the shelf. The rabbit watched, nose twitching, as she opened the leather cover. Blood flowed freely from the pages. She threw the book into the fire and the flames came towards her like Mother's arms outstretched.

Eliza screamed.

Her hands. They were clean. But the floor . . . Why was she on the floor? She looked up at the empty bed. Had she fallen? No. The memory of last night returned to her. She had chosen the floor. She stretched her stiff body as she returned the pillows and top sheet to the bed. It would only be for another night or two, until she grew accustomed to the idea of someone dying in her bed.

After sweeping the north hall that morning, she spent her afternoon repairing the doll she decided to call Victoria. Handling the doll made her uncomfortable, like hearing nails drawn against a blackboard, but, for Rebecca's sake, she needed to repress her own dislike. Ever since they arrived at the manor, Rebecca seemed to be slipping into her old ways, everything the hospital fixed breaking once again. Eliza knew she needed to do whatever she could to hold her sister together. She warmed some paraffin wax in her fingers and inserted it where the eyes belonged. After smoothing it into the gouges, she took up her pen and began drawing Victoria new eyes, trying to think how such damage could have occurred.

She imagined Mr Brownawell as a young man, perhaps attractive. As a wealthy landowner, women would have fought for his attentions no matter his appearance. Yet there was only one woman for this Mr Darcy of Wales – the paintings made it obvious – beautiful, young Victoria. Yet what became of his beloved? An illness, surely, before they could be married. Consumption, perhaps. Mr Brownawell must have sat by her bedside for hours, holding her hand as she succumbed to fever. Day after day he would whisper in her ear, telling her of his love for her, of all the wonderful things they would do together once she was well. It was not to be. Beloved Victoria would pass into eternal sleep, using her last breath to return his declaration of love. He would shake her, beg her to wake, even slap her, to no avail.

Consumed by grief, Mr Brownawell would lash out at anyone who came near, destroy everything that reminded him of their love. In the room meant for children now never to be, there would sit the doll, perched on a small four-poster bed. It was made to match his love, a perfect replica in miniature that was now no more alive than its likeness. He would grab it and throw it across the room, but the doll was too well made and would not break. In his study was a letter opener, the silver one she gave him for his last birthday. He would run for it. Grab it from its place of pride on the desk and thrust it into the doll, desperate to blind it so that the eyes, which were so like hers, would stop gazing upon him.

It must have been this – his fiancée's death – that had made Mr Brownawell such a bitter, twisted old man. Nothing but love could turn men so cruel, and he must be a cruel man to engage a housekeeper such as Mrs Pollard, a caretaker like Mr Drewry. Eliza wondered if that would happen to Peter if she never returned. No, Peter was young. He would find another girl. She glimpsed the unfinished scarf by the wardrobe and felt a pain in her chest. If she hadn't lost their clothing cards . . .

She interrupted the thought. It would do her no good.

The eyes finished, Eliza hurried to the kitchen. Rebecca stood at the sink peeling potatoes. She attacked them with relish, humming as she sliced away the skin. The potato could easily be a rabbit, Eliza thought, and Rebecca would behave the same way.

'Rebecca, look.' Eliza held out the doll.

'Oh. That's nice.'

'I know she's not finished, but doesn't she look pretty now she can see?'

'It's only a doll, Eliza. Dolls can't see. They're not real.'

'No, I suppose they're not. But what do you think about her hair? Is there any particular style you'd like?'

'It doesn't matter to me.'

'I thought you wanted me to fix her?'

Rebecca shrugged. 'That was before.'

'Before what? Suddenly, you don't like dolls?'

'I don't want a doll that looks like that whore.'

Eliza's face flushed. 'You're not to use that word.'

Rebecca gathered the peels into her hands. Eliza saw the rabbit's bloodied fur slipping through her small fingers. She set Victoria aside. 'Rebecca?'

'Yes?'

'You said yesterday, about the . . . rabbit.' Her tongue tripped over the word. 'You said you had done it before. When was that?'

'When we were on holiday,' she said, handling a skinned potato as gently as she had the animal's corpse.

'Holiday?'

'During the war.'

'You mean when we were evacuated?'

'I don't like that word.'

'The family you stayed with, they kept rabbits?'

'They would catch them in the forest. I wasn't allowed to tell anyone because it was the old man's land. But I suppose it doesn't matter now.'

'They were poachers?' Eliza fiddled with the potato peeler.

'They said it was fine because they were poor and the old man had lots of food.'

'But they made you do the slaughtering?'

'Not until the camping trip. Until then, that was Mary's job. She said she came from Brixton, but I didn't like her much. She smelled like vinegar and gave me lice.' She dropped the potato in a bowl. 'I caught her one day, crying as she came out of the bedroom. Mr Meeler followed her out. He had a red mark on his cheek and said Mary hadn't been a good girl. He wasn't sure if he could trust either of us any more, so we had to go on a camping trip to prove ourselves worthy. Could you hand me the masher?'

131

Eliza did so. 'What happened on the camping trip?'

'Oh, nothing too terrible. Mr Meeler made Mary and me sleep alone in the forest for a few nights. It wasn't too bad except it was a bit cold and he didn't give us much water.'

Eliza felt her hand close around the peeler. 'Rebecca, what did you do?'

'Well, it's not my fault she disappeared. There really wasn't enough water for two. And the blanket was quite small.' A little smile appeared at the corner of Rebecca's mouth, which quickly morphed into a frown. 'Really, Eliza, must you always assume I've done something wrong?'

'Was she ever found?'

'Just her shoes. They were by the river, I think.' She considered it for a moment. 'Yes, that's where I last saw them. Mary had big feet, and her shoes were too large for me. Like yours, Eliza.' She smiled.

'Rebecca, why haven't you ever told me this?'

'Well, I don't see why it matters. It's all in the past, isn't it? And Father told us we should forget the past. Only weak men focus on the fuck—'

'Ouch!' Eliza sliced her finger on the peeler.

'Is that blood?' Rebecca hurried to her side. 'Let me see.' She held out her hand, and Eliza obliged her. 'Why, that's not very much at all. Not nearly as much as the rabbit.' She sighed, disappointed almost, and pulled out her handkerchief to dab the red bead away then bent down and kissed the cut. 'There. All better.'

Eliza's eyes fixated on the speck of blood now dotting Rebecca's upper lip.

'I see you've spent the day wisely.' Mrs Pollard held the doll by the leg, pinching it betwixt her thumb and forefinger, her lip curved in a sneer.

Eliza felt a surge of protectiveness and snatched Victoria away. 'I had a few spare moments.'

'Then we'll have to find something to fill them. My office, Miss Haverford.' The keys clanged against her hip as she swept through.

Mrs Pollard's office was a small room off the kitchen with a low ceiling and grey stone floor. A brown trapdoor with a heavy iron ring handle rested in the centre. An antique writing desk sat on the left side before two windows which looked out onto the east lawn. On the opposite wall hung an old tapestry, the colours so faded no image could be discerned.

There was a small fireplace on the back wall with an ash-covered iron grille in front. It was into this fireplace that Mrs Pollard tossed a slip of paper while Eliza stood in the doorway, awaiting her new orders. Mrs Pollard returned to her seat at the desk while Eliza watched the flames consume the rectangular half-sheet. A part of her wanted to cry out that there was a paper shortage. Father's voice told her to keep her mouth shut.

'Mr Brownawell would like to have your dinner in the Ancestral Parlour,' Mrs Pollard said, her eyes on the correspondence before her. 'It hasn't been used in quite some time so you must get it into proper working order.'

'And Rebecca?'

'Does your sister speak English?'

'Yes.'

'Does she have a grasp of basic commands?'

'Yes.'

'Then I will give Rebecca her orders myself. You have a great deal of work to do. I suggest you get on with it. I would hate to see Mr Brownawell's temper if the room is not prepared by Friday.'

133

Eliza left without giving a curtsey. It was a minor rebellion, she knew, but it brought her pleasure all the same. Rebecca stood on the wooden step stool, washing the potato peeler.

'Rebecca, Mrs Pollard would like to see you.'

'All right!' She dropped the peeler onto the drying rack and hopped off the stool, humming as she walked to the office door. Eliza watched, wanting to say something but not knowing what. 'You don't have to wait,' Rebecca said as she entered the office. She smiled at Eliza and closed the door behind her. The doll trembled as Eliza's hands shook. She tried to reconcile the idea that Mrs Pollard – so disgusted with Rebecca when they first arrived – now seemed to take Rebecca in her confidence, and that Rebecca eagerly accepted the woman's guidance.

Despite Rebecca's words, Eliza waited. At this time of the afternoon, when the sun had moved further west, it was dull, dirty daylight that filled the kitchen. Little shadows lay everywhere, cast from the counters and hanging pots and pans. It reminded Eliza of a scene she had seen in a film – of a house that was left empty after the soldiers who lived there went off to die. A giggle sounded from behind Mrs Pollard's door. She could stand there no longer. She deposited Victoria in her room then continued down the hall.

Having armed herself with a Tilley lamp, Eliza stood in the doorway of the Ancestral Parlour. Long and rectangular, the damp room had six floor-to-ceiling windows along the left wall, their dusty shutters all latched shut. A crystal chandelier refitted for electric light hung from a high ceiling surrounded by a pattern of black mould. The number of dust sheets which covered the furniture and paintings made it look like a hospital ward.

Despite its degradation, it was still a grand room and, as

Eliza opened the wooden shutters, she pictured the balls it must have hosted in its prime. She pulled away the sheets with a twirl, imagining lords and ladies and all sorts of aristocracy. Large, expensive dresses draped in silk and lace, sharply tailored dinner jackets and butlers offering champagne on silver trays. A four-piece orchestra playing in the corner. And the dancing! The last time she'd been dancing was in Piccadilly with Peter. But this would've been proper dancing – waltzes and cakewalks. It felt like those guests were here now, spectres keeping her company while she polished the furniture.

As Eliza piled the linen in the hall, a coughing fit shook the walls. She retreated into the parlour. Four days until she had to face him.

'Maybe Death will find him first,' she sighed. The room swallowed her voice, reminding her how empty this place was. There were no royal guests or distinguished gentlemen, and despite the candles and the cleaning, it remained dark. Eliza Haverford, in her dungarees and turned-out blouse, dry hair wrapped in a scrap of cloth, looked more like an army nurse, the kind she read about in *Woman* magazine, preparing a ward for incoming casualties. This place might as well be an abandoned hospital – the stale air, lack of light, that special kind of stillness which only exists in half-forgotten houses. And always that distinct feeling she was being watched.

Eliza shivered. Standing here in this room, alone, she felt more crowded than in Aunt Bess's flat. But Mrs Pollard and Rebecca were in the kitchen, Mr Drewry somewhere on the grounds. Mr Brownawell, where was he? Could he be watching her now? Old houses like these, they always had secret passages, tunnels, spyholes. Just because no one was here did not mean no one was watching. Or waiting.

Someone stroked her cheek. Eliza gasped and turned, but it was only a dust sheet flapping in the breeze. Yet she felt no draught even as the ends of the sheet swayed gently as if hanging on a line outside. Indeed, all the sheets along the wall were waving. The one beside her came loose and floated to the ground.

Eliza raised her eyes to the painting. It was an oil-on-canvas portrait of an older gentleman mounted on a chestnut mare.

Sir Charles Brownawell 1760–1799, read the plaque – the man who built Thornecroft. He had dark hair, and a large moustache spread out from his upper lip to cover his cheeks. An air of superiority emanated from his eyes, a smugness that implied it was beneath him to be in anyone's presence other than his own.

What are you doing here, child? he seemed to say. *Get out of here, harlot. Get out of my Thornecroft.*

No longer able to look at it, Eliza moved to the next painting as Sir Charles watched her.

Go on. Remove it, he whispered. *Maybe he'll prefer your kind.*

The sheet fell to the floor.

Another oil portrait – *Felix Brownawell 1782–1827*. He stood by a table, hand inside his jacket, a spaniel at his feet. His hair was thin and his gaunt, white face stood out, pale like a sick man's. There was something in his eyes, a certain quirk of his lips that beckoned her forward even as she wanted to pull away.

Come here, child. Let me get a good look at you. Yes, yes. You'll do. Come here.

Eliza tripped on the sheet as she hurried to the third painting. Don't remove it, she told herself, leave it there.

Please, please.

She glanced around. She was alone.

Please.

She pulled off the sheet.

Richard Brownawell 1819–1877 – unfinished. His face was completed but the rest of the proposed portrait – the chair, the stack of books at his side – was merely sketched out in black pencil on the brown canvas. There was a kindness in this one's eyes, but something about his mouth implied he wasn't all there, that although he was looking at her, he imagined something else entirely.

Yes, welcome. Welcome, child. Do have a seat. Tea? Where is the . . . oh yes. Here. Have you seen my . . . I'm sorry. Who are you?

Eliza stepped away.

Who are you? Why are you here? Come here, child. Why else are you here? Get out of my sight, wretched girl. What are you doing here? Their silent voices echoed through the parlour.

'I don't need to explain myself to any of you. I don't even want to be here.'

Her lifeless voice caused a shift in the room, as if the men were no longer looking at her but behind her. A pressure formed on her back, the tension that came with being watched. Her breath caught in her breast as she turned. Above the fireplace hung one final portrait. She wanted to leave it covered, but the men, they urged her forward.

He wants to meet you. Let him see you. Yes, he must see you. Go on, child. You must. Yes, you must.

She stepped around the dining table, hesitating at the foot of the fireplace. A cold breeze tickled her back, encouraging her, and she lifted her hand to the sheet. She pulled, but it stuck, caught on the sharp corner of the frame. She reached up further, standing on the edge of the raised hearth, one hand

137

clinging to the mantle for support, as she got a firmer grip on the sheet. Again, she pulled. With a jerk, it came free.

Eliza lost her balance and toppled backwards. She landed hard, knocking her head on a dining chair. She thought she heard laughter as the sheet floated down and covered her legs, but it must have been her own ears ringing. She sat up, dazed, and rubbed her head. No blood, but she felt a lump forming. Wincing, she looked up to see a man twice the size of the others staring down on her. He, like Sir Charles, was mounted on a horse – a pitch-black stallion with a wild grimace. A young man sitting proud, shoulders straight and tall, his face was dark and handsome – the kind Eliza pictured when reading Austen – but his expression was hard, his blue-grey eyes narrowed. This portrait was silent, but there was something in his gaze that held her in place. Something that made her feel that as soon as she turned away, rider and horse might leap from the frame.

A grating cough broke Eliza's trance. She jumped to her feet and ran from the parlour, never wanting to return to that dead man's hall, yet knowing she must.

*

Eliza went to her room straight after dinner, making excuses to Rebecca as to why she wished to be alone. After seeing Mr Brownawell's portrait, the thought of meeting him on Friday weighed heavily on her mind. If a portrait could so torment her, what would it be like to meet him in person?

Tonight, the floor seemed uninviting and the bed still unsound. Eliza compromised and pulled the entire mattress to the floor. Resting her head on the pillow, she looked up out of the window. The days were getting longer now and, despite the hour, some light crept through the dirty glass. As she watched the night grow gradually darker, her thoughts turned to London.

Today was the first day of April. April meant springtime, her favourite season – fresh grass growing in the parks, warm rain showers, no overcoats – and they deserved a good spring after that dreadful, freezing winter. Eliza imagined going dancing, to a film, dinner at a Corner House. The city would pulse with a new energy. If she concentrated, she could feel its rush of life, picture walks along the Thames hand in hand with Peter while black cabs and red double-deckers rumbled past. There were demolished buildings and entire blocks destroyed by bomb blasts, but still the city would sparkle, especially at night with the lights from Parliament and Big Ben and St Paul's – all of them survivors of the Blitz.

Eliza opened her eyes, saw the sky darkening over an empty field, and felt a longing stronger than she had ever known. It was the feeling she'd had when they first arrived at Aunt Bess's, the funeral fresh in her mind as she moved in with a woman she barely knew after being so briefly reunited with the father she missed for years. Yet the feeling now was worse, ten times as strong, because, before, at least she remained in London; at least Aunt Bess was family. Here, the land was unfamiliar and her only family Rebecca, who lately felt more a stranger than a sister.

'This isn't where I'm meant to be.' She didn't realise she was crying until she felt the warm tears on her cheeks. She turned into her pillow, hoping to muffle her sobs, when her hand brushed something foreign against the sheet. She shot up. Another mouse? Or had a piece of rabbit somehow found its way into her room? With shaking hands, she lifted the pillow. There lay the photograph she had left at the cottage. A slender girl with dark hair, one Eliza didn't recognise, had been circled, the name 'Pip' written above her. On the back was a message.

Eliza, I'm sorry. I should have told you. It is not for me that you should leave Thornecroft, but for your own safety.
    As soon as possible.
    — Ruth Owen

12

Horrible thing, that's what the detective constable was saying. It was a horrible thing to see, but verdict of suicide expected. No further inquiries. Peter was having trouble understanding. The station was too loud – PCs laughing over tea, new arrests shouting, phones continuously ringing. This detective, with his pencil moustache bobbing up and down, lips curling to reveal the gap between his front teeth, spat out words which made no sense.

No further inquiries.

The room was hot, stuffed with bodies and whining electric lights and the stench of sweating men. Pain kept shooting down his right leg, made worse by the hard wooden chair he'd been sat in the last half an hour.

Bess Haverford had been in debt. Poor woman couldn't cope. Her nieces leaving must have been a private matter – and Jessica Rolston? Different part of London, different matter, different station. No further inquiries. Now if you please, busy day, busy times. The PCs laughed. A phone receiver slammed down. The detective held out his hand. The man's calloused fingers scratched his skin.

Peter left Fenchurch Street Police Station, the London weather a too apt reflection of his mood. A cold wind blew through the street, chapping Peter's hands and face as he limped to the Rood Lane bus stop. It was supposed to be springtime. Hadn't the winter chill lasted long enough? The sudden change from the warmth and noise of the police station to the cold and muffled sounds of the streets did nothing to clear his mind. Suicide. Was it possible? Was that why she had come to his flat that day? Could he have helped her? What about Eliza? Someone needed to tell Eliza about Bess's death, but how could they if no one knew where she was? He picked at a scratch on his cane and stared at the men passing by in their suits, clutching their briefcases, their faces set in stoic determination. Surely one of them would know what to do, if they were in Peter's situation. If Peter were more like them, he could do something.

He went to the end of the long bus queue. Though the chair in the police station had been uncomfortable, standing was worse. He shifted his weight to his left leg as he tried to process the events of the past few weeks. First the police couldn't find his attacker and now they were calling Bess Haverford a suicide with barely any investigation, despite everything he told them. It was wrong of them to dismiss him so. He might not have the presence of his father, but he was a man – an honest, hard-working Englishman – and it was his right, as such, to have his opinions heard. Something awful happened to those women and if the police were going to sit on their hands pretending it was nothing, then he would have to investigate himself.

He left the queue and walked to Tower Hill underground station. The cramped bodies of the Tube were more a comfort than a bother as he took the District Line to Whitechapel. Pride rose up inside him. He could do something. He could do this.

Outside the Haverfords' building, he stood straight and tall, ignoring the discomfort it caused in his thigh, and struck the handle of his cane against the landlady's door. The woman eyed him suspiciously as he put forth his case.

'We've had all sorts round here lately,' she said. 'All to do with that lady in number seven. How do I know you're not one of 'em?' She chewed on the end of her cigarette, a new utility dress hugging a soft body that had seen better days.

'I understand, ma'am. But I can assure you I am – was – a friend of Miss Haverford. God rest her soul. And I'd never do anything to disrespect the dead. In fact, I saw her just the other day. She gave me this.' Peter pulled out a banknote. The landlady kept her slack posture as she removed the cigarette from her mouth, but Peter saw the change in her eyes. 'I work at the Palladium, you see, and she asked me to get some tickets for the upcoming season. But I suppose she won't be needing them now. She wasn't one to talk about money, but she did let slip that she may have fallen behind in the rent.'

'That she did. Should've kicked her out ages ago. If it weren't for those girls . . .' She kept her eyes on the note.

'Well, I might as well pass this on to you, seeing as Miss Haverford can't repay the debt in person. God rest her soul.'

'God rest her soul.' The woman took the money and stuffed it down her bra. 'Let me get the key.'

Peter waited while she unlocked the door to the Haverfords' flat.

'Mind you,' she said, 'anything goes missing it'll be my head. Policemen asked me to pack it all and send it to her next of kin.'

'You mean her nieces?'

'Some cousin in Manchester.'

'But wouldn't they . . . ?'

The landlady stepped back, allowing Peter entry.

'No idea where those girls buggered off to, but I were told to send it to Manchester, so to Manchester it goes. You get five minutes.'

Peter closed the door behind him. The air of death clung to the flat in the untouched post, the forgotten dishes in the sink, the still-open oven door. It felt as if Bess should be here, as if she still was, hiding just out of sight, disappearing from Peter's view when he turned to see her. But Bess Haverford was gone. The last thing he had seen in this flat was her body. He could still picture her lying on the kitchen floor, see her cold grey legs and smell the rancid gas. The images wrapped themselves around him, choking his will.

'What am I doing here?' he muttered as he sifted through the sitting room, the determination which propelled him on the Tube shrunk to a mere speck. 'I'm not a bloody detective. Can't even find my keys half the time.' His hands shaking, he stopped and took a deep breath before looking through the papers on the coffee table.

Peter's head snapped up. Had he heard something? No, the flat was quiet.

There was no correspondence from Eliza, nothing to say where she might be. There were bills, however. Loads of them. All past due.

'Bess had been up to her ears in it.' He glanced at the clock to see how much time was left, but it was stuck – nine forty-seven. There was no one to wind it. It would always be nine forty-seven in this flat. A bottle of perfume rested on the coffee table. Peter released one short spray. The mist diffused into the air, returning Bess's presence to the flat. He inhaled and remembered the angel that visited him in hospital. She smelled of this. He set the bottle down and grabbed a ball of crumpled paper from the floor. As he flattened out the pages on the table, he recognised the words and handwriting – rough drafts of the letter he'd received from 'Eliza'. The back of one page was covered in Bess's attempt to copy Eliza's signature.

A heavy thud sounded from within the bedroom. Peter started but, upon hearing no other noise, approached the room and used his cane to push the door open.

The room was empty.

'Must've been from upstairs.' He checked the wardrobe and its drawers, but they held nothing save dust and an errant flannel. Across the room, the vanity mirror was broken. Two children's gas masks lay on the floor beside it. The wastepaper bin had not been emptied, but there was nothing there except bits of string and a crumpled pamphlet on bed-wetting.

At the sight of her books, which sat abandoned on their shelves, Peter felt Eliza's presence. They were the only sign she had once existed in this place. Eliza would never go anywhere without her books, not unless she had to. Even if she had run away, like the letter said, she would have found a way to take them with her. Lying separate from the others was the copy of *The King's General* he bought her that day at Foyles, that day he had been so utterly, utterly foolish. He picked it up and ran his hand over the cover, tracing the same route her fingers took after happily plucking it from the cramped store shelf. She hadn't read it yet, he could tell. She never broke the spine or folded the corners, but something happened to a book when Eliza read it, as if she poured a bit of herself into every page. He would give her this book again. He knew he would. He put it in his coat pocket.

His five minutes were almost up, but there was only one place left to search. The perfume lingered in the air. He followed its scent into the kitchen and caught himself stepping over the place where Bess's body had been. There were a few letters on the table, nothing but pots, pans and empty liquor bottles in the cabinets.

Footsteps approached from the stairwell.

Such a fool. There was nothing here. All he had done was waste his afternoon and his money. He closed the bottom cabinet.

Something compelled him to turn back. The perfume was stronger here when it should have dispelled to almost nothing. His eye caught something between the oven and the cupboards. There was just enough space to slip his fingers into the dusty gap and pull it free. A plastic poker chip – green and white with a joker's face on one side. Exactly the same as the one he found with Jessie's belongings.

The key slipped into the front door lock. Peter shoved the chip into his pocket as the landlady entered.

''Less you start paying the rent, best you leave now.'

Peter limped from the kitchen, unable to look back at this, his last connection to Eliza. The smell of the perfume had vanished. The landlady shuddered as she shut the door after him.

'Something wrong with that place. Could you feel it? Weren't for the shortage, doubt I'd be able to let it with the history it's got now. Can barely stand being in there meself. Me mam was always going on about spirits. Thought she were a nutter. But . . . Was hoping that man would come round, collect her things, so as I wouldn't have to.'

'The policeman?'

'Nay. That older gentleman of Bess's. One who covered her rent from time to time. Too bloody tall for a short 'un like her, but to each his own, I suppose.' She held open the front door for him. 'Evening.'

Peter tipped his cap and hobbled down the street, fingering the chip in his pocket as the cold air solidified the ice settling in his stomach. He knew who the landlady meant. Eliza complained about him enough. But why would Mosley be

146

coming round their flat? Eliza never mentioned that. Unless Eliza hadn't known. All those nights at the Palladium, when she wouldn't get home until eleven or later. Peter remembered the last time he spoke to Bess, that bruise around her eye. The poker chip grew warm in his clenched fist. Perhaps today wasn't a complete waste.

The crowds thickened as people poured out of the side streets, filling Whitechapel Road like cockroaches as they scurried towards the bomb-damaged remains of the station. They collided with him, pushing him forward, knocking him back, this anonymous mass of faces that swarmed the street, closing in on him, crushing him till he could not breathe. Till there was no air. Till his cane caught in the pavement, and he tumbled forward, the cockroaches ready to consume him.

A hand reached out, pulled him from the swarm. The blank faces peeled away, leaving behind one that was familiar.

'Stephen?'

'Hello, mate. Blimey, look worse than I thought. Hope you gave as good as you got.'

They shook hands.

'It's not so bad.' A clanging sound echoed in his ears, nearly blocking Stephen's words.

'Went round to see you in hospital, but you'd already gone. Doctors said you can't remember a thing. Is that so?'

Peter nodded, feeling ill.

'What're you doing in this part of town? Eliza come back?'

'No. Stephen . . .' Peter tried to speak, but a wave of nausea nearly brought him to his knees. Only Stephen's support kept him from collapsing.

'Easy, mate. Over here.' Stephen helped him to a ruined shelter. They leant against the corrugated steel as Peter let his mind right itself.

147

'So what is it? What's wrong?'

Peter felt the poker chip in his pocket. He should tell someone, explain what happened to Bess, but every time he opened his mouth, he felt too sick to speak.

'Nothing. It's nothing. Went round to see if Eliza . . . But I better be off.' His nails scratched against the metal as he pushed himself away, sending tremors from his head to his gut.

'Need a hand? I have a few spare hours. Could help you back home.'

Peter swallowed back sick. It burned his throat. 'No, no. It's no trouble. I'll be fine. I should—'

Stephen interrupted. 'The police have any leads on who mugged you?'

'No. No, they say there's nothing more they can do unless . . . unless my memory returns.'

'Bloody typical.' Stephen smiled. 'Well, I'd keep an eye on that head of yours if I was you. Never know what might come pouring out.'

They parted ways on a handshake, the nausea so bad Peter thought he would never make it home. When he did, he used the hall telephone to ring the detective investigating his case. The response was simple – no further inquiries.

*

The street was pitch black except for the orange light of the street lamp. He shivered.

Peter had often had nightmares as a child, even before the bombs began to fall. He often woke in the night, his throat hoarse from screaming. As he stared at the street lamp, a dampness seeping into his back as he lay on unseen ground, he knew he was dreaming. Yet, same as when he was a child, he could not wake himself, not even when Bess leaned over him, looking down with clouded eyes. Her face was covered in wet, dark lines that dripped onto her neck and dress, his angel no longer.

'Leave her,' she said.

I can't, Peter mouthed. There was no sound. Beside him, Rebecca skipped.

'One, two, three, four . . .' she counted. 'Five, six, seven, eight . . .' The ground cracked with every skip. Peter felt it falling apart beneath him. He could not move. Bess's limp, dead hand stroked his face.

'Leave her,' she whispered, lips splitting like the pavement.

'Nine, ten, eleven, twelve . . .'

'Leave me,' Eliza said. She was grey – her dress, her skin, her hair. Black tears ran down her face.

'Thirteen, fourteen, fifteen, sixteen . . .'

'I told you to leave it, didn't I?' Bess said.

'Seventeen, eighteen, nineteen, twenty . . .'

'Let her go,' she hissed into his ear. Eliza was fading, becoming a part of the darkness.

'Twenty-one . . .'

'For your own good.'

'Twenty-two . . .'

Peter reached for Eliza. She closed her eyes and turned to air. A distorted pug-like face in a bright yellow and blue checked cap replaced Bess. Its mouth of broken teeth spat: 'Twenty-three.'

The ground fell away completely. Peter tumbled into an orange abyss, consumed by cold fire, until he hit the rough wooden floor of his bedroom.

He shot up with a gasp, breathing as if denied air for hours. Covered in sweat that made his pyjamas stick to his clammy skin, he leant against the bedside table as Bess's words rang in his ears, foreign yet familiar. Images he thought would be seared behind his eyes forever now faded as his memory of the nightmare dissolved into a single image of the man in the checked cap. He'd not had a nightmare since leaving hospital. He thought they were over. Peter took a deep breath and laced his fingers behind his neck.

It was only a dream, his mother used to tell him. It meant nothing. It was only a dream. Count to ten and go to sleep. That was her advice. Count to ten. Peter couldn't get past one.

13

The grey mare slowed to a stop in front of Davies Market. Eliza climbed down from the carriage and landed in a soft mud puddle. As she yanked her foot free, a smell of sewage wafted up to greet her, bringing memories of home. Was Mrs Hodgkins chucking rubbish onto the street? Did Mr Pendleton still let his canary fly up and down the stairwell? Did Aunt Bess complain Mrs Granderson's wireless was too loud?

'Shop's that way.' Mr Drewry pointed down the road, interrupting her thoughts.

There was no sign of anyone as Eliza walked down the street, shaking the mud from her shoe. London on a Thursday afternoon would be teeming with people. She would have to fight her way down the street just for a box of gravy salt. But here, nothing. Everyone was hidden away as if warned by an air-raid siren. It made her nervy, the silence ringing in her ears becoming the whistle of an incoming incendiary.

She recognised the shop by the blanched sign above the door. Weather had cracked the wood, drawing a line through the word *Drapery*. A pale girl looked down on her from the windows above, stepping out of view when she was spotted.

A bell tinkled weakly as Eliza entered. The shop front was large but bare. Long shelves where bolts of multicoloured fabrics should have rested sat empty. A mouse skittered across the boards, disappearing behind an open cupboard from which flour bags, potato sacks and tablecloths spilled onto the soiled stone floor.

A knock from above caused the wooden support beams to sprinkle dust onto her shoulders. Buildings shook like that when bombs hit, she thought, brushing off her clothes. The dust clung to her fingers, and she searched for something on which to wipe them.

She sifted through the potato sacks, hoping the fresh dirt streaks would go unnoticed. The scent of soapless detergent surfaced from the damp and mildew. That same cheap detergent worked its way into her hands every time she washed Aunt Bess's clothes. If she closed her eyes, she could picture the wooden scrubbing board propped by the kitchen sink, the one Aunt Bess hadn't touched in nearly two years. Eliza doubted she even knew how to use it.

As she reached for a tablecloth, someone grabbed her by the elbow. Before Eliza could pull away, the auburn-haired girl hugged her. Eliza remained stiff, remembering the time during her evacuation when Mrs Littleton's niece had been rude to her the first time they were introduced. The second time they met she kissed Eliza's cheeks and called her pretty, then stole her hair ribbons. Eliza gently pushed away the girl who was not Pip.

'I heard the carriage and followed you. I hope you don't mind.'

'No. It's fine. I . . . I found your note. Ruth?'

She nodded.

'How did you . . . ?'

'Never mind that now. Are you all right? Have you felt at all ill?'

'No, I don't think so, but why do you . . . ?'

Ruth pulled her to the side of the shop. 'Pip was a perfectly healthy girl before she took up with that house. Less than a year later she died of an illness no doctor could name. Or so I was told.'

Someone coughed. Behind the counter, a sallow woman in a pale-green dress carried a bundle of flour bags in her thin arms.

'Oh, Mrs Tew.' Ruth smiled. 'Could you fetch some of that lovely curtain fabric you keep in the back so as Miss Haverford can have a look? Thank you!'

The woman left the sacks on the counter and disappeared without a word.

'Any headaches?'

'No,' Eliza lied. 'No, I . . .'

'Chills? Fever? Nosebleeds? Pip never mentioned nosebleeds, but I wonder . . . any muscle aches or weakness?' Ruth stared into Eliza's eyes as if seeking out any sickness hidden within her.

'No, really. Only I've been a bit tired.'

'Fatigue? Since when?'

'Since long before I came here. Really, Ruth, I'm perfectly all right. You ask more questions than a doctor!' She laughed. A long silence followed.

'My father is a doctor. I know what to ask. What to look for.'

'Is your family still in Ireland?'

'Northern Ireland. Belfast.'

'They must miss you.'

'Not since I married a Catholic.' Ruth continued her questions, but seemed more unsure of herself. 'Is there any history of heart disease in your family? Anyone prone to fainting spells or palpitations?'

'No, not that I . . . My parents both died young. I didn't

153

know you had a husband.' There was no ring on Ruth's hand. She caught Eliza looking and hid her fingers behind her back.

'I don't. He died. After he brought me to Wales. Merchant Navy. If it weren't for Pip . . .' The hard lines disappeared from Ruth's face as she struggled to hold back tears. Eliza handed her a handkerchief. Ruth admired the stitched maroon *E* before dabbing her eyes.

'This is lovely. Did you . . . ?'

'My mother.' She rested her hand on Ruth's arm. 'What happened to Pip?'

'When the war ended, neither of us had any place to go, except here. Joseph inherited the house and when he . . . He left it to me. Told me stories about his thriving village. Plentynunig used to supply miners to pits all over the county, but most have closed. All except Brownawell's. Those who could went elsewhere. Some who couldn't left anyway.' Ruth refolded the handkerchief and returned it Eliza. 'We tried to work as seamstresses, but there simply wasn't enough work for two. I was the better of us both, and Pip couldn't . . . When we heard a job was going at Thornecroft, I encouraged her to take it, even though he told me not to. That Pip should stay away . . .'

Ruth paused, staring at the handkerchief though her mind was elsewhere. Eliza tried to interject, to ask who 'he' was, but before she could Ruth recovered and continued her story, her voice stronger than before.

'Pip was a strong woman – saw her lift a hundred-pound log once, all by herself – and she were always in her right mind. The stories never bothered us. But it only took a few weeks . . . She said it was harder not to believe them once you were out there. And I saw her less and less . . .'

'Stories about the house? About a woman called Victoria?'

'You've heard?'

'I've found her portraits. They're all over the manor. What happened to her?'

Ruth sighed and tucked a lock of hair behind her ear. Her hair was the same colour as Peter's. He had a stray curl that fell onto his forehead that Eliza was forever brushing back for him. She tried to forget Peter as Ruth recommenced speaking.

'According to the townspeople, when Mr Brownawell was young he fell in love with a local woman. Though she was flattered by his attentions, she didn't think it proper – he, English; she, Welsh, and from a poor family as well. She never took him seriously, as Brownawell's father would never allow such a union. Then Richard Brownawell died – quite unexpectedly. His horse got spooked and tossed him into the quarry.' In her mind Eliza saw the quarry's steep edge, Mr Drewry's awful face.

'But, even after he inherited the estate, Victoria refused. She did not love him and never could. It was then that Brownawell's love became obsessive. He threatened her family. Bludgeoned her little dog to death right in the village square. To save her family the same fate, she agreed to marriage. But the wedding never happened. The day prior, Mr Brownawell caught her speaking to one of the male servants. Berwin heard this firsthand from the servant himself down the pub, when he were a young lad. Victoria were only asking him about arrangements for the wedding, flowers or the like. But when Mr Brownawell saw them together, he flew into a jealous rage. Pulled her up the stairs by the hair.'

Romantic scenes of true love separated by tragic illness flew from Eliza's mind. 'He killed her.'

'No one knows. The servants heard her crying all night, pleading her innocence. The next morning she was gone,

155

never to be seen again. Brownawell claimed she fell ill and he sent her away to convalesce. Several months later, he claimed she died. He buried a coffin in the estate's cemetery in a private ceremony. But no one believed he was innocent.' Ruth tapped her nose. 'Victoria's father went mad with grief, tried to convince the whole town she was alive – being held somewhere in Thornecroft as a prisoner – but no one believed him, either, even though her body was never seen. The last anyone saw of him, he was raving about going to confront Brownawell on his own. Mr Brownawell began to unravel soon after. He always had a temper, but every day he threatened to blow up the mines or burn down the village. He broke several windows in the manor, set books on fire. Even started catching rats and stringing them up by their necks, leaving them hanging for the staff to find. Servants left without warning, abandoning him to his rants. They say it's Victoria what drove him to madness. That her vengeful spirit haunts Thornecroft, snatching any woman who resides there as a way to punish him for his crime.'

The air in the room grew cold, as if Victoria's ghost had arrived to corroborate the story.

'And, they say, housemaids have gone missing from Thornecroft ever since Victoria disappeared. That Berwin's own daughter was one.'

'Berwin?' Eliza asked.

'The elderly man who stays with me.'

Eliza pictured the old drunk then wrapped her arms around herself, trying to keep from her mind those feelings she had at Thornecroft – that she was always being watched, the lights and strange sounds . . .

'You said Pip died of an illness.'

Ruth slammed her fist onto a bare shelf, jolting Eliza from her reverie. 'And she did! It's rubbish! All of this. Ghost stories. Nonsense. A fairy tale to hide the misdeeds of others. Pip was murdered, Eliza. Plain and simple. Poisoned, I think, based on her symptoms. But I can't prove it. They never let me see her body, let alone examine it. The locals call her the curse's latest victim. They're more than happy to believe the legend. Don't care what happens to outsiders if it keeps their daughters from entering that place.'

'But you said, your note, you said I should leave. For my own safety.'

'Someone murdered Pip. Someone who hasn't been caught. Who wants to keep the story of Victoria alive. To do that, they need another housemaid. Another victim.'

'What if I can't leave?'

'Then pray to God someone's coming to find you.' Ruth again examined Eliza's eyes. 'Any dry mouth? Double vision?'

Eliza shook her head.

'What about hallucinations?'

'Hallucin—'

'Are you hearing things? Seeing things?'

Eliza laughed. 'Don't be silly.'

'Good. What about your family? Any history of mental illness?'

'No.' Eliza felt herself go still. 'No, absolutely not. Why . . . ?'

Ruth opened her mouth to say more but stopped. Mrs Tew returned, carrying a stack of fabric.

Eliza greeted her. 'I'm sorry. We were . . .'

The front door bell tinkled. Ruth had fled the shop.

*

A haunted air lingered over Thornecroft when she returned. The manor was more than a sad old house now; it was a grieving victim recounting a painful history. As Eliza sat in the kitchen unpicking an old frock, every bump she heard, every groaning floorboard, became an echo of Victoria's memory. She tried to convince herself Ruth was right. The stories were rubbish. Girls didn't simply go missing, not without anyone searching for them. Not in England. Not even in Wales.

Fabric covered the kitchen table. Eliza searched under the mess for her scissors but, unable to find them, walked down the quiet corridor to her room. Mother would never have allowed them to be taken. If Eliza and Rebecca had gone missing, Mother would stop at nothing to find them.

Scissors located, she paused to examine the damaged photo. If Mother were here, Aunt Bess could never have sent them away. If Mother were here, they never would have lived with Aunt Bess at all. When had her aunt become so heartless towards them? Eliza remembered a time when she was a child and Aunt Bess brought her sweets from the seaside. She was always bringing them treats when they were little, rolling her eyes at Father's strict rules, volunteering to take them on shopping trips or to the zoo. How had the war changed all that?

For the first time since leaving London, Eliza missed her aunt – the smell of her perfume, the way she sometimes smiled, her insistence that Eliza could be a beautiful young woman if only she tried harder.

They would see each other again one day. Aunt Bess would ask for forgiveness and Eliza would give it because it was what Mother would do.

A heavy melancholy rested within her chest as she returned to the kitchen and looked at the massive project before her. Her unpicked frock provided a pattern for her to work with, but how would she ever be able to sew all this by tomorrow evening? She knew that Mother could have done it. Mother had been excellent at everything – sewing, cooking, cleaning.

Eliza stuck her finger with a pin. She hissed and sucked on the wound. A carbon copy: at her best that's all she was. She knew how to do those same things but could never get anything quite right. There were always flaws.

She searched through the sewing basket for the right thread. The fabric she had chosen was a nice shade of light blue, only faded on one side, and the silk soft to the touch. If she tried very hard, she knew she could almost make a dress that would impress Aunt Bess.

'What is that?' Mrs Pollard appeared at her side.

'The fabric I purchased in town.'

'I sent you to purchase suitable material for a dress. Not a used sofa covering.'

'They're used curtains, actually.' Eliza smiled.

'Come with me.' Mrs Pollard took her by the arm and escorted her to a small dressing room in the north hall.

The housekeeper positioned her before a mahogany cheval mirror. A streak ran through the dust that coated the glass, as if someone had swiped their hand across it. The floor smelled strongly of wood polish.

'One does not wear curtains when meeting Mr Brownawell. Now, don't just stand there. Undress yourself.'

'I beg your pardon?'

Mrs Pollard opened a large trunk and sifted through clothes wrapped in yellowed tissue paper. 'You're incapable of producing anything suitable for dinner. As I will not have this house shamed because of you, I'll loan you acceptable attire for the duration. Now, undress and put this on. I believe it should fit.' She held out a cream-coloured lace and muslin dress.

'I would really rather not. I'm sorry, Mrs Pollard, but I'd like to decline Mr Brownawell's invitation. It wouldn't be appropriate.'

Mrs Pollard smiled. 'You were talking to that Irish girl today. That little friend of Miss Vlasto's. I needn't tell you she's unstable. The stories she's filled your head with I'm sure made it plain. She's been ever so distraught since Miss Vlasto took ill. Grief does strange things to people, you see, but death is what happens in places like this. The same would happen in India. People you cared for, and people you didn't, alive one day and snatched away the next, driving their families to ruin and despair, destroying everything they hoped to achieve.'

'Is that what happened to your family?'

The dress threatened to tear in Mrs Pollard's grip. She regarded it as if that was what she wanted – to rip it to pieces herself. Almost imperceptibly, she composed herself, stretching her neck from side to side and smoothing back a stray hair that came loose from her plait.

'My family returned to England to pursue better opportunities.'

'So being a housekeeper here is better than India?'

'Tending to Mr Brownawell is the greatest honour one could achieve. And, believe me, Miss Haverford, I have worked very hard to achieve my position.' She plucked a piece of lint from the dress. 'Those who serve Thornecroft well are well rewarded in return. Those who disobey are less fortunate. This house has a way of weeding out the weak. Like Pip.'

She pressed a cloth into Eliza's hand.

'I found that in the hall, by the way.'

It was Rebecca's monogrammed handkerchief.

'Tell her not to leave her things lying about, will you?' She held out the dress. 'Now, would you like to try this on?'

160

For so many years Mother had cared for them, protected them. But Eliza was not her mother. Only a copy. She turned away from the mirror as she undressed and kept her eyes on Mrs Pollard. Exposed in only her brassiere and underpants, she quickly slipped the dress over her head then stared at her feet while Mrs Pollard buttoned up the back.

'There. Now you're almost beautiful.' She took Eliza by the chin and tilted her head up to the mirror.

Mother had been beautiful. Aunt Bess, too, was once a woman others envied. Eliza had never seen herself as such and could not see it now. Eliza could only see Victoria, for it was Victoria's dress she wore.

14

Yes! We have no bananas read the sign beside Peter's ghostly image as he checked his reflection in the shop window. His best suit strangled him. He had grown since he last wore it on VE Day, and it was now too tight in the arms and inside seam. He felt the strain as he reached to smooth a curl which had escaped the Brylcreem's hold. The more nervous he became, the more the suit constricted him. He could barely move his limbs as he crossed the street to Bess Haverford's office.

The pain in his leg wasn't so bad today. His lower back carried the ache as he limped up the building's narrow staircase. Sweat dampened his underarms, and he pictured his white shirt staining yellow. His palm slipped on the banister. He wiped both hands on his trousers and saw them shaking.

It was simple, he told himself as he tackled the next flight. It would be like walking into a pub. An unfamiliar pub where everyone stopped and stared when a stranger entered. Peter paused for breath. He knew he could do this. He owed it to Bess.

No one noticed his entrance. Office boys darted back and forth while secretaries tapped violently on their typewriters. The room filled with the shrill ring of telephones left unanswered and was scented with the sweat of closely packed bodies and gathered cigarette smoke. Peter inched his way into the chaos and tried to stop a passing secretary.

'Excuse me . . .'

She brushed him aside and he bumped into a clerk, who waved him away. No one took any notice as he ventured further in. He approached two ladies towards the back. An older one resembling a canary with her yellow dress and peroxide-blonde hair chirped away at the young girl beside her, who appeared as nervous as Peter.

'. . . can you be out of tea, I told him? No, dear, put it in like this,' Canary said.

'I'm sorry, ma'am.'

'Don't apologise. Just do it properly.'

'Excuse me,' Peter whispered.

'I mean tea,' she continued. 'Of all the things. During the war there was always tea. Why can't we have any now it's over? No, I said like this.'

'Excuse me.'

'How did you get this job, you can't handle carbon paper?'

'Excuse me, I—'

'Not now, lad. Can't you see we're busy?' Canary took the carbon paper from the girl. 'My daughter, Jennet, I've told you about Jennet? She was a secretary in the war rooms and even she can't find work.'

She reminded him of Eliza, the young girl, the way her hand flitted to check the curls of her hair.

'I'm not saying they shouldn't have hired you, but you should appreciate what you've got, you understand?'

Eliza never knew what to do with her hands when she was nervous. Peter placed his on Canary's typewriter. 'I need to see Mr Mosley.'

Canary looked at the hand, then up at Peter. She crossed her arms.

'What time is your appointment?'

'I don't have an appointment.'

163

'Then you won't be seeing Mr Mosley. Now, Gladys, try it yourself this time. This stack here needs—'

'It's about Bess Haverford.'

Canary shut her mouth.

'Who's . . . ?' the girl began, but Canary hushed her.

'Never mind that. Go and fetch us some tea, Gladys. Go on.'

The girl scurried away, smiling thankfully at Peter.

'Who are you then?' Canary asked.

'Peter Lamb. A friend of the family. I'm the one that . . . that found her.'

The woman's face softened. She clasped a hand to her breast.

'Oh, you poor thing. I'm Harriet Wilson. I am – was Bess's dearest friend here in the office. Such a tragedy, isn't it? She never told me how sad she was, didn't want to worry me, the poor dear, but I told Regina over there, I said, "Regina, something is going to happen to that poor old girl. Just you wait and see." And now look. Feel like a prophet of doom. I only wish I'd done something.'

'I'm sure there was nothing you could've done, ma'am.'

'Oh, you sweet thing. You're so kind. Now, tell me, dear,' she leant in close, 'how did she look when you found her?'

'I . . .'

'People say gas distorts the face, bloats the skin, but I think that's rubbish. I bet she looked peaceful, didn't she? Like a sleeping angel?'

The angel of Peter's nightmares, her face dripping . . .

'It's . . . very difficult for me to discuss, ma'am.'

'Of course, of course.'

'Is Mr Mosley in?'

'Oh yes, let me check. You just wait right there.' She

disappeared into a back office, returning moments later, her expression solemn. 'I'm sorry, Paul.'

'Peter.'

'Mr Mosley can't see anyone right now.'

'But it's urgent. If I—'

'He said no. I'm sorry.'

Peter saw the thin, ghastly man staring at him through the open blinds of his office window, clutching a pen. How many times had those knuckles grazed Bess's face?

'Then I'd like to make an appointment.'

A firm hand gripped his shoulder. Peter turned to see a large clerk glaring down at him.

'You were asked to leave, son.'

Peter looked to Harriet for support but, finding none, allowed the burly clerk to escort him from the office. Better to be a gentleman, he thought, until he was thrown onto the pavement.

'Spiv.' The clerk spat on Peter.

He wiped the glob from his cheek. 'I'm not . . .'

The door closed. Wincing, he put on his hat and straightened his coat. Across the street – bright amongst the faded colours of other passers-by – a blue and yellow checked cap, the cap from his nightmares, rested on the head of a man whose face was blocked by the other pedestrians.

Peter was knocked from behind.

'Out of the way,' huffed a silver-haired woman. Peter apologised then looked again. The man in the checked cap was gone.

*

Heavy grey clouds rolled across the blue London sky, bringing a chill to the air as they blotted out the sun. Like Peter's dark mood, they had formed while he rode the crowded Tube. Peter had stood crammed between other passengers as the bumpy tracks jostled his bad leg, with only thoughts of his latest failure to occupy him. His brothers wouldn't let anyone treat them like that, not even Michael.

Peter kicked his feet against the pavement, trying to draw out his anger as he walked up Shaftesbury Avenue. The only man who had any information about Bess and Eliza had refused to even speak to him. He'd had one opportunity and let his uselessness cost him. Maybe there should be another war, he thought. He would be old enough to enlist this time. Perhaps the army could teach him to be more like his brothers instead of the fool that he was.

The day had begun with such promise. Now it was as miserable as the pedestrian-clogged streets and empty shops. All he wanted was to pick up his pay packet from the Palladium, get his name on the next rota, and disappear into the Coach and Horses.

A woman's sobs changed his plans.

'Please, please! You must know. Please!'

Outside the stage door, Mrs Rolston clung to Purvis, crying into his shirt.

'Madam, get a hold of yourself. Madam, that's enough!'

'But she must be here. She must!'

Purvis shoved her away. 'I have no idea where that trollop is.'

'That's no way to speak to her,' Peter said, taking Mrs Rolston into his arms.

'I'll speak to her any damn way I please, Lamb. Look at her. She's hysterical!'

Mrs Rolston cried into Peter's shirt. He could feel her tears soaking into the fabric.

'Her only child is missing, Purvis. How would you feel?'

Purvis brushed off his lapels. 'Children are not my area. Even so, I wouldn't act like some wailing harpy from a Greek tragedy. Especially if my daughter got into trouble as easily as Jessie Rolston.'

'And what's that supposed to mean?'

'It means do something with that woman before she chases away all our patrons!' Purvis disappeared into the theatre. Mrs Rolston pulled back and apologetically dabbed at the wet spot on Peter's shirt with her handkerchief.

'It's all right, ma'am.' He stilled her hand. 'What's happened, Mrs Rolston?'

'Oh, boy. Dear boy. Tell me you've seen her, too. Tell me she's all right.'

'I don't know. I couldn't . . .' Peter paused. 'Too? Mrs Rolston, have . . . ?'

'Just now. In the square.' She pointed towards Trafalgar. 'But I must have imagined it. I must have. I called to her, but she refused to answer. My Jessie wouldn't ignore me. Oh, how foolish I've been.' She blew into her handkerchief. 'I'm seeing things, like Tom says. My Jessie would've answered.'

He squeezed her hand. 'Mrs Rolston, I don't think you're foolish at all.'

*

Peter remained in the square all night, sitting on the steps in front of the National Gallery until his back grew stiff. It was the first time he had witnessed sunlight and lamplight exchange places at both ends of the day. There had been no sign of Jessie, but he knew mothers possessed an instinct about their children. He remembered the times his mother

167

knew his brothers were in trouble – the distant gaze that would dog her for days until they received word John was injured or Michael's squad was missing. If Mrs Rolston said she had seen Jessie, Peter believed her. And if Jessie was still in London, maybe Eliza was too.

His stomach grumbled as the sun rose over St Martin's. Abandoning his post on the stairs, he found a café on Whitcomb Street and settled at a grubby table, the surface sticky from chip oil, and ordered breakfast and tea. The meal took the edge off his night in the square. Some would have considered him a failure. John and Samuel would laugh if he told them he had spent the night walking in circles, searching for a girl. Michael, though ... He thought Michael would understand. Michael would tell him he was only doing what had to be done. Peter's eyes felt heavy, but an extra tea helped keep him alert. If Eliza were in London, there was one person who knew where she could be.

Eliza often complained about Mr Mosley, the way he sneered at her. How he would make Rebecca run errands all over the city. How his eyes would linger on her aunt's chest whenever he spoke to her.

'He has a wife and children,' Eliza said one night after work. 'But I know Aunt Bess wants him. She's always trying so hard to please him. I bet she'd do anything for him. Anything at all.'

Anything at all. That was what she said, that or something similar.

Peter drank a third tea without tasting it and left the remainder of his food on the plate, even though it cost him two coupons.

Michael had told him a story once, about the time he helped capture a German soldier. The man had sensitive information they needed to pass on to their superior officer. Information the man would not give freely. In wartime, Michael said, a man had to do things he wouldn't normally do. Behave in a way that society might frown upon.

Peter passed an alley bombarded by bombsite debris, the ruins of a shop visible beneath the brick rubble and fallen beams. A man on crutches hobbled by, his right leg missing from the knee down. A child with the toes cut off his shoes was dragged down the street by a woman with an empty shopping bag, her coat thin and faded. Up ahead, the queue for a butcher's was already snaking round the corner. London today looked no different than London two years ago. Were they not still at war?

Peter descended into Charing Cross and took the District Line east. The heat of the Tube made his head fuzzy, the soft feelings cocooning him from the sharp edges of the world. Life on the street above was biting by comparison. The wind picked up and needle-like raindrops fell, piercing his exposed skin.

Inside a Corner House, he sat at a table by the window. All day customers came and went, but Peter remained, twirling the poker chip in his fingers and ignoring the newspaper laid out before him. He could have been there days, weeks. He had no sense of time, only the patience that came from waiting for one, singular thing.

The dining-hall clock chimed five times. How many hours had he been awake now? He'd lost count. The lack of sleep only made him more focused. At quarter past, a trio of women exited the building, followed by a few office boys attempting to look up their skirts. An elderly clerk hobbled out, clutching his briefcase to his chest with both hands. At half past, Canary emerged, again dressed in yellow, the door held open for her

169

by Mr Mosley. It felt like only a few hours since he'd last seen them.

He hurried outside, the pain dull in his leg. Mosley stopped at the corner and adjusted his tie, giving Peter the opportunity to catch up. He followed at a safe distance, his stomach churning from too much tea and too little food. He didn't know this part of London, didn't know where Mosley was heading, until he saw the sign for Liverpool Street station. He would lose him there. It was too big. Too many people.

He ran up and jabbed the corner of his ration book into Mosley's back like a knife's edge.

'Don't say anything,' Peter warned. 'Keep moving. This way.' He directed him into a quiet pedestrian street of closed market stalls.

It was a bombsite. A whole side of a house had been blown away, revealing the striated layers within, the empty, pillaged floors resembling a doll's house left to rot. Peter shoved Mosley into the pit, watched him roll into piles of destroyed brick coated in years of discarded rubbish and hit his head on a fallen wooden beam. He climbed in as Mosley, disorientated, tried to regain his footing. Peter knocked him back down.

'Here!' Mosley fumbled in his pocket. 'My wallet. Take it!'

Peter grabbed the wallet and threw it into the empty half house. 'I don't want your money. I want to know where you sent them!'

Mosley turned onto his back, squinting at Peter. 'You. You're that boy.'

'Where is Eliza Haverford? What have you done with her?'

'I've not done a thing. That business is nothing to do with me.'

'But Bess Haverford's bed – that has everything to do with you, doesn't it?'

170

Mosley slipped on the bricks, fell to his knees. Peter grabbed him by the collar, hoisted him as high as his back allowed. 'You were having an affair and, what, wanted her pesky nieces out of the way? Wanted more time with your mistress?'

'No. It wasn't . . .'

Peter punched him. His fist hit the eye socket, returning the favour Mosley had bestowed upon Bess. 'She would've done anything for you. Anything at all!'

'Not for me. Only money. Bess did anything for money.'

The poker chip. The bills.

'She was short on the rent, so I agreed to lend her what she needed in exchange for certain . . . favours. Last I saw her, socially, was the night she sent those girls away. She sent them away herself.'

'Where? Where did she send them?'

'I don't know! Please, I didn't know anything about it. She was drunk. Said she sent them with the one-armed man and that was that and could I lend her money until the payment came. I couldn't put up with her any more. I told her our arrangement was off and I left.'

Peter noticed for the first time how weary the man looked, the blood on his face making the grey of his skin more apparent.

'Please don't tell my wife. Please. That's all I know. Please let me go.'

Peter released him.

Mosley scrambled to his feet and hurried out of the crater, hands struggling for purchase on the loose chunks of rubble. Peter watched him climb onto the pavement, his black suit covered in chalky dust and dirt, and run off down the street.

Peter looked at his hands. They were covered in blood. He wiped them on his trousers, but that only smeared the red around. Peter stumbled sideways into the house and

171

vomited over a half-charred kitchen table. Through a hole in the ceiling, he watched the wind sweep through the exposed rooms, fluttering curtains too high to be pilfered. There he fell to his knees and, on the destroyed lino floor, he wept.

15

The day Mother died was one Eliza often replayed in her mind. She imagined Mother had woken early to make Father breakfast and tea. After he left for work, she must have tidied the kitchen then done the daily shop, stopping to gossip with Mrs Michaels, the young mother who lived next door. The weather had been mild that day in Hungerford and Eliza thought it would be mild in London as well. Then Mother would have worn her favourite blue tea dress with a white cardigan, her hair neatly permed and decorated with a zinnia purchased from the corner market. Father worked late at the office, so she would eat dinner alone – potato pie, with syrup tart for dessert – after which she would listen to the wireless before taking a bath and going to bed around eleven. Three hours later she would be set alight by incendiary bombs – the first night of the Blitz.

Father sent a telegram to tell Eliza the news. It read simply:
Incendiary bomb. Your mother is dead.
Father

She thought he would later post a longer letter, find a way to comfort her with greater words, or even make the trip up to Hungerford to see her. He did neither. It was Aunt Bess who eventually told her more of what happened, though she, too, struggled to make her words a comfort.

Eliza couldn't remember what happened to that slip of

paper. Some days she remembered tearing it into pieces. Others she thought she had thrown it into the fire. And sometimes, although rarely, she pictured herself folding it up and tucking it into her little Bible for safe keeping. It did not matter what happened to the paper because it left its mark inside her – a numbing coldness that lived with her, impossible to shake, and, if ignored too long, made it difficult to breathe. Some days it wasn't there at all. Others, it threatened to overwhelm her.

It was there when she woke this morning, a small speck between her lungs that expanded as the day's shadows grew long.

There was no delaying it any longer. She had to put on the dress. It lay on her bed like a shed snakeskin, every detail haunting her – the lace around the cuffs and collar, the perfect hemline, the embroidery on the skirt.

Her clock continued to tick. Quarter past seven. She slipped the dress over her head, the light fabric weighing heavy on her limbs.

As her shaking fingers struggled with each button, she heard a woman singing. Did Mrs Pollard sing? Yet the voice was too youthful. Eliza peered out of her window. An orange-hued ball of light floated round the back of the manor. She ran out of her room to follow it and bumped into Rebecca.

'Oh, Eliza! You look so beautiful.'

'Hm?' The singing could no longer be heard.

'What will you do with your hair? Are you going to wear make-up? Hurry.' Rebecca took her hand. 'You have to finish getting ready.'

Reluctantly, she let her sister lead her back to the bedroom. There was no light outside. No singing. Nerves, that was all. She was tired, imagining things.

Eliza's last failed perm was fading and, with no kirby grips or wave set, her hair hung limply round her face. She put in a silver hairclip, but it did nothing to illuminate her muddy brown strands. She resembled a child playing dressing up – no beauty, no glamour. She would never meet Peter like this.

She turned to Rebecca. 'Well, what do you think?'

The rough fabric itched her skin. She resisted the urge to scratch.

'I think it's beautiful!'

'You do?'

'It's the most beautiful dress I've ever seen. More beautiful than any of Mother's.'

'You don't remember any of Mother's.'

Rebecca stroked the skirt. 'It's simply wonderful.'

'Isn't it just?' Mrs Pollard appeared in the doorway, her hair pulled back in a neat double plait, accentuating her thin, sharp face. 'Rebecca, your dinner is in the kitchen. Miss Haverford, it's time.'

Passing the paintings felt like passing her own reflection, and her hands began to shake. She felt as if she shouldn't be able to breathe, yet air somehow found its way into her lungs. She expected Mrs Pollard to lay out strict rules regarding the upcoming introduction, and would've welcomed the distraction, but the housekeeper remained silent as she glided ahead on light footsteps.

The early-evening sky looked down on her through Abigale Hall, the stars just starting to appear, each one a beacon, a comfort, reminding her that life existed outside of Thornecroft, if not within, and she gathered whatever scraps of courage she had as she passed out of sight of the dome.

Mrs Pollard flung open the doors to the Ancestral Parlour. The glass chandelier reflected the light of the candelabras covering the dining table. Each flame flickered to its own design. A thousand whispered conversations passed between the candles as Eliza took her place beside the head seat and Mrs Pollard left to fetch the master.

Tonight the portraits were silent but, alone in the parlour, Eliza felt their heavy presence. Only two places were set at the massive table. Frail bone china with pink and red roses and gold trim waited to be soiled, the real silver cutlery ready to wage war. *Say hello to the roses*, that was what Berwin had said.

Outside, Mr Drewry's wolfhound barked in anticipation. She tapped her foot to dispel the anxiety growing within her, but the cold refused to budge. Soon it would grow too large and burst from her skin like the boils in her nightmare. She dug her fingernails into her palms.

All at once, the house stilled. The dog fell quiet. The candles ceased flickering. Even her heart seemed to stop. A screech of metal tore through the silence like a pair of rusty shears. Eliza felt her heart restart to match the steady rhythm of its approach. She focused on a flame and let the rest of her vision blur. Out of the corner of her eye, she saw the dark shape of a person approaching. The sound grew in volume. Eliza closed her eyes as it crossed behind her.

The creaking ceased. Her heart maintained its new momentum.

'Miss Haverford, open your eyes and greet your master.'

Through the haze of the candles, it appeared to be a corpse. Its skin was thin, nearly translucent. The few grey hairs remaining were wisps of cobwebs over a liver-spotted skullcap and the blue eyes milky with cataracts. It must be a corpse, she thought, until she saw him breathing. His protruding chest heaved with every inhalation and the air was released with a rattling sigh. Gnarled hands rested on the armrests of the Victorian wheelchair which supported him, the third and fourth fingers of each curled all the way into the palms. He wore a black dinner jacket, bow tie and a dress shirt tinted yellow with age. A long strand of saliva dripped from his chapped, open lips. He coughed and the strand fell, seeping into the shirt, leaving a moistened, penny-sized spot.

Through his clouded eyes, he stared at Eliza.

She looked for Mrs Pollard but caught only the housekeeper's back as she slid out of the parlour.

The breath rattling in and out of his chest was as mechanical as the roll of the wheelchair. He said nothing, nor did he move. There was only his breathing and the eyes that never left her face. Watching the candles flicker, Eliza tugged at the itching cuffs of the dress, wishing she could rip off the sleeves, tear the whole dress to pieces, and put on her dungarees instead. The portraits smiled at her discomfort. Eliza longed to take her dinner knife and thrust it into each of their faces. Mrs Pollard returned before she had the chance, carrying two bowls of soup in matching rose china. The soup was merely broth – Oxo cubes dissolved in hot water.

She reached for her spoon. Mrs Pollard slapped her hand.

'The master eats first.'

Eliza set down her cutlery and waited. Mr Brownawell did nothing.

'He can't do it himself, now can he?'

Eliza reached across the table for Mr Brownawell's spoon. A candle flame licked close to her sleeve. Mrs Pollard grabbed her wrist.

'Careful. You can't scrub out a burn.'

Eliza dipped the spoon into the bowl then lifted it to his

177

mouth. His cracked lips closed around the silver, Adam's apple bobbing as he swallowed.

'Good girl. And again. He'll let you know when he's finished.'

This was fine. She could do this. It was only soup. Like feeding a baby. She could pretend it was a baby.

When he stopped accepting the spoon, she was allowed to eat, but the broth had gone cold. She managed a few spoonfuls before her stomach rebelled. Mrs Pollard left to fetch the main course.

Feeling nauseous, Eliza reached for her glass of water, hoping it would settle her. One course finished. Soon, this would be over. Then she could hide in her room with *Mrs Miniver* and pretend this night never happened. Everything would be all right after all. Mr Brownawell kept staring. The only movement he made was of his lips and throat as his chest eked out those laboured breaths.

It felt an eternity before Mrs Pollard returned with a brass trolley. She lifted the first silver cloche to reveal a plate of mash and served each of them heaping portions. Potato was good, plain. Her stomach would handle potato. Mrs Pollard lifted the second cloche. Beneath was a small mound of dark, roasted meat.

'Rabbit.' Mrs Pollard served them each several pieces. 'Your sister said it was one of your favourites.'

Eliza smelled blood. The rabbit was rare. Its juices spilled onto the china plate as she cut into the tender meat, revealing the dark pink flesh hidden under outer brown skin. She raised a small piece to Mr Brownawell's mouth. He sucked it off the fork and swallowed it whole, like a snake. No, like a baby, she thought. Same as a baby. As a child. It took over a quarter of an hour to feed him, and by that time Eliza's portion was lukewarm. She took one bite and pushed it away. Mrs Pollard pushed it back.

'We mustn't waste food.' She leant over Eliza's shoulder. 'Be a good girl and finish your dinner.'

The meat was tougher than she expected and, unable to grind the pieces into manageable bits, she swallowed large chunks. The lumps slid down her throat and plopped into her stomach, where she pictured them floating on top of the brown Oxo broth. Every time she paused, Mrs Pollard cleared her throat, refusing to let her finish until all that was left were the remains of watery gravy mixed with leftover pink juices. Mrs Pollard cleared the table. Eliza listened as the brass trolley was wheeled out of the long hall while the food she had eaten continued to bob in stomach acid. When she heard the groan, she thought it was her own body breaking under the strain.

But it was Mr Brownawell, whose eyes were off her for the first time that evening. He stared at the wall and groaned again, a low, dry sound like a dock coming loose from the shore.

'Mr Brownawell?' Was he admiring the portraits? Eliza followed his eyes.

Her chair skittered across the floor as she leapt to her feet.

Victoria stood at the window, her back to the parlour. The candles illuminated her long, brown plait, the pale porcelain skin of her arms, the white muslin dress. She moved away, gliding into the darkness of the night.

'Wait.' Eliza's voice was but a whisper. 'Wait! Am I next? Am I next!' She ran towards the window but was stopped by a cold vice on her arm. Mr Brownawell's fingers curled around her wrist. 'Let me go. Let me go!'

He gripped her harder, stronger than his form suggested possible.

'Let go!'

His lips sputtered, attempting words, his cloudy eyes focusing as he strained to speak.

'Please let go. You're hurting me!'

He maintained his grip, his movements stilted like a broken automaton.

Eliza slapped him across the face. He released her. She staggered back, barely able to maintain her footing.

'What do you think you're doing?' Mrs Pollard stood in the parlour with a dessert trolley.

Eliza felt her face flushing. Her head was light and stomach heavy. Any moment now, she would be sick. 'May I be excused? I don't feel well.'

'You haven't had pudding.'

'Please, ma'am, I . . .'

'Sit. Down.'

Eliza fixed her chair then did as she was told. She could see the mark of her hand on Mr Brownawell's face, but Mrs Pollard made no comment. A heavy treacle tart with thick, yellow custard was placed before her.

'The master isn't fond of desserts, but he insists his guests enjoy themselves.' She placed a spoon into Eliza's hand. 'You wouldn't want to offend him now, would you?'

Though the tart was Eliza's first warm food of the evening, eating it was like swallowing warm sick. She gagged every time she put more into her mouth, but it wasn't until the dish was empty that Mrs Pollard allowed her to be excused.

As soon as she left the parlour, Eliza ran – through Abigale Hall, past Victoria's paintings, and into Rebecca, who waited in their passage.

'How was . . . ?'

Eliza pushed by her into the bathroom. She managed to close the door, but her knees had not hit the ground before the night's meal came pouring out of her.

*

Eliza lay on the mattress, fully dressed beneath the top sheet, and waited for the house to quieten, for Mrs Pollard to fall asleep in her room next door. Then she waited some more. The clock continued its merciless beat into night, bringing a stillness unnatural to those who lived in the day.

Finally, it was time. She slipped on her shoes, threw on her coat and stuffed the family photo into the pocket. She would take nothing else, nothing except Rebecca. Having lain awake, her eyes were accustomed to the darkness. As quietly as she could, she opened her door and snuck across the hall to Rebecca's room. Her sister was asleep, the Victoria doll face down on the floor.

'Rebecca,' she whispered. 'Rebecca, dearie, you must wake up.'

'Liza?'

'Come now. I have your coat. Hurry.'

'What's wrong?'

'I told you we'd leave, didn't I? Well, we're leaving.'

Rebecca was too tired to understand but too sleepy to protest. Eliza snuck Rebecca back to her room. There she hoisted the window and lifted Rebecca out then climbed down herself, taking the Tilley lamp with her.

Guided by the light of the half moon, she hurried them away from Thornecroft. It wasn't until the dark outline of the manor disappeared that Eliza paused to light the lamp. Rebecca was asleep on her feet, but Eliza kept a quick pace, pushing her on. This was easy, like running through Hungerford during a blackout. The fresh, chill air eased her anxiety. Bits of it fell away as they stole through the night. They were gone. She was safe. They would both be safe. When they reached the edge of the village, Eliza extinguished the lamp and waited for her eyes to readjust to the moonlight.

'Liza . . .'

'Shush. We must stay very quiet. Understand?'

Rebecca nodded. Together, they walked through Plentynunig's sleeping streets, stopping outside Ruth's house. The front door was unlocked. Eliza thought everyone would lock their doors here, so suspicious they all seemed, unless they felt they had nothing worth losing. Eliza had barely closed the door when she was blinded by a torch.

'Please. It's—'

'Eliza?' The torch lowered. The spots in front of her eyes cleared as Ruth approached. 'What's happened?'

'Pip was telling the truth. Victoria is real.'

*

Eliza warmed her hands on a cup of tea as she watched Rebecca sleep on the wooden bench below Ruth's kitchen window. Medical texts and sewing fabric were spread over the table.

'This should help warm you up.' Ruth handed Eliza a coarse wool blanket then tucked another round Rebecca's shoulders. 'I like to read while I work,' she said, spotting Eliza's eyes and sweeping the mess aside.

'I'm sorry for disturbing you like this, but, you see, there's no one else. No one we can . . .You must help us, Ruth. I'd walk straight out of here if I could, but I haven't the strength or money to—'

'Hush!' Ruth collapsed at the table, resting her head in her hands.

182

Rebecca's light breaths interspersed with the ticking of an unseen clock before the two fell into synchronicity.

'Nonsense,' Ruth whispered. 'I said it was nonsense.'

'I know it's difficult to believe, but she came to me. It's as if . . . as if she's marked me. From the moment I sat down with Mr Brownawell, she—'

'There are no such things as ghosts.'

'How many girls have gone missing? How many since Victoria died? Since you've lived here?'

Ruth sighed. The circles beneath her eyes were darker than Eliza's own. 'Pip was the last. Before that . . . there was another girl. Jane, I believe. It was her leaving that allowed Pip to take the job.'

'Did she leave? Or did she disappear?'

'She returned to her family in York.'

'And can anyone prove that?'

'Can we prove that she didn't?'

'Before Jane, who was there?'

'There was Berwin's daughter, but that was the thirties, I think, before the war?'

'Can I speak to him?'

Ruth shook her head. 'You won't get anything useful. The drink's ruined his mind.'

'Then who knows how many she's taken?'

'None. Because there is no Victoria. Even in his sober moments, rare as they are, Berwin says his daughter ran off with some gypsy traveller. Saying the manor took her is easier than believing the truth.'

'But you said yourself that Pip . . .'

'Pip died, yes. By another person's hand. A living person. That's what I know to be true.'

'And what I know is that I saw a woman at that window.

A woman who vanished. A woman who looked exactly like Victoria.'

'Our brains play tricks on us, Eliza, when we're under stress. They make us see things that aren't there. Pull out memories we've forgotten and . . . and paste them into the present. Illuminate what's not real. What I told you were only stories. Fictions. Please.' Ruth took Eliza's hands in her own. 'Forget what you saw tonight. Whatever it was, it weren't real. It was all in your—'

'My mind?' Eliza pulled away. 'Are you saying I'm mad?'

'No, that's not it at all.'

'Then don't tell me what I did or didn't see. You weren't there. Maybe if you had, you would understand. I am in danger, Ruth. She wants to take me. And what about Rebecca? What will happen to her if I'm gone? We have to leave.'

There were tears in Ruth's eyes. She wiped them away before any fell. Eliza waited while she reorganised her papers, returned her sewing things to the basket. She was reaching some sort of decision. Finally, she spoke.

'I'm sorry. I should never have . . . Yes. Yes, you must. This is no place for a child. This isn't your fight.' Her worry lines deepened. In the low candlelight, she looked so old for her years. 'Friday. Friday would be best. It's only seven days. What is seven days when Pip lasted a whole year? Every Friday is market day. A delivery lorry comes from Abergwili. I have a friend there who will help if asked. The cart is big enough to hide you both. It's the only way we can get you out without someone seeing.'

'And we can hide here until then.'

'Pollard will find you in an instant.' Ruth fiddled with the page of a journal.

'The people here . . .'

'You cannot trust the people of Plentynunig!' The page tore. Ruth smoothed it out. 'It's . . . They believe that bringing outsiders to Thornecroft is all that keeps their daughters safe. They'll hand you over in an instant. Even Berwin would say you were here. Then Pollard will never let you leave. No, the best thing to do is wait. Do whatever she says. Don't draw attention to yourself. Then on Friday ask to go to town with Mr Drewry. He runs his errands on Friday.'

'But what if he refuses? What if . . . ?'

'He's not from here,' Ruth said, as if that settled the matter. Eliza sipped her lukewarm tea, the cup shaking against her lips as she weighed her options. How could she refuse? What were she and Rebecca to do? Walk to London? They would surely die of exhaustion first, or starvation. Maybe get kidnapped by gypsies. She forgot to bring the little money she had left. She couldn't even afford a telegram to Peter, let alone buy a train ticket. They had nothing. All was at Thornecroft.

'Eliza?'

She never could make these kinds of decisions. It was like the fable of the lady and the tiger, and she always chose the wrong door. What would Mother have done?

'Eliza it will be dawn soon. If you're to get back, you must go now.'

She set down her teacup.

'All right,' she said. 'Friday. But no later.'

'No later.'

Eliza's eyes fell on the torn page. Candlelight flickered over the word 'distressed'.

'No later,' she repeated.

When she went to rouse her sister, Rebecca's eyes were already open.

'How long have you been awake, dearie?'

185

'Long enough.'

'Come on. We have to go.'

With the moon bright above them, they trudged back to Thornecroft, Eliza collecting every bit of anxiety she'd dropped along the way.

16

Coty face powder concealed the circles under her eyes and two tablets of fersolate helped fight her fatigue, but nothing could hide the fact that Eliza had slept less than two hours last night. As she spooned cold porridge into her mouth, she could only hope Mrs Pollard took her exhaustion to be from stress. Rebecca gobbled up her breakfast, no evidence of last night's excursion upon her. Was she really so much younger that she recovered her strength that quickly? When did Eliza get so old?

'Finish your meal.' Mrs Pollard banged a pot into the sink. 'I need you to close up the Ancestral Parlour.'

'Mr Brownawell doesn't want to see me again?'

'I should think not, especially after your behaviour last night.'

He told Mrs Pollard about the slap. Eliza's assault would not go unpunished, no matter if it was provoked.

'Were you mean to Mr Brownawell?' Rebecca's eyes widened.

'No. Of course not.' She felt his cold skin against her palm, tried to rub it away under the table.

'You made him extremely agitated. It took ages to put him to bed. Proper sleep is absolutely necessary for his condition, and I lost a few hours of my own thanks to you.'

Eliza waited for more, for Mrs Pollard to mention his injury, her disobedience, but there was nothing. She suddenly felt very light, as if she could float away from the table, and bit her lip to stifle a giggle. She never got away with anything.

'If he's sick, why doesn't he see a doctor?' asked Rebecca.

'He has, child, but there's nothing to be done. It was the coal mines. That filth seeped into his lungs every time he visited his workers. Now there's no ridding the dust disease, which is why it is imperative he is not agitated.'

'He did seem very upset,' Eliza added, the relief making her bold. 'He kept . . . he kept calling me . . . Victoria.'

Eliza saw Mrs Pollard pale as the implications of her lie took hold. Never had she seen the housekeeper so affected and was pleased it was she who caused it.

'To the parlour. Go. Go! Rebecca, you stay here.'

Eliza left the kitchen with more energy than when she arrived. Perhaps the fersolate was finally working. Aunt Bess swore by it for a reason.

'A week, Victoria,' Eliza whispered to the paintings as she passed. 'Please give me a week.'

As Eliza cleaned the parlour, she wondered what she would do if she were a ghost. Would she pass peacefully from room to room, watching over her descendants as a loving spirit? Or would she scheme against them, harm those that attempted to disturb her? Maybe the choice was not hers. Maybe it depended on how she was taken from this world. If her life ended as violently as Victoria's, perhaps the anger of the act would instil in her a hate that was not hers in life, and she would be compelled to lash out and harm the innocent.

As she recovered the paintings, she hoped Victoria could sense her feelings, understand that Eliza meant her no harm. That all she wanted was to leave this place. That she had no sympathy for these dead men. Her eyes fell on the books sketched in Richard Brownawell's portrait, and she thought of Pip. Had she, too, been forced to dine with the master of the house? Had she worn that dress, eaten that food? Had Victoria come to her as well? Is that when she had sought out the black book, to search for clues in ghost stories to explain that which afflicted her? And Mrs Pollard, in a rage, had torn the book from her hands, perhaps bludgeoned her with it, stealing the last health Pip had left and allowing the house to claim her?

The image of Pip's blood-covered face was fresh in her mind when the screaming started. It came from the back of the house, near the garden. Eliza dropped the sheet and ran down the west wing, out the veranda doors. Mrs Pollard was hurting Rebecca. She knew all along about the slap and was now punishing Rebecca for Eliza's misdeed. It was the only thought within her head. Yet, as she came closer, she realised what she heard was not the screaming of a child, not even that of a person. It was the high-pitched yelping of an animal in pain. She stuttered to a stop on the edge of the west lawn.

Lying on the slim gravel path to the carriage house was Mr Drewry's wolfhound, crying out as Rebecca beat him.

'Rebecca!' Eliza grabbed the wooden club from her sister. 'What are you doing?'

'He's a bad dog.'

'What happened? Did he attack you?' Eliza searched her for any sign of injury, but Rebecca appeared unharmed. The grey dog whimpered and bled.

'Mrs Pollard sent me to collect the eggs, but he was by the henhouse gate. He wanted to get in and eat the hens, I could tell. I had to teach him a lesson.'

Dumbfounded, Eliza knelt by the dog. Her hands hovered over his injuries, unsure how to help. The dog looked at her, his brown eyes pleading. Somehow, he found the strength to wag his tail.

'But what did he do? Did he lunge at you? Anything? Rebecca, why did you beat him?' Slowly, she laid a hand on the dog's wiry head. Stroking gently, she was encouraged when he stopped whimpering.

'Filthy creatures must learn their place.'

'Kasey. Kasey!'

At his master's call, the dog tried to rise but was unable.

'Shh. It's all right,' Eliza soothed him.

'Kasey!' Mr Drewry came running from the north lawn. 'Kasey! Oh God.' He ran into the carriage house and returned moments later with a tin medical kit. He pushed Eliza back. 'Easy, boy. Easy.'

'It . . . it was an accident,' Eliza said. Mr Drewry ignored her as he pulled out a syringe and filled it from a small, glass vial. Gently, he injected it into the dog's leg.

As he tried to bandage the dog's side, difficult with only one hand, Eliza looked towards Rebecca, who stood to the side. No expression crossed her face – no guilt, no pleasure – nothing but a blank stare that hid whatever thoughts were floating in her head as she twirled a strand of her hair in her fingers.

'Help me move him,' ordered Mr Drewry, drawing Eliza's attention back to the injured dog. 'Carry the kit.'

He placed the dog over his shoulder in a fireman's hold while Eliza grabbed the first-aid box. She followed him into the carriage house and up the stairs to his private room, where he laid the dog on the bed. As she helped him tend to Kasey's wounds, her eyes drifted over the spartan loft. It was furnished with only the essentials – bed, wardrobe, table, two chairs. Kitchen utensils hung on the wall over the range. A dog's clay food and water bowls sat by the door. The exposed beams and stone fireplace reminded her of the fairy-tale homes of lonely grandmothers and kindly woodsmen. A window over the bed looked out onto the woods behind the estate. Two windows in the kitchen revealed Thornecroft lurking ahead. She would rather live here than the vast, empty manor.

Mr Drewry calmed as he stroked his dog's head. In the quiet, she could hear him crying.

'I'm sorry,' she said. 'It was . . . He got into the henhouse. Rebecca thought he . . .'

'He hangs about the henhouse 'cause there's been trouble with foxes. It's why Pollard lets me keep him.' There was something different about Mr Drewry's voice. It was softer, younger. His face was a mask of worry, his scars running like tear tracks across his tanned skin. Eliza placed a hand on his shoulder.

He shrugged it off.

'Look what you've done. You stupid, stupid girls.' The dark vacancy returned to his eyes. 'Get out of here! Go before I get me gun. You keep away from me and me dog. You understand? Go!'

Eliza ran from the carriage house. Outside, Rebecca drew patterns in the path with the blood-spattered stick. Eliza took it and threw it into the nearby bushes then hurried Rebecca away through the garden. She had lied for her before, whenever her nervous troubles caused her to act strangely in front of others, but this time Rebecca's actions felt different. This time they felt deliberate.

More than ever, Rebecca needed to remain calm, at least until Friday. Already Mr Drewry could refuse to take them to the village. She couldn't let the problem escalate. Rebecca had to be under control, docile even, in a way Eliza had only seen her once before. No amount of caring or devotion could make Rebecca that calm, which Eliza knew all too well.

The doctor told Aunt Bess to keep the tablets, just in case. Eliza had brought them to Wales for the same reason.

*

Eliza loved the moment before the kettle whistled. She anticipated the change in the water, how the sound of it quieted just before the boil. That brief moment of peace before the whistle blew. She remembered a game she had with Mother – a race to ready the teapot and serving tray before the kettle sounded. If she was quick enough, she would get an extra biscuit. Or had that been Mrs Littleton? Eliza stared at Mrs Pollard's kettle, waiting for that moment.

Though the day had passed without interruption from Victoria, Eliza's lack of sleep made every hour stretch longer than it ought. Her conversation with Ruth could have happened last week or five minutes ago. Had it even happened at all or was it only a dream? Rebecca attacking the dog, that too happened recently, had it not? That was why she stood here now, making tea after dinner, instead of letting exhaustion lead her straight to bed. She had to take care of Rebecca. Even though she was close to falling asleep right here at the counter, her eyelids slipping as her body was lulled by the sound of water boiling, the birds' evensong outside, the breeze brushing against her cheek like a lullaby.

Eliza . . .

The kettle whistled.

Rebecca skipped in from outside. 'Eliza, can I help?' she asked.

'No, no,' she said, rubbing her eyes. 'I'll be mother. Why don't you have a seat? You've been working ever so hard lately, haven't you? What else did Mrs Pollard have you doing today?'

Rebecca circled the table, chattering away about her work in the vegetable garden while the tea brewed. When Rebecca's back was turned, Eliza slipped her hand into her pocket and withdrew two small tablets of lithium bromide. She dropped them into her sister's cup then poured tea for them both. She added a little extra milk and sugar to Rebecca's, hoping to cover up any bitter, medicinal taste, and waited until the tablets dissolved completely before taking their cups to the table.

'Here you are, dearie.'

Rebecca took a sip and shuddered.

'What's the matter?' Had she been caught out already?

'Too hot.'

'Oh, of course.'

'Are there any biscuits?'

'I'm afraid not. Mrs Pollard said we can't waste our sugar ration on mere frivolities. That woman. Well, we'll be free of her soon enough, won't—'

'You should be nicer to Mrs Pollard.' Rebecca stared at Eliza. Her eyes were focused, the muscles tense in her forehead and jaw. Eliza knew that look. The last time she saw it was just before Rebecca attacked Aunt Bess. It had never been directed towards her.

'Rebecca, I . . .'

'She works very hard here. No one appreciates what she does to keep this estate running. You should treat her with more respect.'

Eliza smiled. It hurt, like having her arm twisted behind her back.

'Of course,' she said. 'You're absolutely right. It must be

very stressful for her.' Eliza raised her cup to conceal her face and dropped the painful smile. 'Drink your tea.' She watched Rebecca consume every single drop.

*

The muslin dress wrapped itself around her. She could not breathe, but there was no need. Her body slept below her on the mattress, arms hugging the dead girl. She hovered above, wanting to walk but not knowing how.

I'll show you.

Victoria stood by the door, smiling in the dress that matched her own. Eliza opened her mouth to speak, but Victoria raised a finger to her lips and the collar of the dress tightened round Eliza's neck like a noose made from washing line and her eyes began to bulge . . .

She was back in her body. She was breathing. The mattress held no other body and there was nothing choking her neck. She was breathing, breathing the damp air, the dust from the furniture, the scent of her own perfume. She was breathing, and Victoria was not in the doorway. She was breathing, and Victoria did not want her to leave.

17

Tea was all Peter had to eat. That, a jar of pickled cabbage and a tin of leftover fruitcake from Christmas. If he left the flat, he could do the shopping. But if he stayed inside, no one could find him. No doubt the police were looking for him. A man like Mosley wasn't assaulted without consequences. But Mosley didn't know who he was and, if he did, didn't know where he lived. The police could track him down through the Palladium. Or government records. Everyone was registered. They would find him. Not even the flat was safe forever. Still, it was safe for now.

Peter's hands shook as he rinsed a cup. It slipped from his grip and dropped into the sink but somehow didn't break. He couldn't even break a teacup. How could he break a man? Mosley was fine. A little roughed up, but he walked away. It was a minor thing Peter had done, and for a greater cause. The police didn't lock people up for that, did they? It was only a little fight, a little indiscretion.

These thoughts were like lead pumped into his veins, left to harden under the skin. Lead in his blood. Tea in his stomach. Cigarette smoke in his lungs. His body ached for something more. A solid meal would help, if it was safe to go outside.

Peter checked out the window. Pedestrians, cabs, nothing unusual. Nothing threatening. He pulled his cap low, turned his collar up and cautiously made his way downstairs. The landlady's little dog yapped from behind a door. Sounding an alarm or calling for help? Peter hushed at him to be quiet.

No one assaulted him when he stepped onto the street. He paused and took a good look round. There were so many people about; how could he be picked from the crowd? Barkston Gardens was packed with shoppers. Women with stone faces etched from years counting rations gossiped in long queues while small children ran through the square collecting rubbish and dropping pennies, their high, uncontrollable laughs like chimps at the zoo. Gruff men pushed past him to dash across the street in front of smoky buses.

Peter began to sweat. There was so much noise. Too much, even for London. He would forgo the shop. A Corner House or café would be fine. Anything with food. He tried to hurry, but his limp made it difficult. The faster he moved, the more his leg ached. He needed to get indoors, sit down. There was a café near here, one he wanted to take Eliza to. Why couldn't he remember where it was? He wiped his brow and glanced behind.

The man in the blue and yellow cap stared back.

Peter tasted vomit, smelled the damp pavement, heard the *clang, clang, clang* of the lead pipe rolling. He ran across the street. A horn sounded and he felt the breeze of a car lurching to a stop. He kept running, down to Branham Gardens, into a different crowd.

The man in the cap followed.

Peter remembered being pursued down a different street, a street in darkness, lit only by sodium lamplight. *The first blow struck him in the back.* He felt it now as he turned onto Earl's Court Road and hurried towards the station. The road was crowded, and Peter slipped into the flow of people.

The cap did the same.

There was a cinema up ahead. Cinemas were dark,

anonymous. Peter fished a few pence from his pocket and bought a ticket. He made the usherette show him to a back seat and there he remained, keeping his eyes on the door instead of the repeating newsreels and films. His leg welcomed the relief, and his stomach forgot its hunger. Peter dried his palms on his trousers.

The first blow hit him in the back, he remembered now. He was walking down the street, carrying the bag of Jessie's things. Jessie's things – where were they? Did the police have them? He was walking down the street and was struck in the back and fell onto the damp pavement, scratching his hands and chin. He rolled over. Rolled over to see . . .

All he could picture was the blue and yellow cap. The face beneath it was blurred. No matter how hard he tried, he could not bring that face into focus. Peter cycled through those memories as the programme cycled through on the screen. Never could he get past that point. Never could he see any more than the cap before his memory repeated. The doctors said his mind might mend itself, piece the memories together like a film reel. At the time, it was what he wanted. Now he just wanted it to stop.

It was dusk when he finally left the cinema. The shops had closed and the queues were gone. Men rushed home from work while young couples walked arm in arm from the Corner House to the dance halls. His legs were weak, phantom-like limbs that could barely support his weight. He needed to eat. He needed a good rest. Most likely there had been no one at all, only his mind playing tricks. All he needed was a good meal and a good rest.

Peter took a different route home, just to be sure. Once inside his building, he felt no relief. He locked himself inside his flat and hurried to the window. There was only empty pavement and the occasional passer-by. Nothing which should trouble him. He fell into his armchair, hands shaking too much to light a cigarette. His brother Michael had the same problem when a car backfired or a door slammed or his daughter cried. Peter crossed his arms and tucked his hands into his armpits. Michael said it helped. Peter felt his whole body trembling as he allowed his screen-strained eyes to rest, and he was slipping down into the orange abyss . . .

A gunshot startled him. The light blinded. Peter's heart beat wildly as he shielded his tired eyes. The light – only daylight. His neck and back were stiff. Daylight. Morning. He must have fallen asleep in his chair. But the sound? Letters lay on the floor by the door. The snap of the metal post flap – that was what woke him. Peter checked his hands. They were nearly still.

His stomach groaned as he hoisted himself up. Food needed to be a priority today. Limping to the kitchen, he put the kettle on before collecting the post. A heavy letter rested on top, postmarked last week, no return address. He slid it open. Out fell another envelope, already opened, in heavy grey stationery – a letter addressed to Bess Haverford.

*

The rain began sometime after dusk, turning the park path to mud. A yellow fog coated the buildings in a mustard glow. Peter sat on a bench in St James's Park watching ducks drift on the pond, the letter in his hands becoming wet, the words running down the page like the tears in his dreams.

Businessmen hurried by, shielding their suits with brief-cases and umbrellas. The ducks disappeared, swallowed by fog. The rain crept into his skin, turning his bones to ice, his muscles to brick. The slanted words were hardly legible now, but that didn't matter. He had read it enough times. He knew what it said.

Dear Miss Bess Haverford,

I represent the estate of an influential English landowner located in Wales for which the master requires a housemaid of certain looks and breeding. It has been brought to my attention that you possess a niece who would fit his strict requirements. If she were to be employed, I needn't add that you, personally, shall be satisfactorily compensated for your loss.

Please reply by post to the following address should this arrangement appeal to you.

Signed,

Mrs G. Pollard

Head of Household

The piece of paper with the Welsh address was not included in what Peter received, only a note scribbled on a torn magazine page – *Peter, I'm sorry, Bess*. Possibly the last note she had ever written, her death the same date as the postmark.

Wales. He was wrong. Wrong about everything. Eliza was only in Wales. Mosley was telling the truth. He was innocent. Peter had assaulted an innocent man.

He had to turn himself in. It was the only way to remove the lead weight from his conscience. He would go to the police, admit what he had done, and turn over the letter. Allow them to continue the investigation. They were the professionals. They knew what they were doing. They wouldn't follow false leads, complicate simple explanations. Peter the fool. He should have stuck to accounting. Accounting was simple – maths, numbers. No guesswork. There were rules in maths, rules that need only be followed for the proper outcome to assert itself. Perhaps they would let him continue practising accountancy in prison. His wet trousers clung to his skin as he rose from the bench. He refolded the letter and returned it to his pocket.

It was only then that he saw him. The man in the blue and yellow cap walked through the park, but he hadn't noticed Peter. Perhaps the fog hid him, Peter thought, as he again smelled sick. Felt the lead pipe on his back, the scratch of the pavement on his chin. Nothing was taken when he was attacked. Neither his wallet nor his ration book.

The man in the blue and yellow cap made his way north towards the Mall.

The only items which hadn't been recovered were those belonging to Jessie.

Leave her, the voice said. Leave who?

Peter followed him up Regent Street, where the crowds thickened. The rain became heavier. People rushed to and fro, some with black umbrellas, others only soggy newspaper over their heads. The man in the blue and yellow cap kept a steady pace. In Piccadilly Circus, they went round the statue of Eros in opposite directions. Peter thought he would catch him on the other side.

Instead, the man vanished. Peter searched the fast-moving faces but did not know what the man looked like. He only knew that cap, and the open umbrellas blocked every pedestrian's head. He climbed the statue's steps and scanned the crowded circle.

Black everywhere, colours dampened by rain. One mass of people moving together like a herd of cattle. Not now, he thought. Not when he was so near. He caught sight of him heading towards Coventry Street, the cap untouched by rain. Peter leapt off the fountain, landing hard on his bad leg.

He ignored the pain and ran. He would not let him escape again. He pushed through the crowds, landing in puddles and tripping over cracks in the pavement. There were only a few paces between them. The man headed for a doorway. If Peter was going to prison, so was the man who had attacked him. With a shout, Peter grabbed his shoulders, spun him round and slammed him against the brick wall.

'Why did you do it?'

'Peter?' It was Purvis. 'I . . .'

'So it was you. You've done something to Jessie, haven't you? Was afraid I'd find out.'

'Peter, what on earth . . . ?'

'Tell me the truth!'

Purvis, who always taunted them, pushed them, made them feel like fools in that worthless job.

'Did you have an affair? Is that why she needed to go away for a while? You said she got herself into trouble. How would you know? How! Unless it was you who caused it.'

'I . . . I only meant . . . not that . . .'

Peter raised his fist.

'Oi!' A hand grabbed his and pulled him back. Peter elbowed Purvis's defender in the ribs. 'Easy, mate!'

Stephen. 'What's going on?' he asked.

'He's the one who attacked me,' Peter panted. It was difficult to breathe. 'He's the one . . . He's done something to Jessie . . . He . . .'

Purvis cowered by the wall, raising his flabby arms in a meek expression of self-defence. A small crowd had gathered now – more ushers and theatre staff arriving for work. Peter hadn't noticed they were outside the Palladium stage door. Peter knew these people. They trusted him, bought him drinks and covered his shifts, told him about their new girl or the baby on the way. They looked at him now, their faces showing shock and disgust. One of the electricians went to Purvis's side.

'He . . . He's been . . . I know it was . . .' How to make them understand? How could they feel the black hole inside him? Peter looked at his old employer. Purvis could barely lift a lead pipe, let alone strike a man with it. But it had to be Purvis. Peter followed him here. Following him to the theatre felt right. But the cap. Where was the cap? It must have fallen in the struggle. The crowd around him whispered as he searched the ground. He could prove everything if he found the cap.

'It has to be here. He was wearing it. It has to be . . .'

Stephen put an arm around his shoulders. 'Let us take you for a drink.'

'But I'm right. I know I am . . .' Peter kept his eyes on the ground behind him for as long as possible as Stephen led him away through the rain. He knew the cap was near.

Peter and Stephen ended up in the Dog and Duck, Stephen muscling them into a corner table by the window up on the first floor. A glass of whisky was nudged into Peter's hand.

'I don't drink whisky,' Peter said, shivering in his soaked clothes.

'Looked like you could use something strong.'

Peter slid the glass away. 'I'm fine.'

'Tell that to old Purvis.' Stephen gave it back. Peter ignored the drink and tucked his hands into his sides. 'Going to tell us what this is about?'

Peter looked out the blurred window and stared down at the pavement. Despite the rain, the streets were flooded with people. He couldn't distinguish faces. With the number of umbrellas and overcoats, it was hard to tell which were men, which were women. There were so many people.

'Purvis makes sense. My being attacked after I went to her

flat. Her things being taken. What he said to Mrs Rolston. It all makes sense.' He stamped his foot on the ground, shaking the table.

'No idea what you're on about. Should I call for the bus to Bedlam or do you want to start from the beginning?' Stephen reached for the whisky. Peter stopped him.

'I've been wrong about everything. Bess . . . Bess sent Eliza to Wales.' He withdrew the letter and handed it to Stephen. 'Somehow this Pollard woman got her address. Bess sent Eliza out there to pay off her debts. That's what Mosley said, and he was right.'

'There's no address,' Stephen said, reading the letter.

'I know. It's all so . . . damn foolish. Why should Bess send me this instead of telling me where Eliza is?'

'Maybe it's against the rules.' Stephen put the letter in his pocket.

'I just want to know she's all right.' Peter rested his head in his hands.

'Well, if this has to do with Bess's gambling, I know someone who might know a thing or two.'

Peter's head snapped up. 'How did you know about the gambling?'

Stephen smiled. 'You told me, remember? That day I saw you in Whitechapel?'

'Oh. Yes. Of course. My memory . . . it's been very odd lately.'

Stephen sipped his drink. 'Why keep doing this on your own, ginger? Why not let your mate Stephen help you, eh?'

Peter took one last glance out the window then grabbed the glass. The whisky burned as it made its way down his throat and settled nicely in his stomach.

18

The dress wrapped itself around her, inhibiting movement, strangling breath. Her body slept peacefully below while Victoria beckoned from the doorway, but Eliza could not move. Victoria grew impatient. The dress grew tighter and Eliza thrashed against it. It started to tear at the seams and she was free of it, she was almost . . .

Eliza woke up gasping. When she recovered her breath, she checked it was her nightdress she wore. For two days the dreams had tormented her. Every time she closed her eyes Victoria was waiting, drawing closer, holding her down. The time would come when she would not wake.

Dawn was just breaking over the horizon. Two days and she had not yet spoken to Mr Drewry. She curled her knees to her chest. She could put off apologising no longer. He was their way to Plentynunig. She had thought about what to do, and it was Aunt Bess's advice she kept returning to, the advice Aunt Bess gave just before her first date with Peter.

'You want a man's attention, that's easy enough, but if you want his heart, you go through here,' she pointed.

Several hours later, Eliza stood in the garden wall doorway watching grey ash float towards the sky with Aunt Bess's advice cradled in her arms – a basket of freshly baked rolls. The carriage house was dark, but smoke from the chimney told her Mr Drewry was inside. The rolls were wrapped in a kitchen cloth to keep in the warmth, but the cold air quickly absorbed their heat. This had to be done. They wouldn't be able to reach Plentynunig alone, not in time for the market cart. With each tentative step down the gravel path, she willed her nerves to remain steady.

She was two feet away when Mr Drewry flung open the door, his rifle aimed shoulder high.

'I told you . . .'

'I brought you rolls.' She held up the basket like a shield as his eyes searched for any other intruders.

'Bring 'em here then.' He put the rifle down.

The little confidence Eliza had managed to scrape together vanished as she approached. He grabbed the basket and tucked it under the stump of his right arm, flipping back the cloth with his left hand.

'Pollard tell you to bring these?'

'No. I—'

'Then why did you?'

'I wanted to apologise. For my sister. How is Kasey?'

'Your sister can apologise for herself.' He covered the bread. 'But she won't, will she?'

'It's never been her strength.' Unable to meet Mr Drewry's eyes, she glanced past him into the carriage house. An army officer's trench coat hung from a hook by the stairs. Father's friends wore ones like it when they came for tea. Mr Drewry caught her staring.

'Tell the girl she's lucky me dog ain't dead.' He slammed the door shut. Eliza started back towards the house when the door reopened behind her. Mr Drewry held up a bitten roll. Eliza flinched, afraid he would throw it at her.

'These taste okay.' He disappeared without awaiting her reply.

Pulling her jumper tight around her, she returned to the manor.

Eliza often struggled to understand the ways of men. She had never spent much time alone with Father, not before the war. He would be there at breakfast and dinner, accompany them on family holidays, ask about school, but there was never time for the two of them together. Even on their day trips to museums and libraries, Mother would be there to act as a barrier. When the war ended and she returned home, Eliza came to know his anger. His hurtful words would gather on her skin like paper cuts, wounding her all over till she couldn't move near him for fear of pain. She thought it was because he had not been allowed to go to war, but maybe that wasn't it at all. Maybe that was just who he was.

At least Mr Drewry seemed appeased, she thought, as she began cleaning the dishes. Through his stomach, Aunt Bess said, that was how to win a man. As she never cooked, it was her excuse for not marrying, though Eliza knew it had something to do with her ex-fiancé, that American. The one whose picture Aunt Bess kept in the bottom of her stocking drawer. The one Father laughed about returning to his wife. Yet for once, Aunt Bess's advice appeared to have worked. Mr Drewry would surely agree to take them to the village on Friday, so long as Rebecca did nothing else to anger him.

*

Eliza set the mixing bowl in the sink and ran her hands over her neck. All day, she had kept feeling a tightness there, as if a pair of small hands were strangling her. She rolled her shoulders to loosen the tension and returned to the washing-up. As she did so, laughter sounded from outside – Rebecca's laughter. Worried about what catastrophe Rebecca chose to laugh at now, Eliza went to the window. Rebecca played hopscotch in the grass. Only hopscotch. A simple, childhood game. But Eliza's smile faded when Rebecca started arguing with the air.

She had yet to notice any change in her behaviour since starting her on the tablets. Was there something wrong with them? Had they expired, lost their potency? Or was Rebecca too old for them now? Was that dosage meant for a smaller child? Maybe more time was needed for them to take effect. Rebecca threw a pebble at the window. Eliza jumped back as it bounced off the glass right in front of her face.

'Stop spying on me!' Rebecca shouted, her voice muffled by the walls of the house. She came stomping inside the kitchen, a light film of sweat on her forehead. 'Why are you always spying on me?'

'I'm not spying, I'm looking after you. It's what older sisters do.'

Rebecca seemed pale. 'Older sisters shouldn't be so nosy.'

'Are you all right, dearie? Your colour looks off.' Eliza placed the back of her hand on Rebecca's forehead, but Rebecca turned away.

'I'm perfectly fine, so I'd appreciate it if you left me alone, please.' Rebecca clomped out of the kitchen, knocking over the bin but not stopping to put it right.

Eliza gathered the spilled rubbish. There was no more time. Friday was only two days away. If Rebecca kept behaving this way, Mr Drewry would not want to help them. Maybe an extra tablet would do, just for a little while. Just to make sure Rebecca would be all right.

She called down the hall. 'Rebecca! Time for tea.'

*

Eliza wore a muslin dress, though it couldn't be the same one because this one was yellowed, not shimmering white. The lace was torn and curling and a stain spoiled the skirt. Several buttons were missing and it kept slipping off her shoulders. On the floor below, her body slept on the dead girl's mattress. She reached down to touch it when from the door came a sigh.

There stood Victoria. Eliza opened her mouth to speak, but Victoria raised a single finger to her lips. She reached out a hand and beckoned Eliza to follow. Eliza moved easily.

The train of Victoria's dress led her through the manor like a path of breadcrumbs. She had to gather up her skirt to avoid tripping as she followed. Though the halls were dark, Eliza saw clearly.

They passed through an Abigale Hall filled with floating corpse candles. Eliza let them dance on her fingertips. Victoria called for her.

Come, Eliza. Come with us . . .

Together they snuck into the Ancestral Parlour. Here Victoria stopped at the far end of the dining table. Though the portraits were covered, Victoria pointed to each in turn and again put her finger to her lips. Then she hurried to the veranda. Eliza followed. The doors were wide open.

Outside, all was dark. If there was a moon, the clouds obscured it. Victoria stood on the west lawn, waiting. They continued across the high grass, two ghosts in the night. It wasn't until they reached the iron gate that Eliza realised they had come to the little cemetery at the edge of the woods.

She wanted to turn back, but Victoria would not allow it. She appeared beside Eliza and grabbed her arm. Her grip was cold and froze Eliza's skin. She pulled her forward to the grave marker closest to the trunk of a large yew tree. Eliza could not get close enough to read the name. An open grave lay in front. She tried to run, but Victoria held firm. Her face now resembled the doll's. Bloody holes remained where her eyes had once been and deep gashes ran down her cheeks. The blood dripped onto Eliza's skin.

Come, Eliza.

Father waited in the grave, his face red and purple, swollen, eyes bulging. Victoria pushed her into his arms.

Eliza's knees smacked against the hard ground. She started backwards.

Her first realisation was that she was awake. Her next was that she was not in the muslin dress but her old cotton night-gown. Her last was that she was outside, kneeling in the little cemetery.

She scrambled to her feet, the dream already fading, unsure as to how she got there. It was the middle of the night, but the moon was bright and clear, illuminating the name on the grave marker before which Eliza stood.

Victoria Kyffin.

Eliza ran back to the house, feeling the damp grass on her bare feet, small rocks and twigs stabbing her soles as foxes screamed to each other in the night. The door to the veranda was open. She had difficulty navigating through the black house, having to turn around twice before finding her room. She crawled into bed and curled up under the thin top sheet.

'Please, give me another day. That's all. Victoria, please. Please.'

Tears dried on her face as she fell asleep.

Eliza . . .

A whisper woke her. A pale ghost stood at her side. Eliza nearly screamed, until she saw who it was.

'Rebecca?'

Rebecca opened her mouth as if to speak then vomited all over the mattress.

*

'Easy, easy, dearie. Let it out. It's all right.' Eliza held back Rebecca's hair as she vomited into the toilet, and rubbed slow circles on her back, trying to soothe the convulsions. Rebecca said nothing, merely cried as her body was wracked with another wave of nausea. The sweet stench of bile made Eliza's own stomach lurch. How much sleep had she had since arriving at Thornecroft? She could probably count the decent hours on one hand. Without Rebecca, she could have a few more. Rebecca collapsed into her arms, too weak to continue, as a shadow was cast over them.

'What's going on?' Mrs Pollard kept still in the doorway. Her nightgown hung loosely from her thin frame, the tendons in her neck straining as she stared down at them both.

'Rebecca woke me an hour ago. She's been ill.'

'I can see that.'

'Do you have any stomach medicine?'

Mrs Pollard said nothing at first. Eliza believed she would refuse Rebecca help, but she didn't care. They didn't need Mrs Pollard.

'There may be something. Put her to bed.' She disappeared down the hall.

'Rebecca? Do you think you can walk?'

Rebecca nodded weakly, and Eliza helped her to rise. With one arm around her sister, Eliza pulled the toilet chain.

The first time she had cared for someone with a stomach upset was the night of their return to London. Though she never remembered Father drinking heavily before the war, that night he remained in the pub until closing time then continued imbibing from his private stock of homemade

210

marrow liqueur once he stumbled home. He mistook Eliza for her mother then ran to the toilet to be sick. The next day, he would not even look at her.

As Eliza tucked Rebecca into bed, Mrs Pollard returned with a small brown bottle and a spoon. It was the bottle she had seen Mrs Pollard sipping from on their way to Plentynunig.

'Stomach tonic. Old family recipe,' Mrs Pollard said, catching Eliza's eyes as they scanned the unlabelled bottle. 'One couldn't live in the Indian colony without suffering all sorts of unpleasant stomach ailments. Mother swore by this. Give it to her. Two tablespoons.'

Eliza untwisted the cap and was struck by the pungent odour of herbs and aspic. She poured the viscous black liquid onto the spoon and held it to Rebecca's lips. Rebecca turned away.

'Please, dearie. It will make you feel better.' Eliza tried to force the spoon into Rebecca's mouth but only succeeded in dripping the sticky substance onto the sheets.

'Rebecca. You know what's best for you. Be a good girl,' Mrs Pollard ordered.

Rebecca complied, grimacing as she swallowed.

'One more,' Mrs Pollard said. Rebecca's mouth was open before Eliza could pour another dose.

'That will do for now.' She took the bottle and spoon from Eliza. 'Let her rest.'

Rebecca was already falling asleep. Eliza looked for the bisque doll, wanting to tuck it under her sister's arm, but she did not see it in the small room. She took Rebecca's old plastic cat instead and placed it with her underneath the sheet. Rebecca rolled over and pushed the cat onto the floor. It landed with a smack on the scuffed floorboards. Eliza left it.

*

Between Rebecca's illness and the nightmare, the day was filled with worry. The nightmares had never gone that far before. Was Victoria working harder to keep her here? She tried to keep the matter at the back of her mind, but the vivid dream came flooding back when Mrs Pollard ordered her to sweep the veranda. Eliza looked at the dried muddy footprints on the stone tiling and felt the dirt on her own feet, hidden by stockings and shoes. She had never known herself to sleep-walk. Not even Rebecca suffered from that condition. It was something about this house, about Victoria's lingering presence. Was this how it started? Victoria entering the dreams of those she wished to harm? Was that how she led them away? How was Eliza to control her body while she slept? Perhaps she could lock the door, tie herself to the bed frame. Maybe she could go without sleep tonight. It was only tonight she had to survive. By tomorrow, they'd be in Abergwili.

Father was always threatening to send them away. He was upset with Rebecca's shyness and Eliza's constant references to the Littletons. More than once he snapped at them to be quiet, even when they weren't speaking. It didn't take long for Eliza to recognise that this wasn't the father she'd had before the war. Yet who wasn't changed by those years? Eliza did her best to please him. It was never enough. He never appreciated anything, not his daughters, not his position, not even his own war work. Eliza was sure he had done his bit – Father couldn't help his poor eyesight – but 'too young for the first war, too crippled for the second, too old for the third' was what he muttered to himself when drunk.

As she dumped the mop water, she caught a whiff of marrow liqueur.

By the afternoon, Rebecca felt well enough to eat, so Eliza prepared her luncheon. She put only one tablet of lithium bromide into the tea rather than the full dose, unsure how the medication would interact with Mrs Pollard's homemade tonic. Rebecca did seem calmer today – less angry and more like the little girl she used to be. As soon as they were back in London she would take Rebecca to the doctor, make sure Thornecroft hadn't caused any lasting damage.

London. London as early as next week. She could already feel the bustle of the city. She would welcome it. Peter would meet them at the train station. She would send him a telegram from Abergwili. He would be waiting at Paddington with roses and a ring, and she would run into his arms and right there he'd propose. The whole station would cheer for them. She could stay with his family as they planned the wedding. Peter would have finished his apprenticeship and she would enrol in a secretarial college, or perhaps a teacher training college. They would need to earn as much as they could if they were to afford a house of their own. Rebecca could live with them until she finished school and found a job, or maybe she would go to university. She was so clever when she wanted to be. If Eliza was half as clever as Rebecca, they would be in London already.

'How are you feeling?' she asked, slipping into Rebecca's room. She set the luncheon tray on the bedside table. 'No fever?' She placed her hand against Rebecca's forehead. 'How's your tummy?'

'Stop fussing.' Rebecca shifted away. 'You're always fussing.'

'Only because I care. Do you need anything? Where's your doll?'

'I don't need anything. Especially not a stupid doll.' She rolled away from Eliza and pulled the blanket over her head. The coarse, moth-eaten fabric scratched Eliza's skin as she

213

stroked Rebecca's shoulder. Her sister's wiry frame tensed with every caress, as if Eliza were winding a watch. She pulled her hand away.

'Well, you stay in bed and get as much rest as you can. We have a big day tomorrow, remember?'

The body under the blanket remained still.

'Rebecca, you do remember what tomorrow is, don't you? Friday?'

'Tomorrow we run away.'

'We're returning to London.' Eliza smiled. No reply. 'That's what you wanted, remember? When we first arrived? You told me you couldn't wait to leave.'

'I remember. I always remember.'

'Good. Now try and eat some of this, will you? You'll need your strength. I'll come back in a little while. See how you're feeling.'

More silence. Was Mother this underappreciated? With a sigh, Eliza returned to the hall.

'What did you give her?' Mrs Pollard stood there, hands gripping the waist of her black dress. Now she had seen Mrs Pollard in her nightgown, Eliza noticed how this dress, too, seemed a size too big.

'Some Oxo stock,' she answered.

'And?'

'A slice of bread.'

A chill prickled Eliza's skin as Mrs Pollard took a slow step forward. The keys at her waist jangled once, like a warning bell. The skin of her face was a shade darker than that of her neck. Eliza could see where she had tapered off her make-up underneath her chin.

'And?' Mrs Pollard's voice dropped in octave and temperature.

'Tea.'

'And?'

The pill bottle burned against Eliza's thigh. She slipped her hands into her pockets and took her own step forward.

'Was there something else you wanted me to give her?' She could feel Mrs Pollard's breath across her brow. It smelled of aspic. Eliza did not move, did not breathe, did not blink. Mrs Pollard's face remained unreadable.

From the bedroom came Rebecca's cry. Eliza glanced at the door. When she turned back, Mrs Pollard's eyes were on her pocket.

'Stock and bread and tea sound more than sufficient,' said Mrs Pollard. 'Go to the henhouse. I need the eggs for dinner.'

Eliza calmly walked down to the kitchen, refusing to turn round even as she felt Mrs Pollard's eyes boring into her back. As Eliza reached the kitchen, a door slammed. She turned. The hall was empty.

The day's grey light stained the kitchen. The absence of colour further dampened Eliza's mood as if she, too, had been drained of all colour. If she looked at her hands, would they be pale and pink or grey like the images in a film? She passed through the kitchen, focusing on the damp green grass she could see through the window, but stopped at Mrs Pollard's office. Through the half-open door, she could see a stack of post sitting on the housekeeper's desk. Eliza had received no correspondence since her arrival, but that did not mean none had been sent.

She listened. When the house gave no sound, she slipped into the office and scooped all the letters into her hands. She flipped through them, looking for any message from Aunt Bess or Peter or anyone from London. A few had return addresses unknown to Eliza, and those with no return address were yet unopened. None of the handwriting looked familiar. There was one telegram – a message from Swansea inquiring about a delivery order. Nothing from those she knew.

Eliza placed the post on the desk, careful to return every piece to its exact position. As she aligned the top letter, her eyes fell on an ivory-handled letter opener. Though likely once expensive, the silver file had experienced much mistreatment. Several scratches marred its surface and brittle wax stuck to its tip.

Footsteps thudded on the wet ground outside. Eliza forgot the letter opener and hurried back to the kitchen, leaving the office door half-opened as she'd found it. She continued outside, passing Mr Drewry who was making his way in. Neither acknowledged the other, though she noticed he was eating one of her rolls. The wet ground dampened her shoes as she crossed to the henhouse. Inside the gated grounds, feathers and chicken droppings immediately stuck to her wet shoes as if drawn there by magnetism.

She grabbed the wicker basket from the hook and entered the acrid structure. The thin hens pecked at the vegetable scraps at her feet, some aiming for her hands as she reached for their eggs. Chickens were filthy animals, especially these sickly ones, with their missing feathers and crusted eyes. Eliza could imagine the bugs and mites crawling across their skin, leaping onto her as she passed. Her arms began to crawl and itch. She brushed her skin with her free hand – the hand that came closest to the nesting chickens – and the itching intensified. Had she brushed more creatures onto her arm? The further she went inside the henhouse, the stronger the smell of excrement-soaked straw. What if she inhaled the mites that plagued the chickens? Would they nestle in her lungs? Eat her soft, wet tissue from the inside out?

Eliza started coughing and was certain she could feel the mites rattling in her lungs. They scratched and tore at the delicate membranes as she tried to force them back up her throat. Tears clouded her vision, but she could not stop coughing. She had to get them out. She backed out of the henhouse, the basket dangling from her elbow, weighing her down. She stumbled down the steps and hurried to the gate, the increased squawking deafening. Her lungs felt sore, but she coughed harder, needing to scrape every last intruder from her body. Her feet slipped on the wet ground and she tumbled forward.

The eggs went sprawling onto the grass. Eliza heard them crack under her hands, felt the sticky mess and crunched shells in her palms. She sat back on her calves, wiping the wet yolk on her trousers. The spilled basket lay beside her. Brown eggs – some broken, some whole – dotted the grass.

It was too much today, doing Rebecca's chores as well as her own. Her eyes were so dry, she felt they would crumble into grains of sand if she blinked. She would sleep soon, on the train to London, with a belly full of tea and sandwiches and Rebecca calm beside her. It wasn't long now. She set the basket upright and began gathering the eggs closest to her. Voices came from the kitchen.

'. . . want that girl skulking about . . .' It was Mrs Pollard. '. . . as bad as Kyffin was. And I can't . . . another of those. Well? Are you even listening?'

'Yes, ma'am,' said Mr Drewry. '. . . harmless. Don't even know what . . .'

'I did not ask for your opinion. I asked you to handle it. I must inspect the collection tomorrow, and I can't have her . . .'

Their shadows stretched across the lawn, nearly touching Eliza.

'. . . sure that girl is under control.'

'She's no trouble.'

If they looked out of the windows, they would catch her eavesdropping.

'Remember, I only promised . . .' Mrs Pollard's voice dropped, and she whispered something too low for Eliza to hear. Whatever it was caused Mr Drewry to stomp out of the kitchen. The door slammed hard behind him. He spat on the grass, in Mrs Pollard's direction. As he fixed his hat on his head, he caught sight of Eliza kneeling on the ground. Their eyes met. She held her breath and waited for him to yell for the housekeeper.

He turned and walked towards the carriage house.

Eliza collected the rest of the undamaged eggs and hurried into the kitchen, keeping her head down.

'Miss Haverford,' Mrs Pollard called from her office.

Eliza left the basket on the table and went to the doorway. Mrs Pollard knew. Of course she knew. She always knew.

'Your sister was calling. I suggest you go and see to her.'

Eliza nodded and hurried out of the kitchen, so many thoughts filling her head that she felt no relief from escaping. *Kyffin*. The name on Victoria's grave. And why had Mr Drewry ignored her? What was he planning?

She tried to forget everything. Under control, that's what Mrs Pollard expected of her, and that was what she would be. But only until tomorrow.

*

Having coaxed Rebecca to join her for dinner, Eliza now encouraged her to help with the clearing up.

'It's only a few dishes. Then you can go straight back to bed.'

218

'I don't feel well. Why can't you do them?'

Rebecca's whinging was doing nothing for Eliza's headache. 'Because I asked you to. Isn't that reason enough? And I did all your chores today so you could rest, so could you please just do this?'

'Fine.'

'Thank you.'

Rebecca rolled up her sleeves to wash the dishes, and Eliza noticed the red, raised rash on her arms.

'Rebecca, what's happened to your arm?'

She pulled down her sleeve. 'Nothing. Look, I'm doing what you asked.'

'You can't pretend I didn't see it. Give it here,' she said, holding out her hand. Rebecca ignored her and began scrubbing a plate. Eliza was tired, her head pounding, every muscle stiff and aching. Her temper had grown short. 'Rebecca. Oh, for goodness sake.' Eliza grabbed for Rebecca's arm. Her sister jerked away, dropping the plate. It broke into three pieces on the stone floor. 'Now look what you've done.'

'It's your fault.'

'If you had just let me see your arm . . .'

'It's your fault I have a rash in the first place!'

A lump formed in Eliza's throat. 'Don't be silly.'

'Turn out your pockets. Let me see. You're making me sick just like the doctors did. I know it's you! Let me see your pockets!' Rebecca ran for her and grabbed at Eliza's trousers. She got a hand inside the pocket and snatched the pill bottle. Eliza reached for it but Rebecca was too quick.

'I hate these.' She dumped the tablets onto the floor. 'You know I hate these!' She stamped on them, crushing them into powder.

219

'You needed something to calm your nerves, that's all. For tomorrow.'

Rebecca needed to understand. This was for the best.

Eliza lowered her voice. 'We're leaving tomorrow, remember?'

'Why should I go anywhere with you? You always lie to me. I'm glad we came. I'm glad I did it!'

Eliza froze. Rebecca wasn't making any sense. Or maybe she was too tired to understand. Maybe she wasn't hearing the right words. 'What did you say?'

'I knew you'd be too stupid to catch me. So I burned our clothing coupons and our ration books and I let you think you lost them and I'm not sorry because it's funny. It's funny to see you act so very stupid.'

Eliza slapped her.

She wanted to do it again, hit her until she cried and begged and apologised for being a disgusting little wretch. Rip her hair out and burn her favourite dress. Take away every good thing she ever gave her and watch her weep.

She raised her hand.

Rebecca smiled. 'You pretend you're different, but you feel it too, don't you? Father gave it to both of us. It lives in here.' She pressed her finger into Eliza's heart. 'You can't kill it, so why don't you stop trying?' She twisted her nail into Eliza's skin then walked away, her feet crunching on the broken plate. At the kitchen door, she dropped the empty pill bottle. It rolled across the floor until it bumped into the cabinets by Eliza's foot.

Eliza felt the mark of her sister upon her chest. Inside, she felt the cold spot grow, and while it numbed her, it didn't take the hateful thoughts away. It made them clear and strong and turned them from Rebecca and onto herself as they ate away at her heart.

Ask yourself what horrible thing you've done to be here, Ruth said, and now she knew. She fell to her knees, surrounded by crushed porcelain and pills, and she knew.

19

Huddled in a rain-soaked alleyway on a black, foggy evening, prostitutes offering him their services and his hands red and chapped from the cold, Peter wondered if he could handle war. John and Samuel told stories about mud that went to your armpits, sideways rain that never stopped, heat that would burn your skin clean off. For less than an hour he'd been standing alongside Rainbow Corner, feeling as abandoned as the deserted Red Cross club, and already his feet were soaked through, his freezing hands barely able to keep his collar clasped shut. This was meant to be exciting, but all Peter felt was cold and nerves.

A red door opened in an alley a few feet away. Peter hoped to see Stephen, but it was only a drunken couple sent running by the rain. Peter checked his watch. What time had Stephen gone in? It had to be at least half an hour ago. Twenty minutes, certainly. Maybe only fifteen but no fewer than that.

Michael talked only to Peter about the war, and his stories were very different from John and Samuel's tales of derring-do and amorous French girls – but John and Samuel hadn't been POWs. Michael said war wasn't about action, bravery or romance, but waiting – how his squad would march hours upon hours over frozen French soil, waiting to be shot at, then camp in their foxholes, mending their socks or rereading letters from home, waiting to be bombed. Michael said when the air was still, it was like you could see Death walking amongst the trees and barbed wire and you kept watching for him to turn and point his blackened finger at you. Michael said he still saw Death. He came for him in his dreams, chastising him for living when so many others had died. Peter wondered if Death wore a blue and yellow cap.

A girl in a turquoise dress hurried past him using a news-paper to shield her hair. She stopped on the opposite corner, and turned towards the building to light a cigarette. It was difficult to see her in the dim light and incoming fog, but the dress looked similar to the one Jessie wore on their date. She even wore her hair the same way. But what girl didn't have victory rolls nowadays? Peter stepped forward to get a better look. A private car drove past, splattering his trousers. It stopped in front of the girl and, after a moment's conversation, she climbed inside, discarding the wet newspaper on the pavement. He tried to catch another glimpse of her through the rear window when someone whistled.

It was Stephen, leaning in the open, red doorway. He lit a cigarette then beckoned Peter over.

'Do what I say, when I say it. All right?'

Peter watched the car drive off.

'Oi, ginger.'

'Right. Sorry.' Peter followed him into a dark, narrow hall. One exposed bulb dangled from the ceiling, illuminating cheap wallpaper that peeled at the creases and corners. A thin black carpet beneath his feet reeked of fag smoke, liquor and urine.

At the end of the hall was a little booth – a coat check where a woman whose peroxide-blonde hair and layers of pancaked make-up made her severe age more pronounced. Before her sat a small tin ashtray filled with a few soiled coins. She tapped the tray with a finger ringed in costume jewellery as they passed.

'Leave it, Marjorie,' Stephen said.

Peter's unease grew as Stephen led him up a maze of creaking wooden stairs. Unmarked doors surrounded them at every corner. Always know your exits, Michael said, but Peter could see nowhere out of here. 'Are you sure . . . ?'

'If ol' Bess was into gambling then these would be the people who'd know.'

Peter wanted to ask why Stephen couldn't ask for him, why he had to come at all. His cowardice must have been obvious. Stephen clapped a hand on his shoulder.

'You want the truth, aye? What if Mosley was lying to you? Don't want to be taken for a fool, do you?'

'Of course not.' It had happened too many times already.

'Of course not.' Stephen patted him on the back. Muffled music and conversation seeped into the hall from behind a black door. 'Now you don't owe these lads anything. So, you've nothing to worry about.'

Stephen showed him into a large, windowless room filled with crowded tables covered in cards, poker chips and drinks. Ladies in tight, brightly coloured dresses sat in the laps of men with wrinkled suits and loosened ties. A layer of smoke drifted up from their cigarettes and ashtrays, collecting at the nicotine-stained ceiling. A phonograph in the corner scratched out a Glenn Miller tune barely audible over the chatter and laughter of the punters. Stephen guided Peter to a makeshift bar at the back where a pockmarked barman served what looked to be homemade spirits.

'Matthew.' Stephen leaned against the counter. The barman nodded. Peter tried to act casual, but his arms felt clumsy and unnatural. He settled for standing beside Stephen, arms crossed.

224

'What now?' he asked.

'We wait.'

'For what?'

'Until the boss is ready to see us.'

'I thought that's what I was waiting outside for.'

'You were waiting outside till I could get you in. Now we wait for the boss.'

'But . . .'

'Have a drink. More nervous than a virgin in a brothel.' Stephen looked him up and down. 'Then again . . .'

'Beg pardon?'

'Have a drink.' Stephen nodded to the barman and a glass of liquor was placed before Peter. Tiny unidentifiable specks floated within the off-white liquid.

'Took my pain pills,' he lied.

Stephen shrugged and drank it himself. As they waited, Peter tried to relax. The gamblers seemed like normal-enough people, the kind who came to the Palladium for a show and needed a place to go after the pubs closed. He could imagine he was at the theatre now where he knew every aisle, every row, every exit. But the heat of the room was causing his wet clothes to steam and the smoke itched his eyes, clouding his vision. His mind grew foggy. The questions he wanted to ask about Bess – so perfectly formed when he woke this morning – now became jumbled, some disappearing completely.

After several minutes, he noticed people staring at him. Eyes would glance in his direction then dart away as the person shifted in his chair. It happened several times before Peter realised they weren't looking at him but at his companion. Stephen seemed unaware of the glances, playing nonchalantly with his lighter as they waited.

Peter's cluttered mind began to drift. There was something

about this smoky haze – so much like fog – and the way it clouded the dim electric lights, causing an indistinct glow. And Stephen, the way his brutish hands fiddled with the lighter . . .

A door slammed. Peter caught sight of it at the other end of the gambling hall as it bounced off the wall. A blonde woman in a red dress hurried out, still adjusting her undergarments. A short man with thinning, slicked-back hair, dressed in a white button-down shirt but no jacket or tie, appeared in the doorway, zipping up his trousers. He scanned the tables before resting his eyes on Stephen. He nodded and disappeared into the back room.

'Here we go.' Stephen slipped the lighter into his pocket. Peter followed closely as they navigated the mishmash of tables to reach what he now saw was an office.

Inside, the man leant back against his desk, lighting a cigarette. Stephen closed the door behind them.

'You must be Peter.' The man extended his hand. His skin was tough and smooth and cold. Wet from the condensation on his glass. It felt to Peter the way a shark's would.

'Yes, sir.'

'Angelo. Stephen says you work with him at the Palladium?'

'I used to.'

'Yes, Stephen told me about that, too. Good thing you still have that apprenticeship. You middle-class folk have it all sorted out. But we're not here to discuss social politics, are we?' Angelo moved slowly back and forth across the room, leaving a trail of cigarette ash in his wake. 'I'm told you're an acquaintance of dear Bess Haverford.'

'I am. Or, I was.'

'My wife took her life the same way. Women, eh? So, what is it you wanted to know? Stephen was a bit . . . fuzzy on those details.'

'Well . . . that is, I've been told Bess was a gambler, sir. Or fond of it.'

'Old girl owe you money? Is that it?'

'No. Nothing like that. Only, it was her niece that I was close to.'

'Didn't know she had any family.'

'She, well, see . . . thing is . . . I, that is . . .'

'I haven't got all night, Peter.'

'Right. Yes. I believe she may have sold her niece, to pay off her debts to you. Sir.'

Angelo stopped. 'I never said she owed me.'

'No. Of course not. Beg pardon. But, if she did owe money, to someone, how would, that is, would she have got in contact with the people that offered her the, well, deal? That is what I'm hoping to learn, you see. Sir.'

Angelo crossed his arms. 'Now, how would I know a thing like that?'

'Well, of course, I don't know that you do. But Stephen said . . . Perhaps if you knew other people who ran such establishments then perhaps they might know.'

'Hm. Yes, yes, I think I understand now. So you want to get in touch with these people in Wales, I think it is? Now, if I were privy to such information, how much would it be worth to you?'

'Worth, sir?'

'How much would you be willing to pay for it? What would you be willing to do?'

Peter's mouth went dry. 'Stephen didn't say—'

'Stephen is not in a position to negotiate on my behalf. Are you, Stephen? Now,' Angelo resumed pacing, 'I could ask you for money, but to be fair, I'm earning plenty from those punters out there. If it's all the same to you, Peter, I'd like to ask a favour of you. Would that be agreeable?'

'I suppose it would depend on what the favour was.'

'Ha! Smart boy. I like you. Yes, I like you. Well, let's see. Let's see what would be fair. Yes, I know.' He walked behind his desk and wrote on a piece of paper. 'Bess may or may not have owed me money, but there are others who certainly do.' He handed Peter the paper. It was an address in Blackfriars. 'There's a man there who owes me two hundred quid. You get me that money, I'll make sure you get your information.'

The note quivered in Peter's grip, fluttering like a moth's wings.

'What do you say?' Angelo held out his hand.

In war, Michael said, a man had to make sacrifices for others as well as himself. A real man could do that and anyone who couldn't should be shot for cowardice.

'Well?'

*

The address of the man's flat sat in his pocket. Peter needed to leave soon if he was to make good time, but there was one more thing he wanted to carry, something for luck. From inside his sock drawer, he pulled out the small case which had sat there for so long. It opened with a little click. The engagement ring glittered in the black velvet lining. He snapped the box shut and slipped it into his pocket. There was no more time for cowardice.

The bomb-damaged streets and long queues in Blackfriars were much the same as in any other part of London. Signs of slow rebuilding could be seen in the stacks of disused iron stretchers piled on the edges of pavements, waiting to fence in unfinished estates Peter was sure had waiting lists as long as his arm. Would Eliza want to live here? Or would she prefer the suburbs? Maybe Richmond or his own Shepperton?

Construction workers sat on the edge of the scaffolding, chewing on sarnies from tin pails, watching Peter as he walked past. What was he doing, they probably wondered, walking around down here in a suit and tie while they wore overalls and steel-tipped boots? Their voices fell from the scaffolding as they gossiped like housewives about the awkward boy in the ill-fitting clothes. He couldn't hear their exact words, but he knew they must be talking about him. He drew up his coat collar and continued on.

He had memorised the address and worked out directions using the A–Z, but his was a pre-war version. Some streets he needed were closed for repair, missing their signs or completely blocked by bomb debris. After circling Borough Tube station twice, he ducked into an off-licence for directions. He half expected the shopkeeper to raise an eyebrow when he heard the address, say, 'Oh, you're going to see him, are you?' The only response Peter received was a set of complicated instructions scribbled on the back of an old receipt. He felt the man's eyes on him as he left, but when he turned back, the shopkeeper was busy with a customer.

Despite the cool air, Peter's palms became sweaty and smudged the pencilled directions. The weather continued to turn the closer he came to the address, the darkening sky making the buildings loom taller and shadows stretch longer. All the walking emptied his stomach and made his mouth terribly dry. He debated making a quick stop at the next pub, but before he came across one, he stumbled upon the building.

A discarded newspaper drifted across his path and an air of abandonment permeated the entire street. He reread the address. This was the right place. It was a brown Victorian house now split into flats, the higher windows boarded up, smoke damage staining the bricks. Chunks torn out by shrapnel littered the façade.

The man might not be home, he told himself. He might not be home, then Peter could return to his flat and forget the whole ordeal, at least for today. He rang the buzzer then wiped his damp hands on his trousers. It was a few minutes before the door opened. A mole-like old woman with thick glasses stared up at him in silent regard. Peter's tongue stuck to the roof of his mouth.

'Afternoon, ma'am. I'm looking for Mr Cooper?'

The woman walked away, leaving the door open behind her. Peter was overwhelmed by the stench of cat urine as he entered. The mole stopped and pointed to a poorly painted door then toddled off down the hall to a kitchen. A chorus of meows increased in number and volume as the woman approached, barely silenced when she slammed the door behind her.

Peter knocked where she had pointed. Blue paint flecked his knuckles.

'Come in! Come in!'

Peter saw no one as he descended the steps. Stubs of lit candles sat on the floor, table and mantelpiece. A pile of rags on the bed rose to greet him.

'Sorry 'bout the light there, guv'nor. Bit short of coins for the meter. Now, lad, what can I do for yeh?' The man had a hump in his back which made him stoop low, a web of broken red veins on his nose and an unkempt beard which covered the lower half of his face. The rags he wore were of an old army uniform.

'Are you Mr Leslie Cooper?'

'Aye, that I am. Captain Leslie Cooper, retired. First cavalry. You in the cavalry, lad?'

230

'No, sir. I've never been on a horse.'

'Pah!' The man dismissed Peter with a wave of his hand. He pulled a dented flask from his pocket and took a swig while he waddled back to bed. The smoke stung Peter's eyes as they strained to see in the candlelight.

'Sir . . .'

'Never been on a horse. That's what's wrong with society today, I'll tell you. Men sitting behind desks, no getting dirt under their pretty nails. Wouldn't have been no war, I'll tell you what, if each man in England were forced onto a horse. That's the God's honest truth, that is.'

'Sir, Angelo . . .'

At the mention of the name, Cooper froze – one leg in bed, one out. He took another drink.

'Angelo says you owe him some money. I'm here . . . I'm here to collect it, sir.'

Cooper sat down, the flask dangling from his fingers. 'Go on and do it then,' he whispered, not meeting Peter's eye.

'All right. Well, I'll . . . if you show me where you keep your money, I can . . .'

'I don't have any money.'

'Then, how can I . . . ?'

'Don't play with me, son. I don't have the money. Angelo knows it, aye. Told him so meself only last week. So go on and do what yeh came here for. I won't fight yeh.'

Little tremors ran through Peter's body, breaking him into tiny pieces. 'No. No, I . . . I'm only here for the money.'

'There ain't no money, I told yeh. Now get on with it, else you'll be in as much trouble as meself.'

All he had to do was get the money. Pay back the debt. Then he could find Eliza. That was all he was asked to do. Cooper didn't understand.

231

'No. You have to have it. You have to. There has to be something, God damn it!' Peter searched through the man's things, tossing rubbish and clothes into the air. He had to make him understand. All he came for was the money. Only the money. It all came down to money. A soggy newspaper landed on a candle, extinguishing it with a small hiss. Peter stopped. The smoke in the room seemed heavier than before. His eyes watered. Cooper regarded him with pity.

Imagine that, Peter thought. He's the one about to die and he's pitying me.

No, no one was going to die.

If you don't do it now, his voice said, someone else will. Someone less sympathetic. Someone who will make it hurt.

Cooper waited, his eyes low and sunken like a dog's. A wise old dog who knew why his master had brought him alone to a quiet wood, too obedient to run even at the sight of a shotgun. The fool. He was an absolute fool.

'I won't,' Peter whispered.

'No? What got you here, boy? You ain't like his normal toughs. What's he got on you? What do you owe him?'

'Nothing. I owe him nothing.'

Cooper smiled. Half his teeth were gone. 'We all owe him something. Better to pay your debts now than wait for his reckoning.' He rose from the bed and hobbled towards Peter. 'Don't worry. Killing a man is easy. You won't ache too bad after.' Cooper exposed his neck, offered it as sacrifice.

'I can't.' Peter backed away. 'I can't. I won't!' He ran up the steps, knocking over candles.

On the street, the overcast day blinded him. He squinted against it and ran, not caring what road, which direction. He reached the edge of a bombsite and nearly tumbled in. There was Mosley's body – broken and bloody – resting at

232

the bottom. He blinked and it was gone. He blinked and it was Cooper.

He ran the other way. Buildings passed by in a blur. Voices shouted, at him, he didn't know. His leg sent pain up to his back and down through his calf, but he had to keep running – from the house, from Blackfriars, from his idiotic, foolish self.

Not war, not war, not war.

His feet pounded out the rhythm.

Not war, not war, not war.

War was noble, war had cause. This was not war. This was a fool's errand.

The river stopped him. He collapsed into the rail along the Thames path, let it support his weight. His face was damp, sweat mixed with tears. He watched the gentle pull of the tide as the drops gathered and fell from his face. Barely had he caught his breath when he heard a voice he could not ignore.

'Well, didn't think a little thing like that would be a problem for you. Not after what you did to Mosley.' Stephen smoked a cigarette, eyeing him with a cool detachment Peter had never seen before.

Except he had.

'I never agreed to murder anyone. Never. Especially not over two hundred pounds.'

They were walking alone down Kentish Town Road towards Camden Station on a dark night with only the orange sodium street lamps for company.

'So Eliza's not worth that, is she?'

'What is this, Stephen? What have you got me involved in?'

He remembered how the first blow hit his back and he fell to his stomach, his chin scraping against the pavement as another blow hit his head.

233

'Me? I've done nothing of the sort. You got yourself involved. I'm the one that told you to leave it, wasn't I?'

And how he vomited onto the pavement as the blood began to flow.

'For my own good,' he whispered. He remembered that the pipe was tossed onto the ground beside him, that it rolled into the gutter. 'You said it was for my own good.'

'Aye, I did.'

'When was that?'

'At the pub. After Purvis told you Eliza quit. Or don't you remember that either?' Stephen laughed.

He remembered rolling over, staring up at his attacker, and how the man whispered to him as he fastened a blue and yellow checked cap on his head.

'I remember,' Peter said.

'Good, 'cause you're in it now and you don't want to give Angelo bad news, do you? So let's go back to old Coop's and finish the thing, eh? Before anyone needs to know.' Stephen pulled a cap from his pocket. It was blue and yellow in a checked pattern. He slipped it on as he turned from the river.

Peter punched him in the back of the head and ran.

The Thames guided him. With the blood pounding in his ears, he could no longer hear Stephen but knew he was being pursued. He'd be safe on the other side of the river, that's what he told himself. If he reached the other side of the river, he'd be safe. He ran across Blackfriars Bridge, ignoring the burning in his chest and leg, not stopping until he slipped inside St Paul's. His hands shook terribly as he collapsed into a pew, and he shoved them into his coat.

Only then did he discover a new despair, for, somewhere along the riverside, the engagement ring had fallen from his pocket.

20

Eliza ran her fingers over the scratched image of her mother's face. Behind the damage caused by the broken frame, she could still see her mother's smile. No photograph had ever captured the way her eyes shone when she saw her children. And what horrible children they were. Spiteful, nasty little creatures that could do no right. Perhaps it would be different if she were here to guide them, but her goodness was lost when the incendiaries burned shrapnel into her skin. Eliza now saw why she could never be like Mother. There was not enough good within her. The thoughts she had towards Rebecca had always been there, contained in a small sack stitched the day her sister was born, hidden for years behind her heart. Now that sack was damaged, its contents free to poison and devour her.

She could still try to be the responsible older sister her mother and father expected her to be. She could try to rid herself of the coldness that lived within her.

Eliza kissed the photograph and tucked it into her pocket. There was hardly any room. Her coat was stuffed with hand-kerchiefs, extra underpants, fersolate, Mendahol and what was left of Rebecca's medication. In her handbag were Peter's unfinished scarf, two pairs of stockings and make-up. Her shopping basket held her undergarments, knitting needles and an extra headscarf. She dressed in layers with three pairs of pants and one blouse under her dungarees, legs covered in her newest stockings and her only pair of nylons on underneath. She felt bloated, heavy, but there was so much she would have to leave behind. Departing London, now escaping Thornecroft, she lost things important to her. If she had to leave somewhere else, would there be anything left of her at all?

Rebecca was not at breakfast. Eliza decided to let her sleep and snuck some bread and cheese into her shopping basket for later, feeling the cold block in her chest start to shrink. After breakfast, she checked she could carry no more and tried not to think about all that she had to leave behind. She would be able to replace it all, given time. But it would take so much money and so much time – even thinking on it made her want to forget the whole ordeal. She took a breath to steady herself. This was no time to think about the future. Any loss would be worth escaping Victoria.

She knocked on her sister's door.

'Rebecca? Dearie? Are you ready to go?'

No answer.

'Rebecca.' She knocked again. 'Rebecca, you must get up. We have to leave.'

Silence.

Rebecca's bed was empty.

Perhaps she had gone for a late breakfast after all? Eliza hurried back to the kitchen. It was empty. She went out into the vegetable garden and ran to the henhouse. Rebecca loved the hens. Surely she would be there. Eliza's body trembled as she peeked inside the wooden house and underneath its support stilts. Nothing.

Mr Drewry came across the lawn, leading the grey mare. 'Coming?' he asked.

'Have you seen my sister? This morning? Anywhere?'

'Hard to keep an eye on that little brat, innit?' He stroked the mare's neck, not meeting Eliza's eye. 'I'm leaving in a quarter of an hour, whether you're in this carriage or not.'

'We will be. Just . . . just wait.'

Eliza checked Mrs Pollard's office and the larder. Her bedroom and Rebecca's again. The bathroom. Rebecca was nowhere in their quarters. The quick beating of her heart caused the vein near her temple to pulse. Pressure tightened round her head like a vice.

'Rebecca! Rebecca, this is no time for games. You must come out now.'

Eliza stood in Abigale Hall, face flushed, skin clammy yet warm, not knowing which path to choose next. Rebecca could be anywhere, and the house was too big to search in its entirety now. Her skin itched, Thornecroft's ever-present dust worming its way into her pores. She rubbed her hands, trying to scrub it away.

'Rebecca!'

It started to rain. Water pinged off the glass dome like a thousand pins dropping to the tiled floor. Eliza felt each sharp sound prick her skin as if drawing blood.

'Rebecca, please!'

Her panic turned to anger. How dare she do this, now of all days? If Rebecca wanted to stay, Eliza could leave without her. She could have her own life. Her palms burned. She'd rubbed them raw. Eliza returned to their hall and grabbed her basket. She would do this. She would leave.

'I'm going,' she shouted. 'I'm going to town with Mr Drewry and you won't . . . you won't see me for quite a long time. This is your last chance, Rebecca Haverford.'

Nothing.

Eliza walked patiently to the entrance hall, expecting

Rebecca to come skipping towards her any moment. Rebecca always listened to her sister. When she reached the front door, she counted to ten, waited, then counted again.

Nothing.

'Goodbye, then.'

Nothing at all.

She joined Mr Drewry outside. The mare shook its head, trying to clear the rain from its eyes as the caretaker finished securing a roof to the carriage. Eliza climbed inside.

'Didn't find her?' he asked.

'She's not coming. Let's go.' Eliza gripped the basket tightly to keep from fiddling with her hands.

'Yes, ma'am.' He spat into the grass.

As the carriage moved forwards, she made no effort to look back.

They were over now, those days when Rebecca was her responsibility. Rebecca herself had given Eliza up. Why should Eliza fight to keep her? It was, after all, a responsibility she never fully accepted, that she had tried to give up before. The day they boarded the train at King's Cross, both of their luggage labels destined them for Hungerford. They were supposed to stay together, Mother said, no matter what happened. Yet, when the train arrived, there was a rush to get the children unloaded, and they became separated by the billeting officer as they were lined up at the station. One by one, families stepped forward to claim tired evacuees. The strongest and healthiest went first, Eliza amongst them.

As the Littletons herded her away from the throng of the unclaimed, they asked her if she travelled alone. Did she have any siblings, any cousins, that had been evacuated with her? Eliza looked over her shoulder to where Rebecca stood with the smaller children. Rebecca saw her and waved, and Eliza remembered how Rebecca had taken the last of her chocolate on the train without asking. As Rebecca called out her name, Eliza took Mrs Littleton's hand and whispered, 'No. I'm alone.'

At first she was frightened Mother would be angry, but as the weeks passed it was freeing to be an only child. The childless Littletons doted upon her, made her pretty frocks and delicious cakes. They even had a car and would sometimes take her for trips to the seaside. Several months passed before she saw Rebecca again. By then she was used to not sharing toys or treats, and to sleeping through the night without being woken by screams. She didn't care that Rebecca was thin and dirty, that she wore the same dress she had on the train. Rebecca Haverford was a distant cousin to the new Eliza Littleton, some girl Eliza saw on holidays but never need concern herself with.

*

Water dripped through the roof, wetting her dungarees. She shivered as the carriage approached Plentynunig. The white-washed houses appeared like ghosts on the unforgiving landscape, more of their life stolen each time another pit closed. Many people were out today, but even the market-day activity brought no cheer to the dour faces.

'Don't get lost,' Mr Drewry called as she joined the small crowd on the damp dirt road.

Eliza turned the first corner she came to and rested against a house. She removed her headscarf and dabbed it across her face, suddenly warm under all her layers of clothes. Was Rebecca warm at Thornecroft? Perhaps she had not slept in her room last night but found a hidden, cold corner in which to curl up and rest her head. She would wake, unaware of the hour or day and seek Eliza out only to find empty air and the truth that her selfish sister had abandoned her as she had in Hungerford.

No. She shook her head. No, Rebecca could keep track of the days and hours perfectly well. That had been hatred on Rebecca's face last night. She was happy about what she did, no matter how it hurt them. She was doing this to test Eliza, to see if Eliza would give in and save her yet again. Rebecca was sat by the warm kitchen fire, giggling to herself as she plotted how to next torment her sister.

No, Eliza would not fall victim to her again. She would escape to London then return with Peter to claim her. By then, Rebecca would be so grateful she would be unable to stop crying. She would make all sorts of promises to Eliza, tell Eliza she would be a good girl, never make any trouble again. They would begin a new life then, both of them. Eliza had learnt her lesson. Now it was Rebecca's turn.

She approached Ruth's house from the garden and knocked on the back door. There was no immediate answer. What if Ruth forgot about her? What if the market cart was already gone? What if . . . ?

'Where have you been?' The door opened and Ruth stepped out, wrapping a shawl round her shoulders.

'I'm sorry, I—'

'Where's Rebecca?'

'She's not here.'

'Then are you sure you want to . . . ?'

'Please, let's not speak about it. Where's the cart?'

'This way.' With a sad glance, Ruth led Eliza through the streets of Plentynunig, past housewives wringing out their clothes and crippled men leaning against hedgerows with ciga- rettes dangling from their lips, past children playing hopscotch in the dirt while little dogs nipped at their feet. Eliza had often seen Rebecca in Hungerford, playing hopscotch in the street with the poorer children as she passed by in the Littletons' car.

She had taught Rebecca hopscotch, that summer before the war, soon after they returned from Brighton. Yellow chalk, it was, drawn on the pavement, and the air smelled of hyacinths. Rebecca could not skip, so Eliza made up new rules to keep her happy. They had both been happy. Laughing and playing as Mother watched from the kitchen. Father returned from work, walking up the pavement with the sun setting behind him, the sky coloured in bright pinks and purples. They had all gone for ice cream – Father, too. All of them, a family.

Eliza's foot landed in a puddle, taking her away from that warm summer evening, back to this cold, drizzling day. She saw the large market cart up ahead, waiting for her. It was not horse-drawn, like she expected, but powered by a motorcar – the first she'd seen since leaving London. Its presence was unnatural on these streets, like something from the future come to the past. So fixated was she on it, she didn't hear Ruth speaking.

'I'm sorry?' Eliza asked.

'Do you have everything you need?' Ruth repeated.

In her mind, Eliza recited the list of items she had packed then thought of all the things left behind.

The truck's engine started.

She thought of Rebecca in Hungerford, sleeping outside in dirty clothes, forced to slaughter rabbits while Eliza gorged herself on carrot cake and custard.

A burst of black smoke puffed from the exhaust.

'Eliza, he has to leave. Are you ready?'

Nearby, the little dogs barked. Children laughed. Their mothers called them indoors.

But there was Peter in London, holding roses. West End lights and Big Ben's chimes. And Rebecca in Thornecroft's cold kitchen, hands in blood, with Mrs Pollard watching. Eating dinner with Mr Brownawell, Victoria waiting, and Eliza gone.

'Eliza, he . . .'

'Selfish,' she said.

She felt the temptation to abandon her responsibilities. A part of her, the cold part, wanted to jump into the lorry. Eliza backed away.

'I can't. I'm sorry. I can't.' She ran from the lorry and climbed back in the Thornecroft carriage, hiding her face from the sight of Ruth's house. In the distance, she heard the lorry sputter and pull away – the sound of civilisation leaving her behind.

*

She thought she would detest arriving through Thornecroft's twisted iron gates, seeing its ivy-covered façade. Instead it was as if she was now inoculated against any hate weaker than that she had for herself. She said nothing to Mr Drewry as she exited the carriage and thought nothing as she returned to her room. The presence of Mrs Pollard standing there, waiting for her in the hall with Mr Brownawell in his chair, should have startled her. She felt nothing.

'Went to the village, I see. Shopping?' Mrs Pollard looked into Eliza's mostly empty basket. 'It seems they didn't have what you were looking for. Next time, inform me when you're going out. I was hoping to speak with you this morning. It was about your sister.'

Guilt pierced the numbness that encased her.

'Yes. What about her?'

242

'I'm afraid I've had to send her away.'

Resentment, too, threatened to intrude. Rebecca had been permitted to leave?

'Away?' Eliza asked.

'Well, you know how sickly she's been.'

Rebecca vomiting. Eliza cleaning the crushed bromide tablets from the kitchen floor. 'Yes,' she said. 'Yes, I know.'

'Last night, I had the doctor come up from town to examine her.'

Eliza had heard no one arrive.

'Would you believe your poor sister has contracted polio?'

Her second cousin once had polio. Had he suffered stomach pains? She didn't think so.

'Yes, awfully contagious. So I'm afraid I had to send her away to be quarantined. Only until she recovers, of course. Oh, she did say she wanted you to have this while she was gone.' Mrs Pollard handed Eliza the Victoria doll. 'It looks like it's just us now.' She patted Mr Brownawell on the shoulder. He drooled on his shirt. 'Do let me know if you feel at all poorly.'

Mrs Pollard wheeled Mr Brownawell away, leaving Eliza alone with the doll, whose paraffin wax eyes, those Eliza so carefully created, had been scraped from its skull.

21

Eliza sat on the edge of Rebecca's bed, tipping the toy cat back and forth, trying to make its eyes open and close, but they had broken long ago. Rebecca was much too old for such toys. Eliza could not remember who had bought Rebecca this cat. Mother? Father? Perhaps Aunt Bess? Its half-open eyes caused her to shudder, reminding her of Father's eyes as he swung lifeless in the cellar.

The sky had been overcast that day. She had returned from shopping and began preparing dinner – Woolton pie – shortly before Rebecca arrived home from school in a foul mood, having got in trouble for pulling a girl's hair. As Eliza diced the cauliflower, she asked Rebecca to find Father. When she could not, Eliza decided he must have gone to the neighbour's for a cigar, as he sometimes did after work. Then came the crash from the cellar.

It was at that point her memories became fragmented, unconnected vignettes linked together by fear.

Rebecca running. A potato rolling across the kitchen counter. The broken jar of marrow liqueur, the syrupy brown liquid seeping into the dirt floor. The taut cord of the washing line. Rebecca staring, eyes fixed on his body as she counted his feet tap-tap-tapping against the shelves. The stool tipped on its side, the spreading liqueur inching towards its wooden legs. A look of fascination on Rebecca's face as the sweet, smoky scent of the spilt liqueur mingled with the sulphur of the wet coal in the cheap furnace, stinging Eliza's nose. His eyes bulging, face red and engorged. Shouting for the neighbours. The line of spittle dangling from swollen lips. His feet tapping. Rebecca watching them, still counting, counting for the first time. His bulging eyes unable to close. Telling Rebecca to come away. His feet tapping the shelves twenty-three times before she managed to drag Rebecca upstairs as the smell of the marrow liqueur fermented in her brain, etching itself a permanent place in her memory.

*

Eliza set the cat aside and searched the room. All of Rebecca's clothes were missing, as was her suitcase and those damn too-small shoes. Eliza didn't know what else to look for. Rebecca had so little. How did Eliza have so much to pack? So much to leave behind?

'We need to burn it.' Mrs Pollard stood in the doorway, hands clasped neatly at her waist, her thin figure draped in a plain brown dress. Her face was solemn, but her eyes hid a smile.

'Burn what?' Eliza looked away, too tempted to strike her.

'Everything in this room is contaminated by your sister's disease. Mr Drewry is building a bonfire on the east lawn. Take everything to him.' With a scuff of her boot on the carpet, she was gone.

Mrs Pollard was wrong. It wasn't Rebecca who was contaminated.

Eliza stripped the bed and gathered what little remained – Rebecca's hairbrush, a headscarf, the toy cat. The bottle with the surviving bromide tablets rattled in her pocket as she carried the items out through the kitchen. In the centre of the east lawn, Mr Drewry put a torch to a pyramid of sticks and kindling. He circled it, prodding the fire in various places as she approached. The stack was ablaze by the time she reached him.

He indicated the bundle in her arms. 'Leave it.'

'No. I'll do it.'

He looked for a moment as if he would argue, then appeared to think better of it. 'Maybe . . .' He spat into the fire, his voice changing to the one she heard in the carriage house. 'Maybe she'll recover,' he muttered then threw the torch into the bonfire and walked away.

Eliza laid everything on the ground as the increasing heat seared her skin. For the first time in months, she began to feel warm. One by one, she tossed items into the flames, waiting until each was sufficiently burned before adding another.

The fire suffocated her. Her lungs filled with its smoke. She breathed it in and held it. This was what Mother experienced, she thought. This is how she died. Eliza coughed, feeling the smoke coiling in her lungs. She thought it might choke her. Father choked, by wrapping that washing line around his neck. She put a hand to her throat to ease the fresh soreness there.

Rebecca had choked, too, choked that little boy in her school. His face went dark and red before the teacher separated them. Aunt Bess was so embarrassed. A schoolyard scrap, that was what she tried to pass it off as, but they both saw the bruises on the boy's neck, the fear in his eyes, the lack of remorse on Rebecca's face. Why, Eliza asked. Why had she done such a thing? There was never any answer. Rebecca hadn't even known the boy. Aunt Bess rang the doctor that evening. They were on a train to Portsmouth the next day.

Eliza stared into the bonfire, Rebecca's plastic cat in her limp hands, and listened to the crackle of the wood.

Rebecca was her responsibility, Father said so in his letter, that very last letter of all, which Eliza found crumpled in the bottom of his drawer the day she packed away his clothes. The paper was so cheap and thin it nearly dissolved in her hands as she smoothed it out on his writing desk. The ink was blotted and smudged, obscuring the meaning of sentences that made little sense to start with. The father so elegant with his words when describing a painting, whose hand was so neat in the inscriptions on the books he gave his daughters, that father was gone, replaced with an incoherent madman. Or maybe she simply had not understood. Maybe his words were meant for an adult's eyes. Aunt Bess perhaps, but Eliza never showed it to her. She never threw it away either. She folded it into quarters and stuffed it into the hollow leg of Aunt Bess's bed, as if by hiding it there she could keep him close, and remember the only words which made sense.

Eliza is responsible for Rebecca. Eliza, you are responsible for Rebecca. You are responsible.

The cat looked at her with its half-open eyes as Victoria's voice whispered in her ear, *You are responsible.* Eliza never took her responsibility seriously, never understood why she should. When it came time to truly help her little sister, she was unable to for she did not know how. Instead, she pretended. Played the role of the loving sibling.

She tossed the cat into the flames. It remained whole for a moment. Then the heat took hold, melting the hard plastic shell. The shape of it dripped away as its ears shrank into white liquid stubs. The wax-like plastic covered its eyes. At last it could sleep, she thought, feeling a cold breeze caress her back. Only one item remained. Eliza pulled out the pill bottle and ran her thumb over Rebecca's name. Never could she do what Father wanted. Eliza threw the bottle in and watched it burn.

*

The veg was tasteless and overcooked. She mashed it in her mouth, pressing it into a soft ball with her tongue before swallowing the lump. However, she did not complain, as she did not deserve decent food.

With the table to herself, she sat facing the windows, watching the bonfire burn itself out. The first time she had ever eaten dinner alone was the day Aunt Bess took Rebecca to Portsmouth, but it had not been this quiet. It was as if a heavy curtain had descended upon Thornecroft, sequestering it from the world outside, sheltering its inhabitants from each other. No, London was never like this. Even tucked in their bed, a cab would sound its horn or a night bus would rattle past, hitting that pothole. That *thunk thunk* – the noise which so annoyed her – Eliza's world now felt empty without it. Not even the fire outside, now faded to a mere red glow, made a sound.

She looked down at her food. The veg was smashed into one gobbet and the mutton was cold. The fat separated from the gravy, congealing on top of the brown meat like a layer of wallpaper paste. She went out to the compost pile and scraped the plate clean.

A shadow passed before the bonfire's dimming embers. Eliza first thought it was Mr Drewry coming to check on the flames. As she looked closer, she caught a glimpse of an orange-hued ball and a trail of white heading round the back of the house. She dropped her plate and followed.

The high stone wall which protected the overgrown garden was missing a chunk in its side, as if an artillery shell had pounded through its edifice. More bricks succumbed to the harsh Welsh weather, leaving a hole large enough to climb through. Eliza glanced through the shrubberies but saw nothing save the disused fountain.

The squeak of a door opening broke the quiet like a gunshot. Eliza shrank behind a hedge and waited for the silence to reassert itself before risking a closer look. Past the main garden doors, she spotted a raised sash. It was a window, then, that had opened. Seeing no one, she crept closer and peered through it into an unfamiliar room. It was too dark to make out any details except for the dark, square shape in the centre.

Eliza climbed through a window and hurried to the object – her copy of *Mrs Miniver*. Tucked in the front cover, marking the faded table of contents, was a handkerchief. She recognised the embroidered *R* immediately. There was no reason Rebecca should have been here. The place was completely bare, like a prison cell. She tried the door but found it locked. Lowering herself, she peeked through the keyhole, but the hall on the other side was too dark.

Eliza turned back to the window and stifled a shout.

There she stood outside, her back to the room.

'Victoria?'

The woman lowered her head in recognition, shame, or both. Eliza held out Rebecca's handkerchief.

'You took her, didn't you? Why? She's only a child. Why not me? You could've taken me.'

Victoria moved away, her long dress sliding against the ground.

'There must be a way to get her back. Tell me how to get her back!'

A key turned in the door.

'What in God's name are you doing in here?' Mrs Pollard

grabbed her by the arm, digging her sharp nails into Eliza's skin. 'Answer me!' The lantern dangled dangerously over Eliza's head.

'There was a bird.' It was the first thing she could think of.

'A bird.'

'Yes, ma'am. I was passing by outside and saw it in the room.'

'And what kind of a bird was it?'

'I'm not certain. A crow?'

'You saw a crow.'

'Yes, ma'am.'

'And how would a crow get into a locked room?'

'The window was open.'

Mrs Pollard's eyes darted to the window, searching. Eliza too, looked, but Victoria had vanished.

'For how long?' She shook Eliza. 'For how long was it open?'

'I don't know!'

'And where is this bird now?'

'I don't know. I scared it off.'

'You don't know much, do you, Miss Haverford?' When she spoke, her voice came as a soft hiss. 'When you first arrived, I thought your sister was the imbecile. Now . . .' She tilted her head from side to side, examining Eliza's face. 'Now, I rather think it's you. Someone should keep an eye on such unfortunate souls. Simpering idiots who cannot keep their hands off other people's property.' She reached for the book, but Eliza pulled it away.

'This is mine. I brought it from London.'

'Is it now?' she sneered. 'Well, I suppose you'll need something to occupy your time.' Mrs Pollard dug her nails deeper into Eliza's arm as she dragged her back to her bedroom.

'This is really unfair to me, you know. I have responsibilities that don't involve keeping an eye on snooping, ungrateful housemaids. I do deserve time to myself, which I can't have when I'm wasting hours chasing you around this house.'

Tossed inside her room, Eliza listened as the door was locked.

'I'll release you in the morning, once you've had time to think about what you've done.'

She ran to the window, but it was nailed shut from the outside. She pounded on the door. 'Let me out! You can't keep me prisoner here. Let me out!'

The door refused to give. Eliza banged her fists even harder.

'I'll get her back! From this house, from Victoria. Do you hear me? She is my sister and I will take her back!' She shouted until her voice grew hoarse and night fully fell.

Eliza turned her back on the door and slid to the floor. Her knuckles were covered in scratches. On her arm, half-moon punctures from Mrs Pollard's fingernails welled with blood. She dabbed at them with Rebecca's handkerchief until the bleeding stopped.

*

Victoria, Pip and Rebecca held hands and surrounded her, singing 'Ring a Ring a Roses'. Their eyes were gouged out, the empty sockets bleeding, but they smiled and laughed as the blood stained their white dresses.

'Give her back to me,' Eliza demanded. They kept singing. 'How do I get her back? Tell me! What must I do?'

Faster and faster they spun, their faces blurring together until they became one and their smile stretched like a snake's and their mouth spoke in Mrs Pollard's voice: 'You must be responsible. You must break the curse.'

251

A thin, clawed arm reached out from the blur and grabbed her by the hair, pulling her into the vortex. Eliza felt her body being torn apart, her soul consumed, until she woke on the cold floor, sweat plastering her dungarees to her skin as she failed to dislodge the scream in her throat. She could feel Victoria watching her from somewhere in the darkness.

Something clattered to the floor in the room next door – Mrs Pollard's room. Eliza listened to her footsteps as the housekeeper retrieved the object. Thoughts of Victoria still occupied her head as she rubbed at the fingernail scratches on her arm. Victoria, Pip, the other housemaids, now Rebecca. Every woman seemed to vanish from Thornecroft, all except one.

'What deal did you make with her?' Eliza asked Mrs Pollard's footsteps. 'Why doesn't Victoria take you?'

22

Peter pulled on a cigarette to stave off his hunger. Three-quarters of an hour and the queue had not moved. For forty-five minutes he had stood by this same lamppost, staring at those same scratches in the paint while either side of him women gossiped about the latest fashions, the new looks ladies were wearing in Paris. But he had no choice. He had eaten the fruit cake, opened the pickled cabbage and reused the same teabag four times. This was his last cigarette.

The queue moved one step forward. Peter kept his collar turned up and his cap pulled down. Although the grey sky had held off so far, there was nowhere to go if it did rain. A solid concrete building stood on his left. The pavement to his right was a constant flow of mothers and prams, old ladies and shopping trolleys. Little children clutching wooden toys stared at him as they passed, their small faces blank and innocent. Michael said the Germans used children as spies. You'd see all these raggedy little urchins crawling about in the rubble and offer them a bit of your ration, then suddenly a German troop would know your position or a bomb would go off beside you.

Another step forward. The lamppost was beside him now, not before him. Progress.

No one knew his face. London was anonymous like that. It was easy to hide in such a mass of people. Especially queues. A queue was probably the safest place in all of London. There were so many of them and all the people standing there looked the same. It was easy to hide in a queue. Easy to stay anonymous. Easy to stay safe.

He flicked ash onto the pavement. How long till he would move past that dusting of ash? Till it, like the lamppost, would be behind him?

A pair of turquoise heels stepped on the ash.

'Got a light?' a woman asked.

'Oh. Yes, of course.' Peter fumbled for the lighter. It fell from his pocket. As he bent down to retrieve it, the woman did the same. 'I'm sorry, I . . . Jessie?'

She wore a turquoise dress to match her shoes and a pillbox hat with full veil which shielded her face. They rose slowly, both holding the lighter. Peter let go.

'Cheers.' She lit her cigarette, her fingernail polish chipped and uneven. 'Are you still looking for Eliza?'

Peter nodded.

'We can't talk here.' She walked away down the road.

The queue behind him moved forward as Peter stepped out. Jessie's high-heeled shoes knocked against the pavement, echoing off the surrounding buildings. Peter remembered their date – how she ran ahead, trying to be flirtatious, when all she did was give him a headache from the sound of her shoes. There was no running today. Jessie wobbled once or twice, as if she could barely stand. The stockings decorating her legs were merely stains of gravy browning and eyebrow pencil, and the smell of stew wafted from her, making Peter's empty stomach churn.

This was a trap. It could only be a trap, but she mentioned Eliza and, like a starving dog, he couldn't resist following the scent. He kept alert, glancing either side for the ambush, the way Michael had taught him. His mind shouted at him to turn away, to run, that every step with Jessie down narrower and ever more deserted streets was a step towards death.

I know, announced her heels. *I know, I know, I know.*

What happened to Eliza, they left unspoken, but Peter could hear it. They stopped outside an old church. Jessie nodded for him to enter. Through the open door, all he could see was darkness, an open mouth wanting to swallow him whole.

'So they're waiting in there to kill me?' he said.

'No one wants to kill you, Peter.' She adjusted the strap on her handbag.

'I don't believe you.'

'Then why did you follow me?'

'Eliza.' The mention of her name could get Peter to follow anywhere. Jessie knew this. She had to. 'Do you know where she is?'

'Not exactly.'

Peter walked away. He wouldn't be lured into a friendly trap, not again. Not ever again. He heard Jessie hurry after him, those damn wooden heels clacking on the cobblestones like gunfire.

'Peter, wait.'

'If you have nothing to tell me . . .'

'That's not what I said.' She ran in front of him, blocking his path the way the veil blocked her face. They both were trapped. 'I need you to listen. Come and sit with me.'

Peter looked back at the darkened church. How cold such a place would be. So able to absorb a man's screams, even in the daytime. Jessie's shadowed face held a trace of that gloom.

'Not there,' he said. Across the road was a dismal tea house. He led her inside.

Once they were seated, Jessie pulled up her veil. Cheap make-up poorly concealed a bruise on her cheek.

'Where did you get that?' he asked.

Jessie took out her compact and refreshed the black-purple skin. 'Same place as Bess. Our friend Stephen.' The compact snapped shut.

'He killed her.'

'I couldn't say.' Jessie glanced at the counter, trying to catch the waitress's eye as she removed her lace gloves finger by finger. Turquoise used to bring out the colour of her eyes. Their shine had faded as much as her clothes.

They remained silent until the waitress brought them dry biscuits and tannin-stained cups. The tea was no more than beige water, but Peter, needing something in his stomach, drank quickly.

'I'm listening,' he said.

Jessie ignored her tea and played with her food. 'After I started work at the Palladium, Dad kept taking my pay. Said he needed it for family expenses. Mum didn't agree but kept her mouth shut like she was told. I got sick of it. It was my money. I should be able to do what I like with it. So when I saw an advert in the paper – a girl looking for a roommate – I moved out. And it was alright. For a while.'

Across the road, an old man wearing an old Great War uniform limped out of the church. Was Cooper still alive? Peter tasted blood. He finished his cup and poured another from the pot. The steam from Jessie's cup faded as the tea cooled.

'Is that when you started gambling?'

Jessie broke a biscuit, pressing her painted nails into the crumbs. 'Not like we have anything else to spend it on, is it? I paid my rent, fed myself. Why not have a little pleasure?'

'And then you started losing.'

'Kept thinking my luck would change. Didn't realise it already had. Stephen said Angelo would forget my debts if I did a little work for him. Lucky me, eh? Two jobs when all these girls can't find one. Thought all I had to do was work at the club for him, smile at the gents, serve a few drinks. That sort of thing.'

The biscuit was dust. Jessie brushed off her fingers, finished her cigarette and pulled another from her handbag.

'Then Angelo said I needed to earn money, to make up for what he lost. But there's only one skill I have to sell, and it ain't my needlework.'

Peter choked on the tea. Sell. Like Bess sold . . .

He set down his cup. 'Eliza's in Wales. She's working as a housemaid in Wales.'

'They said you knew that. They said . . .' Jessie looked out of the window towards the church then quickly down at her lap. 'They said a lot of things.'

Peter reached for her hand. Jessie latched onto his touch. The crumbs stuck to her fingers scraped against his skin.

'Peter, there are rumours Angelo . . .'

The church bells tolled a mournful chime. Jessie released him and lit her cigarette. Her hands shook.

'Never mind. That's not why I'm here.'

'Then why are you?'

'To settle my debts.' She checked her watch.

'What rumours?' He reached for her hand again, but she moved it under the table. 'Jessie?'

'I want to go home, Peter. To my mum and dad. I don't want to do this any more.'

'You don't have to. What rumours, Jessie? What is he doing?'

257

A tear ran down her cheek, taking her mascara with it. Peter handed her his handkerchief. The tears made her eyes glisten, reminding him of the Jessie he used to know.

'They say Angelo keeps an eye out for . . . girls that have a certain look. For a special client.'

'Pollard?'

'I don't know the name, or what happens to them. But whoever it is pays Angelo a nice fee for finding them.'

'So he can get in touch with Eliza. Or whoever took her.'

Michael said there was a certain thrill that came with going on an offensive, a lightness in the chest coupled with a hardening of the soul. Eliza wasn't lost. He wasn't a failure.

Jessie tossed the handkerchief at his chest. 'Peter, why can't you leave it alone? Haven't you learnt yet? The house always wins. But if you walk away now, it might let you live. Just walk away. Now.'

'Don't cause trouble? Is that what you're saying? Let those in power do what they will? I thought the Germans never invaded.'

'I'm trying to help you.' She flicked ash into her teacup. 'But you men. Always making this about the war. Always wanting a fight. Well, I'll tell you what, Peter Lamb, I've spent my life fighting – my parents, my bosses, myself. And where has it got me? You want to see the other bruises? Pay a few quid and I'll even let you touch 'em. Fine. You keep fighting, if you like, but they'll find a way to bring you down. That I can guarantee.'

She extinguished her cigarette into her biscuit crumbs and grabbed her handbag. She reached for his lighter, too, but Peter put his hand over it before she could take it.

'Don't pretend Eliza wasn't your friend,' he said. 'You were going to tell her, weren't you? That Saturday after she

258

disappeared. Ask her for help. Look, I'm sorry for what's happened to you. For what Stephen did. But if I leave it alone, it means giving up on the woman I love. I'd give my life for her.' He pushed the lighter towards her. Jessie hesitated then tossed it into her handbag.

'No one's life is worth another's.' She glanced at the church then pulled down her veil. 'But if that's how you feel . . . let's go out the back.'

*

The filth of the club was clearer in the daytime. Black stains from coal dust and car exhaust plastered the red door, the dried vomit on the entrance hall carpet unmistakable. Peter's shoes stuck to the wooden stairs, and he could smell the heavy dust collected on the wall sconces. This place was not meant to be seen in the light.

He followed Jessie up to Angelo's office, keeping an eye out while she unlocked the door with her hairpin. He didn't like the quiet. London should never be this quiet. Quiet in London meant something was wrong. Jessie struggled with the lock. He wanted to slap the pin from her hands and try it himself, but his were shaking too badly.

The door clicked open. Peter rushed in ahead of her. The light switch didn't work, and quickly he drew back the curtains. Together, they searched the desk.

'He must have an address book,' Peter said as they rifled through the drawers.

'He is an organised man. Likes things a very particular way.'

Downstairs, a door closed. Footsteps travelled up the staircase. Peter and Jessie froze.

'You told them I'd be here.'

'No, Peter. I . . .'

Someone entered the gambling hall. Peter crept to the office door, listening. No one approached the office. Whoever it was might leave on his own time. He and Jessie would have to wait. There was no other way out.

A heavy thump sounded behind him. Jessie stood in shock by the overturned desk chair. The footsteps hurried towards the office and the door swung open.

The barman shook off his surprise and lunged for Peter. Peter dodged the first blow but caught the second on the chin and went sprawling to the floor. He rolled away from the barman's foot, but a second kick landed on his ribs. His breath rushed out of him. On the third kick, he caught the foot in his hands and shoved the barman back. Peter crawled to his knees but was grabbed by the shirt collar and hauled to his feet, the man's fist primed and ready to strike.

A shower of glass came down over the barman's head. He lost consciousness as he fell to the floor, blood already seeping from a gash in his head. Jessie stood behind him, holding the remnants of Angelo's desk lamp. She dropped it then grabbed a small leather-bound book from the desktop and tossed it to Peter – an address book.

'Let's go,' she said. He raced after her out of the building and into the alley. 'Don't go straight home,' she said, pushing Peter away. 'And don't come looking for me.'

'Jessie . . .'

'Go!' She ran off into the crowds of Shaftesbury Avenue before he could thank her.

*

Though it was hours after the assault at the club, Peter remained dazed as he exited Earl's Court station. The address book was tucked safely in his jacket pocket, but he hadn't looked up Pollard, afraid that if he opened the book, it would somehow signal his whereabouts to Stephen and Angelo. Jessie had not sought him out in the hours that followed. With no way to contact her, he could only hope she was somewhere safe. He debated writing to Mrs Rolston, but thought the truth could be more devastating than her uncertainty. Jessie would tell her parents in her own time.

The bruise on his chin garnered him unwanted attention from weary glances as he walked home. Though it was only early evening, he was exhausted. He still hadn't found time for a proper meal. So when he spotted the grey smoke billowing into the sky, he thought he was imagining things. Then he noticed other people pointing at the rising ash. As he walked more quickly towards his flat, he drew closer to the smoke. He wanted to deny it, wanted to hold on to the hope of a different possibility, but as he reached the fire brigade's barricades, he was forced to accept the truth.

His building was in flames. Fire shot out of the windows as water hoses battled to keep it from spreading. His landlady stood to the side, gaping at the destruction while her little dog barked in her arms. Nearby, a body covered in a white sheet was being loaded into an ambulance. A pair of turquoise high-heels stuck out of the bottom.

Stephen stood across the street. He tipped his checked cap to Peter then slipped away as another body was carried from the building.

23

Eliza sat at the table watching her porridge run off her spoon the way the rain ran down the glass. Her eyes felt swollen and sore. She wouldn't touch them for fear of itching them raw. One of these nights, she needed to get some decent sleep.

Mrs Pollard mashed up fruits for Mr Brownawell's breakfast. The squelching they made reminded her of the butchered sheep's carcass. Eliza lost her appetite and took her bowl to the sink.

'Has there been any news concerning Rebecca?'

'I'll be informed if she dies.'

'Is there an address so I could send her a letter?'

'If you wish to write to her, I'll post it for you.'

The bowl threatened to break in her grip. 'I would send it myself if only you gave me the address.'

'If you're so keen to write to family, why don't you send a letter to your dear aunt? I'm sure she's missing you terribly.' There was laughter hiding in Mrs Pollard's voice, like a background conversation on a crossed telephone line. Eliza dropped her bowl in the sink, enjoying the displeasure on Mrs Pollard's face as it clattered against the porcelain.

'I've heard that several of the children from town were sent to the hospital in Swansea. I'm sure someone in the village has the address. Or even the 'phone number.'

'Why don't I make it easy for you?' She motioned for Eliza to enter the office. The trapdoor was slightly ajar. Mrs Pollard slammed her foot down, closing it properly, then continued to her desk. She opened a small tin box full of index cards, flipping through it until her fingers stopped and drew one card from the stack.

Cefn Coed Hospital

Cockett

Swansea, SA2

'Children love receiving post, don't they? It's only when we're adults that we fear the day the letters stop.' She stared at the card, rubbing her finger along its edge.

'And what day did your letters stop?'

Mrs Pollard thrust the card forward. 'Write to her all you like, Miss Haverford. But do remember there is a paper shortage.'

Back in the kitchen, Mrs Pollard finished preparing Mr Brownawell's breakfast tray, and left Eliza alone. It took Mr Brownawell approximately thirty to forty-five minutes to finish breakfast, depending on his mood, which gave Eliza plenty of time. When she was certain Mrs Pollard had left the east wing, Eliza hurried into the hall and tried the door to Mrs Pollard's room. It was locked. She peeked through the keyhole, though she could see little. There was, however, a window.

Eliza returned to the kitchen, slipped on the oversize raincoat and wellies Mrs Pollard left by the door, and waded through the mud to the window. The rain made the sash slick and Eliza's fingers kept slipping as she struggled to get a good hold. Once she managed to draw up the window, she crawled through the opening then sat on the sill, removing the wellies and setting them outside. If Mrs Pollard noticed tracks of mud across her room, Eliza would have more to worry about than wet stockings. She felt no shame as her feet slipped quietly to the floor. Mrs Pollard had stolen her privacy; Eliza was only returning the favour.

The room was the same length as Eliza's but about a foot or so wider. The bed was small with a wooden frame, plain headboard and brown top sheet. The single nightstand had no drawer and held only an alarm clock, oil lamp and two books. Out of habit, Eliza examined the titles. One was a book on archaeology. The other's name had faded from the spine. Eliza opened the cover page, but the title had been scratched out. *Useless* was scribbled underneath the censored title. At the bottom, in a different hand, someone had written *Property of Thornecroft Reading Room*. Footsteps sounded above her. Eliza returned the books and continued searching. The floor underneath the bed was empty and spotlessly clean. Nothing hung on the bare and yellowed walls. The electric lamp awkwardly installed in the ceiling was the only item gathering dust. The final piece of furniture was an immense Victorian wardrobe too big for the small room.

That's where you are, she thought, approaching it with caution. There was a noise from the hall. Eliza paused, her mind racing through acceptable excuses should Mrs Pollard find her. There were none. She listened, but heard nothing more. Nothing but an old house sinking into its pains.

Eliza opened the wardrobe doors one at a time. All of Mrs Pollard's black and brown dresses were neatly hung, her shoes aligned in a strict row. She flipped through the clothes.

'You must have something,' she whispered.

On the floor sat a sewing box. Eliza unlatched the lid and sorted through the items. Needles, thread, scraps of fabric in assorted colours. At the bottom was a small brown bottle, similar to the one Mrs Pollard kept on her person. She unscrewed the lid and sniffed – the same strong smell as the syrup given to Rebecca. Eliza returned the bottle and sewing box then searched the top shelf where the undergarments and night things were stacked and folded. Though she wanted to search behind them, she was too short to reach all the way back. Instead, she ran her hand along the front of the shelf.

'You must have been a person once.'

Her fingers fell on a key.

She turned it over in her hand, trying to determine to what it belonged. There was a keyhole on the wardrobe, but the one she held was much too large. Eliza searched the room again but found nothing else that would require unlocking. Of course Mrs Pollard would have nothing here. She probably knew Eliza would sneak in as soon as she had the chance.

Eliza was closing the wardrobe when something caught her eye – a slip of paper stuck inside the frame near the bottom. She tugged it free.

It was a photograph of a young girl, aged six or seven, with familiar dark eyes and distinctive sharp cheekbones, holding the hand of a beautiful Indian woman. Eliza ran her fingers over the dust coating it and turned it over. The words 'Georgina and nanny' were written on the back of the photograph. This nanny, she must have been important to the family if they chose to photograph her, she thought. Eliza stuffed the photo and key into her pocket.

There was only one other place Mrs Pollard kept any of her belongings. Eliza climbed back out of the window, her stockings landing in the thick mud. The wellies were filled with water and her feet were soaked through as she sloshed into the kitchen. She returned the coat to the hook and went quickly to change her stockings before returning to the quiet kitchen. Still no sign of Mrs Pollard. Eliza snuck into the office. A multitude of locks adorned Mrs Pollard's desk, but the key belonged to none. As she stepped back, her foot bumped against the iron ring of the trapdoor.

Eliza had been everywhere on the ground floor of Thornecroft. Everywhere except that cellar. She hadn't been in any cellar since Father's death. Since she ran with Rebecca's hand in hers. He wouldn't be down there, of course he wouldn't. There would be no body, no marrow liqueur, no tapping of feet. Yet no matter how much she called herself a coward, she couldn't bring herself to reach for the handle.

A voice in the hall made the decision for her. Eliza hurried into the kitchen, pretending to clean up her uneaten breakfast. As footsteps approached, Eliza realised it was not one voice but two. Mrs Pollard and another woman. Her heart leapt for Rebecca but quickly extinguished its excitement. Rebecca was still a child.

The kitchen door swung open with a violent lurch.

'Ah. There you are,' Mrs Pollard said. 'Well, Miss Haverford, you'll be happy to hear your sister's absence will not lead to your solitude. Someone else is apparently eager for the job.'

She yanked Ruth into the room. Ruth refused to meet Eliza's eye.

'I would give you time to get to know one another, but I have it on good authority you already do. Miss Haverford, go see to the veranda. Mr Drewry says the doors are leaking again. Mrs Owen, you'll be so kind as to stay here with me.'

Eliza scurried out of the kitchen. Before she could take another glance at Ruth, Mrs Pollard slammed the door in her face.

*

She stood in the doorway, the mice scampering around her feet, drawing her deeper into the room.

You know what you must do, said Rebecca.

It's him keeping us here, not her, Pip added, her smile obscured by the blood trickling down from her nose.

It's him, Rebecca agreed.

It's him, Pip said.

It's him ... It's him ... It's him, they repeated back and forth, speaking in time to their feet moving through the empty air as their bodies swung from the meat hooks in the larder. Eliza wanted to leave, but the door had vanished, a grey brick wall in its place. She ran her hands over it, unable to find an escape.

It's him ... It's him ... It's him ... A high voice followed by a low.

There must have been a way out because more mice had found their way in, and they were crawling up Rebecca and Pip's legs to their faces, where the first few had begun to nibble at the soft whites of their eyes.

Eliza shot up in bed, gasping. Breath came to her in shallow gulps, the lack of air keeping her from screaming. When she first heard the gentle tapping at her door, she shrunk in the bed, fearful of the mice, but then she heard the voice.

'Eliza, are you awake?'

She recognised immediately the soft, Irish accent and hurried to open the door.

'Ruth!' She spoke louder than intended. Ruth pressed a finger to her lips and nodded to Mrs Pollard's door. With a single candle to light their way, Eliza and Ruth crept down the hall to the kitchen, quietly closing the door behind them.

Though the nightmare still clung to her, the images of Rebecca and Pip's bodies visible every time she blinked, she felt minor relief in Ruth's presence.

'I've wanted to speak with you all day,' Eliza panted, still recovering her breath.

'I don't think Pollard wants us alone together at all,' Ruth said.

The house creaked. A footstep? Eliza couldn't tell. Ruth took her hand and led her deeper into the kitchen, and into the larder. Eliza wanted to protest but couldn't find her voice. Instead, her body trembled. She pretended it was from the cold, and avoided glancing at the wall where the too-familiar meat hooks were embedded.

'We must be quick,' Ruth said, closing the door behind them. 'If she finds us, she'll do worse than snatch me from my home.'

'Is that what she did?'

'She somehow got word that I tried to help you leave. Berwin, I suppose. Yesterday, everyone in the village whom I sewed for, they all said they no longer had need of my services. The money I'd saved . . .' Anger brought her pause. 'It's all gone missing. And who should turn up at my door? Mrs Pollard. She practically kidnapped me and brought me here.'

'You couldn't have run? Your friend in Abergwili . . .'

'Aye, but . . .' Her anger left her with a sigh. 'When I saw her at my door . . . I heard Rebecca was gone, I felt responsible for not doing more to help you both.'

With those words, Eliza turned away. Though her eyes remained averted from the walls, the smell of raw meat began to sting her nose.

'We're not your responsibility,' she said. Outside, heavy rain pounded on the manor, muffling all other sounds.

'You are now. And if I'm stuck here, too, I might as well be useful to you.' Within the rain, they thought they heard another sound. Another footstep? A cough? Ruth spoke with more urgency. 'Word is Rebecca fell ill like Pip. What were her symptoms?'

The smell of the meat continued to assault her. Eliza could almost feel the fresh blood upon her. She absentmindedly began rubbing her hands together.

'I don't know. She was barely speaking to me these past few days.' Eliza remembered the hatred on Rebecca's face as she stamped her foot, crushing the tablets.

'Since she beat Kasey.'

'How did you . . . ?'

'Was she prone to violent outbursts?'

'No. I don't know. Did you ask Pip all those questions?' Eliza turned away. She appreciated Ruth's desire to help, but not this interrogation. Rebecca's history was a family matter.

'Aye. But she swore it were only the dust making her ill. The dust and . . .' She ran a hand across her face.

'Victoria?'

Ruth ignored her question. 'What did Mrs Pollard say happened?'

The smell was beginning to make her sick. Eliza tried to distract herself and toyed with a tin of tongue on the counter. 'That Rebecca caught polio and had to be sent away for quarantine.'

'Polio? But I thought . . . That could be the truth.'

'You trust Mrs Pollard to say anything that's true? If she's right about Rebecca, why was she wrong about Pip?'

'Keep your voice down. Of course I don't trust that woman. It's only . . .' Ruth sighed. 'There has been a small outbreak of polio in the village. Some children have been sent to the big hospital in Swansea.'

'When? When was this?'

'Wednesday. By Friday, the sick children were being taken away. It is possible Rebecca . . .'

'I was there on Friday. I saw no one there collecting children!'

269

'Eliza, please.'

She had been shouting. They both fell silent and listened for any approaching footsteps. There was only the rain, but the smell was nearly unbearable now. Was the meat rotting?

Ruth reached for her hand, but Eliza pulled away. 'Did Rebecca seem ill at all?'

'No.' Eliza hesitated. 'It was nothing.'

'Tell me exactly. Fever? Chills? Any flu-like symptoms?'

'It wasn't polio.' Her voice resembled Father's before an argument. The smell itched its way under her skin. She started scratching at her arms.

'Okay. I believe you. But Pollard could have lied to or even bribed the doctor to take Rebecca along with the others.'

'Or it was an outright lie and Rebecca's not at any hospital. Whatever this . . . illness is, I think Mrs Pollard has it, too. At first I thought it strange that if all women go missing from Thornecroft, why hasn't she? But I think she is succumbing to it, finally. Perhaps she made a deal with Victoria to last this long, but her time has run out. She barely eats, is pale, I think her stomach often bothers—'

Ruth shook her head. 'You're talking about the curse again. Mrs Pollard is no ghost's victim, Eliza. You wouldn't believe all this nonsense if you were in London.'

'I wouldn't have to.'

'Fine. If you're so set on believing that, fine. But can you do one thing for me?' She placed her hands on Eliza's, stopping her from itching. 'I need you to search Mr Brownawell's rooms for any tablets. Any medications. And bring a sample of each to me.'

'She's not poisoning anyone with Mr Brownawell's medication or anything else. I've prepared my own food, and Rebecca's, for the past few weeks.'

270

'This is about more than poisoning. I would do it myself, but she'll be keeping too close an eye on me. It's you she's used to now. Thinks she knows you. She underestimates you, Eliza.'

Eliza dabbed the sweat from her face. Whatever it was hanging from those hooks, she would not be eating it.

'I promise I'll tell you more. But for now . . . are you alright?' Ruth asked. 'Eliza, you're shaking.'

'It's nothing. It's the smell, that's all.'

'Of potatoes?'

'No, the . . .' Eliza lifted the candle. The meat hooks were empty. 'Excuse me.'

She abandoned Ruth in the larder and hurried down the hall to the bathroom, trying not to let the candle blow out. She balanced it on the edge of the sink and turned the water on as far as it would go. She scrubbed her fingers and underneath her nails. She rubbed water over her face and neck then grabbed the hard bar of soap and ran it over her hands like a cheese grater. She rinsed her hands once, but it wasn't enough. She scrubbed them again, getting in between every finger, into every crack and crevice, and rinsed once more. Her hands were red now, but still the dirt remained. She washed again, another three, four, five times, until she felt she had removed an entire layer of skin and exposed a clean, fresh surface to the air. Only then, when the feel and the smell of the nightmare had been cleansed, was she able to return to her bedroom and a restless night.

24

Smoke rose from the Vickers-Armstrongs aircraft factory in nearby Brooklands. The grey tendrils gathered into clouds which marred an otherwise pale blue sky. How many times had German bombers nearly hit his house trying to destroy that building? Peter looked away from the smoke to his mother's blooming garden. The horrible cold of the past winter was finally retreating. Tree buds were flowering into leaves, the grasses turning brown to green, the garden now fragrant with the expectation of the coming summer.

He wrapped the old wool blanket tighter round his shoulders and thought of the four people who died in his fire as smoke continued to fill the sky. He reached for the tea Mother had made him but pulled back inside the blanket when he noticed his hand shaking. Nothing could keep out the chill. Withdrawing the address book, he thumbed through pages now stained with his fingerprints. P for Pollard. There was only one. Number 5 Adelaide Street, Swansea. There were telegram offices in Swansea. Post offices. If Eliza wanted to write to him, she could have done so weeks ago. Unless she hadn't been allowed.

A truck lumbered down the road, the heavy engine sputtering as it stopped near their house. Moments later, there was a faint knock on the front door. The smoke rose ever higher. Mother would handle it. Some minutes later, she appeared next to him in the garden. He felt her watching.

'How was your tea?' she asked. Peter glanced at his full cup.

'Fine, thank you.' He waited for her to leave. Instead, she sat in the wicker chair beside him.

'That was the recovery company. They've delivered your things that survived.'

'Small box, is it?'

'Go take a look.'

'Throw it in the bin. I don't care.'

'Well, that's quite careless. When all of us are hurting from want, I'm sure there's something we could salvage.'

'You do it then.' He felt so cold, as if something had been extinguished within him.

'Peter, God knows what happened was a terrible, terrible thing. But we must be grateful that you survived and move on. Your brothers saw much worse during the war and none of us are strangers to tragedy at home . . .'

'Stop comparing this to the war. This is nothing like the war.'

'I agree. This is much less severe.'

Peter threw off the blanket, knocking over the teacup. It fell onto the grass, the brown water seeping into the ground, staining the fresh green sprouts.

Mother sighed and gathered the cup. 'Peter, you've had a very stressful time of it of late, but we must put things in perspective. You should be grateful you're alive.'

'And what of the others who aren't? What should they be grateful for? What do their families have to be happy about?' He thought of Mrs Rolston. What would happen to her now her greatest fear had been realised? He pictured her wandering the streets, begging strangers to help find her daughter's killer – to find him. And here he was, safe in Shepperton. Both hands were shaking now. Without the blanket, he could not hide them. He crossed his arms and tucked his hands into his sides. A look crossed his mother's face, the same she had when Michael first came home. It was the look he saw every time he glanced in the mirror.

'I'll go and get my things,' he said and hurried into the house.

The small wooden crate sat on the centre of the kitchen table, his name and parents' address stamped on the top. Peter carried it up to his bedroom and used a screwdriver to lever off the lid. He was right. There wasn't much – a few items of clothing Mother could salvage with a good washing; one Glenn Miller record, warped by smoke and water damage; the biro Father bought him when he joined the accounting firm; his frying pan, the only thing he knew how to cook with. Eliza's book was gone, the one he had promised to return to her. Another promise he couldn't keep.

Peter tossed everything back in the crate. A smoke-stained shirt unfolded as he grabbed it, spilling a separate item to the floor – a black jewellery box. Eliza's ring. The ring he lost in Blackfriars. He opened the lid. The ring was gone. In its place sat a folded piece of paper. He set the box aside and read the message.

Jessie begged. Will Eliza?

Peter reread the words, memorising them against his will, and tore the note into scraps. He threw them into the crate, but he could still see them. He covered them with the salvaged shirt and, using the screwdriver, hammered the lid back on. Yet, even with the box closed, he felt no peace. He hoisted up his window and breathed in the clean, country air. The smoke from the factory wasn't visible here. The sky remained calm and peaceful. He grabbed the crate and pushed it out of the window.

It crashed into Mother's rose bushes. His clothes hung like bunting from the stems. The corner of the record peeked out from the thorns. He wanted to throw the address book down there as well, but his hands couldn't manage to pull it from his pocket. He shut the window and went down to join his parents for dinner.

'What was that noise?' Mother asked.

'No idea.' He sat patiently while she served the hot food. All he could smell was smoke.

'Peter,' Father began, 'I know we've been discussing it, but housing in London simply isn't an option. Every place is full and those that are being restored have quite the list. We were lucky to have that flat. Such a loss. You'll simply have to commute like your uncle and I, until something affordable becomes available. Lord knows you've had enough time off now. Uncle Marvin says you're falling behind in . . .'

Peter wasn't listening to his father, to these incessant ramblings about housing and commutes and all those things that didn't matter. His mother made some sort of response, but he paid her no attention, either. It was claustrophobic sitting here between these two people talking about him but not to him. If he did anything but agree with them, they wouldn't hear what he said.

Be reasonable, Peter. Be agreeable, Peter. Do as we say, Peter. Yet all he heard was Stephen's warning, Angelo's offer, the old captain's acceptance of death. Was he dead now, like Jessie? Had Stephen completed the job of which Peter was incapable? Were Jessie and the fire the final consequence of his disobedience or the first?

'. . . think, Peter?' Father was addressing him. Peter hadn't heard.

'Think what?'

'The seven thirty-seven train tomorrow. That should get you to the accounting office in plenty of time, wouldn't you say?'

Peter stared at his dinner plate. The untouched sausages were overcooked, burnt. Two stubby legs protruding from lumpy gravy-covered mash the colour of fire-scarred furniture. The colour of her legs stained in gravy browning, the same colour, the same smell . . .

Fingers snapped in front of his face.

'Pay attention, son.'

Peter flipped over his plate, smashing his meal into the tablecloth and spilling his water glass. He wanted to shout at Father, at both of them, but his anger paralysed him. He knew they were waiting for him, waiting for him to scream and curse so they could speak and appease him, but he couldn't. The anger choked him.

His muscles relaxed as the quiet descended, and he regained control of his body. He fixed his plate and began scraping the food off the table as best he could. The rhythmic scrape and tap of his fork fell in line with the ticking from the grandfather clock.

'Jenny rang today,' Mother said, her soft voice sharply interrupting his rhythm. 'She thought it would be nice if you came to visit Michael while you're home, the other boys being so far away.'

Peter felt Father's disapproval before it was spoken.

'Darling, I don't think that's the best . . .'

'I'll do it,' Peter said. 'I'll go see him tomorrow.'

'You have responsibilities to . . .'

'To my brother. I have responsibilities to my brother.' His fingers clenched the fork so tight, he thought his knuckles might break.

'Yes. Yes, I suppose you do.' His father dabbed his mouth with his napkin then excused himself from the table. Peter released the fork and flexed his fingers, the relief in his joints the only joy he felt.

'Well,' Mother said, 'what would you like for pudding?'

*

'Want to go outside?' Peter asked. They stood in the shadowed kitchen watching Michael's wife and daughter play. Little Grace ran about in the back garden with Jenny and the spaniel pup. Peter couldn't remember its name. He doubted Michael knew it, either.

'No,' Michael replied after a time. 'It's better here, in the dark.' He sat at the table and lit a cigarette with steady hands. The tray before him was spilling over. Michael wouldn't allow Jenny to empty it.

'How is Mother?' he asked, drawing circles in the ash.

'Fine.'

'And Father? Has he found you a new flat yet?'

'He wants me to commute.'

'Poor Peter. Will he ever stand on his own two feet?'

Peter took one of Michael's cigarettes without asking. 'There's a housing shortage.'

'We have a house.'

'Aren't you lucky?'

'Lucky that Jenny's parents died. Funny. You survive a war and decide you're invincible then BAM!' Michael slammed his fist on the table. 'Here comes a lorry. Right through the crossing. Funny old world.'

Peter held the cigarette smoke inside his lungs, letting it burn before releasing it.

'She won't let me in her bed,' Michael said. 'Her parents

277

slept in separate beds and she's inherited their foolish little habits.' Michael poured water from his glass into the ashtray, dampening the powder, and began building sandcastles. 'We're in modern times. A man should be able to sleep with his wife, in his house, in their bed. We did it often enough in hotels before the wedding. What about that girlfriend of yours? Rumour is she took off. Not that we expected any different.'

Peter stubbed out his cigarette in the centre of Michael's ash castle. Michael smiled. He wore the expression poorly.

'What are you going to do about it then?' Michael asked, moving Peter's butt and beginning again.

'I've already tried.'

'And?'

'And I had my flat burnt down.'

Michael's fingers were covered in ash. He brushed a hair from his eye, leaving a grey streak across his brow. He sighed.

'You always gave up so easily. Even when you were a child. Mother and Father always ended up helping you, didn't they? It's why Father got you the job with Uncle Marvin. He knew you'd never be able to do it on your own.'

'They killed a girl because of me! Killed her in my flat because I . . .' Peter rose from his chair and pushed it in hard, shaking the table. He still didn't know why Jessie had been in his building. Had she been waiting for him, thinking it would be safe? Had Stephen killed her and left her body there as a warning? Would he really go after Eliza next?

Outside, the pup barked as little Grace chased after its tail. *Yap, yap, yap.*

'I never said you were weak,' Michael continued. 'Don't think that. Don't ever let anyone think that of you.'

The pup continued to bark, each shrill noise like a cigarette burn on his skin.

'Then what do I do?'

Yap, yap, yap. Michael opened his palm and flattened it on top of his house of cinders. *Yap, yap, yap.*

'You fight.'

Yap—

'Shut that dog up!' Michael shouted. Unsatisfied, he wrenched the glass door open, leaving ash on the handle. 'Shut that mangy dog up before I get my gun and shut it up for you!'

The pup cowered behind Jenny's feet. Little Grace began to cry. Michael calmly closed the door, leaving more ash on the floor.

'Stay for dinner, if you like,' Michael said, wiping his hands on his trousers and lighting another cigarette. 'Jenny would like it if you stayed.'

That night they ate in silence, offal sausages and carrot and potato pie, but it was the smell of wet ash that lingered in Peter's nose as he felt the corner of the address book digging into his thigh.

25

Eliza stared down the hall at the carved doors leading to Mr Brownawell's rooms while the rain pelted the manor like shrapnel. Last night, in her nightmare, these doors had bled. Though she could see now they were clean, every time she blinked, she saw thick red blood running down through the carvings. She stuck her hands in her pockets to keep from scratching her arms. For now, these pockets were empty. Soon, if she followed Ruth's instructions, they would contain Mr Brownawell's tablets.

She still could not understand why Ruth wanted them. Last night in the larder she'd been too distracted by her own fears to question Ruth's intentions. Now in the daylight, with no strange smells bombarding her, the questions filled her mind.

Voices sounded from below – Mrs Pollard and Ruth taking more towels to the leaking veranda doors. Eliza waited until the sounds had passed then crept forward down the carpeted hall. Given time, Ruth would come to understand the true terrors of Thornecroft, just as she had, but they did not have time. Not if they were going to save Rebecca and stop Victoria from claiming Eliza as well.

Eliza looked at the carpet before her. How many times had the living Victoria Kyffin walked these halls? Had the carpet softened her steps as they did Eliza's or were the floors bare? Did her shoes smack against the wooden boards, marking her path in sharp beats that drilled fear into her heart? Eliza found the presence of an aged Mr Brownawell distressing. What must have it been like here when he was the strong, youthful brute seen in the portrait hanging in the Ancestral Parlour? Victoria had been unable to defeat him in life. No wonder she haunted him in death.

Eliza paused at the staircase that winded back to the east wing. Victoria stole girls because of him. To torment him. What would she do if he no longer existed? If he joined her in the netherworld? Would his torment finally cease or would he descend to the hell he so rightly deserved? If she were Victoria, Eliza would want him to live as long as possible. Let him suffer in body as well as mind. Perhaps that was the deal Mrs Pollard had struck with the ghost of the manor. Why she remained so concerned with the health of the old man even though she never seemed to speak to him kindly – so long as she kept Mr Brownawell alive to suffer, Victoria allowed her to live. Mr Brownawell's death could mean her own destruction. Perhaps it also meant the freedom of the taken.

Eliza became lightheaded and paused in the stairwell. If her theory were true, Rebecca's freedom would mean the death of another. And who would be responsible for that death? She looked at her hands. They had started to shake. These hands she used to cook, to clean, to mend – could she use them to kill? Bile rose in her throat. A man as terrible as Mr Brownawell deserved to die, didn't he? But murder was an equally terrible act. An act for the likes of men such as Mr Drewry, not little girls like Eliza Haverford. And suppose she did find a way to commit such an act, was it worth it for Rebecca? Would Rebecca, once rescued, rush into Eliza's arms, proclaim her thanks, show true remorse for the behaviour that had led them to Thornecroft in the first place? Or would she shrug her shoulders, turn away and say this was what she expected in the first place?

A vein pulsed in her throat, constricting her thoughts. Air barely passed through her lungs. Her mind became clouded as the smell of sulphur and marrow liqueur passed under her nose. Blindly, she made her way down the stairs. She had to get as far from these thoughts as she could – leave them behind with the dust in the north hall.

She found herself in the kitchen, her hands under the running water with no recollection as to how she had arrived or for how long her hands had been under the tap. She turned off the tap and reached for a flannel. Her fingertips were white and wrinkled. As she dried them, she walked to the kitchen door and opened it to let in the fresh, rain-scented air. She inhaled deeply, feeling her mind unravel, when she spotted Mr Drewry crossing the lawns with a bulky burlap sack tossed over his shoulder. The sack, tied at one end, was about the size of a small child. Eliza dropped the towel.

When Mr Drewry passed out of sight, she followed him out onto the grass and around the crumbling stone wall of the gardens. He kept a steady pace towards the little cemetery, grabbing a shovel from its resting place against the wall on his way. He was going to dig a grave.

Who would need a grave, except the girl Victoria had stolen away, kept locked up somewhere in the dank and cold, where she caught a chill? No blankets to warm her, no food to maintain her strength. Victoria had let her waste away in the darkness, and the tiny girl was unable to survive.

Hot tears welled in her eyes as she ran back to the kitchen. The guilt weighed down every muscle, every desire she ever had, winning control. With Rebecca gone, what would she do? How could she earn forgiveness? She would have to live with the guilt and let it consume her. Become a spinster to atone for her sins. Maybe take in orphaned children. Help them in ways she could never help her sister. She saw herself with grey-white hair pulled into a tight bun, wire spectacles balanced on her thin nose. Dressed always in black, like a widow. Losing what little looks she had in her youth to become a witch-like crone.

'The dog.'

Mrs Pollard stood beside her. Eliza hadn't heard her approach. The housekeeper nodded towards Mr Drewry.

'It was the dog. It never recovered from its injuries. I must thank your sister next I see her.'

The vision of her spinster self faded as another thought took its place. Rebecca had another innocent death to her name.

'Stop staring like an imbecile, Miss Haverford. I need you to take luncheon to Mr Brownawell. The veranda doors are proving particularly troublesome today, and Mrs Owen and I are going into town to fetch additional supplies. Besides, it's time you took on more responsibility in this house. He is waiting in the north hall study.' Mrs Pollard swept out of the kitchen, leaving Eliza to prepare the tray.

Still recovering from the false shock, she lost herself in the luncheon preparations and did not let her mind linger on the thought that she and Mr Brownawell were to be alone together, again.

The silver tray was heavier than she expected, and it wobbled precariously as she carried it to Mr Brownawell's study. She smelled him as soon as she entered. The stench of sour milk and urine was so embedded in his skin no amount of bathing could remove it. She avoided breathing too deeply as she approached the red calfskin armchair in which he sat before the fire. He made no acknowledgement of her presence. His milky eyes were focused on the flames, each breath more difficult than the last. She set the tray on the side table.

'Good afternoon, Mr Brownawell. I've come to give you luncheon.'

Eliza pulled up a chair and placed the bowl of cold porridge in her lap.

'Have you heard that the veranda has flooded?' she asked.

He breathed in and out, the reflection of the fire bringing the illusion of light to his eyes.

She sunk the spoon into the porridge. 'But you don't much care, do you?' She stuck the spoon into his mouth, not waiting to see if he was ready. He swallowed.

'You don't care about this house. Only what hides inside it.'

She fed him again, her headache returning along with the thoughts she'd had upstairs only several minutes earlier.

'Victoria. That's all you think about, isn't it?'

His head turned slowly towards her. She fed him another spoonful.

'What you did to her is horrible. The worst thing one human being can do to another.'

She fed him again. The porridge dribbled down his chin. Maybe he wouldn't need to die. Maybe a confession would be enough.

'But what she's doing now is just as wrong. These girls she's taken, they're innocent. She's only doing it to punish you.'

Eliza remembered their one, terrible dinner. Having to wear that dress. Eat that nauseating cold food. Another spoonful. Porridge dripped onto his shirt. He groaned.

'She's keeping you trapped here, isn't she? She and Mrs Pollard? You should be dead, but she's making you suffer by keeping you alive.'

He closed his mouth, but Eliza forced the spoon in. He would not get off that easily.

'If I can stop her, I'll get my sister back and you can finally die. Though I can't say you deserve it.' She dropped the spoon into the bowl. 'Admit what you've done. Admit you killed her. Then you'll be free. Her curse will be broken.'

Mr Brownawell opened his mouth. She leant in close.

'Yes?'

He coughed, spewing regurgitated porridge over Eliza's face and clothes. She dropped the bowl, the remainder of his food spilling to the floor. He continued coughing while she searched desperately for a handkerchief.

'You wicked old man! You did that on purpose. No wonder Victoria didn't love you. How could she?'

Mr Brownawell groaned in displeasure. More porridge dribbled down his chin.

'No one ever loved you and no one ever will.' Eliza rushed out of the room, wiping away the disgusting, creamy lumps, and grabbed a towel from the nearest linen cupboard. She walked blindly down the hall, wiping herself clean but unable to rid her skin of that sour milk smell.

She came to rest at the damp and water-damaged veranda doors. Towels were stuffed into the doorframe, but more water kept trickling through. With her eyes closed, she could smell where rot had already begun to take hold. She never would have treated a person like that before, no matter how cruel they were. A customer once purposely spilled his drink on her uniform, but had she cursed him and dumped hot tea down his suit? No. She walked away, informed Mr Purvis, and continued on with her shift.

This entire place was rotting from the inside out, and she was rotting along with it. What she couldn't decide was if Thornecroft was infecting her or if it was the other way round.

*

Eliza hid in her room for the remainder of the afternoon. Though she looked for *Mrs Miniver* to keep her company, she could not find it anywhere and so occupied her thoughts by darning a hole in her green dress. When Ruth and Mrs Pollard returned in the late afternoon, Mrs Pollard relegated Eliza to the kitchen, where she was to prepare the evening meal, while Ruth was to continue fixing the veranda doors. As soon as Mrs Pollard left to check on Mr Brownawell, Eliza abandoned the kitchen and hurried out of the east wing towards the veranda.

When she passed the garden doors, she saw Ruth weaving her way through the overgrown hedges. Eliza immediately ran out to her, cornering her beside the fountain.

'Eliza!' Ruth glanced at the windows as if afraid of being spotted. 'We can't be seen together in the daytime.'

'We'll be fine. Mrs Pollard is with Brownawell in the north hall study. Aren't you supposed to be at the veranda?'

Ruth looked away. 'I needed Mr Drewry's help. But now you're here, tell me, what did you find?'

Eliza felt the weightlessness of her still-empty pockets. 'Nothing.'

'We were gone for hours! You had plenty of time to—'

'I have my own concerns here. And I suppose I don't see why Mr Brownawell's medications are so important since you won't tell me.'

Ruth sighed and fiddled with a stray lock of hair. 'Mr Brownawell is said to have silicosis.'

'Yes, from visiting the mines.'

'Not according to the old miners. They say he never went down the pits and only came to the sites if he had to. There's no way he could have a miners' disease.'

'So he has something else. You said you came here to help me find my sister and yet all you do is ask questions about everyone's health. So either tell me why or forget about helping us at all.'

Ruth grabbed Eliza's hands. They were damp and cold. 'I am here to help Rebecca. I'm here to help her by catching Mrs Pollard in all her lies. She's hiding something about Mr Brownawell. I don't know what it is, but if – when I find it, it could be the key to discovering what happened to Rebecca and Pip. And I may have already found something.' Ruth pulled out a burnt glass pill bottle. 'Do you know what this is?'

Eliza recognised it instantly. The guilt she had so carefully controlled these past few days could no longer be kept at bay.

'It's a prescription for lithium bromide. The name's been scorched from the label, but . . .'

'Where did you get that?' Eliza asked, finding it difficult to breathe.

'Mr Drewry found it cleaning up the bonfire. You wouldn't give it to a silicosis patient. Lithium bromide is used in the treatment of mental disorders.'

'I know exactly what it's for.' Rebecca's pale, placid face rose up and took hold of Eliza's memory.

'I don't know why Mrs Pollard had it. It could be for her or she's using it on Mr Brownawell. But this could be what Mrs Pollard used to poison Pip! Bromism causes weakness, ataxia, nausea and vomiting, erythematous rashes . . .'

She slapped the bottle from Ruth's hand. 'No one cares about Pip! Pip is dead and they'll never prove who did it, but Rebecca can be saved. And instead you're . . . you're fixated on some poisoning theory. I was wrong. I don't want your help and I don't need it. You never came here for Rebecca. You only came for yourself. You must feel so guilty, making Pip take the Thornecroft job. Well you should.'

Eliza left the garden, stamping the bottle into the ground

287

as she went. If Ruth called after her, she couldn't hear. There was only the sound of blood in her ears, the throb in her temple indicating a headache was looming, as she forced the remaining coldness back into its safe.

*

She was running – running through the halls, catching glimpses, hearing footsteps – but Rebecca remained just ahead, out of sight, out of reach. The dog was barking, chasing after her, after them. Blaming them. Eliza ran through the north hall, Rebecca chasing the dog that led the way. The carved doors lay ahead, but Eliza ran too fast to stop. She crashed straight through and teetered over the edge of the quarry. Wisps of mist reached up to greet her and she leant back to stay out of their reach. Rebecca, smiling, pushed her in.

*

Eliza didn't know where she was. Her clothes were soaked and she shivered in her nightdress. It was too dark and there were no landmarks to guide her. She scrambled to her feet, slipping in the mud, and saw the light ahead. As her eyes identified the outline of the manor, she spotted the open kitchen door.

She was on the east lawn, and the light came from the highest floor of Thornecroft. It hovered, stationary in the window. Mrs Pollard, she thought, but then saw lamplight and a thin figure moving through the kitchen. Mrs Pollard came and shut the kitchen door then vanished into the darkness. The light above remained.

'What is it?' Eliza asked. 'What is it you want me to see?'

The kitchen door remained unlocked. Eliza crept down to her room and hid herself inside. Drenched and freezing, she changed into her warmest jumper and trousers and crawled onto her mattress.

She could hear Mrs Pollard moving about next door. The clock read 1 a.m. Eliza lay still, letting her wet hair soak the pillow, and listened to the rhythmic ticking of the clock as she waited for the housekeeper to settle. Time was merciless, each minute moving slower than the last. A larger gap of silence appeared between the ticks of the second hand until the clock stopped moving entirely. The room was all in silence and stillness. Time froze. Nothing moved. Nothing except the ghost-white hand reaching towards her chest.

Eliza shot up and rubbed her eyes. The clock ticked loudly above her head. Time had released her, she thought, then realised it had never held her in the first place. She tipped the clock face towards the moonlight – three in the morning.

Even a familiar home changed when the hour was so late, when all life within slept and moonlight transformed simple objects into complex shadows. Walking through Thornecroft at night was like entering a different world. Every corner hid a secret. Every shadow was alive. This was the time when the second inhabitants of the house came out to play, took free reign of the rooms and halls. Eliza joined them.

With her Tilley lamp, she ascended the east-wing staircase. The light she had seen was directly over the kitchens. This surely had to be the way. She climbed like Jack up the bean-stalk, following the staircase as it twisted and weaved into the unknown world above.

She reached the top, no giant to be seen. The halls were unfurnished, the floor bare. Here the ceiling was slanted, like an attic, making Eliza cautious of hitting her head. The journey up the winding staircase disorientated her, and she no longer knew if she faced the east lawn or not.

'Victoria?' Her voice bounced off the bare walls. She thought it would boomerang back to her, it travelled so quickly in the quiet. She waited for a responding echo, but none came.

She began trying the doors. The first was locked. Eliza peered through the keyhole but saw only an empty room illuminated by moonlight. She tried the next. Nothing more than a half-empty broom cupboard. The following two were also locked and peeps through the keyholes revealed nothing. Eliza turned the handle of the last, expecting the same result, but this one gave under her hand. Before opening it, she glanced at the wooden sign mounted to the door and brushed away the dust.

Reading Room

Holding her breath, she pushed the door in and stepped back.

Books were stacked floor to ceiling, covering every wall, reaching to the highest corners. They filled the entire room like a hedgerow maze, leaving only narrow passages through which a person could walk. Almost all were bound in leather, stamped with faded gold. The first spine she touched belonged to a Shakespeare folio. She swung the lamp to and fro trying to read every title, every name as she passed – Wordsworth, Browning, Keats, Stevenson, James, Molière. The vast collection cramped into this tiny space – she felt the books crying out in pain, unable to be read.

When she arrived at a small clearing, she set the lamp down and picked up the first title she could reach. She sat on the floor by the lamp, admiring the cover. This was a moment that needed to be appreciated. She placed the book to her nose and inhaled deeply. It smelled of nights warmed by a roaring fire, cups of tea and a soft armchair. She ran her fingers over the spine – *Seven Curses of London* by Greenwood. How long had Mrs Pollard kept these trapped here? How long since someone gave them purpose? Careful of the thin paper, she opened the cover, feeling the book's knowledge already passing through her fingers as it pulsed with a desperate desire to be read.

She stared at the table of contents and frowned. Someone had defaced the page, scribbling out the words in heavy blotches of black ink. She turned to the next page. This, too, was ruined with ink. A third, a fourth. She skimmed the entire book only to find horrid marks across every page. Most were illegible scribbles with the occasional word – *bird, cantor, coal* – that made no sense. Perhaps a child? But when had a child last lived at Thornecroft?

Eliza set the book aside and chose another, *Imaginary Conversations – 1825–1826*. She opened to a random page. It was written over in red and black. As was the next and the one following that. The entire book ruined. This kind of defacing was deliberate. It took time.

She closed it and took another, *Memorials of Human Superstition*. Red lines like scars tore many of the delicate pages.

She tossed it onto the ruined pile and opened another – *Law of Husband and Wife*. This too was destroyed, though the words were clearer – *harlot, trollop, disease, filth*. The handwriting here was different, thin and feminine. Though hurried, Eliza remembered that same spider's scrawl from the letter in Aunt Bess's handbag. She snapped it shut and left it at her feet.

She found a French title – *Le Magasin des Enfants* by Jeanne-Marie Leprince de Beaumont. Eliza remembered the author's name. She once had a copy of this same book in English. It contained one of her favourite fairy tales, one Mother would read her every night before bed, before Rebecca was born. Eliza turned to 'La Belle et La Bête' and dropped the book

291

in horror. The Beast had a sword protruding from his back, blood spurting from the wound, and a grotesque tongue dangling from his mouth. A noose hung round Belle's neck while blood dripped from an incision down her chest. She looked at Eliza with eyes scratched out in red ink. The word *WHORE* was scrawled on the page opposite, written over and over again. But this was not Mrs Pollard's writing nor the heavy male hand of the other books. It was simple, untrained, like a child's. A young girl's.

No. She would not think it. Eliza scrambled to her feet, bumping over another stack. Several books tumbled to the floor, every open page defaced with violent words, graphic drawings. As Eliza grabbed the lamp, something soft fell onto her head and to the floor. A dead mouse lay at her feet. She backed away, deeper into the darkened room, eyes fixed on the mouse as if the books themselves had somehow poisoned it. But from where had it fallen? Eliza raised the lamp. A loose strand of twine dangled above her. She turned slowly about the room. The light fell on a pair of tiny feet – doll's feet. The Victoria doll hung from the rafters with twine. Beside her hung a squirrel, another mouse, a fellow doll, a pigeon, a rabbit. Like ornaments from a tree, their bodies hung in neat little lines all across the ceiling as far as Eliza could see. She looked away and covered her nose with her hand, desperate to block the sudden smell of sulphur.

On the floor, across from the fallen mouse, lay *Mrs Miniver*. She reached for it with a shaking hand and opened the cover.

For my girls. No day is complete without a story. With love, Father.

Eliza dropped the book. She felt rats gnawing on her skin as she ran from the room, the books closing in around her as she frantically navigated the maze.

She never stopped running – all down the twisted stairs, down and down through the hall to her bedroom. The door was locked. She tried the handle several times, but it refused to turn. She ran through the kitchen, out into the rain and to her window, forgetting it had been nailed shut.

'No, no,' she panted, setting down the lamp. She tried to lift the sash, but it would not budge. 'No, please!'

She gave up and went back through the kitchen, where the Tilley lamp faded, depleted of oil. In the dark and quiet, shivering in her wet clothes, she rested her head against her door in despair.

It clicked open.

Eliza entered cautiously. It was empty. The door was never locked, she thought, as she shut it behind her. It couldn't have been.

Ruth was right. There was a poison here. It thrived within the walls, infecting every room. The house itself was poisoned with madness, and she could no longer allow herself to succumb to it. The longer she remained here, the more it ruined her mind. She could still save Rebecca, but she could not save her if she remained within Thornecroft.

*

Mrs Pollard was preparing breakfast in the kitchen when Eliza approached. She already wore her coat, her suitcase in hand.

'I'm leaving,' she announced.

Mrs Pollard cocked her head to the side and smiled. 'Are you now?'

'I came here on the condition that it would be to care for my sister. As Rebecca is no longer here, there is no reason for me to stay. Consider this my notice.'

The housekeeper would no longer have any hold over her.

Eliza knew now where the source of the hate came from, and she was no longer afraid.

Mrs Pollard set down her spoon. 'Well, then, if you're so certain. There is one thing, however, before you go.' She untied her apron. 'Something I've been meaning to tell you.' She disappeared into her office and emerged a moment later with a slip of paper. 'Where, may I ask, are you going to go?'

'I'll return to my aunt in London.'

'Ah yes, quite a good idea. Although that may be some-what difficult as your aunt is dead.' Mrs Pollard handed her a telegram.

Eliza forgot about the books, about the poison, about Rebecca.

She couldn't be. Aunt Bess couldn't be. The words of the telegram, the sender's address in Swansea, were blurred. Only the date remained clear.

'This . . . this is dated weeks ago. Why didn't you tell me straight away?'

'It kept slipping my mind.'

'Our last living relative – Rebecca's guardian – dies, and it slips your mind?'

'You'll watch your tone, Miss Haverford.'

'No I will not! You had no right to keep this information from me or Rebecca!'

Mrs Pollard smiled. 'Rebecca knew. Her guardianship was transferred to me upon your aunt's death. Would you like to see the paperwork? Rebecca was quite pleased. I thought you would be, too. You never seemed to like her much.'

Eliza struck Mrs Pollard. It hurt her hand, but the pain felt good.

Before she could hit again, Mrs Pollard backhanded her twice across the face then grabbed her by the hair and yanked her head back, straining her neck. Eliza cried out and clawed at Mrs Pollard's arm, but her head was thrown forward into the countertop. She crumpled to the floor, a fresh wetness on her forehead. Mrs Pollard took her by the hair and pulled her across the kitchen floor to the office. Eliza kicked and screamed, but there was no one to help her. Ruth. Where was Ruth? Mrs Pollard yanked open the trapdoor and kicked Eliza into the dark hole. All the air was knocked from her as she hit the packed dirt floor.

'You'll remain there until you learn a little respect. No one touches me. Not in this house.'

The door shut, leaving Eliza in darkness, the smells of the cellar morphing into the smell of sulphur and sweet marrow as she lost her battle with consciousness.

26

Ticket queues wound through the station while passengers hurried to and fro, bumping into one another from lack of space. Smoke wafted to the ceiling and the smell of coal dust was nearly unbearable. The only sound that carried above the loud crowd was the whistle of departing trains.

There was too much noise, too many people. To Peter it all sounded like screams. The smoke from the train was the smoke from his building; the hurrying passengers were tenants desperate to escape the flames. All eyes watched him, blamed him.

It had been better in Shepperton, that fear someone was always watching him. Shepperton was so quiet. He knew every neighbour, every shopkeeper. There was no place for strangers to hide. In Paddington, every face was unknown to him. He used to love the contact of strangers on the bus or underground, the odd sense of camaraderie that they were all surviving London together, each in their own way. Now it felt like survival was not a group effort but a competition pitting man against man, one where not everyone could survive.

The queue inched slowly forwards. The address book felt heavy and solid in his pocket. There was a train to Swansea leaving within the hour. If the queue was quick enough, he could make it. He felt exposed, as if Stephen would know precisely when he crossed London's borders. He had asked Michael to join him – the journey safer with two – but Michael refused. He knew how dangerous leaving the house could be.

Peter felt trapped. Michael said it was better being a moving target, but Peter could only move as the queue allowed. He kept his eyes on the faces around him. Two men bowed heads to whisper to each other about Peter. A pair of old women laughed at his discomfort. The mass of coats, shoulders, caps, umbrellas all blurred into one beast. One smirking, snarling beast with a pug-like face . . .

Someone tapped on his shoulder. Peter's breath caught in his throat else he would have screamed. The old woman politely asked him to pay attention. The queue had moved forward. Peter obliged, removing his handkerchief to dab his face. His palms were sweating and he closed his eyes to try to block out the sights and sounds around him. He opened them and wished he hadn't.

Lurking at the entrance to the platforms was Stephen. His ragged blue and yellow cap was pulled low on his head, hands jammed in his coat pockets as his eyes searched the crowd. Peter turned up the collar of his coat and moved forward with the queue. Stephen made eye contact with someone. Peter followed his line of sight to a man down the station. The barman from Angelo's, a bandage on his head. He shook his head once – no – and Stephen did the same. Stephen looked the other way, making eye contact with another, but this time Peter did not see who.

Peter used the crowd to his advantage, keeping his head down, staying turned away from the platforms.

The queue was interminably slow. Policemen loitered about, but Peter ignored them as they did him. He moved closer to the counter as Stephen moved closer to the queue.

Peter bought his ticket just in time for the train. The warning whistle sounded. No longer could the queue protect him, but the path to platform four looked clear. He kept his head down as he hurried across the station and didn't see the man he bumped into.

'Hello, mate.' Stephen smiled.

Peter struck him in the face with his suitcase. The bag fell to the ground and burst open, scattering its meagre contents. His ticket clutched firmly in hand, Peter ran for the train but was grabbed by the arm. The barman. Peter elbowed him in the stomach. The train whistled. Smoke burst from the chimney. Peter ran. The crankshafts began to move, the coupling rods pulling the train forward. Someone snagged his coat collar, the third man. Peter snapped his head back and smacked the man on the nose. Freed, he ran and leapt onto the last carriage.

The train pulled out of Paddington as Stephen and the two men were accosted by the police. Peter watched until the train left the station then found a place to stand in a crowded coach. He couldn't see London as they left, but it didn't matter. He and Eliza would see it together when they returned.

27

You know what you must do.

Eliza woke in darkness to the feel of hard-packed dirt beneath her hands as the smell of damp lingered in the air. She could not see where she was, but, as her thoughts returned, she remembered her fight with Mrs Pollard. She was in the kitchen cellar. She felt the ground around her, but could not find the stairs. From her pocket, she withdrew her matchbox and shook it, trying to discern how many were left. It rattled lightly. The scent of marrow liqueur tickled under her nose. No. No, there was no time for those thoughts. In utter blackness, she willed her hands to calm as she slid the box open. A drop of sweat, or blood, trickled down her face. Her fingers, less nimble than she liked, grasped one of the small matches. She closed the box, nearly dropping the small match onto the hard ground, where it would have been lost forever. She struck it. It took three times to light.

Father's feet dangled above her.

She screamed. The dropped match extinguished in the dust.

'Stop it! You saw nothing. Nothing.'

She found another match and lit it. The smell of marrow faded away. Cupping the fragile flame with her hand, she tried to get her bearings. No one's feet hung from above. She glanced a wooden staircase that led up to the trapdoor. She scooted towards the nearest wall and used it to pull herself up. Her head felt like it had split open where Mrs Pollard smacked it on the kitchen counter. The match burnt down and nipped her fingers. She dropped it and lit another. There were shelves beside her, and she found the stub of a candle just as the second match burnt out. Her fingers failed to find another. The marrow smell became strong again.

Eliza drew back her hand, took a breath, and searched again. There was one match left, stuck in the inner edge of the box. As careful as if handling a sick animal, she drew the stick out, lit it, and transferred the flame to the candle.

She searched the wooden shelves for any other tools, hoping for a torch or a lamp. There was an old lantern, but it held no oil. On a bottom shelf, she found another candle. This she lit and, after melting its bottom wax with the fire from the first, stuck it to the lowest stair. Carefully, she climbed up to the trapdoor. It wouldn't budge. She put her shoulder into it. Not even the slightest movement. Perhaps there was another way out.

After crawling down to the floor, she took more time to examine the modest cellar. It ran from underneath Mrs Pollard's office to the width of the kitchen. Wooden shelves lined both sides, but they were mostly empty, home only to dusty, disused items – broken lamps and gardening shears, bits of chicken wire and rusted meat hooks. Eliza crossed underneath the staircase, hoping for a second entrance, some other means of escape, but there was nothing save a cold, white brick wall turned yellowish-grey from centuries of soot and dirt.

She turned and spotted the trunk. It was large and domed, made from some type of metal. Faded stickers decorated the top and sides – Cunard Line, White Star, Paris, Belfast, India.

It was locked, but the key from Mrs Pollard's room was still in her pocket. It slipped straight in. Eliza lifted the lid.

The entirety of Mrs Pollard's life lay before her for the taking. Old children's clothes and toys. Clothes for a young woman, hair clips and a box of jewellery. Books on archaeology and Ancient Egypt, their pages left unscarred, hand brooms, line levels and a trowel. At the bottom was a cigar box filled with photographs – names and dates scrawled on the back. The top photograph, dated 1907, featured Mr G. Pollard, wife and infant daughter. A family portrait for each year followed, and Eliza saw Mrs Pollard's sharp features in the growing girl. She removed the photo of *Georgina and nanny* from her pocket. It fitted between the years 1913 to 1914. The family portraits continued until 1919. The final photograph had only mother and daughter, dressed in black.

A second cigar box contained frail, yellowed letters. Eliza skimmed through, stopping when her fingers fell on a piece of familiar grey stationery. She held it to the light. The envelope listed an address in Dover.

6 June 1919
Dear Mrs Lilith Pollard,

Thank you for your recent correspondence. I am sorry to hear of your unfortunate circumstances. It is indeed true that I seek additional help at my estate. While your daughter is young to perform the duties required of this house, she is of a prime age to begin proper training for the position. Send Georgina upon receipt of this letter. Her salary will be sent directly to you as per your request. Your daughter shall work hard, but you shall want for nothing.

Sincerely,
Mr E— Brownawell

Eliza reread the letter until she heard the footsteps above her – heavy and hurried. Another pair followed – lighter but firm. The voices were muffled but loud enough for her to hear.

'Which was it? Which?' Mrs Pollard. Eliza wasn't sure if it was the distortion of the cellar, but the housekeeper sounded panicked.

'New Cware.' Mr Drewry.

'Have they gone through old Cware? Well, have they?'

'That's all the information I have.'

'You must take me there immediately.'

'It'll be faster . . .'

The footsteps moved, carrying into the kitchen. Eliza moved with them, missing only some of the conversation.

'. . . that is final.' Mrs Pollard again. '. . . would you go? Who would take in a worthless murderer such as you?'

A murderer? Of course. What if Mr Drewry was entirely responsible? Maybe she and Ruth were both wrong.

'What about the girl?' he asked.

'She's been taken care of for now.'

'For now?'

Mrs Pollard's voice came again, but she spoke too low for Eliza to understand. There was no reply from Mr Drewry that she could hear. The footsteps resumed. She made to follow them but was distracted when wax dripped onto her hand, scalding her skin before cooling quickly. She peeled it off and flicked it away. As she watched it fly off into the darkness, something else caught her eye – a large black shape frozen in the far corner. An old, iron furnace. Though it was cool to the touch, the ash smelled fresh, like a bombsite in Hungerford visited the day after it was hit, not old, like the ruins of her parents' home.

She opened the door. Unidentified bits were half-buried in soft grey peaks of ash. Eliza reached in and pulled out a piece of leather. She dusted it off. It was the cover of a journal. The pages inside had all been destroyed, but an embossed inscription could still partially be seen.

. . .*lasto*

'Vlasto,' she decoded. 'Sorry, Pip.'

She set the piece aside and looked again. Another book emerged from the ashes, this one still mostly intact, enough for Eliza to recognise it immediately. Rebecca's Bible – the child's Bible Father gave her the day prior to their evacuation. Its once white cover was now black and grey, the gold cross on the cover turned brown. She opened the first page, which, protected by the heavy leather, still had Rebecca's name written in Father's familiar scrawl.

Rebecca surely would have taken this with her, Eliza thought, if she was sent to hospital. Unless Eliza overlooked it when cleaning Rebecca's room, and Mrs Pollard decided to dispose of it.

A dog barked.

It could be any dog, a stray from the village. Any dog at all.

Mr Drewry shouted. 'Kasey! Stay!'

The dog fell silent.

The Bible trembled in Eliza's hands. If Kasey was alive, who was buried in the new grave? Eliza looked from the charred Bible to Pip's journal. Pip, whose belongings were burnt in this same furnace. Pip, who was dead. Rebecca, who was . . .

'No!' Eliza dropped the Bible and candle to the ground. The flame went out, leaving only the light on the stair. She ran up the cellar steps and banged on the trapdoor.

'No! No, she's not! She's not!' Eliza screamed, pounding

303

her fists on the rough wood. Rebecca wasn't. She couldn't be. Eliza threw all her weight into the door again and again. It jerked then snapped back down. Eliza launched herself at it again, feeling no pain.

A crack of light. She shoved her hands into it. Something sat on top of the door but it was moving, sliding. Eliza shouted as she pushed. Whatever was holding her down fell over, and the door flung itself back under her force. She climbed up the last few stairs, shoving aside the overturned crate of potatoes which had been her barricade. She went to the garden shed and grabbed the shovel then ran for the little cemetery.

Kasey was lying alongside the garden wall, panting happily. He saw Eliza and wagged his tail. As she ran for the cemetery, he followed at a trot by her side. Her nausea increased the closer she came to the grave. Behind the cemetery, the silent wood watched her approach. She wiped the sticky blood from her forehead.

The freshly turned ground was easy to spot. It was just below Victoria's grave. Eliza began digging. Kasey sat across from her, watching. The ground, still loose, moved easily but was heavy from the constant rain. She kept going, down and down. The sun moved in the sky, but Eliza did not look at it. She only knew by the changing shadows. The ground rose above her as she sank into her self-made pit. How deep would it have to be? How far into the earth would he have buried her? Her muscles ached. Sweat dripped from her forehead, mingling with the blood from her cut. The mixture dripped into her eyes. She felt nauseous, but she would not stop. She must be close now.

Kasey began to bark. Someone was approaching. She did not stop. Let it be Mrs Pollard. Let it be Mr Drewry. She did not care, not about any of them. She kept digging.

'Eliza?' A woman's voice. 'Eliza, what are you doing?' Ruth's shadow fell across the grave.

'You see him, don't you?' she asked.

'See who?'

'The dog.'

'Kasey? Of course. He's right here.'

Eliza spared a brief glance upwards. Ruth stood beside Kasey, her hand stroking his head. She looked back at her work.

'Mrs Pollard said he died. I saw Mr Drewry digging a grave and she said it was for the dog, but it wasn't. It couldn't have been.' She kept digging.

'Oh, Eliza, you don't think . . .' Ruth could not complete her sentence, and Eliza would not finish it for her. Her shovel hit something soft.

'Eliza, stop.'

She tossed the shovel aside and brushed the dirt away to reveal a large canvas sack.

'Eliza, please.'

As she already felt sick, the smell from the sack made her no worse. She tore it open with her hands and staggered back against the grave's dirt wall. Eliza looked away, taking in the dirt and blood covering her clothes, legs and arms, her chapped and bleeding palms, the grey sky so far above her, and she laughed.

The sack was filled with dead foxes and the maggots which crawled through their eyes.

*

It took Eliza longer to run her bath than it did for her to bathe. She let the water reach above the five-inch line, let it go all the way to the brim, then scrubbed herself clean. After she pulled the plug, she watched the muddy, warm water spin down the drain.

Ruth waited for her in the kitchen with two cups of tea. Eliza ignored them and walked straight into Mrs Pollard's office.

'Eliza, you must sit down a moment. You've exhausted yourself,' Ruth urged, following her to the office doorway.

'There's no time for that.' Eliza kicked a potato away and rummaged through Mrs Pollard's desk.

'There is. The entrance to one of the mines has collapsed. Mrs Pollard and Ben will be there the rest of the day, possibly most of the night, trying to clear it.'

'Why would Mrs Pollard care?' Eliza said, remembering the housekeeper's frantic response. 'And who is Ben?'

Ruth looked away. 'It's Mr Drewry's Christian name.'

'Murderers aren't Christian.'

'You mean the foxes? They're vermin.'

Eliza opened a drawer and pulled out a blank piece of heavy grey stationery. 'My aunt had a letter written on this.' She set it aside. 'And it's not the foxes that worry me. Don't you ever wonder why he's here?'

'He's the caretaker.'

'Some job of it he's doing. The lawns, the gardens, even the cemetery. It's all a mess. So what is he taking care of except Victoria's dirty work? If she's stealing their souls, that would still leave the body behind, wouldn't it?'

She dug deeper into the drawer and pulled out a small, well-worn Moleskine notebook.

'Leave him alone. You shouldn't judge people you don't know.'

The book's pages were filled with names and addresses. Those towards the front had faded, but those at the back were

306

not. Some were crossed out in a single line of red ink. Others were left alone.

Ruth peered over Eliza's shoulder. 'Is that your great discovery? An address book?'

'But how did she get my address?' Eliza pointed to the last page. Aunt Bess's name was written in a neat, slanting hand along with the address of their Whitechapel Road flat. A line of red ink ran through it. Eliza turned to the page before. 'And why is Pip's name here?'

Pip Vlasto's name also had a red line through it.

'Do you recognise anyone?' Eliza handed the book to Ruth. Ruth scanned through it, shaking her head.

'No. No, I don't . . . Wait. Here.' She pointed to a name above Pip's. 'Hawthorne. I don't know an Eric, but Jane, her surname was Hawthorne, I think. And this one – Marsh. When I first came to Plentynunig there was a Marsh girl. I remember now, her talking in the pub about wanting to join the Land Girls but not being permitted to quit the manor. Molly, I think. Where do these names come from?'

Eliza took the book back and slipped it into her trouser pocket. 'Knowing her, probably the Devil himself. Do you still think Rebecca's at Cefn Coed?'

'Cefn Coed?'

'The hospital in Swansea. Where Mrs Pollard says she sent her.'

Ruth placed her hand on Eliza's arm. 'No children with polio would be sent there. Cefn Coed is a mental hospital.'

A mental hospital. Rebecca's worst fear.

'She gave me that address as a joke.' As if her family was a joke. Rebecca's condition, a joke. Their entire lives, a joke. She took a glass paperweight and threw it against the wall.

'Why don't you lie down . . .'

'Don't tell me what to do.'

'You've had a shock, Eliza. If you don't allow your body to rest . . .'

'Just because your father is a doctor doesn't mean you are.' Eliza paced. 'Maybe Victoria doesn't have her. Not yet. Maybe that's what she's been trying to tell me. The handkerchief. Rebecca was locked in that room until someone moved her. And why would Mrs Pollard care so much about the mine collapse unless . . . Do you know what a *cware* is?'

'*Cware*? It's Welsh. The Welsh word for quarry.'

'When she heard about the collapse, Mrs Pollard was upset. Worried. I've never known that woman to be worried about anything.' Eliza pulled Ruth along.

'And you think . . .'

'I think that's where she's hidden Rebecca.'

*

The ground was bumpy and wet, making it difficult for Eliza to balance on the frame while Ruth pedalled. She would have preferred to walk, but Ruth's old bicycle was the fastest way. After nearly twenty minutes, they reached the top of a hill, where they dismounted.

'There.' Ruth pointed to the west. The red pit head stood out from the green hills while smoke stacks puffed more grey into the air. The shouts of the men below echoed, bouncing off the landscape. A few old horse carts were parked haphazardly on the main gravel drive, but the view of the mine's entrance was blocked by a brick outbuilding where Thornecroft's familiar carriage waited. The mare stood patiently, oblivious to all the activity. Beside them, the gaping wound of the quarry rested. Without fog, Eliza could see the treeline on the opposite side, and the narrow shelf path that led to the unseen bottom.

'Where is Mrs Pollard?' Eliza asked.

'I can't see her.'

'We must get closer.'

Ruth held her back. 'We can't go down there.'

'I'm not here to admire the view.' Eliza started down the hill. She heard Ruth following.

'If the mine's shut, there's no getting any of the men out, let alone your sister. They could be trapped there for hours. Days, even, if they're alive at all.'

'They'll get through eventually, and I'll be there when it happens. I'll be there for her.'

'But she mightn't be there, Eliza.' Ruth ran in front of her. 'Your sister could already be dead.'

The smell of coal dust grew stronger as they came closer to the mine. Eliza tasted it on her tongue. The shouts of the men were clearer, a mix of English and Welsh. An explosion shook the ground. Eliza struggled to stay on her feet as a great puff of black smoke flew into the air.

A brief cheer went up amongst the men, who began clearing more debris. Eliza continued to feel the vibrations as she and Ruth made their way to the outbuilding. The mare looked at them, disinterested, then lowered its head and returned to sleep. They hid around the corner of the outbuilding and tried to watch the rescue. More men were disappearing into the mine. No survivor had yet come out. Mr Drewry directed the proceedings, wearing the army trench coat Eliza had seen hanging in the carriage house.

Mrs Pollard stood beside him, eyes fixed on the men running back and forth. There was an uneasy calm about her. Whatever was being done at the mine entrance did not concern her. It was the movement of the men. She stood as if guarding something.

Eliza continued to watch, unnoticed amongst all the activity. One miner hurried from the wreckage carrying what appeared to be a bundle of fabric. Mrs Pollard stopped him. Eliza's mind transformed the bundle into a child. She could see its lifeless arms and legs, a shock of curly blonde hair. Maybe Ruth was right. Maybe Rebecca . . .

Mrs Pollard grabbed the bundle from the man. It was only a mass of canvas. It contained nothing. Mrs Pollard threw it aside then dusted off her hands.

'Ruth!'

A large man, face black with dust, stood behind them with a pickaxe.

'What're you doing here?' he asked Ruth, throwing Eliza a glance.

'We heard about the collapse. Thought we could help.'

'Nothing you can do here.'

'Davey!' Another man whistled at them and the miner hurried off. 'Best get yourselves home 'fore you get in the way,' he called over his shoulder. Eliza watched as he ran past Mrs Pollard. Mrs Pollard, who thought Eliza was still trapped in the cellar. Mrs Pollard, who stared directly at her.

Eliza saw the anger blooming on her face for only a moment before Ruth had her by the hand, pulling her up the hill. She wanted to look back, see if the housekeeper was following, if she had sent anyone after them, but as soon as she turned her head she stumbled. Her body hit the damp ground and began rolling down the hill. Ruth caught her and yanked her to her feet. They reached the bicycle, and Eliza was barely seated before Ruth was pedalling off.

She struggled to maintain her balance as Ruth sped away.

She clung to the frame, but her arms were weak from the digging and threatened to lose their hold. She gritted her teeth and gripped tighter, using her pain as a focal point. They could do this. They could get away. They could.

All she noticed in the crossroads was the presence of something large. Then she was on the ground, tumbling towards a ravine.

28

Harsh winds blew in from the Bristol Channel, battering Peter as he walked down Stryd Fawr. Glass crunched beneath his feet. London had been hit badly by the Blitz, but Swansea was devastated. Building after building was completely razed. Others were mere shells – smoke-stained façades hollowed out by fire and bomb blasts. Their charred skeletons towered either side of him as he battled against the heavy incoming winds. When he reached Castle Street, there were no buildings at all, only piles of rubble, the ruined remains of homes and businesses. He caught the glowing eyes of stray dogs keeping warm in dens of crumbled brick and mortar, their faces hungry and pleading.

Peter had no room, no map and little money. Adelaide Street could be beside him or on the other side of the city. He opened the address book, but there was no new information to guide him. He passed the ruins of a castle that now matched the city it called home. Maybe no one would notice if he spent the night there. Castles were strong, defensible.

Just beyond stood one surviving building, the words *Castle Cinema* gleaming from the red brick. Peter sheltered in its doorway, though there was no escaping wind which seemed to blow in every direction. If only Eliza knew he was here. If only she could guide him the rest of the way.

Voices carried on the wind. A group of girls hurried past the closed cinema. Their smiles vanished as soon as he stopped them.

'Excuse me, ladies, I don't mean to bother you, but I'm afraid I'm a bit lost.'

'Long way from home, are you, English boy?' A girl in a peacock-blue coat stepped forward and took the book from his hand. Her boldness faded as she read the address. She shoved the book into his hands and stepped back into the safety of her companions.

'Why would you want to go there?' she asked. Her friends whispered questions, and she responded in a low Welsh burr.

'So you know it?' Peter asked. He couldn't hide his excitement. Eliza was getting closer with every passing second.

The girl on the right spoke. 'Everyone knows Tŷ Marwolaeth.'

Peacock Blue nudged her in the arm, urging her to remain silent.

'I'm sorry. Tie—'

'Looking for work or what?' Peacock Blue asked.

'No. No, I'm looking for my girlfriend.'

The third, silent girl's face softened though the two others remained sceptical.

'Likely story. Come on, girls.' They changed direction and started walking back the way they came. They couldn't leave him. Not now. Not when he was so close.

'Wait, please! Her name's Eliza. Eliza Haverford. She and her little sister, Rebecca, they were sent here. I need to find them. Please.'

At the mention of a little sister, the quiet one detached herself from the group and came forward.

'Anwen, wait,' her friends urged, but she ignored them. From her pocket she withdrew a small notebook and began scribbling in it.

'Here,' she whispered, tearing out the page and pressing it into his hand. Directions.

'Thank you,' Peter said. 'Thank you. Wait. What does it mean? Tŷ . . .' He pointed to the words she wrote at the top.

'Death House,' she said, and was gone. They were all gone.

Peter stood alone on the pavement, receiving no shelter from the brick cinema as the winds threatened to steal the paper from his grip.

Death House. Superstition, he told himself. All the people out here were superstitious. The name had to do with the war. Perhaps the place was used to house those wounded in the Blitz, many of whom later died. They probably thought the place was haunted.

The heavy rain fell straight down despite the wind, but he had no umbrella or even change of clothes. If he were home now, he'd be settling down for dinner inside his warm, dry house, eating hot food and drinking hot tea. He could almost hear the whine of the wireless, the crackle of a fire, could smell the scent of a freshly cooked meal.

He passed another gutted building, its façade completely torn away and only some of the inner dividing walls standing, like a mews for giants' horses.

Beside it was Tŷ Marwolaeth. It was three storeys tall and all the windows were boarded up, like a body with its eyes glued shut by the undertaker, a body void of life. It reached out to Peter and, like a vacuum, drew him close while stealing what little feeling he had left.

The door stuck but eventually yielded. The house wanted him, Peter knew. It would not bar him entry for long.

Inside it was silent except for the rain outside and, although it was dry, it was cold. His damp clothes clung to his skin, and he shivered as he inched his way into the foyer. The girl called this Death House, and there was a smell about the place, a kind of musty coldness he remembered from his grandfather's

314

wake. Peter breathed deeply though it felt as if he weren't breathing at all. He could feel the air, yet couldn't, as if his body were a ghost. There was only one certainty – Eliza was not here.

As his eyes adjusted to the gloom, he could make out the walls and doorways, the stairway before him, but there was no furniture, not so much as a coat stand. This house was empty. Eliza had never come to work here.

Peter fell forward into the banister and lowered himself onto a step. It was lost. She was lost. There was nothing he could do for her, no way he could find her. And what would he do? Return to London, where thugs wanted to kill him? To parents who were ashamed of him? He had forfeited his apprenticeship by coming here. The firm would find another man to replace him, a trustworthy man, a reliable man. He had nothing. He should have left it alone.

Peter's fear and exhaustion began to morph into anger. Anger towards Bess, towards Eliza, towards the men who tricked him into coming out here. He wanted to find them, every last one of them, and make them suffer the way he had suffered. He gripped the banister and pulled himself to his feet. No longer did he feel cold or tired or hungry. There was only anger. That was his fuel now.

He climbed the stairs. He would search this house top to bottom for clues, for anything he could use. He would inter-rogate every person in Swansea until he found Pollard, track down those Welsh girls, make them tell him everything they knew. They must have known more. Why else would they have run away so quickly? He should have made them wait. Peter stumbled, banging into corners, tripping on loose floor-boards. His cigarette lighter was too weak to burn a hole in the darkness.

Somewhere on the first storey, where the damp wallpaper peeled and cockroaches skittered home across the floor as the rain continued its heavy assault outside, Peter's legs could no longer hold him. He was close. He could feel her near, but the anger had burnt out. He was empty, hollow. He crawled into a corner of the room, rested his head against the wall and allowed the house to envelop him.

29

She was lost inside their house in London. Except it wasn't
their house. Everything was familiar but wrong. Doors in
the wrong place. Rooms on the wrong floor. This was Aunt
Bess's bedroom. There was a woman there. A body. Pip
Vlasto's, and her eyes were missing. Eliza ran. Every hall had
the same paper, the same carpet. Candles lit the way through
Thornecroft, and if she reached Abigale Hall, she would be
safe, but there was nothing save long, empty corridors.

You know what you must do, Victoria whispered.

The large, carved doors appeared before her. She could get
closer now. She could see what was wrong. The wooden figures
moved, acting out their idyllic scenes. A cough like a monster's
scream shook the doors and the figures writhed in pain.

You know what you must do, Rebecca said. Eliza looked but
did not see her. The doors were open. She had opened them,
cut them in half with the knife in her hand, and they bled.
When she screamed, her voice made no sound. She could
hear Rebecca counting, but her voice was distant.

'Hush. It's alright.'

Eliza opened her eyes to a dark room. A candle flickered on
the nightstand beside her. She was in a bed, dressed in clothes
that weren't hers.

'It's fine. You're safe.' Ruth sat beside her, holding a lamp
and a tray of food. 'A lorry knocked us down. You've a few
bumps and bruises but nothing serious.'

The room was warm, but there was a chill Eliza couldn't account for. It seemed to come from within her. She wrapped her arms tight around her torso.

'How long have I . . . ?'

'A few hours. Past dinnertime, but I thought you might be hungry.' She handed Eliza the tray.

'The mine?'

'What I've heard, all the men are out. At least the ones they could find.'

'Rebecca?'

'No one saw a little girl.'

Eliza had no appetite. She pushed the bread around her plate.

'Eliza, you must leave Plentynunig. Mrs Pollard has it in for you. It's not safe for you here.'

'I understand,' she said. It was the truth, but sense had no meaning for her now. Sense could not erase the duty she had to her family.

'Good.' Ruth smiled. 'Now rest. You need to get your strength back.'

Eliza forced the food down her throat then fell into a fitful sleep. Though she should have felt safe in Ruth's house, she could not rest. A million different thoughts crawled around inside her, trying to catch her attention, but she could never focus on one. There was not a part of her that did not ache. She was itchy and feverish, her clothes scratching against her skin. The bed sheets became too warm. She kicked them off, nearly knocking over the candle. Every time she closed her eyes, she heard her sister crying, saw the knife in her hands.

'Rebecca,' she whispered to the dark. 'Rebecca, I'm sorry. I'm coming.' The dark never replied.

You know what you must do.

Though she never felt herself fall asleep, when she next opened her eyes, the candle had gone out. Eliza swung her feet off the bed. The cotton nightgown she wore was damp from sweat and stuck to her skin. On a chair by the door she found a pile of clean, folded clothes – dungarees and a work shirt. Ruth's old Land Girl uniform. She dressed, the clothes baggy on her smaller frame, and tied back her hair in a headscarf. Her shoes were beneath the chair and she laced them up quickly. She knew what Victoria was telling her to do, yet she could not do it. Rebecca could, but Rebecca would not return until it was done.

As Eliza made her way down the narrow attic staircase, voices drifted up from below. A man and a woman. The woman was Ruth, and the man she assumed was Berwin. Yet, as she reached the first floor, the man's voice became clearer. It was much too young to be the drunk.

Their voices remained hushed as Eliza crept down the staircase to the ground floor. Ruth and the man were in the kitchen. Eliza remained quiet, as if Victoria were standing beside her pressing a finger to her lips, and placed her ear to the closed kitchen door. She could only make out a few words.

Time. Girl. Swansea. Wait.

The man's voice was familiar. She knew it but couldn't place it, though it made her heart quicken in fear. So familiar. Something nudged her leg. Kasey stood beside her, wagging his tail. Eliza pushed open the door.

Ruth and Mr Drewry were held in each other's embrace, kissing. The kitchen door bounced off the wall, and they broke apart.

'You lied to me,' Eliza whispered, unable to move. 'I should have known. How you got those notes to the house. Why Mrs Pollard hired you. It was to keep an eye on me, wasn't it?'

Ruth stood silent, unable to defend herself.

'Belfast. The label on Mrs Pollard's trunk. Is that where she recruited you?'

'Eliza, wait.'

'Your name isn't in the book. Your name . . .'

Mr Drewry moved towards his rifle. Eliza ran. She heard them shouting after her, chasing her, Kasey barking, but she did not stop. She did not see where she was running to, but she did not stop.

Betrayed. Betrayed. Betrayed.

The word pulsed inside her head as her feet flew across the ground. She should have known better than to trust anyone. But she had been so desperate for someone to talk to, for someone to help her. It was so obvious now. Not knowing what happened to Pip, the children having polio – they were lies. All of them lies. And she had believed them. Despite everything, she had believed them. Gullible, weak, just like Father said.

Tears clouded her vision. She no longer heard them chasing, but she didn't turn to look. In the distance was a treeline and she ran for it. She was a few feet into the forest when the burning in her legs and lungs forced her to stop. She fell to her hands and knees and screamed. The sound tore out of her, deep and primal, ripping her throat to shreds. She didn't care. A little girl. That's all she was. A silly little girl, always believing everything she was told. The world laughed at her, spat at her, buried her under the weight of its lies, of the false belief that if she muddled through, made the best of everything, it would all turn out alright.

Tears kept rolling down her face, but she didn't bother to wipe them away. Let them fall on the ground and nurse the wicked soil, she thought. The world was wicked and cruel. Let it feed on her weakness and purge her hollow soul. Let her become as hard as the earth. Let her turn to stone. No, to coal. Turn her to coal and let her burn. Let her dust contaminate the earth, stain those who would harm her. This was what Rebecca understood. Why she treated the world the way she did. Rebecca understood how easily everything could turn against you but refused to let it get the better of her.

Eliza knew then her sister was alive. Rebecca would never stop fighting. She would do whatever she could to live. Rebecca was nothing like Father, Eliza saw that now. Rebecca would fight. Now was Eliza's chance to show Rebecca that she, too, was strong.

She let her tears dry, waited until the burning in her legs receded. Then she retied her headscarf, brushed the dirt from her hands and made her way back to Thornecroft.

*

The creatures of the night came alive around her as she waited in the woods at the edge of the little cemetery. Owls hooted. Foxes darted across the lawn. Shadows, which earlier seemed innocent, grew more sinister. She blended in with the darkness. Blackouts had once terrified her. Anything could have been lurking in Hungerford's darkened streets, so she would keep herself nestled snug by the Littletons' fire, sewing dollies from scrap and pretending the world beyond the blackout curtains was filled with light. She never saw London in blackout, but Aunt Bess told her how eerie it was, like an abandoned ancient city. One could never find one's way, she said, and if you were stuck in an unfamiliar place with no street signs to guide you, you had to wait until morning and hope you were still alive. The one good thing, she said, was that if it was a quiet and clear night, you could see the stars. They shone bright and

321

clear and filled the sky, allowed you a moment of beauty in an otherwise ugly time.

There were no stars now. The clouds were a curtain pulled across the sky. She debated how long it would be until she could be sure Mrs Pollard was asleep. The answer in her heart was never. She pictured the woman coiled like a snake, ready to pierce her venomous fangs into the most unsuspecting victims.

Movement in the garden refocused her attention. Eliza thought it was Victoria, but the figure moved with too much purpose. Mrs Pollard walked out the back gate and into the dark carriage house. Mr Drewry had not been home all night. He and Ruth were probably out hunting her, tracking her across the countryside.

Mrs Pollard emerged riding the grey mare faster than Eliza had ever seen it move. So captivated was she by its speed, it took her a moment to realise it was headed in her direction. Eliza ducked behind the nearest tree and crouched low. She heard the hooves pounding on the ground, the heavy snorting breaths of the overworked animal. Closer and closer it came, nearly on top of her. She thought of Ichabod Crane hiding from his Headless Horseman, and hoped hers would be a dissimilar fate.

The sounds of horse and rider veered away. Eliza peeked round the tree and caught a glimpse of the mare's backside before it was swallowed by the dark. She could hear its galloping grow fainter and was tempted to follow. Perhaps Ruth and Mr Drewry had contacted Mrs Pollard, told her Eliza was gone. How furious she would be at them.

Eliza needn't worry now whether the housekeeper had gone to bed. She emerged from the woods and ran down to the house. The kitchen door was locked. She grabbed the rock they used for a doorstop, feeling the smooth spots where the rabbit's blood still stained, and tapped it against the handle. It remained intact. Forgoing silence, she slammed the rock again and again, until the old handle broke off and fell to the ground.

She moved through the familiar kitchen with ease, grabbing the Tilley lamp off the wall and the matches kept nearby. After lighting the lamp, she chose the largest knife from the block and headed into the hall. Her bedroom door was open. Though the furniture remained, the room had been emptied. All her things were gone, the bed sheets changed, ready for a new occupant. Eliza thought of the address book and wondered who the next girl was to be.

Sickened, she continued through the house, pausing only in Abigale Hall. This had always been her favourite place, the only spot that felt untouched by the evil eroding the rest of the manor. She never saw Mr Brownawell here and Mrs Pollard chose to pass through quickly, as if they could not bear the comfort of the place, its carved-flower wainscoting and delicate dome the antithesis of the rest of Thornecroft's heavy brutality. It was as if Victoria's spirit had taken solace here, imbuing the hall with the same strength that drove the girl's ghost. While the halls of Thornecroft threatened to destroy, twisting around Abigale Hall like choking bindweed, the hall maintained its strength, a strength Eliza now let fill her as she climbed the north hall staircase.

The shadows of the carvings ran down the grand double doors. The figures remained still as Eliza put her hand on the polished brass handle and pushed. The door stuck, then gave way.

The room was deep and dark, with towering ceilings and oversized furniture. Everything seemed designed to dwarf the occupant. Eliza refused to feel small. At the far end of the cavernous bedroom was an immense four-poster bed, the kind Eliza saw in books on French royalty. Heavy curtains were drawn all the way around. She approached, afraid the creaking floorboards would give her away. She reminded herself that he was a crippled old man. He could do nothing to harm her. She came round the side of the bed, gripped the curtain firmly and yanked it aside.

The bed was empty. The sheets were neatly made, tucked into the mattress with precision. The pillows were smooth, perched and waiting. Eliza touched the bed. It was cold. When she drew back her hand, it was covered in a fine dust. She looked closer at the bed and realised the pillows and top sheet, too, were dusty.

A cough echoed from next door. Eliza took one last glance at the bed then hurried after the sound. On the far side of the room was another door. This one was plain, with scuff and scratch marks around the bottom. A low groan sounded from behind. She turned the knob.

It was a windowless cupboard with only three pieces of furniture – a bedside table, the antiquated wheelchair and the simple single bed in which Mr Brownawell coughed and writhed. The room was freezing, but he had only worn flannel pyjamas and a thin blue sheet. The pillows beneath his head were flat and uncovered. He coughed into a handkerchief already coated with globs of spit then weakly dropped his head.

Eliza pushed the wheelchair aside and held the lamp over his head, staring at his gaunt face and liver-spotted skin. He coughed again, and she stepped back to avoid getting sprayed by spittle. She didn't know how long Mrs Pollard would be gone but was starting to feel as if she'd been here too long already. She knew what she must do.

'Wake up,' she said.

Mr Brownawell did not move.

'I said wake up.' Eliza kicked the bed. He startled awake. Disorientated, he cowered at Eliza then seemed to recognise her.

'This is the only way, isn't it? The only way to break the curse.'

Mr Brownawell wheezed.

'I once told Rebecca that I couldn't hate anyone, but I was wrong. I didn't know men like you existed.'

He reached for the call bell that rested on his nightstand. Eliza grabbed it.

'Mrs Pollard isn't here.' She dropped it to the floor. 'Whatever deal she made with your ghost is at an end. The girls – they'll all of them be returned.' She positioned the knife above her head.

With great effort, Mr Brownawell spoke: 'Victoria.'

'I am not Victoria! Your Victoria is dead.'

He took a deep breath. 'No. I . . . know.' He pointed a crippled hand at the nightstand. 'Drawer,' he rasped. 'Please.'

The man in that portrait would never have begged. Eliza kept the knife primed while she opened the drawer. It was empty save a single photograph. A smiling girl about Eliza's age stood in front of a simple stone house. Because she was smiling, Eliza did not immediately recognise her. A younger girl stood in the foreground and the older man beside them wore a suit that did not fit his weathered face and deep-set eyes.

'My . . . Victoria,' he wheezed.

Eliza turned the picture over.

'My . . . daughter.'

Reginald Kyffin and daughters, 1876

There was no doubting the similarity between the man in the photograph and the old man lying on the bed. Eliza dropped the knife.

'You're not . . . You're . . . Reg Kyffin.'

He closed his eyes and nodded.

'But, but no . . . You died. They said you . . . disappeared.'

'Came . . . came to find her . . . Can't leave till . . . till I find her.'

'Why is Mrs Pollard keeping you here? Why is she pretending you're Mr Brownawell? Where is he?'

He did not answer.

'Is he with my sister? Do you know where they are?'

A deep breath. 'No.'

'Did the house take her? Take her like it took Victoria?'

'Not like . . . Victoria. P-Pollard. Like Pollard.'

'But is she here? Is Rebecca here?'

Reg Kyffin did not answer.

'Have you seen her ghost? Mr Kyffin, have you seen your daughter's ghost?'

'Ghost . . . ghosts. No . . . ghosts.'

The old man was exhausted, losing his battle against sleep. He reached out his hand. Eliza gave him the photograph. He pressed it close to his heart and was asleep.

30

The thump from downstairs woke him. Only the rain, Peter told himself, until he heard the voices. Someone had entered the house. He kept still. The slightest movement would make a sound in an old, empty building like this. Their words were muffled, but Peter heard the men spreading out as if looking for something. Someone.

A street lamp cast a thin ray of artificial light into the room between the gaps in the old wooden boards. Hoping the men were making too much noise to hear him, Peter quietly made his way to the window. He was only on the first floor. Not a long drop. If he could get the boards loose without them hearing, if he didn't injure himself, he could hurry off into the shadows before they could find him. There wasn't much time to think. He reached for the boards.

A hand clamped over his mouth. Peter struggled as the person whispered in his ear.

'Shhh.'

Peter was allowed to turn. An old man held him. He slowly released Peter and put a bony finger to his lips. Together they waited as the footsteps echoed, drawing closer and closer to their little room at the back of the house.

The old man indicated for Peter to remain still then walked to the door and flung it open, attracting the attention of the intruders. Peter wanted to run, but there was nowhere to go. The man shut the door, leaving Peter in darkness.

'What you lot coming round here for?' the old voice said.

'What is it? You find him?'

'No, it's only ol' Addy.'

'What're you doing here, Addy?'

'My *tŷ*. My house,' the old man said. 'I've a right to be here more than any of you.'

'Phew! Take a whiff of him. Been drinking again, Addy?'

'Oh, leave him alone. He ain't doing any harm.'

Peter recognised the last voice. He'd spent hours down the pub with it, drinking and chatting. A voice that once carried friendship, now only fear.

'Say, Addy, is it?' Stephen continued. 'You seen any strange blokes about?'

'Besides you *tair*? *Na*, quiet as a mouse here. I keep mae *tŷ* nice and quiet. She likes it nice and quiet.'

'Yeah, I'm sure she does,' Stephen said. 'So, no one's been round? No one about my age? Ginger hair? Skinny lad?'

'Could be you, but you're not so lean, are you *mae bachgen*? Your mother feeding you up nice and proper, she is.'

'Come on, let's go,' the first voice said.

'Yeah, come on. I'm bloody starving,' said the second.

'You'll let us know if you see anyone, won't you, Addy?' Stephen asked.

'Course I will. Course I will. Report all visitors, I do. Always and forever.' The old man kept rambling while the heavy footsteps descended the stairs. The front door banged heavily and the house grew quiet once more. Peter listened for the old man but heard nothing. Cautiously, he opened the door. The man stood there, staring at Peter.

'You've caused them *tair* a spot of bother, you have.' He looked Peter in the eye as if assessing his very soul. Finally he nodded and walked away. 'They should be gone now. Come

328

upstairs and join us for *cinio*. No meat on your bones, *mae bachgen*. No meat at all.'

Peter followed the man to the top floor of the house. This place, too, was dusty and sparse, save one room at the back. Here a rudimentary living space was set up – a mattress on the floor with a few bare sheets, a gas-ring stove, bucket with water, clothes piled in the corner. A second bucket held human waste.

'Come and sit. Come and sit.' He pointed to a table with two chairs. When Peter made to sit, the man stopped him. '*Na, na*. Can't sit there. *Na*, that chair's not for you. Here, erm, here . . .' He spun round, looking for a suitable alternative.

'The floor will be alright,' Peter said.

'*Na, na. Na* way to treat a guest. We treat our guests well. Here. You have my chair. Yes, you sit there. *Na, na*. Don't mind me. Don't bother me at all. Guests come first. What we always say, isn't it, *m anwylyd*?'

Peter sat in the chair and waited in silence as the man lit the gas ring, scooped water from the bucket using a saucepan, and set it to boil.

'That was very kind of you,' Peter said. 'For not telling them.'

'Oh, nonsense. Don't listen to them. Never listen to them. Bastards,' he spat, his expression turning dark.

'My name is Peter. Peter Lamb.' He held out his hand.

'Yes, yes. Of course. How foolish of me.' They shook hands. 'Addison Marsh. Pleased to make your acquaintance. I hope you enjoy your stay here. Not as grand a guest house as we used to be, but we do our best for our visitors, don't we, *m anwylyd*? Afraid you caught us at short notice, though. Not much food in. Have some noodles. They brought us noodles, so that's what we have. Funny little word, isn't it? Noodles.'

'That's fine. Thank you.'

There was no heat source in the room, nothing but the few candles and the stove. Peter felt his teeth chattering. His clothes were still damp and the wetness seeped through his skin. The anger that warmed him earlier had yet to be reignited.

'You've brought us news, I suppose,' Addison said, his voice suddenly solemn.

'Beg pardon?'

'News about our Molly. That's why you're here. Hush, *m anwylyd*.'

'I'm sorry, sir. But I don't know any Molly.'

'Are you sure? Lovely girl, lovely. Loveliest girl you'll ever meet. Couldn't forget her if you met her so I suppose you haven't. Quiet, woman! He said he doesn't know her.'

'Is Molly your daughter?' Peter asked.

'Oh yes. Our only one. Only child, our Molly. *Ein merch. Ein cariad.*'

'Has she . . . has she gone missing?'

Addison dumped some noodles into the saucepan and watched the water boil over.

'She's not missing,' he said. 'Not to us. No. We know exactly where she is. Exactly where.' From beside the stove, Addison pulled out a bottle and took a swig. He knew. This old man knew. Peter inched forward on his chair.

'And where is that, sir?'

Addison slammed the bottle onto the stove, dangerously close to the flame.

'I'm sorry,' Peter apologised.

'What have you lost?' Addison whispered, his eyes on the ring of flame. 'Wouldn't be here 'less you lost something. What have you lost?'

'Her name is Eliza.'

330

Addison lowered his head. Then he turned down the flame, slowing the boil. He joined Peter at the table.

'They take them,' he said. 'They sniff you out, like ruddy dogs, sniff out those with nothing to give and something they need. You say *na*. At first. Say *na*, *na*, *nac oes*. But these are hard times. Hard times. My drink. Fetch my drink.'

Peter grabbed the bottle from the stove and handed it over.

'*Iechyd da*.' Addison raised the glass then took a long sip before continuing. 'Did you say *na*?'

'It wasn't my choice to make.'

Addison nodded. 'You would've said *na*. Then you would've said yes. We say yes, always. It's only work, that's what we tell ourselves. She's a big girl now. She could do with a proper job, that's what you say. And the money, the money is a little bonus. Something for our trouble. No trouble. And then . . . and then . . .' He took another drink. 'And then you never hear from Molly again. Hush, dear, don't cry. Don't cry.'

'Where did Molly go, Mr Marsh?'

'You can't get her back. Not once she's gone. Once she's gone, she's gone. She's gone.'

'Is it nearby? Is it somewhere in Swansea?'

'They don't tell you where. I thought they might. If I let them use the house, if I said they could use it, use it to lure others, they promised to tell me. I know they lie, woman! Stop saying it!'

'Do you know anything, Mr Marsh? Please. I have to find her.'

'You have to.'

'Yes.'

'You'd do anything.'

'Yes. Anything.'

331

'Anything just to see her again. Hold her. Keep her close. Love her.'

'Yes. Please.'

Addison pushed the bottle across the table. 'Then you might as well start on that, because you won't ever see her again, *mae bachgen*. Except in your dreams.'

*

Peter spent a restless night in Tŷ Marwolaeth. Addison allowed Peter use of the mattress but then spent the whole night pacing the house and speaking to himself. Peter had only brief recollections of his dreams, all of which involved Eliza. He took a few sips of Addison's whisky and found that it helped.

He was only half awake when someone banged on the front door. Peter glanced at his watch – half past seven in the morning. He listened carefully but, being on the top floor, could only hear garbled voices. He was certain, though, that neither was Stephen's. He crept out of the room and into the hall.

'. . . said no one's been here but us. Why don't you believe us?' said Addison.

'Who else was asking?'

'Your compatriots. Came here last evening, looking for *dwili*. Nonsense. Trouble. All you lot ever cause.'

Peter snuck to the railing where he could peer down onto the ground floor. Addison cowered in front of a taller man whose face was hidden by a cap. But Peter needn't see his face. The man had only one arm. This was the man Mosley told him about – the one who took Eliza away.

Apparently satisfied with Addison's answers, the one-armed man left. As soon as the front door was shut, Peter ran down the stairs. He grabbed Addison by the shoulders.

'Who was that?'

332

'Why, him? Calls himself Drewry. Pay him no mind. Same as the others. Take, take, take.'

Peter opened the door and spotted Drewry at the end of the street, turning left. Addison grabbed his arm and pulled him back.

'Don't. You won't see her again. We never do, do we, *m anwylyd*?'

Peter pulled his arm free and ran after Drewry. He thought Addison might yell after him, but he heard nothing. He glanced behind. The old man was gone.

He was afraid he'd already lost Drewry when he spotted him at the next corner. Last night's heavy rains created deep puddles in old bomb impact sites. If Peter stepped in one, the splash would be enough to draw the one-armed man's attention. Drewry rounded another corner then entered a pub.

It was hours before opening time. The shutters were closed and Peter couldn't see in, but, in the quiet morning street, he heard voices down a nearby alleyway. Peter followed them and ended up round the back of the pub, where he saw Drewry shoving Stephen up against the wall. Two other men stood idly by.

'My business is with him,' Stephen said.

'You're to stay in London,' Drewry replied. 'He comes out here, they'll handle him. He comes to Thornecroft, I'll handle him.'

'This is personal.'

Drewry punched Stephen in the gut.

'I don't care if he shat in your mam's bed. You do as you're told according to the agreement, else our business is done. There're plenty of other toerags in that cesspool who'd be happy to have our business. You think I came out here for my health? They sent me to tell you they don't like the trouble you're causing. That means you're in their eye, and that's a more dangerous place than you've ever been. Put yourself on the first train back to London or I'll put you in hospital.' Drewry spat at Stephen's feet then went inside the pub. The other two bruisers followed.

Peter hurried out of the alleyway and watched Drewry head towards Castle Street. After waiting to see if Stephen and the others would follow, he went after him, tailing him all the way to the train station. Peter hid in the crowds there, keeping close to Drewry until he saw him board the train at platform three. Peter bought his ticket with minutes to spare.

Addison Marsh was wrong. He'd be seeing Eliza again very soon.

31

Heavy rainfall on the carriage house roof woke Eliza. Though she was dry, the temperature dropped, and she shivered in the thin shirt. She wrapped a horse blanket from the mare's stall around her shoulders and went to the carriage doors. The top of the manor towered over her.

Inside, Mrs Pollard would be preparing breakfast, plotting with Ruth to bring the next girl to Thornecroft. Did Ruth help capture all the girls or was Eliza a special case? Perhaps Eliza was wrong about the curse. If the real Mr Brownawell was gone, who was Victoria trying to punish? Maybe she fed off the souls of the young in order to remain on Earth. Or maybe they were only taken once they learnt the truth about Reg Kyffin. But how could Rebecca have known? What had she done all day while Eliza completed chores?

The garden door was left open and, through the rain, Eliza glimpsed the overgrown shrubberies. The world looked different in the rain, like a series of photographs moving quickly before her eyes, each slightly different from the last.

The singing was clear – a child's voice coming from the garden. Eliza dropped the blanket. Climbing through the tangles of weeds and bushes, she ignored the fresh scratches on her skin as she ran to the latticework doors. They were already open.

A flash of white. Victoria's dress? Eliza looked, but the figure was gone.

Rebecca's voice rang through the hall.

'*Run rabbit, run rabbit, run, run, run . . .*'

Eliza placed one foot inside.

'Rebecca?'

The moment her name was spoken, the singing ceased. Eliza took another step. All she could hear was her own breathing, the rain dripping from her clothes, the wind outside.

A woman screamed.

Eliza ran back through the garden, wiping the rain from her eyes as she rounded the garden wall. The shimmering white figure came towards her. Victoria stumbled and fell, red blossoming on her dress as a wig fell from her head.

Eliza saw her ghost's face.

'Help me, please,' Ruth gasped, clutching her side.

It was another trick, a way to trap her.

'Eliza, please. Please, she's coming for me.'

'You're Victoria.'

'I'll explain. Please! Help me.'

A dark figure walked briskly towards them, shaking Eliza from her inertia, and she hoisted Ruth to her feet. The blood was sticky against her rain-soaked hands. It was real.

'The carriage house,' Ruth panted. Eliza obeyed. She supported Ruth and together they hobbled across the east lawn. Eliza resisted the urge to look behind her.

'The key,' Ruth said, pulling at her dress collar. Eliza removed it from Ruth's neck, quickly opening the door then locking them inside.

'But she'll still get in,' Eliza said.

'No. Ben changed the locks. Her key won't work. Upstairs. There are bandages. Ah!' Ruth cried out and fell to her knees. Eliza helped her up to the loft and sat her on the bed.

'By the basin. There . . . there should be . . .'

'I'll check.'

Eliza found a roll of bandages and some clean rags. When she returned to the bed, Ruth was lying down, eyes closed.

'Ruth. Ruth, you must stay awake.'

Ruth opened her eyes. Eliza could see now how glazed they were. Blood had seeped through most of the dress. The wig was lost somewhere outside. Eliza ripped apart the fabric where the knife had torn it. She couldn't see the wound for all the blood. It was a darker colour now, more black than red. Eliza placed a wad of cloth against the worst part of the bleeding.

'We should have told you. More pressure.' Ruth's breathing was laboured, her skin whiter than the dress.

'You've been Victoria this whole time.'

Ruth nodded, but the motion made her paler still.

'When Pip was murdered, I . . . I knew it was Mrs Pollard.' She struggled to take a deep breath. 'Thought I could . . . use the stories . . . make her feel . . . haunted. Punished.'

The blood poured over Eliza's hands. She grabbed another cloth and pressed it against Ruth's side. It made no difference.

'Guilt can't harm those who feel nothing . . . Victoria was never for . . . you. I tried to tell you . . . there was no ghost. But I . . . thought it safer if you . . . you didn't know the whole truth. Wanted you to stay away . . . cause . . . dangerous. She's dangerous.'

'You must rest now, Ruth. Don't try to speak.'

'Ben. Trust him. He's . . . a good man. He'll . . . he'll . . .'

'Hush now.' Tears, not rain, now dampened Eliza's face.

Ruth's eyes snapped open. 'Rebecca. She was there. There with . . . You were right . . . We had no . . . idea how . . . how . . .' Ruth released a shuttered breath. She never took another.

337

'Ruth?' Eliza shook her by the shoulder. 'Ruth, what about Rebecca? Ruth? Please, don't go. I'm sorry. I'm so sorry.'

It was no use. Though her eyes were open, Ruth would never wake again. Eliza retreated from the lifeless body, saw her hands, her Claddagh ring, her clothes – Ruth's clothes – covered in blood. Some water was left in the basin. Eliza plunged in her hands and the water turned red. The ring fell from her finger. She left it at the bottom of the basin. Outside, the rain continued to fall. It was the only sound in the loft until she heard the barking below.

She moved cautiously to the window. Kasey growled at a figure about a foot away. Mrs Pollard stood stock still in the rain wearing a cloak and hat, staring at the dog. Kasey refused to let her near. The housekeeper's head tilted upwards. She smiled at Eliza then turned on her heel and returned to the manor.

Mrs Pollard wouldn't need to get into the carriage house to destroy her. She could burn the place down, threaten to kill Rebecca. Anything to coax Eliza out.

Kasey sat sentry at the door, awaiting his master. Eliza could wait no longer.

32

The train was nearly deserted. Interspersed amongst its empty compartments were an elderly couple, a soldier and a young mother with two children silent from hunger. Peter glanced at them through the windows as he passed, every sombre face a reflection of the tired landscape outside. Wherever they were headed, it was not a place many wanted to go.

Drewry sat alone in the front compartment of the forward coach, where the engine was the loudest. Peter stayed back when he spotted him. The compartment behind was empty. He could ride there for the remainder of the journey, but he stood in the corridor, watching this man whose cap was pulled over his eyes, his arm draped across his lap. When had that calloused hand last touched his Eliza? When had those eyes last looked upon her face?

She was getting closer. Peter could nearly smell her familiar scent. Roses and old books. That's what she always smelled of to Peter, even when a night at work made her sweat through her uniform or she'd been cooking with lard and Oxo all morning. Roses and old books. That was Eliza.

Drewry rolled his shoulders and rested his head against the compartment wall. Peter wondered how much of an interrogation it would take to get the truth. The man had more muscle than Peter, but he was damaged. How much fight could a man with only one arm have? Peter was young, fit.

His leg hadn't bothered him for days. He could take this man. He'd been able to take Mosley.

The train turned round a steep bend, shaking the carriage. Peter stumbled against the wall, catching his hand on the window ledge. His palm cut on a splinter of wood, and he shook it to dispel the pain. Drewry stared at him, as if the scent of blood had drawn his attention. Peter curled his hand into a fist and slipped back into the shadows of the train.

From the next-door compartment, Peter watched the sun's descending red rays. It was beautiful to see the colourful light over the hills, but it wasn't long before the sky filled with clouds and streaks of rain dashed the windows. The storm continued as the train pulled into a station. Peter saw Drewry leave the coach and waited a few moments more before doing the same.

On the platform, Peter turned up his collar as he studied the worn wooden sign – Plentynunig. He had never heard of it. He looked for Drewry but the platform was empty. Had he not disembarked here? It was too late to board the already departing train. He followed the Way Out sign. Someone might know where this house was.

Peter descended a set of rotting wood stairs onto a grassy bank and spotted a pub across the road. As he stepped towards it, someone grabbed him by the collar and shoved him against the station wall.

'I know who you are,' the man growled. 'And it would do you best to leave this place now.'

Peter wriggled free and turned to face his attacker.

'I'm not leaving without Eliza.'

'You can't help her. And it'll only be tears for you if you try. Go back to London, lad. This ain't your war.'

'I won't let you keep her prisoner. Do what you like to me, but I'll free her, even if it's the last thing I do.' Peter raised his fists and braced himself for a fight. This was his purpose, and he would no longer allow any man to come between him and his Eliza.

Drewry regarded him a moment, his expression unreadable, then started towards the pub. 'Put those away.'

'Why? What are you going to do? Get some help from your friends because you're too cowardly to face me on your own?'

Drewry called over his shoulder, 'I'm going to buy you a drink,' and continued across the road.

'You're . . . what?' Peter hesitated then jogged after him.

He entered the pub a moment after Drewry. Only the publican and the one-armed man were present. Candles and lanterns lit the dim, wood-walled space. Peter walked across the grey stone floor, unsure of where to stand. Drewry took two tankards of beer in one hand and walked to a high-backed corner booth. Peter followed, the publican eyeing him with mistrust as he passed. Drewry pushed a tankard towards him as he sat on the creaking wooden seat.

'No one else's ever come this far. I'll give you that, Lamb.' He sipped his beer.

'Where is Eliza?'

'Up the road at the manor.'

Peter rose.

'Sit your arse down and listen, will you?'

'Why? You work for her, don't you? This Pollard?'

'I've a feeling my employment will soon be at an end.' He drank more, tilting his head far back, downing most of his pint. 'Look, Lamb, I'm on your side.'

'Are you? Why?'

'Why else? A woman.' He leaned in. 'There are things in motion. Things you don't need to understand. But I give you my word, I'll bring Eliza back to you.'

'When?'

'Tonight.'

'And her sister? Rebecca? She won't go anywhere without Rebecca.'

Drewry leaned back. Worry crossed his face. 'I'll do what I can about . . . that.'

'Brilliant. Though of course I have no reason to trust you.'

'Course you don't. And I ain't got time to try and make you.' He reached into his pocket and pulled out an old notebook and pencil. 'Here are directions to the house. It's called Thornecroft.' He scribbled down a few notes and a rudimentary map then tore out the paper and handed it to Peter. 'If we're not here by closing time, then come and find us.'

'Of course. And it will be another false address. Another trap, like Death House.'

'Swansea ain't a trap. It's a safety net. A way of hiding the trail when girls go missing. Of keeping little shites like your old pal Stephen away from here.'

'How many girls have you helped to disappear?' He expected Drewry to deny it, to proclaim some noble intentions.

'Three. Including your Eliza. And one I shouldn't have . . .' He drank the rest of his beer then glanced at the clock sitting on the fireplace mantle. 'I gave someone else my word that I'd not let this happen again. That I wouldn't let Eliza disappear. And if it gives you any comfort, I care about this person a great deal more than you.' He rose and threw some coins on the table. 'Get yourself another drink. You look like you need it.'

He was gone before Peter could protest.

*

Time passed slowly in the strange pub. Few men entered and those that did looked nearer to death than life. Like old Addy

342

back in Swansea, their skin was taut and grey. Sunken eyes glanced at Peter then stared into stale pints. No one spoke, not even to order. The bald, pale-faced publican simply set a beer on the bar for whoever approached. The longer Peter sat, the more uncomfortable he became. He could feel his skin shrinking like that of the other patrons, his complexion changing to grey. The cold pub felt like a cocoon transforming him into one of these moth-like men who hovered by the lantern lights as if they were their only salvation.

Peter was on his second drink when he realised he was an idiot. Trusting a man like Drewry? Believing his nonsense about bringing Eliza back? All Peter was doing was giving him a head start. But it hadn't been too long, only an hour. No other trains had come or gone. He would've heard them at the station. He left his unfinished beer and Drewry's remaining coins on the table and walked out of the pub. Some men loitered outside with their pints, staring at Peter as he passed, the smoke of their cigarettes becoming lost in the fog.

With every step, the word echoed in his head – Thornecroft. Thornecroft. Thornecroft. Something was pulling him towards that word. Towards Eliza. The fog swallowed the world around him and he felt safe, alone with his thoughts. It was only him and the road. He would be there soon.

It suddenly struck him how silent the world was. Where once there were birds chirping, now there was nothing. He listened for the wind, but that, too, had fallen still. The silence broke Peter from his trance, and he realised he had no idea where he was. He looked at his feet. He wasn't even on the road any more. At some point, the fog had become heavier and he hadn't noticed. Yet in the distance was a light, a round ball hovering in the air. Peter stepped towards it.

A twig snapped behind him, and a figure emerged through the fog.

'Hello, mate.'

'Drewry told you to go back to London,' Peter said.

'And leave my dear old friend on his own?' Stephen took a step forward.

'Why did you follow me?'

'No choice. If you had stopped all this when I told you, we wouldn't be here now. Could still be friends. Teasing Purvis at work, going to the pub at weekends. You had to go and spoil everything.'

'I couldn't let her go.'

'You should have.'

'How long? How long have you been kidnapping girls?'

Stephen laughed. 'I've never kidnapped anyone. Girls need work, I find them work. Usually it's a matter of putting them on the streets. Like Jessie.'

'And how many have you killed, like Jessie?'

'She broke the rules and got what she deserved. Once the police finish their inquiries and find out she were strangled, in Peter Lamb's flat, then you'll get your chance to suffer. Or rather, your reputation will.' His hand reached into his pocket.

'And what about Eliza?' Peter asked as he searched the fog for an escape.

'Eliza was the first of the special ones I found. Was supposed to get a nice cut of the profits. But you had to go snooping about, and now Angelo won't give me my share until this business with you is settled.'

Peter had nothing to defend himself with except for his fists. Stephen might have a knife or even a gun in his pocket, and he was now only an arm's length away. Peter steadied himself.

'If you needed money, I could . . .'

'You made me look weak! Like I didn't know what I was doing. Like I was stupid! You're my friend. You're not supposed to make me look stupid.'

'I'm sorry.'

'Well, it's too late for that. So be a good lad, Peter, and let me do my job.'

Stephen lunged and they both fell to the ground. Hands clasped around Peter's neck and pressed down, cutting off his air. Peter jabbed his knee upward, hitting Stephen in the groin. Stephen's grip loosened enough for him to roll out from underneath. He could have run then, but Peter was tired of running.

He kicked Stephen in the head, knocking him backwards. He went in for another kick, but Stephen caught his ankle and yanked him to the ground. The air was knocked from his lungs, but he dodged Stephen's next blow. He coughed violently, forcing his lungs to work, until Stephen stomped a foot into his back.

Peter was pressed into the ground. He scrambled for purchase but could find none on the wet grass. Stephen kicked him and shoved him onto his side.

'You won't forget it this time,' Stephen panted, drawing a gun from his coat pocket. 'But you won't have long to remember it, either.'

Stephen drew back the hammer. Peter launched himself at his legs. The shot went harmlessly into the air as Stephen tumbled backwards then disappeared. Peter thought he vanished in the fog, but as the sound of the shot dissipated, he heard Stephen screaming – a faint sound growing further away. Peter crawled forward, panting, towards the spot where Stephen had just stood. His hands met air. Peering down, he saw the fog swirling in a bottomless quarry. Soon, the screaming died.

Peter crawled to his feet, regaining his breath as he stared into the abyss.

'You should have listened to Mr Drewry.'

33

The gunshot faded into the night. Someone hunting foxes, Eliza thought, as she forced the veranda door open. She used one hand to guide her along the hall. The other held the fire poker from Mr Drewry's loft. Her clothes were heavy and stiff, stained in Ruth's blood.

The house gave no sign of Rebecca or Mrs Pollard or Victoria. Then she remembered, and the house no longer held any fear over her. There were no ghosts keeping it alive, only Mrs Pollard. Thornecroft was another dead thing, like the rest of Plentynunig.

At Abigale Hall, she paused. It held no feeling any more. It was just another part of the sickened house. The echo of warmth and protection she once thought existed here – of the heart of the house fighting some encroaching illness – was as much an illusion as Ruth's ghostly Victoria. No part of Thornecroft held any care for her. Abigale Hall would give her no strength. She skirted its circular edge, avoiding the illumination of the night-time sky now cleared of clouds. She wanted to remain a part of the shadows.

The east wing was darker and colder, as if Mrs Pollard's presence sucked all the warmth from the air. Eliza passed Victoria's portraits, gently touching each frame. Her ghost might not roam Thornecroft, but the poor girl was murdered here. She deserved retribution.

The doors in the servants' passage were closed tight. Once,

they all would have appeared the same, but Eliza had learnt this house and learnt it well. Quietly, she twisted the handle to Mrs Pollard's room. It was unlocked and swung soundlessly inward. Silently, she approached the single bed and peered over it. Only pillows and air.

'Looking for me?

Eliza spun round and swung the poker. She felt it hit hard flesh. Mrs Pollard cried out. Eliza swung again, but the poker was grabbed before it struck. Mrs Pollard yanked on it, trying to tear it from Eliza's hands, but she clung tight until she was shoved into the door frame, the poker arm pressed up against her neck, choking her.

She kneed Mrs Pollard in the stomach, and the poker fell. Eliza ran for the kitchen. She slammed the door and turned the key. It wouldn't hold Mrs Pollard forever, but it would give her some time. She lit the stove and cranked the flame all the way up.

A metallic scrape filled the kitchen as the key twisted in the lock. The door sprang open. Mrs Pollard entered. By the gaslight, Eliza saw a pair of needle-nose pliers in her hand and the blood dripping from her forehead.

Eliza held the address book over the open flame. 'Don't step any closer.'

Mrs Pollard paused. 'Do you even know what that is?'

'The list of your victims.'

'Potentials, Miss Haverford. Potentials. I keep track of the chosen in an entirely different matter.'

'So you won't mind if I burn it then.'

'Go right ahead. There are always more where you came from.'

Eliza tossed the book onto the flames. Mrs Pollard didn't flinch.

'Where's my sister?'

'I assure you she's perfectly safe.'

'That's very little comfort.'

'You've never seen how special she is. She told me so.' Mrs Pollard took one step forward. Eliza took one back. 'I must say, I was quite annoyed with your aunt when the two of you were presented on my doorstep, but Rebecca . . . She has proven to be more useful than I could ever have imagined. You might say she's what I've been waiting for.'

'Where is she?'

Mrs Pollard came another step closer. 'Nearly thirty years I've been here. Can you imagine what that does to a woman?'

'Why did you kill Mr Brownawell?'

She laughed. 'Quite a dim child, aren't you? After all your time here, you think I'd ever harm my master?'

'Perhaps. Maybe I should ask Reg Kyffin what he thinks.'

Mrs Pollard feigned surprise then smiled. 'Ah, so you've discovered my little secret. How ingenious of you. No one else has come that far.'

'Except for Pip. And the other girls you murdered.'

'Pip never knew nor did anyone else. Oh. Is that why you think they died? Oh, you poor, simple thing. Those girls died because they needed to. In death, they found their purpose. As will you. Come along, child. It's time to end your tenure here. There's already a new girl on her way.' Mrs Pollard held out her hand.

Eliza stepped back. She felt a hard object, the rolling pin, on the counter behind her. 'Don't you remember? I already resigned.'

She swung at Mrs Pollard but missed. The housekeeper grabbed Eliza's arm and twisted it until the pain caused her to drop the rolling pin. Mrs Pollard kicked Eliza's feet out from under her and began dragging her out of the kitchen. Before Eliza could struggle free, a gunshot sounded.

Mrs Pollard shouted and dropped her. Something wet dripped onto Eliza's face. Instinctively, she wiped at it. Her hand came away with blood. There was another shot. Eliza turned and saw the end of Mrs Pollard's dress as she ran away.

A dog barked.

Eliza turned to see Mr Drewry standing over her, Kasey at his side, the rifle pointed towards where Mrs Pollard had departed. He lowered it and slung it over his shoulder.

'You alright?' he asked.

'Did you hit her?'

'Just grazed. Should have killed her.' He offered his hand. Eliza hesitated then took it.

'Ruth . . . she's . . .' She stuttered, unsure how to tell him.

'I've been to the loft.'

Eliza noticed the blood on his clothes. 'I tried to . . . It was too deep . . .'

He reloaded the rifle. 'We have to go after her.'

'She could be anywhere in the house. We'll have to . . .'

'She won't be hiding in the house.' Mr Drewry headed out of doors.

Eliza followed. 'How can you be certain?'

'I know the old snake better than you.'

They crossed the east lawn, heading for the treeline.

'Ruth said I could trust you. Should I believe her?'

Drewry paused. 'Not before. It's different now.'

'How so?'

'Pollard broke her promise. You coming or what?' He walked off without waiting for Eliza's answer. She followed. Together, they entered the woods.

Kasey stayed behind to guard the carriage house but to guard it from what, Eliza did not know. There were thousands of questions she wanted to ask Mr Drewry, but the man was silent, brooding. Eliza supposed he was mourning the loss of his love, but she had assumed such things before.

'Did you love her?' she asked, breaking their silence.

'What does it matter?'

'It matters a great deal. It matters because I want to know whether you're going to help me or whether you're taking me out to a quiet place to kill me.'

'Could have killed you at the house if I wanted. Only Kyffin would've known.'

'So you know that isn't Mr Brownawell?'

Mr Drewry didn't respond.

'Do you know what happened to the real Brownawell?'

'Gone before I came here. And yes.'

'Yes what?'

'Yes, I loved her. Pollard promised to let her be, so long as I stayed out of her way. Not ask any questions.'

'Even about Pip?'

He coughed and wiped his mouth on his sleeve. 'If I had, Ruth would've died a lot sooner than she did,' he said softly. 'Ruth is . . . was a good woman, but she was like everyone else in the village. Didn't care what happened at Thornecroft until it took someone that meant something to her. I even warned her not to let Pip take the job, that I knew Pollard had plans for her, but Ruth insisted. Said Pip could handle herself. When that woman got an idea in her head, Devil himself couldn't talk her out of it.'

They walked in silence for a few steps before he spoke again. 'Do you love him?'

'Who?'

'That boy from London. One who's been following me round.'

'You've seen Peter?'

'Picked him up in Swansea, like a bad smell. He's been looking for you. Told him to wait at the Old Hare. Safer for him there.'

Peter, who got lost in his own town, who could hardly order a different sandwich at the Corner House without panicking, he had tracked her all the way to Wales. He had not forgotten her. He had fought for her. Her own fairytale prince.

'I suppose I do.'

'There's no supposing about it. You either do or you don't.'

Her hand felt bare without his ring. She rubbed her palms together as they walked the path Eliza had seen Mrs Pollard take the previous night. 'Where do you think she's going?'

'To check on the collection.'

'You mean the books? But they're . . .'

'I don't know what it is. But I know where it is.'

After a long walk, they came to a clearing. Eliza realised where they were – on the opposite side of the quarry. She could see the pithead and outbuildings from the site of the mine collapse. It was calm now, but the hectic signs of the previous day's events could be seen in the leftover debris.

'This way,' said Mr Drewry.

She followed him down the steep incline that led into the quarry. The path was narrow and Eliza clung to the rock wall, careful of the loose stones beneath her feet. Mr Drewry made a torch from a fallen branch and handed it to Eliza. She looked across the quarry, towards the main road that led to Thornecroft. The ground was so flat here that a light on the quarry path would be visible from that road, even in the fog.

Halfway down they reached an old mine entrance excavated into the rock. There was a fresh smear of blood on the wooden frame supporting the opening. Together, they went inside.

All night-time sounds dropped away, leaving only their breathing and the scrape of their footsteps against the rocky ground. By torchlight, she could see broken lanterns strung along the wall, the indentations where pickaxes had been used to carve the way. It was numbingly cold as they descended deeper into the earth and only her hand, by the heat of the torch, was kept warm. Above them, rotting wooden beams supported the tons of dirt gravity wished to descend. She pictured how easy it would be for one to break and bury them alive.

For fifteen minutes or more they walked, becoming ever more shielded by layers of earth until suddenly the claustrophobic narrow tunnel opened onto a massive underground cavern.

Eliza stumbled to a stop. Above her a ceiling of stalactites hung like blades, ready to drop on any unsuspecting creature below. The bottom of the cavern was too far down for the torch to light. They stood on a narrow path that clung to the side of the cavern wall. Before them were a few rusted mining carts covered in bat droppings. She and Mr Drewry kept close to the cavern wall and followed the path's descent.

They were halfway down when Eliza noticed a dim light on the opposite side of the cavern. She tapped Mr Drewry on the shoulder and pointed. He nodded and continued onward. Eliza was careful to make her steps silent. Silence was their only protection.

They wound their way to the cavern floor. It was a mess of twisted tracks and abandoned mining equipment, and Eliza trod carefully for fear of tripping.

The other light came from a separate tunnel. A quick-moving shadow darted back and forth. Eliza heard it muttering to itself as they drew nearer.

'Insolent child . . . as she's told. No matter. No matter . . . the others. Never changes . . . for you . . .'

Mr Drewry slowly removed the rifle from his shoulder. Eliza stood back with the torch as he aimed.

'That would be a mistake, Mr Drewry.' Mrs Pollard remained out of sight, but her voice was clear. 'There was quite a bit of explosive material left here when we shut down the entrance in '31. Miss Haverford's exposed flame is worrisome enough. We don't need to be adding gunpowder and sparks to the mix, unless you want to blow us all to pieces.' Her skeletal frame appeared in the entrance to the tunnel. 'But you've done that once already, haven't you? Or are you still blaming the Germans for unpinning your grenade?'

Eliza saw the sweat that was forming on Mr Drewry's face despite the chilling cold. His arm began to shake.

'How many of them did you kill? Wasn't it your entire squadron? Amazing what a grenade can do when you drop it by accident. All those men who looked up to you. Depended on you. All of them dead. What were their names? Oh yes. Scott. Galloway. Benge. Davis. Shall I continue?'

The rifle quivered back and forth.

'Put it down, Ben. You'll only hurt someone else.'

It clattered to the ground as he buried his face in his hand, cowering from ghosts only he could see.

'Don't forget, Mr Drewry, this is your home, too. If anyone ever discovered you dropped that grenade, accident or not, there would be no end of volunteers to walk you to the gallows. Come now, Miss Haverford. It's time for you to meet the real master.' Though her voice was confident, Eliza could see the unhealthy paleness of her skin, the wet stain on her dark grey dress. Eliza stepped forward. A hand held her back.

'Don't,' said Mr Drewry, his body shaking, face wet with tears. She knelt down to meet him eye to eye and clasped his hand in hers.

'It will be alright.' She leant closer and whispered in his ear. 'You were a better shot than you thought.'

Mrs Pollard waited patiently as Eliza approached her.

'Show me the way.'

The women walked side by side in the wide tunnel.

'Why is Mr Kyffin in Thornecroft and Mr Brownawell in the mines?' Eliza asked.

'The master prefers the cold. And to be close to his collection.'

'Why not keep the collection in Thornecroft? Wouldn't that be more convenient?'

'He did. Before I came along and convinced him it would be more discreet to store it elsewhere. One of the many contributions that changed my fate.'

'You must have been so young when you first came here.'

Mrs Pollard paused. 'I was Rebecca's age. Had I not proved myself useful in other areas . . . I wanted to be an archaeologist, you see. It was all the rage when I was a girl. The world had other ideas.'

Eliza remembered the archaeology books untouched by cruelty.

'I found the reading room,' she said as they came to a sharp bend in the tunnel.

'I thought you might. You're so alike, you and your sister.'

'You said books should be properly maintained. Then why destroy them in that way?'

Mrs Pollard laughed then grimaced and gripped her side.

355

'That's not destruction. That's salvation. His father built the library and put those books there, but all they did was shout at the master and cause him pain. He could hear his father's voice in every one, he used to say. His father's or Victoria's. I helped to silence them. But my time of servitude is at an end. I've been waiting for so long for someone suitable to take my place. I thought she wouldn't arrive in time, but for once fate has decided to show me kindness.' She smiled, and Eliza saw the solemn girl from the photographs. 'Still, there are a few things we need to put in order. You'll have to change before we begin. It's so much easier when they die already dressed.'

They turned the corner. The fear Eliza had lost found her again.

The wall was lined with corpses. Each stood propped against a metal pole with a noose to hold her head back against the wall, like porcelain dolls on a stand. Dolls wearing Victoria's dress.

'My talents for organisation proved very useful. Before I came, the master could only manage one every decade or so. This is the real Victoria Kyffin.' Mrs Pollard pointed to the first corpse. Her dress was yellow and tattered. All her skin had rotted away, leaving only a blackened skull and matted tangles of brown hair, her jaw locked open in a smiling grimace.

'When Mr Kyffin came to claim her, the master let the fool believe he would see his daughter if he waited long enough. The man lived in that cellar for years, poor thing. Until I discovered a better use for him. The master isn't much for entertaining these days. It makes him so weary. But a house must have its presumed leader.'

Each corpse they passed was less decayed than the one

before. They were all so similar – same build, same hair – it was like watching a sick reconstruction of Victoria returning to life.

'Someone would notice. All these girls. Someone would care.'

'But that's the wonderful thing, Miss Haverford. No one did. No one who mattered. And the war made it easier. All those refugees. Before, most of them were from the kingdom – English, Welsh, Scottish. Even an Australian. But Olenka here was Polish. Amelia after her, French.' They reached the end of the line. 'And then there was dear Pip.'

The freshest of the corpses, only Pip's eyes had completely decayed. The skin of her face was grey – sunken and drooped – but the scream she held as she died was visible on her dried, receding lips.

'She was holding that book you found when I stabbed her. Thought it could act as a shield. But it was easy to slip the boning knife up between her ribs.'

Beside Pip was an empty metal stand, a noose dangling above. Hanging from the pole was the dress Eliza wore to dinner, the dress that haunted her dreams.

This was to be her resting place.

As Eliza stared at the waiting space, Mrs Pollard continued down the tunnel.

'Mr Brownawell, aren't you proud of me? I've brought you another bride.' A silent wheelchair rolled forward.

This corpse wore a red dinner jacket and bow tie, his skeletal hand adorned with a gold ring while his face held the permanent smile that matched his brides'. Eliza's eyes met his empty sockets.

'Nineteen forty-five wasn't a good year for his condition. But you're holding up admirably, aren't you, my dear?' She stroked his shoulder. 'For nearly thirty years, I've been his one, faithful companion. I promised I'd serve him till death. Sadly, that day has come sooner than expected.' She coughed into her handkerchief. Eliza glanced at the bloody wound staining Mrs Pollard's side, but the woman merely smiled. 'No, not that. I have the cancer. Known it for some time. But, unlike others, I'm able to make my peace with death. For in death, we can be together.'

She leant down and kissed the decayed scalp of her master. Eliza pictured the germs that must have transferred onto Mrs Pollard's lips, saw them sinking into the delicate, thin skin of her lips and worming their way into her bloodstream. Eliza understood why the woman had cancer. What shocked her was the thought that she had ever tried to reason with or appease Mrs Pollard. One could not reason with irrevocable madness. Mrs Pollard reached into the darkness and pulled forward another chair over which another gown, one different to Victoria's, was draped.

'I will be his true bride. The only faithful woman he has ever known. And remain here with him forever.' She caressed his cheek.

'If you're his wife, then he won't need any more brides,' Eliza said. 'So why need someone to carry on his work?'

Mrs Pollard laughed. 'Because of the children, of course. We both want children. And we have plenty of space for them down here. But first things first, Miss Haverford. I promised him you, and I've never broken a promise to my master. That's why he loves me.' She stepped forward and fingered the dress that was to be Eliza's. 'I've already decided the best way to go about it. A hanging. In honour of your dear father. Won't that be nice? Now, put on the dress.'

'No.'

'Alright. Put on the dress or I kill Rebecca. She'll die willingly if I tell her to.'

Eliza couldn't move.

'You would do anything for your sister, wouldn't you? You've hurt her so much already. The only way you can make it up to her is if you sacrifice yourself. She'll never forgive you otherwise. I know. She told me.'

Eliza felt the coldness within weaken her. She reached for the dress.

'That's a good girl.'

It had to be eradicated. She pulled the dress from the hanger.

'I told you, sir. There was no need to ever doubt me.'

There was only one way to remove it. Eliza held the dress to the light.

'I always do as you ask.'

The delicate lace caressed the lick of flame from the wall lantern, and the dress caught fire. Eliza tossed it onto Mr Brownawell. Mrs Pollard screamed, and Eliza ran, yanking lanterns off the wall and throwing them onto the corpses. The passage burned behind her. Each body became consumed by flames as the fire crackled. The orange light behind her grew like the oncoming dawn as black smoke drifted ahead of her, trying to block her path. The heat boiled her skin as sweat coated her like a shield, and she struggled to breathe in the oxygen-starved air. Through the smoke, she could see the exit to the tunnel of flame, and the figure of Mr Drewry waiting beyond. Only a few feet stood between them.

Mrs Pollard tackled her. 'You will do as you're told. You will take your proper place!' She tried to pin Eliza's arms behind her back. The smoke scalded her nose. All she could smell was ash. She tasted it on her tongue.

Eliza rolled over and kneed the gunshot wound. Mrs Pollard gasped, and Eliza punched her again. The housekeeper fell backwards. Eliza got to her feet and ran until she reached the cavern. Mr Drewry sat on the ground, rocking back and forth. Eliza grabbed his arm.

'We have to go! Mr Drewry!'

He wouldn't budge. Eliza took his face in her hands, forcing him to look her in the eyes.

'Ben, it's time to go.'

He responded, noticing for the first time the fire in the tunnel.

Mrs Pollard hobbled from the flames, coming for them. Ben grabbed the rifle and fired. Mrs Pollard fell then pushed herself up to her knees.

Together, Eliza and Ben pushed one of the heavy mining carts in front of the entrance. Mrs Pollard threw herself at it but was too weak to move it away. Her bloodied fingers reached for them as Eliza took her torch and lit the wooden tunnel entrance. The fire climbed up either side and lit the top of the frame, surrounding Mrs Pollard in flames.

'She'll never forgive you!' she screamed, blood spitting from her lips. 'She knows the good work I do here. She won't fail us!'

A flaming beam cracked and fell on top of Mrs Pollard. Her angry shouts turned to screams of another sort as Eliza watched the flames engulf her body, sending her to the same end as the brides in the tunnel. Her dying wish, at last.

'And they lived happily ever after,' Eliza whispered. Ben pulled her away.

Together, they ran from the burning cavern and through the tunnel, not stopping until they reached the outside quarry path. The clear, fresh air on the surface calmed her.

An explosion shook the ground. Eliza fell sideways towards the gaping quarry. Ben grabbed her and pulled her back, losing his grip on the rifle. It tumbled into the void as the ground rumbled again. They kept running, the path threatening to collapse under them. Behind them, the path fell away. They were almost on solid ground.

Eliza reached the top first and helped Ben up after her. They ran from the unstable edge as the ground continued quaking beneath them, the underground flames burning away the last of Mr Brownawell's poison. At the treeline, they paused and watched the quarry breaking apart as a multitude of stars looked down upon them.

34

Peter walked for hours, his legs going numb from the effort. Many times he thought he was only wandering deeper into the unforgiving Welsh countryside. He had images of walking all the way to the sea or stumbling across the English border, his collapsed body found by miners, gnawed on by foxes.

When he saw the manor house, he wept. The place appeared abandoned, half-hidden as it was behind a high brick wall. He wiped dirt away from the plaque mounted by the front gates.

Thornecroft.

He laughed. He had found it. After all this time, despite what everyone said, he had done it. He had found her. Peter pushed open the heavy iron gates and approached the house. All was pitch black except for a small light glowing in the window to his right. Someone was home.

He rang the doorbell but heard no sound. Thinking it broken, he knocked. No one answered. He tried the handle. The unlocked door opened onto a dark entrance hall.

'Hello?'

His voice echoed through the blackness.

'Eliza?'

No answer.

'Anyone?'

To his right was the small orange light.

'Hello?'

It moved deeper into the house.

'Wait!' Peter ran after it, bumping into walls and furniture, finding it difficult to navigate the twisting passages. He entered a hall decorated with old paintings. Each he passed depicted the same woman and scrolled like a film reel as the woman drew closer and closer to an entrance in the distance. Peter stopped at the last painting. It was the entrance to a mine. Ahead, someone coughed, drawing his attention. The light hovered there.

'Hello?' As he approached, he saw the illuminated face. 'Please. I need your help. I . . .' He paused. 'Rebecca? Oh, Rebecca! Thank God you're alright.'

Rebecca's face was blank. The poor girl must be traumatised, he thought.

'Rebecca, it's me. Peter. Don't worry. You're safe now. I've come to save you.'

'You're not supposed to be here,' she said.

'I know. But we'll move quickly. I'll have you out of here quick as a flash. Where is Eliza?'

'You'll have to go. We don't need you here.'

'Rebecca,' he laughed. 'What's got into you? Stop being silly. Here. Take my hand and show me to your sister.'

Rebecca set down the Tilley lamp then reached for Peter's hand, keeping the other behind her back.

What a queer motion, he thought, before a sharp pain erupted in his stomach. A knife handle protruded from his abdomen. He tried to speak. Only blood came from his lips. Rebecca pulled the knife out. He staggered back. A doorframe. He tried to support himself. His feet slipped on the bloody floor.

'This is our home now. You don't belong here.'

'R . . . Rebecca . . .'

She plunged the knife in again. This pain was less than the

first but caused more blood to spill. She pulled out the blade. He fell back onto something soft. He was sweating. It must have been from the heat. The blood was so warm. But he was so cold.

Rebecca stroked his hair.

'Don't worry.' She smiled. 'It'll all be over soon.' Gently, she tilted back his head.

The knife went through his neck.

He was choking and drowning all at once.

Michael held his hand. Mother kissed him on the cheek. But where was Eliza? Eliza was close. Roses and old books. He had to give her the book. Her book. She needed. He needed. He promised. His mouth filled with blood.

Rebecca's smiling face became preternaturally clear then blurred as he slipped away to the sound of her counting.

35

Dawn was breaking as Eliza and Ben returned to the estate. The sky grew warm with a golden-pink tinge. Today would be beautiful. They parted at the carriage house. The grave she had dug yesterday would be useful after all. Eliza took the long way round to the kitchen. Crossing the garden only made her think of Ruth, and right now she didn't want to think. She wanted to rest.

When she spotted Rebecca waiting for her in the kitchen, Eliza rushed inside.

'Rebecca!' She threw her arms around her and held her close. Rebecca returned the hug with equal ferocity. 'Are you alright? She didn't hurt you, did she?'

'I'm fine, Eliza. Where is Mrs Pollard?'

'Oh, she's gone, dearie. She's gone. And we'll never have to worry about her again.'

'Did you kill her?'

Eliza kissed her hand. 'Let's get some rest. I'm exhausted. You must be, too.'

'Because it's alright if you did. Some people deserve to die.'

'It's nothing you ever need worry about. Now, we'll rest today, and tomorrow Mr Drewry is going to help us return to London.'

Rebecca led her out of the kitchen. 'I made you a present while you were gone.'

'Really?' Eliza yawned. 'Can it wait till tomorrow?'

'But I've already put it in your room. Go on. Go and see!'

'Alright, then.'

The smell of blood was embedded in Eliza's clothes. She wanted to change, take a warm bath, but most of all she wanted sleep. She wanted to curl up in her bed and sleep until the afternoon. Today, she felt she'd earned it. Yet she owed this to Rebecca. She could no longer be selfish.

Eliza opened her bedroom door. Between the shock and exhaustion, she could not scream. She could only stare at the mutilated body, his skin and clothes soaked in damp blood, his cloudy eyes staring vacantly at the ceiling. The half-finished scarf lay neatly across his chest.

She did not run to him. There was not even a chance he was alive.

'Peter . . .' Her hand felt bare.

'Do you like it? I made it just for you.' Rebecca smiled, and Eliza felt herself tumbling into the quarry.

'You . . . you murdered . . .'

'Yes.' Rebecca cocked her head to the side. 'And?'

'I loved him.' The fog reached up and took her in.

'He came to take you away.'

Eliza backed down the hall. Rebecca followed.

'You're not allowed to leave, Eliza. Mrs Pollard wanted to kill you, and I very much disliked that idea. She could be very queer sometimes. But now you've taken care of her, we can live here together with the master. Carry on his good work. Doesn't that sound splendid?'

Eliza noticed Rebecca was carrying her hands behind her back. She caught the silver glint of a knife.

'But, Rebecca,' she said, 'why would you want to stay here when we can go home to London? Don't you like London?'

'Well, it's alright. Perhaps we can visit every now and then.

366

But why should we leave when this whole manor is ours now? Thornecroft can be our home. We'll have our own bedrooms and bathrooms and no one to bother us!'

'A house like this, it's too much work for just the two of us.'

'That's why we hire girls to help. Mrs Pollard showed me how it works. She showed me everything. Doesn't the collection remind you of Father? All their faces look so peaceful as they sleep. Father's face was peaceful, too.' Rebecca pulled the burnt address book from her pocket. 'Now see, we hire them, they work, then we give them to the master. Our own place. Isn't that what we've always wanted?'

Eliza neared the main hall of the east wing. Her eyes darted for an escape. Rebecca noticed.

'You don't want to stay, do you?'

'I think we need to sleep on it, weigh our options.'

'You want to lock me away and forget about me. Don't you? You're always happier when I'm not around. Admit it. I found the address for that hospital amongst your things when I cleaned your room. Mrs Pollard told me what kind of hospital it was. I didn't want to believe her, but she was right, wasn't she? Mrs Pollard is always right.'

Rebecca's eyes went black and dead. Her face contorted into a twisted snarl, revealing the vicious beast she was inside.

'Let's calm down,' Eliza said. 'Be reasonable.'

'I am perfectly calm. Dearie.' Rebecca leapt at her with the knife. Eliza dodged it then ran.

'Run, rabbit, run!' Rebecca shouted.

She headed for the kitchen, but Rebecca pounced on her. Eliza felt the knife sink into her shoulder as she fell to the floor. She got to her knees and threw herself against the wall, knocking Rebecca off. She pulled out the knife, dropped it and kept running. Outside on the lawn, she shouted.

'Ben! Ben!'

The sun peeked above the horizon as Rebecca's grey figure continued advancing towards her. Kasey galloped in from the other direction. He went straight for Rebecca, grabbing her by the leg. Rebecca swung the knife at him, but he refused to let go. When Ben appeared round the corner, he saw Kasey attacking and ran to Rebecca's aid.

'Ben, no!'

He reached the pair.

'No, Ben. Let him!'

He looked at Eliza in surprise, and Rebecca stabbed him in his hand. The knife stuck. Rebecca abandoned it and retreated, limping through the damaged wall into the garden. Eliza rushed to his side as he removed the knife.

'I've lost her. She's mad. She's killed . . .' Eliza used her handkerchief to bind his hand, and pushed the fog away. 'The sedative you used for Kasey. Is there any left?'

'Some. But it's only meant for animals.'

'It's all we have.'

They hurried to the carriage house. The mare, unperturbed, watched as Ben extracted a vial from the first-aid kit and drew the liquid into the barrel.

'She could be anywhere in that house,' he said.

'Then we'll have to smoke her out.' Eliza took the syringe. 'Get Mr Kyffin, then burn it to the ground. All of it. She can't call it home then.'

She threw a length of rope over her shoulder and headed out into the garden. The dawn light made it easier to see but cast strange shadows over the ground. Her shoulder bled sluggishly as she crept through the hedges, remembering the games of hide and seek they would play in Gran's garden. Eliza always won.

Eliza peeked round the fountain. The latticework doors were open. She approached cautiously and saw drops of blood leading inside.

Thornecroft was silent. She inched her way through the house, following the bloodstains to the north hall. When she reached the staircase, she heard a familiar creaking. Mr Kyffin's wheelchair. The sound quickened until he appeared at the top of the stairs. Eliza was powerless to stop the wheelchair as it was pushed over the edge.

Both Mr Kyffin and the chair tumbled. Eliza leapt to the side, but not far enough. The heavy metal contraption landed on her leg, pinning her down. Mr Kyffin continued to breathe, though Eliza saw how badly broken his body was. She manoeuvred herself so she could hold his hand.

'I found her,' she whispered. 'I found Victoria. She's at peace now. She said you don't have to wait any more.' Eliza kissed his hand. Mr Kyffin sighed, and his pain finally ended.

Rebecca looked down on them from the top of the staircase.

'Did you hear that, Rebecca? The collection is gone. I destroyed it.' Eliza pulled her ankle free. Already it started to swell. 'Mrs Pollard, Mr Brownawell. I destroyed all of it. You have no home here. No purpose.'

'Liar!' Her voice boomed through Thornecroft's empty halls.

'Yes, but not this time.'

Rebecca ran at her. Eliza rolled out of the way, leaving Rebecca to punch the floor instead. She cried out as her hand met the hard surface then ran off down the hall, cradling it to her chest.

Eliza pulled herself up by the banister, wincing as soon as she placed weight on her ankle. Ben ran into the room, tried to get her to sit.

'There's no time,' she said. 'Light the fires. We'll keep her contained. Go!'

He paused over Kyffin, crossing his chest, then hurried off. Eliza hobbled in Rebecca's direction. She would never be able to run her down now. Ahead of her, she heard a door close, followed by whispers. Rebecca was counting again.

'Eighteen!' Eliza shouted. 'Twelve! Forty-three!'

'Stop it!' Rebecca screamed from the opposite side of the door. 'One two three four five—'

'Twenty-two!'

Rebecca cried out. Eliza heard her run away from the door. She opened it just as Rebecca disappeared behind another.

'One two three four—'

'Six seven eight nine!'

'Stop it! I hate you. I hate you!' Again she ran.

Eliza limped into Abigale Hall just in time to see the door to the Ancestral Parlour slam shut. On the other side she heard weeping.

'One . . . two . . . three . . .'

'Rebecca?'

'Stop it! Stop it. Stop stop stop! One, two, three . . .'

'Open the door, dearie.'

'Four five six!'

'We don't have to fight.'

'Seven eight nine!'

'Sisters aren't supposed to fight, remember? It's against the law.'

Rebecca stopped counting.

'I know you like it here, Rebecca. Let's talk about it. We can work something out. Like grown-ups. You're all grown up now, aren't you?'

There was a long pause.

'You're not angry at me for what I did to Peter?'

Eliza let the coldness numb her. 'No, of course not. I could never be angry at you. Please, let's talk.' She waited.

The door handle turned. Rebecca's face appeared. She looked calm again – the Rebecca who had been scared of Aunt Bess, not the one who stabbed Peter Lamb to death – but she remained in the doorway.

'Will your shoulder be okay?' Rebecca asked.

'I'm sure it will heal fine.'

'I'm sorry. I didn't mean to hurt you, only I was angry.'

'We all get angry now and again. Now, may I have a hug?' Eliza outstretched her arms. 'I love you,' said Eliza.

Rebecca hesitated then came forward to embrace her. She held her a moment. She let the syringe slip down from where it was hidden in her sleeve and jabbed it into Rebecca's neck, pushing the plunger in one fluid motion.

Rebecca shoved her away and yanked the syringe from her neck.

'You . . . you fibbed.'

'You'll be alright now, Rebecca.'

Rebecca staggered into Abigale Hall, her face contorting once again into the monster. Her eyes glazed over as she struggled to remain on her feet, her breathing becoming laboured, and she fell to the floor beneath the dome. Eliza gathered her into her arms.

As dawn shone through the dome, the hall was filled with reflections of light, the unique pattern of the bevelled glass creating unusual round spheres that danced in mid-air.

'Hush now, it's alright. Shh. Look, Rebecca. Look, the sun is coming up. Look how it shines through the dome. And we'll

371

be the last people to ever see it. Isn't it beautiful?' She stroked her sister's hair until she fell unconscious. Gently, Eliza used the rope to secure her arms and legs. She lifted Rebecca into her arms as the smell of smoke drifted in from the east wing. Ben had lit the first fire.

EPILOGUE

'It's called a transorbital lobotomy. We take one of our surgical instruments – an orbitoclast – and insert it under the upper eyelid, against the top the of the eye socket. Then we use the mallet to gently drive it into the brain here – the frontal lobes.'

Eliza watched Rebecca sketching on a piece of paper. It was difficult to even notice her. Her white pyjamas blended in with the white walls, the white floor. Everything was so very clean and white here. Not a speck of dirt or coal dust could be found.

'Will it be painful?' she asked, clutching her handbag. She loved the white, but the smell of disinfectant was beginning to bother her.

'There will be some minor discomfort, but she'll hardly remember a thing.'

'How soon can you do it?'

'You should take some time to think about—'

'How soon?'

'I believe the operating theatre is available on Friday.'

Eliza nodded. 'Friday then. No later.'

'Miss Haverford, I must say, while this procedure is at the forefront of mental health treatment, the outcome is always uncertain. This could cure Rebecca's condition, but she may never be your sister again. We can't guarantee any miracle cures or happy endings.'

'Happy endings are for fairy tales, doctor. I only want this to end.'

Rebecca turned, saw Eliza and waved. The new sedative they were using worked remarkably well. Eliza smiled back as she took the clipboard and signed the papers.

'Goodbye, dearie.'

Outside, the harsh sun blinded her. It was the hottest summer England had seen for years. It made Eliza uncomfortable. Made her dress itch against her dry skin. Made her feel dirty. She wanted rain, just some soft rain to cool her. A fog to block the harsh rays. She walked across the airless car park, the blood overheating in her veins as she opened and closed the latch on her handbag. Open and close. Open and close. Open and close. Slow and methodical. Once for each of the girls in Mr Brownawell's collection. By the time she reached the car where Ben waited, the fog had descended within her, cooling the blood, and making her feel so much better.